The Illusionaires

Brian T. Marshall

missppelled press   2021   Paradise, CA

Most characters in the following work are fictitious. Some are not. Neither the thoughts, words or deeds of any such parties are purported to be real.

ISBN 978-1-7371562-1-5
Library of Congress Control Number Pending

Fiction/Action and Adventure
Fiction/Fantasy/Historical
Fiction/Magic Realism

First printing 2021, missppelled press, Paradise, CA
www.missppelled.com

Formatting: BB eBooks
Cover Image: K. S. Ferguson

Also by Brian T. Marshall

Table of Contents

There are two crafts practiced in this our world
As distinct as prayer and blasphemy
With both laying claim to the very same word
And calling what they offer Magic

The one is a means to rob men blind
Or charm them with cheap deception
And the sooner its students depart this Earth
The happier we'll all be

But the other?

Ah, yes, the other

Sir Samuel Watloe, 1872

1938

1

THE HOUSE LIGHTS dim. The curtains pull back. An empty stage is revealed.

A second passes, then two, then three. A murmur fills the hall. Next up it's the chatter of programs, gripped in impatience, and a couple of coughs ringing out. And yes, of course, tricks were expected, but not this kind of trick, the transmutation of hard-earned cash into waiting for God knows what. Finally someone, a well-dressed man, exits from the third row, then hesitates as he reaches the aisle, contemplating his next move.

Find an usher? Inform the promoter? Each option is scrutinized. Until, all at once, he spins around, heading for the stage. The lip of the proscenium itself is a good five feet off the floor, but without a moment's hesitation the man leaps into the air, only to land on his outstretched arms and then roll into a tumble. There's an audible gasp—from a woman, it sounds like—one that catches the man off-guard, and what had been a moment of consummate grace ends in an ugly pratfall. For a second he lies there, splayed out on the stage, feeling the sting of comeuppance. Then, in a stiff-lipped show of resolve, he climbs back to his feet.

There is, however, a problem. His left arm is detached from his body.

He stares down at the severed limb; a child who's acting naughty. Then he bends down, right arm extended, and both hands grip one another. There's a playful moment of *mano a mano*, no clear winner in sight, which ends when the man attempts to return the lost limb back into the sleeve of his jacket. But wait. Another problem. A second arm has already sprouted. Is now emerging from the empty sleeve as a bulb breaks through the earth. Revealing a hint of annoyance, he glares at the renegade arm, then jams the stump atop his head, spoiling his perfect coif.

A man with an arm growing out of his head. A disquieting prospect at best. But that, of course, is his very intention, his modus operandi as it were; to delight and disturb in equal measures, to draw them in and then chase them away.

"Ladies and gentlemen and whatever else you may be, I am Richard Constairs."

His voice rings out, not loud, not forceful, yet it reaches the back of the building. Daring anyone there, anywhere in that hall, to challenge this declaration.

So, of course, somebody does.

"Liar!"

This second voice is more of a snarl. A gauntlet

hurled down. From out of the wings, a man appears, a gate-crasher on the stage.

"*I* am Richard Constairs," he declares.

The same patrician features. The same dark hair, streaked with grey. The same handkerchief, the same red rose, tucked into the same black silk jacket. But whereas the first claimant sports an extra arm, with his rival, it's a third leg instead.

Noting this, the entire hall inhales a collective breath, aghast at the sight of this travesty, this perversion of Mother Nature. But rather than acknowledge that reaction, evidence any hint of shame, the figure decides to compound his affront by crossing the stage towards his twin. To call it walking would be a misstatement. It is more like some shambling shuffle. The off-kilter waltz of a damaged toy, or a puppet with crossed strings. Within it can be seen every cruelty of life, every cripple, every palsied mistake. A sight that bids one to turn away, yet invites all to keep on staring.

Finally, mercifully, the figure halts, a few feet from his all-but-double.

"Correct me if I'm wrong," he states, "but are you in fact claiming to be the same Richard Constairs, late of Newcastle, England, who is currently engaged in a tour of these United States?"

"I am," the first Constairs concedes.

"The very same Richard Constairs who has studied at length with the swamis and katapoors of the Indian Sub-

Continent, and thus mastered their skills of illusion, self-deception and the deception of others, such as may be evidenced on this very stage?"

"None other," is the reply.

"And in doing so, are you therefore suggesting that I, this person, an amalgam of flesh and blood, am in fact mere illusion instead, a phantasm generated by your vivid imagination, a trick being played out even now on the fine folk seated before us?"

"How could I pretend otherwise?"

"Very well," the three-legged man retorts. "I can see no other option. Pistols at twenty paces."

With that the two figures line up, back to back, each staring out into the wings. Needless to say, they are the exact same height, not including that extra arm, and both are now clutching brass trumpets which have conveniently appeared out of nowhere. As all eyes watch, they are then joined by a third instrument, a snare drum suspended mid-air, along with a pair of wooden sticks that begin to rattle out a slow, almost martial rhythm.

Moving in concert to that tattoo, they pull away from each other, only somehow their respective black silk jackets have fused into a single garment. Stretching between them, like a banner held taut, the jacket slowly elongates, until the two figures finally come to a halt on opposite sides of the stage. At the sound of a final, propulsive blow delivered to the snare, both figures wheel around, then raise their trumpets to their lips, chests swelling tight with air.

A single light tap on the drumhead. A second, moments later. And then, with a third, the crack of two pistols, and the acrid sting of burnt powder.

Twin figures suddenly grip their chests. Twin spouts of blood erupt. A red so red it becomes something else, a new color unto itself. Both men are falling, tumbling downward, collapsing to the stage, and still the blood is gushing forth, pooling on worn oak floorboards. A few seconds more and this tide will spill over, violate the lip of the stage, a crimson wave lapping the aisles, staining the hems of all present. But no. Wait. It isn't blood. Isn't even liquid.

Instead both bodies are buried beneath a massive mound of roses.

AFTER THAT IT'S time for some harmless piffle. A little break in the clouds. His own variant on the Marston Twist, but with poodles filling in for the pillows, followed by a couple of levitation numbers that earn him some light applause. Which, of course, he can't stand. Better to have them catcall, walk off in droves, burn the old dump down, than to be merely polite, or condescend in any way.

An intermission. A small spot of gin. Five minutes to put his feet up. With the HM, a rude little runt of a man, giving him the eye. Then it's time for the second act, when Karla will join him onstage.

A couple of years back, when the crowds had started to thin, he'd finally bitten that bullet. Swallowed his pride, or what little was left of it, and hired on an assistant. Because stage magic was entertainment, after all, and nothing entertained like a glimpse of skin, with the men never spurning a quick peek or two, and the women preferring to have their husbands seeing it at a remove rather than chasing after it in the office, not that all that many of them still had an office, or a job, to go to.

But Karla wasn't just a pretty face. The promise of fleshly delights. Yes, she had all the right parts in all the right places, no denying that, but far more importantly she had that awareness, that aura, the thing that turned a bit of stage dressing into a full-on performer. Any woman could connive a man. That much was a given. But to make him a willing accomplice, to have him sit there, grinning away, as all the while she lured him in, tightened the knot, well, that was more than just artifice, that was art. An art as complex, as demanding, as any he could claim as his own.

Plus she was a joy to work with. For their latest number, they'd revamped the classic knife-throw, switching roles so that she'd be the one who would wield the blades, while he'd serve as her helpless target. The first step was her costume. A black fishnets and garters number that got everyone's pulses going. Then there was her shtick.

The icy demeanor, that severe, furrowed brow, the fact that she spoke not one word. And lastly, there was Constairs own contribution to the act. The dapper, droll man-about-town who is slowly turned into a quivering puddle of nerves as each knife skirts that much closer. People want their magicians to be cool. Implacable. Always in charge. While secretly hoping that someone will come along and finally put them in their place.

"And now, to close our show, I would like to introduce you to a most gifted individual. Several years ago, my continuing studies carried me to Vladinstock, a rather insular, inhospitable village tucked away in the Ural Mountains. Since time immemorial, the people of Vladinstock have practiced the art of the blade, both the crafting of fine knives themselves and of their use as deadly weapons. Needless to say, these skills are typically the province of the men alone. Which was why it came as such a shock to discover that the greatest practitioner of these arts should prove to be a woman, almost a girl."

He motions to the wings, stage right.

"Ladies and gentlemen, Miss Karla Livotski."

A slow parade to center-stage, halfway between stroll and strut, her slender frame all but hidden beneath a floor length cloak.

"Miss Livotski would like me to thank you in advance for bearing with her silence. She speaks little in the way of English."

Karla follows this with a stately bow, acknowledging

the hall. As she straightens back up, the cloak tumbles off her, as if by accident. Every single man who is present leans forward in his seat.

"She also hopes you will be so kind as to let her knives speak for her."

He snaps his fingers and a table appears, and atop it a wooden box. Exquisitely milled and lined with felt, its hinged lid is already open, allowing a gleam of burnished metal to steal across the hall. Then a second percussive snap summons up yet another platform, this one much larger than the first, with its top tilted to a near vertical, thus displaying the outline of a body painted on its surface, and four sturdy clamps, bolted in place, where ankles and wrists will soon rest.

"On a typical evening," he explains, "I would at this point ask for a volunteer from the audience. But after what happened in Chicago I cannot in good conscience allow anyone but myself to proceed."

Nothing happened in Chicago, of course, except that it didn't snow.

He slips out of his silk jacket. Hangs it on thin air. Places his body on top of the outline, clamps snapping shut on their own accord. Silent, unmoving, he awaits his fate. The hall is deathly still. He can feel the frisson they have carefully crafted, the pickle they've put them in. All those men who fear her prowess, while at the same time wanting to swap. To take his place there on the table. To feel her touch, her sting.

Meanwhile Karla, mannequin still, stares back at the audience. Allows the barest hint of a smile to play across her features. Then, like a child, bored and indifferent, she wanders over to her wooden box, letting her fingers play over each blade, as if trying to choose the right chocolate. Still staring downward, she snatches one up, tosses it more or less towards him, then fails to notice as the blade sails right past and clatters to the floor.

Snared by that sound, she looks up, embarrassed. Shrugs once to the hall. Picks out a second knife from her assortment and sends it after the first. Only this one finds wood, not failure, sinking in a good inch at least, right between his left thumb and index finger. Seeing this, she smiles again, reaching for the box, and then there's a sudden flurry of motion, too quick for the eye to follow. When it ends a few seconds later, there are now eight knives embedded in the table, each perfectly centered between one finger and the next.

From that point on it's a steady escalation, each feat more impressive than the last. From out of nowhere, a pocket mirror appears, allowing Karla to turn her back to the table, and then use the reflection in its glass to direct a couple of knives to either side of his head. Raising both hands in excitement, she carelessly drops the mirror, watches it shatter on the floor, and then celebrates her bad luck by blindly tossing four more knives over her shoulder. All of which somehow find the table, a mere hand's width below his groin.

One knife thrown straight upwards, bound for the heavens, hit instead by a second knife, which sends both of them spinning back down to earth and, one-two, into the table. A third knife that she drops from her hand, kicks with her heel, and which lodges directly between the first two. And through it all, this amazing display, it's not like he's been idle. No, he's been working on his own escalation, a showy surrender to terror, as if he actually doubts her skill, or is uncertain of the outcome. A white shirt beginning to darken with sweat. That twitch in his left eye. The fine art of playing to the back of the house without losing the folks up front.

Or perhaps it's not mere performance. Perhaps something *can* go wrong. And if you don't give them real blood now and then, pretty soon they'll stop showing up.

There's one knife left in the felt-lined box. One last chance to get things right. For a moment she regards it, her face almost tender, feeling its weight, its heft. Then, staring straight into his eyes, she hurls it into space. Can you actually hear it, the sound of the impact, how it's subtly different this time? Or will their first clue be the trickle of crimson, soon to dribble down his neck? Thanks to his first trick, that bit with the roses, they're all pretty jaded by now, and have to come to expect that nothing is real, it's all just smoke and mirrors. Which has always been his problem. The problem of every magician. You can only lie to people so often before they start growing bored.

He watches as she slowly moves towards him. Feels himself still leaking away. Hopes the blood won't get on his shirt, he's down to his last two clean ones. And he wonders, like always, how many will sense it, see the affection there, the way she bends over, finding his neck, finding the wound she'd just rendered, and then slowly start to lap away, like a child at the tit.

A second later the curtain falls.

There's a round of scattered applause.

And a total of thirty-eight paying patrons begin to file out towards the exits.

2

"DOES ANYONE IN this God-forsaken hellhole know where to procure a drink?"

Max Bettlebum knows. Has known, in fact, since before his birth, still bobbing away in the womb. Known because such knowledge, such expertise, comes with the territory, falls under the purview of those brave souls who called themselves theatrical agents. No, the real trouble is having to decide whether or not to tell Constairs.

"Hellhole?" he counters. "Only people born in St. Loo are allowed to call it that. People like yours truly, I might add."

Constairs lifts his gaze from the mirror, abandoning his reflection.

"Really, Max? That explains a lot. And you have my sympathies."

They are backstage in his dressing room, with the show now a half-hour dead. In better times, his so-called heyday, they'd still be clamoring away, lining up with their programs, clutching a pen, or waiting outside the stage door, ignoring the rain or the snow. But tonight?

No one but a guy with a push-broom, sweeping up the last few rose petals. All those mice, burrowed deep in the walls.

"And as to watering holes," Max resumes, "it would help if I knew which kind. You want someplace noisy, lots of distractions, get your mind off tonight's big flop? Or are you looking for something quiet and maudlin, you crying away in your Boodles?"

Constairs rises to his feet. Grabs his topcoat from the rack. "Since you'll be paying for our drinks, I'll leave that choice to you."

Missouri. Misery. Surely it wasn't mere coincidence. So why hadn't he noticed that awful pun when they'd first mapped out the tour? And the Midwest. He'd always bombed in the Midwest, even in sunnier times, a place where the cattle could outsmart the people, where they grew corn, then actually ate it. And yes, technically, St. Louis might not even be considered the Midwest, but really, in the end, wasn't the whole damn country stuck in the middle of somewhere? A bland, flat place where the merest hint of something new, something different, flew over their big fat heads.

"Laramy's" Max tells the cabbie. "16th and Danvers."

Traffic is light, it's a Wednesday after all, and, God forbid, after ten. Then again, the traffic is always light nowadays, ever since Black Friday, and as if to drive the point home even further, they cruise by a small Hoover-ville. Canvas tents sagging in the light rain, and the cops clustered at each corner, and in one hovel the light of a candle, leaking out past a cardboard wall.

Laramy's, it turns out, is neither small nor big, busy or quiet, one thing or the other. How like Max to split the difference and give him a little of both. A waiter, one button shy of a vest, escorts them to a booth, a hulking affair of dark, pleated leather, well past the line into vulgar. Constairs orders a skirt steak and a side of pommes frites. Max a glass of seltzer. And while the kitchen beats said steer into submission, a Boodles martini, please.

"Thirty eight," Constairs announces to no one.

"Better than thirty-seven."

"Is it? I sometimes think an empty house would be better than one with mere crumbs."

"Or better yet," Max suggests, "just stay home. Make do with some nice, safe IM gig, and a paycheck every two weeks."

"Me? Industrial Magic? Coming up with this year's Miracle Floor Wax, or helping them build some bridge?" He snaps his head once. "No. I don't think so."

His martini arrives, a far cry from frigid. He'll drink it anyway.

"So how did it come to this?"

"How? Simple." Max pecks at his seltzer. "You stuck your head in the sand."

Only then does Constairs get it. Max is actually pleased. Pleased that the night was an all-but-disaster, pleased at this slap in the face, pleased that his victim has been sufficiently humbled to finally listen for once.

"So what's it cost, just a ballpark, to open up the Palladium?"

"Haven't a clue," Constairs admits.

"Just a hair over three bills. Utilities, staffing, what have you. Which, I might add, doesn't begin to include fixed costs, even if they stay dark. And which, I might also add, means that even if you were willing to work gratis, wave any percentage of the door, they'd still have to get a hundred-plus warm bodies in there just to break even."

Warm bodies. Warm gin. Does life get any better?

"So let me guess," Constairs suggests. "I pay people to show up."

"Well, sure, you could. Or you could just do the math. Take a couple hundred Palladiums, scattered all across the country, and pack them full of people at a dollar a head. And even if your cut is only a point or two, you're suddenly in the black. Maybe not serious money, but enough to keep you in gin."

"Not this. Not again."

"Yes this. Yes again."

A reprieve arrives disguised as his steak, or perhaps it's a spare tire instead. Procured from the very same yellow cab that had dropped them off out front. Soggy potatoes, limp and indifferent. A pretense of a salad. If tonight's show weren't disheartening enough, it seems

Max is going for broke. Showing his client, just like Marley's ghost, the dismal future that awaits him.

"Look," Constairs says, rallying now. "I'm a performer, not an employee. And a performer needs his audience. Probably a lot more than they need me."

Max sighs back in disgust. "So did you even see *King Kong*?"

"Yes," he tells him. "Of course."

"And what did you think?"

"It was brilliant," Constairs admits. "Absolutely brilliant."

"Well, there you go. Did Carl Simmons tell the studio, no, sorry, have to pass, I'm a performer, not an employee? No. He got off his high-horse, looked at the numbers, and saw where the whole world was headed. Realized that that he could touch a hell of a lot more people by working with the future than by pretending it didn't exist."

He saws off a small portion of Goodyear. Gives his jaws something to do. Is there anything worse than some old friend trying to help you out?

"But it's Hollywood," Constairs finally says.

"So?"

"So they're all Jews out there."

But even Jews can turn a cheek. Max merely smiles back.

"You want me to be offended? Fine. I'm offended. And yes, there are a lot of Jewish assholes out there, in

Hollywood and everywhere else. A lot of gentile ones too."

"Jews, gentiles, what does it matter. By now all the good jobs will be sewn up. And me, I'd just be some old dog, trying to learn new tricks."

With that Max lights right up.

"Finally, some honesty. You admitting that you're scared."

He tosses his fork onto his plate. Dabs at his chin with a napkin. "Not scared. Not exactly. It's just that I'm a magician. Been one all my life. But magic, it's more than just knowing the right spell. It's winning people over, letting them in on the con, showing them that sometimes the impossible happens, no matter how grim things may look. Otherwise, why get up in the morning? Why face another day?"

"You'd still be doing all that," Max insists. "Just in a different way."

THE WAITER RETURNS to steal back his plate. Eyes most of his meal, uneaten. All three of them knowing that those scraps, those remnants, will fend off hunger elsewhere. At Max's insistence they both order brandies, even though he seldom drinks, implying they're about to seal some pact, commemorate some moment. Don't get your hopes up, Constairs wants to tell him. I haven't agreed to a thing. And I still reserve my God-given right to be a foolish, obstinate pig.

"*The Wizard of Oz.*"

He shakes himself from his reverie. Turns his gaze towards Max.

"Pardon?"

"*The Wonderful Wizard of Oz.* You've heard about it maybe?"

Constairs dismisses that with a shrug, arrogant to the end.

"Yes, I suppose so. Some kind of children's book."

"A whole series of them, in fact. And don't go looking down your nose. If you could guarantee one-half of one-half of one percent of the books Baum's sold, the Palladium would've been packed."

They pause long enough to sample their Remy. Even Laramy's can't ruin good brandy.

"Anyhow, it's just been announced, big news in all the trades, MGM is planning this major production, pulling out all the stops. Rumor has it that Mayer's dead-set on luring Shirley Temple away from Warners for the shoot. There's even talk they might go color when they film the thing."

"I thought color film stock was exorbitantly expensive."

"Like I said, a major production."

A children's book. Nothing but pabulum. More corn to feed the hogs. With none of them knowing how to tell real magic from some charlatan's parlor tricks. Then again, winter was coming, only four more stops on their tour, and they claimed California was always sunny, even on Christmas Day.

"And I suppose," he tells his glass, "you'd have a few connections out there."

"A few," Max says, nodding back.

He downs the rest on his drink in one shot.

"Let me think about it."

They part ways out front, on a deserted sidewalk, left damp by the steady drizzle, one of them as slender as a bowling pin, one more rotund, like the ball. For Max it'll be a train ride north, another client in Chicago. For Constairs a modest room at the Midland, and perhaps a second nightcap. For a moment he lets his eyes roam the street, a habit he'll never outgrow, until they settle on a shadowy figure, peering back from beneath a cloth awning. A reporter? Fat chance. His newsworthy days are over. So maybe, like him, he's awaiting a cab. A hot date in a lukewarm city.

"So I'll give you a call in KC," Max tells him. "In the meantime, you do that thinking."

He lets Max snag the first cab—he's still on the clock, after all—then glances once more across the street as a second hack pulls up to the curb.

"Go ahead and start the meter," he tells the driver. "This should only take a second."

Moving quickly, with a dancer's grace, he cuts across

the pavement, looking neither right nor left for traffic that isn't there. Seeing his approach, his gumshoe falters, contemplating a quick escape, but then with a visible show of restraint he relaxes both shoulders. Pretends to study the curb.

"What's up, sport?" Constairs calls out. "Picked a bad night to stay dry."

The man glances up, only he's not a man. More like an oversized kid. A big Adam's apple, a bigger cowlick, baggy clothes from a Sear's catalog.

"Wait," Constairs says, "I've seen you before." He pauses stock-still in the street. "Tonight. The Palladium. Fifth row back."

"That's pretty good," the kids says, nodding. "With most folks, I'm just plain invisible."

There's more than a trace of self-pity there. Buck up, he feels like saying.

"So what's the play?" he asks instead. "You want an autograph? A souvenir? Or have you got some sister waiting back home, claiming I got too frisky?"

"Nothing like that," the kid insists. "I just want you to teach me."

"Teach you? Teach you what?"

"Magic."

He barks out a quick laugh.

"Try the Guild, why don't you. They love telling people what to do. You work hard enough, you'll even get a diploma, something to stick on the wall."

"But I don't want to be like them. I want to be like you."

The drizzle is starting to pick up. His overcoat's growing damp. Across the street the driver, impatient, gives the horn a light tap. For a moment he stands there, studying the kid, feeling his heart break a little, then reminds himself that when it comes to good deeds, they never go unpunished.

"Sorry, kid. I'd really like to help. But the very last thing I'd wish on somebody is having them turn out like me."

3

SO WHAT EXACTLY is magic?

For the last twenty years, he's been asked the same question, phrased a thousand different ways. Delivered sometimes with no trace of guile, in total sincerity, courtesy of a kid on the high school newspaper, dreaming of his first big byline. And then, a day or two later, it might be one of the winkers. The sly conspirators. Some guy who's convinced it's nothing but hokum, on a par with picking pockets, but you and me, we're both grownups, so let's not spoil all the fun.

An outright lie. A subtle illusion. The willful suspension of disbelief. Call it whatever you want to call it, but the question still remains. What exactly is magic?

And always, his answer's been the same. So transparent it throws them all off. Because the simple fact is, in this world of ours, few things are outright impossible. Finding true love. Being happy. Managing not to die. But a great number of things are instead what we might call highly unlikely. And magic is nothing more than altering the percentages, massaging the numbers, enacting all the minute incremental changes that move any given outcome from that one column—highly unlikely—to another, whether that be labeled as possible, or likely, or downright inevitable.

Does water flow uphill? Not usually, no. But given the right circumstances, and sufficient osmotic pressure, it will do precisely that. Or sometimes even part in two, like the Red Sea itself, as the Bible assures us it did. Can lead be turned into gold? Of course not. And yet the constant transition of all matter from one form to the next is the very engine of existence, which means that such transmogrification is a matter of degree, not kind. Stack your column high enough, your culmination of unlikely events, and pigs can fly, won'ts become wills, disbelief turns into amazement.

Still, like always, there's a catch. Magic doesn't happen on its own. It needs a spark, a catalyst, what the ancients called a prime mover, and what we call a magician. Someone arrogant enough, willful enough, to insist that they can break the rules, beat the house as it were. Because such interventions are dicey, unpredictable, many prefer a safer path, a reliance on cause and effect, especially now that scientific advance can promise such miracles. Plus, there were other factors at play. Most magicians are insufferable narcissists. Convinced they're God's right hand. Leaving their patrons to ask themselves, was that pound of gold really worth it? Worth the price they'd paid? Sitting there, helpless, as some fool droned on, telling them just how great he was.

Many believe that the Sorcerer's Guild was formed for that very reason. To serve as a brake for runaway egos. To make magicians seem more palatable. To provide a codified framework, a modicum of discipline, for what was ultimately the most self-centered of all endeavors. Some had thrived under this form of stewardship. Others bridled instead. And the same divisions of caste and class that had plagued mankind since its inception began to manifest in magicians as well. White and black and sometimes grey, legit or fly-by-night, magicians who could win your war, or just clear up your blocked drain, some revered, some reviled, some ignored.

And Richard Constairs?

One day, years back, when but a child, he'd realized he was a certain kind of person. One who'd never pretend to know who he was, but knew damn well who he wasn't. Not a boot-lick. Not a lackey. Not a company man. Not one to climb a ladder. But by the same token, not much of a rebel either. There was no fire burning away in his chest, just a restless melancholia. Something that seeped out through his pores, like a kind of psychic sweat. So call it the Magician's Curse. The downside of their trade. Because when you live and breathe magic, you no longer notice the stuff, much as a fish, consigned to the sea, is unaware of that substance called water.

THE NEXT TEN days pass by in a blur, or maybe make that a jumble. An unlikely mix of hope and regret, battling it out inside him.

Part of that are the shows themselves. The fact they're so well-attended. Fully half the seats sold out in advance, and the sound of real applause. Back in his twenties he'd dabbled at theatre—light drama, comedies, even a stab at Shakespeare—and so he understands it well, the pacing of a run. The way things began in a total panic, the terror of opening night, then that long, slow middle when you're perfecting your timing, your craft, to the point you're almost sleepwalking through the role, and then, right at the end, the sudden realization that wait, hold on, something's wrong, can this really be our last night?

That being the case, it doesn't surprise him. How life is determined to taunt him. That the privilege of being a working magician, of finding himself on the stage, would grow sweetest just as he's considering moving on.

Karla, of course, can sense his turmoil. Knows that something's up. Approaches him after their show in KC, trotting out her best third-degree. But after twenty years of pulling the wool, he's mastered the art of dissemble, and so pretends to have no clue as to what she's talking about. From that point on it's cool looks and cold shoulders, the Joneses having a spat, and the only time they make eye contact is when she's tossing sharp objects his way.

Stuck on his own, needing diversion, he drops by a

theatre. Not a real one, mind you, with curtains and stage, but the kind where they show motion pictures. Of course, he'd heard about the defections, magicians sneaking Out West, the desperate ones with no real prospects, the famous ones, just on a lark. Had also heard that such magicians, even those lucky enough to find employment, would rarely receive much on-screen credit for their work. That an arcane set of union rules, or the jealous machinations of director and cinematographer, wardrobe designer or make-up man, had all but assured that these individuals worked in the dark.

That afternoon's feature is a horror film, *The Bride of Frankenstein*, and a perfect opportunity for Constairs, a magician, to catch his brethren at toil. That sequence with the miniature people? It reeked of Charles Magnot. Which might explain why he'd disappeared, abandoned the world of touring, only to settle for job with the studios, and a guaranteed three squares a day. All the same, he can hear the audience chuckle. Sense their wonder and delight. Know that, for them, who or why doesn't matter, all that counts are the results. Which means it is there, in that darkened hall, surrounded by perfect strangers, that Richard Constairs finally sees the light. Realizes that it wasn't money, or security, or the glorious weather that had lured his compatriots westward.

No, it was something else.

Because the very thing that made performing in front

of a live audience so, in a word, magical, was also its greatest failing. Every show was ephemeral. Fleeting. As short-lived as a mayfly. A moment of brilliance, of style and grace, and then a memory, soon to fade. But film? Film was for the ages. And thirty or forty years down the road, assuming he's still alive, he could sit back in another darkened room and watch Doctors Pretorius and Frankenstein still at it, still scheming away. And even if your name never made the credits, even if nobody knew the truth, it was nonetheless a form of immortality, the one trick that no magician had ever managed to pull off.

Cheating death. Living forever. Leaving your mark behind. Just the kind of improbable dream that could appeal to a couple of mad scientists, up there on the screen, or a man, not quite as deluded, with no heir, no mate, no prospects. He's been having a dream lately. Or to be honest, more of a nightmare. One that finds him sitting in an empty hall, after one of his shows has concluded. Glancing over at the seat next to his, he spies an abandoned program, then reaches over, snatches it up, peruses the cover sheet. And of course there's the usual verbiage, the overblown theatrical prose, only there, dead center, where his name should be, there's a blank spot instead. As if that name, his very existence, had been erased from memory.

Lost in thought, it takes him a moment to realize that the film is over. That with the raising of the lights, it's time for him to go. He starts to stand, then suddenly pauses, feeling a gaze fall upon him. That awareness every performer has of knowing eyes are directed his way. Playing it cool, he finds the aisle, slowly ambles forward, pretending to study the murals on the ceiling while scrutinizing his fellow patrons. He's almost reached the lobby, and the end of his search as well, when something tells him to turn his head, and glance down the very last row.

A slender frame. A prominent cowlick. Eyes that refuse to meet his. The boy had declared himself invisible, and he very nearly is. Still, St. Louis lies a couple hundred miles to the east, and it's been a full week since his date at the Palladium, which probably mean it's not really him after all, just another Midwest yokel, ditching classes or playing hooky from the farm, or doing whatever it is such youths do. But that word—probably—it doesn't hold much weight, or least not for Richard Constairs. Not for a man who's spent his whole life making the improbable real.

"So JUST OUT of curiosity, were you ever going to tell me?"

The blow-up had finally erupted in Des Moines, the last stop of their tour. Not that you would've needed a mentalist to see it coming down the pike. By the time dear Karla finished her act, his silk shirt had been in tatters, with the sight of his bare chest, nicked and bleeding, provoking its share of cat-calls.

"Tell you? Of course."

"When?"

"Tonight."

They'd bowed together, their hands gripped tight. Found smiles that were more like a grimace. And the moment the curtains kissed the stage, she'd stormed off in a huff. They were both staying at the Metropol, on separate floors this time around, and he'd spent a good ten minutes outside her door, pleading like some errant cad. Which he was, after all.

Still, he'd had an ace to play. Throwing knives always left her half-starved. Pretending to give up, he had loudly trounced off, and then waited by the lift for room service. Intercepting her tray, a Spencer cooked rare, he'd slipped the bellhop a five-spot. Three light raps on that same closed door and the drawbridge came crashing down.

"And who told you?" he asks.

"Max," she shoots back. "Not that he had to. You've been sleepwalking this whole week."

She's wearing some kind of Chinese robe, with probably nothing on beneath it. Bare feet, no make-up, her dark hair in disarray. In other circumstances, all that could prove awkward, or alluring, but there's too much raw emotion in the air for imagining that kind of nonsense.

"Look," he tries to explain, "I didn't even know for sure myself. Not till just yesterday. And besides, if I'd told you sooner, would it have done any good? The two of us going out there, faking it each night?"

"Better than just one of us faking it."

And, as always, her aim is dead-on. She knows her target too well. The way he always needs a secret, something that no one else knows.

"OK. Fine. I was a heel. Probably still am. The question is what do we do now? Now that it's out in the open?"

Ignoring her steak, she picks up a bottle. Her friend, her Traveling Companion. Pours two more fingers into her glass, then makes one of them disappear.

"I could always try talking you out of it," she offers. "Assuming you're worth the trouble."

"Or I could talk you into coming along."

They pause. Study each other. It's hard to say who smiles first.

"Really," he insists. "It could work."

"Spoken like a true magician."

Prompted by that, he conjures a glass, a twin to the one she's holding. Leaning closer, she blesses it with the bottle, daring her robe to fall open.

"So say we both go out there," she counters, "one of three things will happen. Either we'll both flop, and end up crawling back on our knees, or we'll both hit big, meaning we'll be too busy to ever see one another again, or, worst of all, one of us makes it and the other one doesn't, in which case we'll hate each other even more than we do now."

He helps himself to a sip. "I never said I hated you."

"You're right. You never did."

He watches as she leaves her chair. Finds the light switch on the far wall. Her hand reaches out, a flip of the toggle, and the room is suddenly dark, with the sole illumination, a candle or nightlight, softly glowing in the bath. A figure, a shadow, slowly moves towards him, swaying with each step, then two white shapes, what must be her hands, grab hold of the robe's cloth belt.

At which point he knows he's been forgiven, deservedly or not.

"What's this?" he asks the figure in the dark.

"This is me saying goodbye."

SOMETIME LATER THEY both come around. Remember who they are. Remember why they shouldn't have done whatever it was that just happened.

"Miss Livotski."

"Mr. Constairs."

"It seems I'll have to skip town more often."

Hunting around, she finds a pillow. Props herself upright.

"Just to be clear, that wasn't a bribe, or trying to trick you into staying."

"No, I didn't think it was."

"But still," she goes on, "we didn't exactly take precautions and maybe I need to do something. Soon."

Grabbing a pillow of his own, he reaches out. Pats her shoulder.

"Don't worry. I took care of it."

Just like that, he can feel her stiffen. Her body pulls away.

"What do you mean?"

"I didn't think either one of us wanted that. A baby, a child. So I went ahead and did what I do. Played with the percentages."

He's seldom heard a silence that heavy. That fraught with implication.

"That could have been your daughter," she hisses. "Your son."

"And here I thought you said no tricks."

The words had slipped out on their own. His way of saying goodbye.

"God, you are such a bastard."

Five minutes later he's fled the room, his jacket tucked under his arm. Feeling just like what she'd called him, a bastard through and through. It's late, three or four in the morning, and the hallways are mercifully empty, just a tipsy Shriner who gives him a wink, one scoundrel to the next.

Room 213. He hunts through his pockets, front and back, then tries patting down his jacket, only to finally realize that his keys must still be upstairs. No matter. He's a magician. He can open up locked doors. But before he can focus on that task, he turns back to face the hall. Calls out in a mocking voice, fueled by his own self-hatred.

"Come out, come out, wherever you are."

One second it's a potted palm. The next a gangly young man. Constairs stares back, trying to remember if he was once a young man too.

"You know, you're getting better at that."

"Thanks."

"It wasn't meant as a compliment."

Probabilities. Percentages. So if you screw up one life, but save another, does it all even out in the end? And what about if you screw up both? He pauses. Shrugs. Only one way to find out.

"Hey. Kid. You want to go see Hollywood?"

4

IMAGINE A JEWEL out on the horizon, where the sun goes to bed each day. A place built of falsehoods and fakery, where nothing is as it seems, where dreams are stamped out like subway tokens, then sold for their weight in gold. To get there you board a fulmination, a serpent made of iron, cross endless plains, and towering peaks, and arid miles of desert, only to enter a land of date palms and citrus, of wish-for and make-believe. In a time of darkness and deprivation, it refuses to bow down, resolute instead in its sacred mission. To hoodwink. To entertain.

For someone like Richard Constairs, it should feel like coming home. Finding a land as cunning, as conniving, as the confines of his heart. But, in fact, these last two weeks, they've been a bit of a trial. Strangely reminiscent of when his family had returned to the States from overseas, with him but seven years old. That sense of disorientation, confusion, to find everyone else using a different word, dressing a different way, all of them at home in their surroundings, and him on the outside, looking in.

In an effort to cope, young Richard had started a notebook. Jotted down each day's mistakes. Only to find, almost forty years later, that he was back at it again. Compiling a list, or call it a primer, of Hollywood Do's and Don't's.

Never wear black, except at a funeral. Never wear suit and tie. Dress instead like you're on a vacation, like you've already got the part. Always use contractions. Every third or fourth word should be slang. Such slang to be picked up while drinking alone in a supper club or bar. Get a tan, but not, of course, a dark tan, not unless you want to play ethnics. Never appear desperate, seldom appear even interested. Use every social interaction, however slight, to suggest that you would rather be with someone else, someone who is more interesting, glamorous or connected than whomever you happen to be with.

Smile, but never sincerely.

It helps a bit that he has a companion, Charlie the Invisible Boy. Someone who's even more at-sea than Constairs, his putative mentor. By explaining things, showing Charlie the ropes, he massages his own self-esteem, convinces himself that, compared to some, he's not a complete ingénue. And the truth is he likes the company. Someone to dispel the silence. They set up court in a small bungalow, tucked away in a steep ravine, but just a few blocks from the nearest bus stop, twenty minutes to downtown proper. Their neighbors are a mixed lot, day laborers and aspiring extras, and each day begins with the cry of stray peacocks, echoing through the hills.

Soothed by their music, he starts to relax. To surrender to the spell. His street, the ravine, the whole damn town just one enormous back-lot, a kid who's always playing dress-up and invites you to come along. Finding some diner, sitting there at the counter, the next stool might feature a cowpoke, while glancing outside it's two harem girls, sharing a cigarette. As a performer, he knew it well, that giddy sense of excitement, the fact no one suspects who you are, behind the mask, the curtain. Only now, instead of an audience, he's surrounded by people like him, images from a house of mirrors, as brilliant as glass, and as brittle.

He buys new clothes. Studies a street map. Pores over a handful of trades. Decides he should talk to their landlady soon, see about having a phone installed. True to his word, Max has passed along a few names; fellow agents who owe him one, scramblers and fixers and cons. But The Industry—and yes, you must always use caps—is so volatile, so addicted to the now, that yesterday's leads are today's dead-ends, and most of Max's contacts prove useless. Finally, on a lark, he tracks down the Guild's local chapter, an ugly, off-pink blob of stucco in a two-bit town called Rosemead. Back east, just the name Constairs would raise a few eyebrows, or an escort back out the door. But here in LA he's just one more nobody, with no rep, good or bad.

He's soon shaking hands with their Second Mage, hair pomaded as tight as a skullcap, and all it takes is a minute or two to finally glimpse the big picture. To realize that the Guild, always opportunistic, had pretty much leased itself out as a talent scout for every studio in town. Finder's fees, and quiet kickbacks, and a percentage on each contract, with someone like Constairs, a freelance, a loner, frozen out for good. *So what do you say?* the Second asks him. *Ready to sign up?* Constairs thanks him for their little chat, says he'll think things over. Finds himself wondering, once he's left, how long it will take anyone to notice that the picture in their waiting room, that pitiful seascape, is now hanging upside-down.

THE PLACE, A restaurant, is called the Brown Derby. Named after the hat it resembles. But seeing it there, bigger than life, he's reminded instead of a bra cup. That or a scoop of chocolate ice cream somebody left out on the sidewalk.

It has taken four phone calls, and an equal number of lies, to arrange this rendezvous. And, in all honesty, he doesn't really expect it to go anywhere, or at least not initially. No, it will probably take multiple forays, repeated exposures, before people start talking, comparing notes, asking themselves who exactly is this Constairs fellow and why is he so determined to be a pain in the ass?

The maitre d' glances up as he enters. Gives him a smile, insincere. A look of appraisal, or is that contempt, hiding behind all those teeth.

"Good afternoon. Is the gentleman meeting some-one?"

"Actually, the gentleman has a reservation. Con-stairs."

He doesn't bother consulting his ledger, tucked dis-creetly out of sight.

"I am sorry sir, but I'm afraid there is no such reser-vation."

Maybe not yet. "Are you sure? Perhaps you'd better check."

With a sigh, he retrieves the leather-bound notebook. Takes a moment to scan its contents. A moment later his brow creeps up, and a flush steals over his cheek.

"Please forgive me," he says, eyes averted. "I must have overlooked it somehow."

"Happens to the best of us."

It's a spacious booth parked near the back wall, which, like the whole building, is curved. Punctuated by a series of plate glass windows, each one framing a view of the hills. He orders a martini, Boodles, no olive, then examines his fellow diners. Small clusters of men, all substantial, middle-aged, their voices hushed and mellow.

"So this is how the other half lives."

No one, of course, has seen Charlie enter, following just a few steps behind him. Even Constairs himself, knowing he's there, detects just an empty booth.

"Like what you see?" Constairs asks.

"Not bad," Charlie replies, keeping his voice to mere whisper. "Now all I got to do is convince you to order me one of those martini things too."

"Not till you're twenty-one."

His drink arrives. He takes a sip. It's exquisitely, glacially, cold. Almost as cold, he reminds himself, as the reception he's about to receive.

Myron Goldfarb. Goes by My. Seven years at MGM. Which practically makes him an elder statesman in high-turnover Hollywood. Started out as an Assistant Director, twelve-week, B-slot filler, till he finally saw the way things worked and switched over to Production instead. He'd been hooked up with the Oz proposal since before Louis Mayer even secured the rights, and rumor has it if you needed an in, he was the man to talk to.

And don't forget the red hair.

Constair's barely put a dent in his drink when he spots it coming towards him. A curly thatch of caramel curls that would look right at home in a circus.

My stops. Stares.

"Where's Lenny?"

"Five minutes," Constairs replies.

"Five minutes what?"

"Five minutes of your time, and then we can both track him down."

And that's one more thing, besides the red hair. He can never turn down a dare. Once drove a stretch of Highway One blindfolded, just to prove he could.

Shrugging, My throws himself down in the booth, almost slamming into Charlie. His eyes dart over, as if sensing him there, then lock onto Constairs' instead. "So how'd you get my private line? How'd you get past Charlene?"

"My five minutes, my questions. Question one: how's the shoot?"

"What shoot?"

"Oz."

My shakes his head, amused. "Read about it in *Variety*."

"I already did. Sounds like you've got a few headaches. Only I can spare you one."

"Really."

"Yes, really. Who's doing your specials? Your magic?"

My replies by raising his arm, flagging down a passing waiter. He jabs two fingers towards Constair's glass, then finally turns his way.

"Our specials? Why should you care?"

"Because I can do them better."

Arrogance is a tricky thing. It attracts and it repels. And when arrogant men are brought together, one of two things will happen. Either they can go after each other, determined to play top dog, or else they find a bond instead, maybe even see eye-to-eye.

"Flying monkeys."

"Say again," Constairs replies.

"Flying monkeys. Monkeys with wings. We need at least a couple dozen. Only our guy, the bozo we hired, he can't seem to come up with anything we can use. All we get are these ugly-ass things, like a toupee fucked a bat. Think you can give it a crack?"

Constairs takes a moment to think that over. Dabbles at his drink.

"How big a monkey?"

"How big?" My throws up his hands in consternation. "How should I know? Organ grinder big."

Closing his eyes, Constairs concentrates. Begins to compile a list. Hair gathered up from those seated around him, including My himself. Flesh, viscera, stolen in bits and drabs from the expansive meat locker tucked away in the Brown Derby's kitchen. The almost bones of a broken plate, a bright costume composed of torn linens, with two glittering orbs, marbles in fact, borrowed from the dishwasher's pocket.

Two seconds later his monkey appears, upending a glass salt shaker.

My jumps back, his hazel eyes bulging. "Not bad. But where are the wings?"

At that very moment, outside their window, a crow alights in the parking lot. Begins to poke at a small piece of trash, what looks like a silver gum wrapper.

Sorry, Constairs offers up.

It's hard to tell which erupts first, that godawful squawking from beyond the plate glass, or the flutter of wings, much closer. Both men instinctively lower their heads, raise their hands to protect their eyes, as a shape, fur and feather in equal parts, rises up off the table.

And talk about a commotion. At every booth, they're calling out. Pointing towards the ceiling. A waiter rushes out from the back, drawn by the raised voices, then freezes in place, gazing upwards, dropping his towel to the floor. The ceiling is almost twenty-feet high—it's a giant hat, after all—with the crow, or the monkey, or whatever it is flapping away at its apex, shrieking away in a panicked voice that strangely enough sounds human.

"I think I get it," Constairs tells My, "Why God didn't give monkeys wings."

But apparently his creation is just getting started. Mere clamor is not enough. Hanging by one arm, it dangles the other directly beneath its ass. Begins to fling what look like dried berries at anyone within range.

"I read about this," My says, ducking. "In *Geographic*, I think."

Only then, out of nowhere, Charlie is there, looking completely unfazed. Grabbing a knife from off the table, he takes a brief moment to aim, then hurls it, spinning, towards their assailant, still jabbering overhead.

One last squeal, the loudest yet. A dark shape tumbles

downward. The sound of shattering glassware rings out as it lands in a vacant booth.

"Good shot!" My cries out.

Then he turns. Realizes no one's there.

"What happened to him?" he asks Constairs.

"To who?" Constairs replies.

THE TWO OF them, with a possible third, reconvene in the parking lot. There will apparently be no charges filed, no involvement with the police, since no one's quite sure where the flying monkey came from, or where its body ended up. And this is Hollywood, after all. No one bites the hand that feeds them. Even if that very same hand ends up flinging a little poo.

"So you always good for this much excitement?" My wonders.

"Actually," Constairs tells him, "I generally try to keep a low profile."

He watches as My slips a hand in his jacket. Pulls out a leather billfold. The cardstock is heavy, a creamy off-white, embossed with three initials. MGM.

"Give Charlene a call, why don't you. She can set up a little make-nice. Maybe you and LeRoy and whoever else, see what we can work out."

Constairs takes the card. It becomes a carnation. He tucks it into his lapel.

"Thanks. I appreciate that."

And then he lets the smile fade. Assumes a more somber mien.

"But just to clear, the Guild and I, there's not much love lost between us. That's not going to a problem, is it?"

The billfold disappears once more. My gives an off-hand shrug.

"There are problems, and there are problems."

5

"SO AREN'T YOU going to thank me?"

Normally he'd just take a cab back home. Maintain the illusion of wealth. But sadly, his nest egg is dwindling fast, and the bus is a whole lot cheaper.

"Thank you for what?" Constairs asks.

"Getting rid of that monkey," Charlie replies.

A man at a bus stop, talking to no one, with no one answering back. Anywhere else, people might wonder, but Hollywood wasn't anywhere else. Plus, the kid was right. He did owe him one. And even if they missed the next bus, there'd always be another.

"You still interested in one of those martini things?"

An invisible Charlie nods back.

They wander for a block or two. Find a suitable watering hole. A dinky place that's probably not much bigger than one of the Derby's rest rooms. In an hour the booths will most likely be packed, an after-work crowd cutting loose, but for now there's just a single patron, staring a hole in his Manhattan. Ignoring him, Constairs flags down the barkeep, orders two Boodles, dry. Notes how the guy sniffs away at that, the question he doesn't quite ask.

"What can I say?" Constairs observes. "I feel especially thirsty."

He carries both drinks to a booth in the corner, Charlie mirroring his every step, then feeds a quarter into the juke, punching up some Artie Shaw. Me? Talking to myself? Are you sure it just wasn't the music? And lucky for them the booth-back is tall, blocking any view from the bar, which means the keep won't get all hot and bothered, watching the glass levitate, or the way, seconds later, a small sip of its contents disappears into empty air. There's a sudden gasp, barely audible, as the Boodles hits its mark. Constairs should probably warn the kid to go slow, but he'll catch on soon enough.

"So this thing you do," he tells him, "being invisible, it's kind of interesting. The way it obviously includes the clothes you've got on, but not any objects you're holding. And back at the restaurant, the way you became visible just for a second, when you threw that knife."

"Yeah," Charlie admits, "I still got trouble doing it. Doing two things at once."

"Well," Constairs suggests, sampling his drink, "we could probably fix all that. Assuming you'd want to."

He watches the glass float up yet again, not quite as steady this time. "But I thought you said that could never happen," Charlie points out. "That you didn't want to be no teacher."

The opening bars of *Begin the Beguine*. He'd always found them hopelessly sappy.

"So you know that woman, Karla, the one who was part of my act. We were quite close for a while. But the second I heard about coming out here, maybe having a chance to start over, I dropped her in a hot second. Because that's what magicians are like. Ruthless. Completely self-centered. And I don't think it would be possible for someone like you, someone so self-effacing, to ever become one. Because the one thing we need, more than anything else, is to be noticed. To be seen."

Charlie thinks that over. "But what if there's another way?"

Already his words are slurring a bit. His tongue doesn't want to behave.

"I mean, maybe that's how it works for you," he continues, "but not for everyone else. Like in that book they're making the movie from, the one about Oz, there are two kinds of witches, good and bad, and so maybe there's two kinds of magicians too. And you, you're one kind, and me, I'm the other, and maybe we both end up at the same place, only we start out from opposite ends."

It's the most words the kid has managed to string together since they first met weeks ago.

"Why, Charlie," Constairs says, surprised, "did you just call me bad?"

"Hey. You said it first."

And perhaps it's merely his second martini, consumed in less than an hour, but just for a moment, a fraction of time, he can see the logic there. Because he'd known his share of good magicians, decent and honest and kind, and had always assumed it was part of their act, the mask they showed to the world. But what if it wasn't an act after all? What if they really were good? Had once been bumbling bumpkins like Charlie, still were in their heart of hearts?

"You've heard, I assume, of Waterloo?"

"Not really," Charlie admits. "Is that somebody's name?"

Kids these days. What they did—and didn't—teach them.

"It's a name alright, only not of a person, but a place. A place where two famous people, two generals, fought a decisive battle. And one side, the French, they relied on magic, and the other, the British, not so much, only the magicians the French used, they were having a bad day, and, in the end, they lost, which is why we're both speaking English."

"Better than French, I guess."

"And ever since then, and in fact long before it, people have never quite trusted magicians. Which, it turns out, is smart. Because, with magic, you can never be sure how things will turn out. And even with the best of intentions, a good person can make some very bad things happen. Do you think you could live with that, Charlie? Live with knowing the truth?"

Their *Beguine* is now long finished. Only silence fills the air. The muted sound of late-day traffic bleeding through the slotted blinds. Constairs watches as the glass rises floats up, born aloft on invisible wings.

"Guess I won't know till I get there."

Hearing that, Constairs takes the plunge. "An hour a day," he announces.

The barkeep suddenly glances over. Constairs lowers his voice.

"We'll start with what you already know. How to disappear. But we'll improve it, refine it, put you in charge. Then we'll move onto the basics. Axiomatic essences. The Marsten Protocols. Tennent and Swift, of course. Everything I had to figure out, only I was on my own."

"You mean it?" Charlie spits back. "This ain't some kind of joke?"

"Just one I'm playing on myself. And don't go thinking there won't be a price tag. If I really do become involved with this film, we'll be walking into a minefield. The scheming, the plotting, the petty jealousies, like the theatre, only far worse. Which means it would be of considerable benefit to have a second pair of eyes and ears, and invisible ones at that, keeping me abreast."

"Kind of like a spy, huh? I could go for that."

Charlie's glass lifts off the table. Constairs raises his own in response. Rims clinking, they knock back the last of their drinks, sealing an accord.

"Still," Constairs warns, almost whispering now, "there's one more thing you must realize."

He stares into what could be Charlie's eyes, seeing only empty space.

"At some point I will probably hurt you. Disappoint you. Not because I want to, or choose to, but because of who I am. Do you think you can live with that?"

A voice, a whisper, from out of thin air.

"It ain't like I got much choice."

TWO DAYS LATER, on a bright, breezy Thursday, they pull into the MGM lot.

No bus trip, no transfers, not this time around. Even a cab won't do. When entering a world where image is all, appearances must be maintained. But stealing a car, or borrowing one instead, really isn't a challenge, not for a man who can alter what is, or another who can't be seen. It might be a Packard, or perhaps a Hudson, to be honest, neither one of them cares. All that matters is that there's plenty of chrome, and, of course, a convertible top.

"Constairs," he tells the guard at the gate. "I have a ten o'clock with Myron Goldfarb."

He's done his share of homework. Learned the lay of the land. But no amount of reading or gossip could prepare him for what's waiting there. There are five major studios that call Hollywood home, but MGM is clearly king, qualifying as a city unto itself, a place that makes its own rules. There are tennis courts. Swimming pools. A huge vaulted commissary. Almost a dozen enclosed shooting stages, each the size of an aircraft hangar. And then there's the staff. Plumbers, electricians, cooks and valets, seamstresses and exterminators, a literal army of hundreds, of thousands, all on the company payroll. Some of the smaller outfits, Paramount and Columbia, have been gutted by the Depression, are barely hanging on, but for MGM, the woes of a nation are money in the bank. An acknowledgement that Mayer and crew can guarantee the public the one thing that even Roosevelt and his New Deal couldn't deliver. A reason to laugh, or to smile.

They park their wheels in the huge guest lot. Get lost a couple of times. Ask an overweight man in a sweat-stained toga where Goldfarb hangs his shingle. Near the lot's west side, where the breeze blows cooler, there's a cluster of bungalows, with red Spanish tiles, and white plaster walls, and big cascades of bougainvillea.

Constairs inspects his white sport-coat. Adjusts his boutonniere. "No talking, no cute stuff," he reminds Charlie. "You're just a fly on the wall."

Each bungalow has its own number, with Myron's a lucky seven. When Constairs gives the door a rap, a voice yells for him to come in. The décor is West Coast Casual, lots of teak and pale rattan, suggesting that this is a place for play as much as it is for work. From behind his desk,

My glances up, throws him a sly smile, and then returns to his phone call, head bobbing up and down.

"Yeah … yeah … you got it … not that he'll even notice … so, look, Sol, I gotta go … catch up with you on the flip."

My parks the receiver back in its cradle. Jumps up from his chair. Between the slacks and polo shirt he's ready for the fairway.

"Richard," he says, extending his hand, "thanks for making it in. And even on time, no less."

"You sound surprised."

"Do I?" he shrugs back. "It's just that some of you guys, magicians I mean, they come off like prima donnas. Last on the set, first to leave, you know what I mean."

"Well then please let me apologize on their behalf."

"Not that *they* ever would, right? Anyway, as to this morning, I thought we could have us a dog and pony, I'll show you around the set, and then, good news, it looks like we might sneak in a minute or two with LeRoy."

"LeRoy?"

"The Producer. The Big Kahona."

There's a golf cart parked in a slot out back, Gold-farb's name stenciled on the rear bumper. It turns out the lot is teeming with them, plus a legion of bicycles, all supplied by MGM, which makes for some interesting traffic rules, or rather a lack thereof. My, for his part, pretends to not notice, driving by brashness alone, content to assume that everyone else will clear out of his way.

"So just to warn you, things might be tense," he shouts on over to Constairs. "They're yanking Fleming in a couple of days."

"Fleming. He's the director, right?"

"Through tomorrow anyways. Then he's switching to *Gone with the Wind*."

"So who takes over *Oz*?" Constairs asks.

My shrugs his shoulders, almost clipping a bike. "TBA. To Be Announced."

Their journey concludes at one of the hangars, sealed up as tight as a drum. My nods towards what looks like an airlock door and the red light that's burning above it.

"Should be just a second."

True to his word, the light snaps off, and all three of them slip inside, entering a dim and cavernous world, its upper reaches lost in shadow. And while outside it's a pleasant seventy-two, thanks to the nearby Pacific, inside those walls it's hot and stifling, the air thick with a black, burnt smell and an underlying odor of horse flesh. As Constairs trails My, eyes scanning the floor, on the lookout for any stray cables, he now sees that at the room's far end, still dozens of yards distant, it's blindingly bright instead. Glancing up, he spots a series of catwalks, suspended from the ceiling, each crowded with white-hot arc lights. A sear as bright as the mid-day sun, unleashed on its unwitting victims.

For victims is what they are. At first he thinks it's a

trick of the light, some kind of false perspective, but then a worker, a stagehand, walks out from the wings, providing a sense of scale. Constairs stares in disbelief. Tries to comprehend what he's seeing. The set, the stage, is filled with midgets, forty or fifty at least, crowding together, fanning themselves, all decked out in elaborate costumes, festooned with buckles and bows. Seeing them there, sweating and teeming, it's like a dream, or more like a nightmare. One that's rendered even more surreal by My's complete nonchalance.

"They may be little people," he notes, "but they sure do stink pretty big."

Eyes still glued forward, Constairs pulls closer. "What are they supposed to be?"

"Be? They're Munchkins."

By now they've all started to grumble a bit. A buzz like an angry hive. Apparently there's some kind of technical problem and the cameras are no longer filming.

"And where on earth did you find them?"

"All over," My shrugs back. "Carnivals. Freak shows. Vaudeville acts. Even rigged up this special bus to get them here, drove halfway across the country."

For a while Constairs just stands there staring, thinking how strange it is. That it has taken something small, shrunken, something like these people, to demonstrate how big it is. How making this picture, a trifle at best, could touch so many lives, demand so many sacrifices, generate a world of make-believe that was, in its own way, quite magic.

"And did it ever occur to you," he asks My, "that with the right spell, you could have taken another fifty or sixty people, normal ones I mean, and reduced them down into whatever size you wanted?"

My peers back, studying him. Shakes his head in what could be dismay.

"You really don't get it, do you? How there's a war going on. How most everyone who works the lot, they can't stomach you magicians."

Before Constairs can even begin to respond, their exchange is interrupted. Some kind of altercation or spat has broken out under the lights. One of the midgets is shoving another. Voices, high-pitched, ring out. Not only are they as tiny as children, they're every bit as ill-mannered.

"Which means," My admits, "having to put up with this kind of nonsense."

They survey the scene a few seconds longer. My glances at his watch. Nodding over his shoulder, towards the back exit, he starts to beat a retreat. Once they're outside, Constairs pauses. Turns to confront their host. Before he gets in any deeper, he needs to know just where they stand.

"What you said back there about a war. I assume you were being melodramatic."

My reaches up to scratch his ear. For once he seems tongue-tied.

"Look at it this way. You use that spell of yours, and all those poor schmucks in there are suddenly out of a job. Then multiply that by a hundred. Because every time a magician replaces an optical, or eliminates some matte painting, that's one more guy off the payroll. So go ahead, go ask John Henry, was it just being melodramatic, him and that machine?"

Good intentions, bad results. Just like he'd told Charlie.

"Either way," My declares, "we'd better get going. Don't want to keep the big man waiting."

They all clamber back into the golf cart. Dodge and weave through a maze of back-lots. Finally home in on their target, what looks like a spanking new three-story building, blinding white in the late-morning sun. The cars parked out front put any Hudson to shame; two Cadillacs and a Bentley. A couple of men in grey coveralls are pruning a long row of hedges.

The lobby is small but well-appointed, and sports a glass display case. A row of twelve gold statuettes study My as he rings for the elevator.

"And where," Constairs wonders, "does the big man stand on all this? Is he going to hate me too?"

"What LeRoy hates is wasting money. That and making a bad movie. You convince him you won't do either one, and you can pretty much walk on water."

Walking on water? He'd done his fair share. Even managed to keep his shoes dry. After a brief ride up to the top floor, they kill time in LeRoy's front office, as an icy blond in a tight pink sweater hunts and pecks at her Smith Corona. Glancing over at a vacant chair, he can see a faint indentation, what must be Charlie sitting down, barely weighing in at one-twenty. Neither My or the blond seem to notice.

"Mr. LeRoy will see you now."

LeRoy looks like a businessman, which, of course, he is. Black-framed glasses, thinning dark hair, the beginnings of a comfortable paunch. But his eyes are shrewd, bordering on cold, and his words are clipped and concise, and based on the way he's ignoring his guest, Constairs is invisible too.

My and LeRoy banter a while, reviewing the latest disasters, and then, finally, introductions are made, and the latter gives him a nod.

"My says you can make a mean flying monkey. Care to show me one?"

"Actually, that could get pretty messy. Let's try this instead."

From out of nowhere, a Munchkin appears, complete with outlandish costume. There's even a hint of that stink My had mentioned, just to complete the illusion.

LeRoy barely blinks. "And can he move? Talk?"

"Depends," the midget croaks his way. "What do you want me to say?"

"I'm impressed," LeRoy claims, without looking it. "And how many more can you conjure up?"

"It's like a tea bag, magic is. You can only stretch it so far. And the more simulacras you create, the less detailed, the less real, each one then becomes." He pauses a moment, snapping his fingers. The munchkin disappears. "With a production of this size, you'd want to employ at least a dozen or so illusionists, all working in tandem off the same basic template."

LeRoy thinks that over. Nods once to himself.

"I won't lie to you, Constairs. So far I haven't been too impressed with the quality or abilities of the individuals the Guild has been sending our way. Plus, there's the bad blood they generate. Problems with our own personnel, whom, of course, we value highly."

"Yes," Constairs tells him. "Myron was just mentioning that."

"But my real beef is this. For being so-called magicians, you people aren't very magical. Quite frankly, you don't seem to *believe* in much of anything." He pauses. Consults the ceiling. "Tell me, have you even read the book?"

"*The Wizard of Oz?*" he asks back. "No, I'm afraid I haven't."

For a moment LeRoy looks like an old school marm, scowling over his response.

"Then I suggest you do so at once. And if, once you're done, you can walk in here and tell me what it's about, well, maybe then we can talk business."

"WELL THAT WENT pretty well," My declares.

They're back at the visitor's parking lot. The Hudson is still there. With any luck they'll have it back to its owner just in time for lunch.

"You really think so?" Constairs replies. "Felt more like a brush-off to me."

"Brush off?" He waves that aside. "So read the book. Come up with some kind of hokum. What have you got to lose?"

The two shake hands and My speeds off, leaving terror in his wake. Once he's safely out of range, Constairs consults his companion.

"And what did you think?"

"Man, those little people gave me the creeps," Charlie tells him. "The way their faces were all scrunched up."

Scrunched up. Exactly. Climbing back behind the wheel, Constairs lays his hand on the dash. Is rewarded by the sound of all those horses, summoned back to life. After a quick glance over his shoulder, he slips the Hudson into reverse, and only then spots the man who's approaching, moving at a determined clip. He looks to be in his late thirties, a touch of silver in unkempt dark hair, and radiates a palpable air of resentment, of anger tightly held.

"So you're the new one, aren't you?"

By now he's leaning on into the car, exuding a sour

tang. The smell of a body needing a shower, and too many drinks last night. Not that Constairs can really complain. He's smelled just as rank sometimes.

"The new one?"

"Give it a week. Two if you're lucky. Then it'll be your turn. Telling the next guy what I'm telling you, not that he'll listen either."

With that he abandons his grip on the door. Begins to storm away. Only to halt a few second later, a mocking smile on his face.

"And tell your friend the Invisible Boy I can see him anyway."

6

LEARNING MAGIC IS no picnic.

Because no matter how you dress it up, how many instructors you throw into the mix or how many academies you may attend, in the end it comes down to a single moment, repeated ad nauseam. You and the Universe, locked in a room, decided who's going to be boss.

For Richard Constairs that room had been an attic, tucked atop a humble row-house, illumined by a single dormer window, overlooking a quiet side street. Downstairs his mother would be parked by the fire, completing her daily correspondence, while their once-a-week, dear old Sally, might be polishing up the silver for a dinner party that never came. And Richard? Richard, age twelve, would be cursing no doubt, or muttering under his breath, laboring over a Spanzeti Duplication—his twentieth attempt, his thirtieth?—and still not getting it right.

Learning magic can make you hate things. Hate them with a passion. Hate the coin that keeps slipping out of your hand, hate wrapping your tongue around Latin, hate everyone who's come along before you while mostly just hating yourself. Which means, of course, that the real trick is taking all that hatred, that frustration, and using it as fuel. Motivation. Since his parents were too scrape-by to afford a decent school, magical or not, he'd had to imagine one instead. The smarmy students, privileged all, regarding him with derision. The pompous prig who led the class, with Richard his whipping boy. Some frail old fool of a Headmaster, telling him to buck up, toe the line, soldier on. They'd served as his straw men, his would-be foes, the spur that goaded him onward, and one day he would show them all, prove he was a true magician.

But what if you'd never learned how to hate? Never learned how to stoke those flames? If winning or losing, triumph or failure, left you happy either way?

"Hold on," Constairs declares. "This clearly isn't working."

Their bungalow is in disarray. The kitchen is a shambles. They've been eating canned hash for the last three days and the whole place smells like a diner. One corner of the so-called living room is now devoted to physical magic, repeated attempts to convince a bucket of beach sand that it would much rather turn into flour. And that deck of Tarot, fanning across the floor. Another tribute to lost causes. At least they'd had a little luck with Charlie's invisibility, gotten things to the point where all he needed was to touch an object, however briefly, before it too would disappear. A one-trick-pony that might get him onstage, but never once as the headliner.

"What's not working?" Charlie asks back.

"Me. You. This."

The couch has become their de facto wardrobe. He shoves a few shirts aside. Rather than wash them once they're dirty, he's been conjuring up clean ones each day.

"So. Charlie. Didn't you ever get beat up in school? Picked on by somebody?"

Charlie parks himself down in their one good chair. Shrugs those coat-hanger shoulders of his.

"Well, sure. Curt Simmons and a few other guys. Used to drive me crazy."

"So what did you do about it?"

With anyone else, thinking back on bad times, their face might cloud up a little. But Charlie merely shakes his head. Chuckles to himself.

"My foster mom, the one in Nebraska, she had this thing she did. Called it killing someone with kindness. And every time they'd make fun of me, or try to get my goat, I'd just stand there, smiling back. Or even worse, sometimes go right ahead and agree with them. Admit I had chowder for brains."

Which was, of course, the very essence of Charlie. The Man Who Isn't There. All at once, it's suddenly ten years ago, and Constairs is back on tour. That hideous three-night run in Manaus when it never seemed to stop raining.

"Jui Jitsu," he announces.

"Chew what?" Charlie asks.

"Jui Jitsu. It's a Brazilian fighting technique. The idea being that you never trade blows with your opponent, merely redirect their own attack. I saw a demonstration once in the Amazon. Damnedest thing you ever saw."

Leaning back, he studies Charlie. Perhaps he's Brazilian too. A visitor from a far better world where anger or hate have no place. It's obvious now, despite all his efforts, that the boy will never follow in his footsteps. Never find joy in besting another, or in practicing deceit. Which means there's only one path left open. The mountain must come to Mohammed. And if Charlie can't ever learn to be bad, then Constairs will be forced to do good.

"Look," he tells him, still lost in thought, "I've got something I need to take care of. Something that could take an hour or two, or keep me out till midnight. Either way, when I get back, I don't want to see a bucket of sand. I want to see a bucket of flour. Maybe you'll kill it with kindness, maybe you'll just walk on down to the store and steal a bag off the shelf. The point is, I'm kind of curious to see what you come up without me breathing down your neck."

Charlie thinks that over. Nods once to himself.

"And what if I end up drawing a blank?"

"Then I guess I'll be disappointed."

HE TAKES THE next bus out to Culver City. Walks the five blocks to MGM. Spots a snarl of traffic up near the front gate and decides that rather than trying to talk his way through, he'll simply steal a page from Charlie's book and turn invisible for a few seconds. The only problem being that, once past the gate, he almost provokes an accident when he materializes right in front of a harried extra, speeding along on his bicycle.

The personnel office, he soon discovers, is located in the main administration building; a sprawling compound, vaguely Moorish, that's the size of a city block. After spotting the entry up a short flight of steps, he kills ten minutes in a plush vestibule, only to hear his name being mangled by a hesitant contralto.

"Carstone," it calls out.

There's a brass nameplate parked there on her desk, declaring she's Rose Mahoney.

He summons up a dozen in scarlet. Hands them over, and then sits down.

"Really," she tells him, clearly pleased. "You shouldn't have. Now if only I had a vase."

He keeps it simple, white porcelain. Cold water with an aspirin to boot.

"So let me guess," she says, taking the vase. "You're one of those magicians."

She's pretty enough to be in a movie, or close enough

anyways. He wonders if all the women on hire are like that, near-misses and not-quites, contenting themselves with desk work, the next best thing to fame.

"And speaking of magicians," he counters, "I'm trying to track one down. He would have been recently terminated, I believe, but before that I'm pretty sure he was working on *Oz*."

She slips the roses into the vase. Clears a small spot on her desk. Has she noticed they're the exact same hue as the lipstick that she's wearing?

"Well, it's a good thing you came to me. You see, none of the magicians are on standard payroll. They don't want them on the books. So they're paid cash instead, out of a separate account, what they call miscellaneous expenses. And good luck tracking them down."

"But something tells me," he hazards, "good luck is your middle name."

"Actually, it's Claire." She pauses. Smiles. "But give me a second anyway."

A second becomes a minute. A minute is soon more like two. Telephones ring, and typewriters clack, and voices murmur softly, all the busy, muted sounds of a well-oiled machine at work. As before, on his visit to the set, he can't help but be impressed by the sheer scale of the place. All the myriad, multiple talents at play, contributing to the whole.

She returns, slightly winded, her pale cheeks flushed,

clutching a small log-book.

"I swear, you'd think we were Fort Knox or something, the way they cover their tracks. Which means I'd probably catch hell if they knew I was showing you this."

This is some kind of ledger, the corners lightly frayed, chock-full of names and addresses, and the occasional telephone number. A few of the entries are in rendered in ink, far more in pencil instead, but all of them share one thing in common when it comes to the signatures themselves. No one on earth, or at least no mere mortal, signs his name quite like a magician.

"And these dates here," he asks, pointing. "Is that when they were hired?"

"Beats me," she offers back. "I just work here."

Rather than rely on memory alone, he conjures up a memo pad. Jots down the most recent entries, comprising a dozen or so. Watching him work, she's visibly nervous, veiled looks cast over her shoulder. He'd hate to think that her fears are well founded. That she might actually lose her job.

"I can't begin to thank you enough," he tells her. "What can I do to repay you?"

She responds with a smile, coy and inviting. "Ask me on a date?"

He reaches out and pats her hand, chaste as any priest.

"Why, Rose, didn't your mother ever tell you? Never date a magician."

THE FIRST TWO entries are both dead-ends. Rooms rented out by the week. Seedy hotels where the manager's paid to never remember a face. At first it strikes him as odd that such places could exist hand-in-hand with Hollywood's showy glamour, or at least until he realizes that the one gives birth to the other. That for every star the machine creates, a hundred more are left behind, and that tending to this effluvia, giving them respite, however poor, has become an industry onto itself.

It's mid-afternoon by the time he locates the third address on his list, a three-story hulk of one-bedroom apartments with a tavern on the ground floor. Nobody answers at 217, and he's tempted to just move on, but decides to play a hunch instead and check out the action downstairs. Two men, older, are at the bar, each nursing a mug of beer, while one more patron inhabits a booth, tucked in back near what must be the restrooms.

Without even asking, Constairs plunks himself down. The man stares up from his drink.

"The new one," he says, as if they're old friends. "Should've known we'd cross paths again."

The only thing worse than a successful magician is one that's gone to seed. And there's something about that combination—over-inflated ego meets rampant self-pity—that can clear a room in seconds.

"So, how'd you do it?" he inquires of Constairs. "You

use a tracking spell?"

"No," he replies. "Just charm and a little shoe leather."

The man—Anston Williams if the ledger is right—thinks that over. Nods in appreciation.

"I'm impressed. We all get so lazy, after a while. Forget how to tie our own shoes." He takes a stab at the amber liquid sulking in his glass. "So who'd you study with anyway?"

"No one. I'm self-taught."

He purses his lips, letting out a low whistle. "One of those, huh? Well, all I can say is good luck. If you're really that pig-headed, there's no way you'll cut it with the studios."

Constairs nods down towards his glass. "Get you another?"

"Sure. Why not. It's not like I'm going somewhere."

Crossing the room, he flags down the bartender. Orders another drink. Watches the man fill a fresh glass with ice and a splash from a bottle, unlabeled. Once that's done with, he gives Constairs a look: better you than me. Leaving his change along with a nod, Constairs makes his way back to the booth.

"So a few weeks ago," he tells Williams, "I had someone tell me, an agent I work with, that Hollywood was the place to be. That they were dying for decent magicians out here. Steady work and good pay to boot."

"You always believe what you're told?" Williams asks.

Constairs ignores the question. Continues on, unperturbed.

"Then out of nowhere you show up, with this giant chip on your shoulder. Plus I've just heard word that MGM is playing cute, keeping any and all magicians off their books. Almost like we're persona non grata. Something they're trying to hide."

Williams reaches down and lassoes his drink. Downs half in a single gulp. A quick wince when it hits his tongue, a shudder as it finds his stomach.

"So you really don't know, do you?"

"Know what?" Constairs asks.

"The way the whole thing works. How the studios and the Guild, they're working in lockstep. How everything's sewn up. How you first have to pay your standard dues, then a booking fee on top of that, and even then you're just one more guy in the pool, hoping you'll get some piecework. The whole point being it's divide and conquer; they've got us working against each other. And if you say anything about it, raise a stink, they put you on a permanent blacklist."

"So go around the Guild," he counters.

"You can't," Williams sneers back. "If you do, the studios won't hire you. And meanwhile, they're setting us up as the bad guys. Telling their own people that if they can't keep up, the optical guys, the set designers, they'll go ahead and hire us magicians. Which means, if we ever did try a walk-out, we'd get zero support. They'd just be cheering instead."

Hearing all this, Constairs should feel discouraged. His Hollywood dreams are now scuttled. So why is he registering something else, a quiet, clandestine thrill? Maybe by accident, or call it fate, he'd stumbled onto something. A way to do good, but still be bad, all at the same time.

"So granted I just walked in on all this," Constairs tells him, "but the answer seems obvious. If the Guild isn't going to bat for you, it's time you got someone who will."

Williams kills his drink. Shakes his head. Stares back in disbelief.

"Like what—a new union? Out of thin air?"

"Why not?" Constairs counters. "That's why they call us magicians."

BY THE TIME he makes it back up the hill, the sun is beginning to set. The sky has that syrupy butterscotch glow that seems to define California. He'd read some-where, back in the old days, that was how Hollywood first got started. How it was that same sky, the transcendent light, that had sucked them in like so many moths.

He arrives to find Charlie stretched out on the couch, feet up and eyes half-closed, looking entirely too relaxed, like a cat that ate the dog. Before he can sit up, or say a word, Constairs pulls a quick detour. Glances into the bucket. Sees that it's no longer filled with sand, but contains no flour either.

"So where you been?" Charlie asks him, stifling a yawn.

"Around."

Constairs finds a seat in the armchair. Slips out of his shoes, then sighs.

"So. Charlie. What do you think of the Wobblies?"

"You mean like when you drink too much?"

"No," he replies. "The Wobblies. Industrial Workers of the World. The pinkos, the commies, the reds."

"To be honest, I never much followed politics."

And the thing was, neither had Constairs. Which means that, whatever happens, it really wouldn't be about summoning the future, or making the world a better place. No, like always, it would be about him. Sticking it to some convenient foe, real or imagined.

"But you do believe in collective action."

"Collective action?" Charlie inquires.

"Sure," he tells him. "One for all and all for one. That a handful of people, working together, can accomplish pretty much anything."

"Well, sure. I guess."

"Like turning sand into flour."

Can a silence really sound guilty? No, of course it can't. Which means that said guilt must reside in one's mouth, or someone else's ear.

"So about that," Charlie replies. "You said you didn't want to see a bucket of sand. So we're good on that point, right?"

"I suppose so," Constairs concedes. "But I still don't see any flour."

"That's cause the sand is still in the bucket. I just made it invisible. And as for the flour, I admit I cheated a little, went to the store like you said, but then I went ahead and did something extra to make it a little more special."

With that he nods towards the kitchen counter. Constairs follows his gaze. Spies a sad, misshapen loaf of bread, too ugly to be store-bought. But even though it looks a little flat, a little defeated, in fact, surely whoever baked the poor thing has shown some initiative.

Leaving the couch, Charlie hunts down a bread knife, then saws off two generous slices. Hands one of them to Constairs, who hasn't eaten a thing since breakfast.

He takes a bite. Starts to chew. A minute later he's still at it.

"Are you sure you put in enough yeast?"

Charlie stares down at his own hunk of bread.

"Knew I forgot something."

7

LIFE IS FULL of surprises.

Like Charlie for example. After that fiasco with the home-baked bread, you might suspect he could barely boil water. Find yourself tempted to head for the hills every time he starts eyeing the kitchen. Yet despite such misgivings, Constairs is now enjoying the most delicious rendition of Eggs Benedict he's ever stumbled across, and yes, he's tried quite a few.

"So what's the secret?" he wonders aloud.

"Secret?" Charlie scoffs back. "They're ain't one."

For a moment it seems he'll leave it at that, but temptation proves too strong.

"Or maybe it's like how you talk about magic. How if you do all the little things right, the big thing can't help but go along. Getting the roux just perfect, not too thick and not too thin. A little pinch of nutmeg in there, like this cook he once showed me. And, of course, you need good eggs. The yolks deep orange, not yellow."

It's a cool morning, or at least by California standards. A hint of fog stealing in from the coast. Close your eyes and you can almost believe there's an actual ocean out there, a place with waves, and storms, and sheets of rain, and the occasional crack of thunder. But up here in the chaparral? Just another perfect day parked outside their window.

"You know, Charlie, it just occurred to me. You don't talk much about your past."

"What's to talk about?"

"I don't know. Everything, I suppose. This cook of yours, and how you learned about roux, and why you never mention your family. Most people, you invite them to go out west, and they don't just say 'sure, why not?' They have jobs to quit, and people they'll miss, and a life that won't let go."

Charlie shoves his plate aside. Gazes out the window.

"You mean like a home?"

"Yes. Exactly. Like a home."

And all at once, Constaris can sense it. A wall, or more like a rampart. Something that's always been there with Charlie, but is usually tucked out of sight. Push it a little, he instinctively knows, and the rampart will grow firmer. Pushed harder, it becomes firmer still. Protecting a place, tender and raw, behind that aw-shucks act of his.

"I guess that's because I never had one" Charlie admits. "A home, I mean. Or maybe I had too many."

Bony fingers, scabbed and calloused, start to pick at the frayed tablecloth.

"Passed around from place to place, like you're just

some hand-me-down, and by the time you get used to calling some guy 'Dad', you're getting shipped off to wherever's next." His fingers slow, then still. "So no, I don't truck much with words like home, or family. They belong to somebody else."

Somebody else. All on their own, Constairs' eyes steal across the room. Settle on the thin, cloth-bound volume awaiting him on the couch.

"I know a girl who might disagree."

"A girl?" he asks back. "What's her name?"

"Dorothy. And according to her, there's no place like home."

"I thought that's what I just got finished telling you."

Only then does Constairs see it. The way the statement can be read two ways. An affirmation of where it is we come from, or insisting that it doesn't exist. Maybe Baum wasn't such a sap after all. He just had an odd sense of humor.

"Well, sometime you can bring her on over," Charlie suggests. "Me and her, we'll compare notes."

"Sorry, but she'll have to decline. She only exists in a book."

A smile flits across his face. Like a butterfly, just passing through.

"A book, huh? How's it end?"

"I'll let you know when I get there."

SO IMAGINE A girl, trapped in a prison. A prison that has no walls. A flat, grey place that goes on forever, as barren as the sky.

For warders she has an aunt and an uncle. Both of them are grey as well. Bean-pole people, brittle as corn stalks, sucked dry by the endless wind. Each day begins in a house still dark, cold grits or else hot porridge, and she can taste the dust as she swallows, the same dust she will soon become. Five days a week it's a three-mile walk that ends with a one-room schoolhouse, where a dozen children wait for life's lessons to be carefully doled out. Their teacher is a bitter crone, she hates them with a passion, and her only satisfaction is knowing that soon they'll all be as desperate as she is. Resigned to a life that starts, then stops, with not much in-between.

But somehow there's been a mix-up. One weed that has managed to flower. The girl is granted a special gift to lighten her burdensome days. The dog's name is Toto. He is small, scruffy. Irrepressible. Ignoring the blight that surrounds them both, he embodies the girl's rough spirit—her innocence, her joy—all packed inside ten pounds of gristle and fur, scampering underfoot. The schoolmarm shrew can't stand the mutt. He's a constant source of trouble. And though Uncle Henry would've scared him off ages ago, Aunt Em had instead interceded, pointing out how the dog kept the rats at bay, protecting their meager harvest.

And then, one day, disaster strikes. A cyclone levels

the farm. The girl, Dorothy Gale, finds herself carried off to a world too wild to dream. There are witches afoot, both good and evil. Tiny people who dance and sing. A wizard who lives in a great emerald city, at the end of a yellow brick road. Through some miracle, a divine act of mercy, Dorothy has been reborn, and soon she and Toto have both embarked on an unexpected quest. For this journey she is joined by three comrades, each one on a hunt of his own, but no matter what happens, what mishaps enfold, the reader is always reminded that it is Dorothy's search, her quest, almost sacred, that matters above all else.

The search for a place called home.

At which point, with an audible sigh, Constairs sets the book aside.

Home? Really? That same bleak patch of farmland she woke to every morning? The same grim life she'd been forced to endure, with no hope of moving on? It seems a strange lesson, willfully perverse, to pass on to some young reader. That the evil you know, what feels familiar, trumps a chance for trying something new. Still, all you had to do was read the papers, follow the news, to realize that it happened all the time. Women stayed on with the same men who beat them. Men wallowed in weakness and vice. And the prisoner who finally wins freedom finds him- or herself in a panic, longing for the same iron bars that had defined their lives for so long.

Which might well explain Constairs' own life. A life

lived on the road. An endless parade of union halls, theatres and opera houses, traded out year after year. Ever since he'd left the UK, settled in the States, he'd always pretended he was moving forward, on the hunt for better things. Bigger crowds. More applause. A greater claim to fame. When, really, if he were honest, all along he'd been fleeing instead. Fleeing an ordinary life. And home? Home, in a word, was a coffin. A place where you settled, then died. And to imagine it as anything else was a fiction, a fairy tale. One as outlandish in its own way as any fable set in Oz.

And if he knew this, knew it by instinct, Charlie knew it too. Was possessed of a kind of inherent wisdom that belied his brief tenure on earth. So perhaps they should both be reading the book. They could write their critique together. And when Constairs returned to the MGM lot, and pleaded his case to LeRoy, they could take turns explaining why two out-and-out cynics could help make their movie a smash.

"So what do you know about the Guild?"

"Pretty much zip," Charlie tells him.

They're on a bus, destination Rosemead, waiting out a red light. And why no cab? First off, as always, he can't stand wasting a dime, especially when that dime is his. And second off, he's discovered that he actually likes rubbing shoulders with the hoi polloi now and then; plumbers, and housemaids, and short-order cooks, people who work for a living. A break from all those Hollywood hustlers, getting paid to be someone they're not.

Leaning past his companion, Constairs cracks the window. Is greeted by a wash of exhaust.

"So the first thing they do, if you're thinking of joining, is to give you a book to read over. Nicely bound, with a burgundy jacket, and the title in bright gold leaf. *Tome of the Mage.* A couple hundred pages of Abyssinian sorcerers, and evil pharaohs, with a little Merlin thrown in for good measure, all letting you know what an honor it is, that they'd even consider letting you in the ranks."

The bus begins to lumber forward. Progress, or the next best thing.

"But what they fail to mention," Constairs continues, "is a fellow named Samuel Watloe. How, back in 1860, he was two-steps away from debtor's prison, or a ticket to Botany Bay, when inspiration struck. Why settle for being just a failed magician, living in poverty, when you can round up all the rest of the failures and have them pay you to be in charge. One year later the Guild was born. The rest is history."

"So they tell a fib or two," Charlie counters. "I thought that's what magic's all about."

"Lying to them is one thing. The audience. The marks. But lying to each other, your fellow magicians, that's another thing altogether. Besides which, they committed the ultimate insult. Told me I didn't pass muster."

He stares through the glass, remembering that day. The way it still stung, years later. With him a mere boy, not much older than Charlie, left to wander adrift.

"Still," he goes on, "we'll forgive them for now, because they've done us a great favor. Compiled a list of all the magicians who've come out here looking for work. A list which, I might add, we'll find extremely useful in the next few weeks."

Charlie sniffs at this. "And because you're all such good buddies, they just hand it over?"

"No, of course not. Which is why we're going to steal it."

He'd thought about sending Charlie out solo. His maiden flight, so to speak. And a chance, just like with that bucket of sand, to figure out things for himself. But even an Invisible Man can require a diversion or two, lest somebody wonder why that door, that drawer, is opening all on its own. Besides which, after all those decades of simmering resentment, Constairs couldn't stomach the thought of farming the job out to someone else. Gaining revenge by proxy.

A one-story building dipped in tan stucco. A few struggling privets out front. Maybe it's just the time of day, but the Guild offices look even shabbier than they did on his first visit there, weeks earlier. In the meager shade of a nearby date palm, they plot things as best they can, even though Constairs knows quite well that planning can only take you so far. That unlike a stage act, carefully conceived and rehearsed to death, this will be an improvisation. A lark.

They enter the front door, moving in lockstep, and then Constairs hesitates. Feels a draft as an invisible Charlie moves past him, footsteps muffled by thick carpeting. Rather than pausing at the reception window, or acknowledging the woman behind the glass, Constairs targets a second doorway that opens onto a short corridor.

"Sir? Sir, excuse me."

Pinned by her voice, he pretends at confusion, then takes a quick step back. There's plenty of room left for Charlie to slip by. At that point he's on his own.

"Sorry," Constairs offers up with a smile. "I'm afraid I'm a bit distracted."

Unlike dear Rose at MGM, this woman is no starlet-in-waiting. Just a chubby, middle-aged mother of two, stuck with manning the gates.

"I was hoping," he tells her, smile still in place, "to talk to someone about one of your members."

He's also hoping this someone won't be the same mage he'd met on his previous visit. Not if it means another sales pitch. But the man who appears a few moments later is a stranger, and, Constairs senses, by no means a fellow magician. Like they say, it takes one to know one.

"Simon Hayes," he tells Constairs, offering his hand. "My office is a little more private."

Private or just deprived? The sparse furniture, dating back to the twenties. A Ficus with dust on its leaves. And, of course, the family portrait, staring out from atop a bookshelf. For a godawful moment Constairs starts to feel pity, a spark of outright compassion, thinking how bleak the prospect must be, coming in here five days a week. Then he stops. Steels his resolve. The key to keeping your enemies straight is never admitting they're human.

"So I met with a man," he tells Hayes, "a magician that is, about a small project I had lined up. But I was hoping, before I hired him, to check with your office first."

"Check with our office?" Hayes parrots back. "I'm not sure I understand."

"To make sure he's qualified. That there haven't been complaints filed. Angry clients. That kind of thing."

"I'm afraid we don't keep those kinds of records."

Now it's his turn to dissemble. "Really? Why not?"

"Ours is a professional organization. We're here to serve the aims of our members, not the public at large. I'm sure you understand."

Constairs stares past him, through the thin, slatted blinds, at what looks like some kind of park. Wide swaths of grass, and gnarled pepper trees, and a sandbox, complete with kids. The so-called Public at Large.

"Funny you should say that," he counters. "About serving the aims of your members. Because this same man claimed you were doing just the opposite. Selling them out to the big studios. Working both sides of the street."

With that Hayes' face, blandly complacent, shows the first little hint of ire.

"And this man of yours. Does he have a name?"

"That's the problem. I didn't write it down. Can't quite remember it right. But I'm sure if you've got a list of your members, seeing it might jog something loose."

For just a split second, Hayes' eyes dart downward. Steal a glance at his desk. Then they're back, almost glaring at Constairs, no longer playing nice.

"Our records are private, unless you have a court order. And if you don't, I'm afraid I'll have to ask you to leave."

But Constairs is already out of his chair. He smiles down at Hayes. "Afraid? That's her job."

It's a short, piercing, four-alarm scream. The best one he's heard in ages. And while the matron up front might not be a beauty, you've got to admire those lungs. Hearing her at it, Hayes jumps to his feet. Bolts past him towards the door. A second scream, not quite as polished, rings out a second later.

Rats. Norway rats. They never fail. But you have to call up the right ones. Not the white pure-breeds favored by labs, but the wild strain, dark and mottled. And the fangs. Strictly speaking, these ones are way too large, totally out of proportion, but guaranteed to get a rise out of even the most hardened slum-dweller. Constairs watches as Hayes yanks the door open. Sees a woman go hurtling past. Notes a man, equally rattled, as he climbs up on top of his desk.

Constairs steps out into the hallway. Cups both hands to his mouth.

"In here! Bottom drawer, left side."

Hearing this, Hayes spins around. Throws his voice towards the back of the building.

"Carl! We need some help."

Carl, it turns out, is a Teutonic blond, as lean, as lithe, as a race horse. One of those uber warrior-types that's all the rage in Germany lately. And, far more importantly, Carl is also a magician, one they must keep on hand for just this kind of nonsense. For a moment the two men study each other, dogs with their hackles raised, and then, all at once, Constairs is down. His legs no longer exist.

A Half-Marsten, it feels like. Or maybe a Sciatic Burn. Either way, he'd best find a way to contain it before it can climb any higher. In the blink of an eye, his rats all sprout wings. Just like those flying monkeys. Working in tandem, they home in on Carl, targeting that haughty face.

The Marsten starts to weaken. Constairs launches a second attack. A Neural Cloud that should put his foe under without any permanent damage. But by the time the Cloud has materialized, the last of the rats is dispatched, freeing Carl up to engage the Cloud, to bend it to his will. Being magicians, they both can see it there, a swirling mass of darkness. But anyone watching, any civilians, would merely see two men, standing in silence, glaring away at each other. Showing no sign of their ongoing struggle, an encounter in search of an outcome.

Carl is good.

Constairs is better.

A blond head hits the floor.

Winded, he slowly gets to his feet. Makes for the front door. Barely catches a glimpse of Hayes, trying to rush him from behind. Moving by instinct, he darts to one side, some of that old jui jitsu, then gently directs his clumsy attacker into a teak end table.

"Ouch," he offers in parting.

The bus stop is a three-block walk. His legs feel almost normal. Just a bone-deep exhaustion from employing his Talent, or falling victim to somebody else's. Which is, of course, one potential downside of the scheme he's got in mind. That by seeking to help his fellow magicians, free them from their servitude, he will instead incite an ugly little war. Brother on brother, mage versus mage, with no victors left behind.

He finds a spot on the concrete bench. Senses he's no longer alone.

"You get it?" he asks the empty air.

"I got it," a voice answers back.

8

THE FIRST FEW are sent out via postcard. A handful more in sealed envelopes. And then, already growing bored, Constairs decides to spice things up a bit.

Matthew Armstrong has just finished bathing, and is about to embark on a shave, when he sees what appear to be letters taking shape in the steam clinging to his mirror. For Issac Myers, it's a moment of confusion as the front page of that week's *Variety* shimmers, then fades, then reappears seconds later with an invitation meant only for him. And for Karen Fields, one of the few female magicians who's made Hollywood her home, it's a bowl of Campbell's—alphabet soup, of course—that is bound and determined to spell out a message, one she can't ignore.

As for the content of Constairs' announcement, each invite reads the same.

GALLED BY THE GUILD?

If So, You're Not the First. And Probably Not the Last.

Unless You Decide to Do Something About It.

Join Your Brethren, Magicians All,
And End Your Servitude.

Thursday, November 12
North Hollywood Longshoreman's Hall
7:00 PM

Too jocular? Most likely. Too verbose? Perhaps by a hair. But that was always the risk one ran when trying to appeal to magicians. To pretend that a ragtag assortment of self-centered egoists could share anything in common. Win over one, you offend the other. Find a third, and it's open warfare. The only thing they can all agree on being the fact that they all disagree.

Which means that the meeting risks being a fiasco. A waste of their time, and his. A deliberate act of provocation that the Guild will not let go ignored. Plus, there will be risks. The simple fact is, in his face-off with Carl, it had been touch and go for a while. A reminder that after years of being a mere entertainer, Constairs had forgotten how to fight. To play dirty. And should Hayes and his crew decide to crash the meeting, they'd have their spells at the ready, determined to quash any insurrection before it could even begin. And then? There's a reason why magic is the blackest of arts. A dark side to its parlor tricks. A fascination, centuries-old, with all the ways of inflicting pain.

Knowing all this, he has two options. To be or not be scared. To spend the next few days lost in trepidation, or do what a better man would do; buck up and go on with his life. He conjures himself a navy blue Borsalino. A red carnation for his lapel. As he makes for the door, Charlie glances over, still half-asleep on the sofa.

"Where you headed?"

"Out," is his reply.

EACH TIME HE swings by the MGM lot, the place seems a bit more familiar. Somewhere he could put down roots for once and forget his nomadic ways. The guard at the front gate, nodding him in. The milling crowd of extras. That cheerful little ring of a bell, interrupting his reverie, a warning that someone on a filched bicycle is about to run him over. In a way they'd constructed a perfect world, or at least for someone like him. A land where no one was what they seemed, where every act was a performance.

"Richard Constairs. I have a ten o'clock with Mr. LeRoy."

And that newfound ease, others can sense it. It puts them at ease too. The woman, a knock-out with auburn curls, lets her eyes linger on his.

"Have a seat, why don't you. He's always running late."

Late? Hardly. The whole place runs like clockwork. Which means the waiting, the implied social ranking, is just one more part of the game. A way of informing the supplicant—Constairs—that his benefactor—LeRoy—is far more important than he is. And really, that name: LeRoy, the king. But the king of what exactly? When in the end they're both just lackeys, working for Louis B. Mayer.

As per suggestion, he finds a chair. Summons up a deck of cards. Starts to lay out a solitaire hand, suspended in midair. More kings, some queens, diamonds and spades, a bit of mindless distraction, but engaging enough that when LeRoy speaks up, it catches him off-guard.

"Who's winning?" he asks Constairs.

"The cards. Just like always."

LeRoy leads him back to his office, decorated with quiet restraint. Its focal point being a wall of celebrity photos and movie posters, each one framed behind glass. From behind a cluttered desk he offers Constairs coffee or tea, both of which are declined, then takes a moment to study his guest, the ghost of a smile on his face.

"You know, to be honest, I didn't really expect to see you back here."

"And why's that?" Constairs inquires. "I'm not up to reading a book?"

The smile broadens. "No, not that. It's just you magicians, you're an arrogant bunch. You don't like doing what people ask."

"I know. It's our greatest flaw."

Declaration and confession both, it provokes a moment of silence. At least these two men, however different, can agree on this one thing.

"Well, I appreciate you proving me wrong," LeRoy tells him. "And what did you think? Of the book, I mean."

Constairs lets his gaze slip past his host. All those photographs, beckoning back. People, some famous, clutching each other's hands, dishing out smiles for the camera. But look beyond the glassy stares, the white teeth tightly clenched, and you can see something shadowy there. A darkness no flashbulb can ever dispel. Fate overpowering fame.

"I think that Baum," Constairs replies, "he hit the nail square on the head. We're all born with something missing. A hole we carry around inside us, that we spend our whole lives trying to fill. Only thing is, he claims there's a way out. That happy endings are real. As for me, I'm not convinced."

LeRoy stares back, surprised by his candor. Such a rare thing in Hollywood.

"Plus, to my mind, he sold the girl short. Had her settle for going back home. Even after she's been given a chance to call her own shots for once. Is that really the message you want to send to every kid in America? Dorothy Surrender?"

The man behind the desk shrugs once, looking almost sheepish.

"Funny you should mention that. So far we've had three different guys working on the script. And the one thing they all agree on, we've got to make Kansas less bleak. Otherwise why go back?"

Constairs leans forward, pressing his point. Clutching the Borsolino.

"Exactly. And from what I've heard, those initial scenes of Dorothy at home, you plan on shooting them in black and white, and then once she's in Oz, everything shifts to Technicolor. So how about at the end of the movie, when she does go home, you make that in color as well. Let her, the whole audience, see it's not the same Kansas that she left behind. That when Dorothy changes, the whole world changes with her."

"Nash already suggested the very same thing," LeRoy admits. "We've been batting it around."

A minute ago both were wary. Two enemies facing off. Only now each has found an ally of sorts, someone they could work with instead. For Constairs this would be terra incognita. He's always performed alone. Or at least until that day, three years back, when he'd brought Karla into the show.

And LeRoy?

"Well, I've got to admit, this is a surprise. You and I being on the same page. Most magicians, all they care about is a chance to show off. Highlight their favorite trick."

"Don't get too excited yet," Constairs warns. "You haven't heard the closer."

LeRoy tents his fingers. Doesn't say a word.

"Along with a handshake, I get a peek. The Man Behind the Curtain."

LeRoy pauses, his face clouding. "If you're asking what I think you're asking, the answer's going to be no."

"Oh, come on," Constairs insists. "Forget about all that 'no place like home' nonsense. If Baum had a single point to make, it was that you can't trust the guy upstairs. That the more someone hides out behind his flunkies, the less we should all kowtow. And if that goes for the Wizard of Oz, what's it say about Louis B. Mayer?"

"But that's just the point," LeRoy counters. "When you run the whole damn studio, you've earned the right to sit things out. And the last thing Mayer wants is to get dragged into some petty squabble."

"Squabble?" Constairs asks, feigning surprise. "I don't see any squabbles. Last I checked, you and I are getting along like thieves."

"Fine. Then let's keep it that way."

"As long as I get my five minutes with Mayer."

IN THE END they reach a compromise. LeRoy will make some calls. Lob a few balls at the castle walls and see what comes bouncing back. In the meantime, it is suggested,

Constairs might as well bug off, kill an hour or maybe two, seeing how movies are made. And while he's at it, LeRoy offers, why not drop by the set? Margaret Hamilton's working today. A Witch of the West that's so darned Wicked it will give him nightmares for days.

Nightmares? Wonderful. Thanks but no thanks. So perhaps that's why he gets lost. Finds himself parked in a Denver saloon instead of the Land of Oz. He watches an ornate fistfight, impressed by some first-class stunt-doubles, then throws a monkey wrench into the works by transporting a horse onto the set. Seeing the chaos this generates, he realizes he has options. That if LeRoy falls through, if he can't finagle a meeting by legitimate means, Constairs could hold the entire studio hostage. That when you're running a railroad, sometimes all it takes is a single grain of sand to send the whole thing off the rails.

Leaving Denver, he wanders on. Finds another set, this one dark. A cavernous structure, big enough for a blimp, with nary a soul inside it. There's nothing as lonely as an empty hall, a theatre stripped of its actors, a place that holds a thousand ghosts, all of their words now silent. Back in LeRoy's office, for the first time in weeks, he'd forgotten to forget. Had let his thoughts drift back to Karla, another hole that would never be filled. So instead he'd found a sad, lost boy. Made him his companion. Pretending he might be the very same son he had willed out of existence.

Only then from somewhere, all that shadowy gloom,

he can hear a voice, softly singing. A woman's voice, or more like a girl's, and a melody he can't place. Moving through the pitch black room, he lets that siren lure him, for once the victim of a spell, and not the one who'd cast it. Rounding a stairway of plaster and lathe, a short flight of steps leading nowhere, he can now detect a single light shining down from the overhead catwalk. Caught dead-center in its sapphire glow is a tree, now mere silhouette, with a simple rope swing hanging off one branch, and on that swing, a girl.

She looks to be in her early teens. Twin pigtails sprout from her head. A gingham dress with blue and white checks adds to the illusion. But her soul? Her soul, he can sense, is ancient. Old when the world was still young. Countless years you can hear in each phrase, each note, in the depth of her lament.

His shoe finds a chair leg, provoking a squeal. All at once, the singing stops.

"Hello? Is somebody there?"

Her speaking voice is hesitant. He can hear a trace of alarm.

"Sorry," he says, stepping into the light. "I didn't mean to intrude."

She abandons the swing seat, standing instead. Almost like she's been caught out. "No. That's fine. I was just practicing."

"Practicing? Why bother?" Her shyness is contagious. He feels like he's all of fifteen. "Not when you sound like you do."

"Well, thanks," she says, coloring a bit. "That's awfully kind of you."

Two strangers, they stare down at the floor. Actors awaiting their cue.

"So you must be making a movie," he suggests. "A musical, am I right?"

She gives him the oddest look, hearing that. For the first time she almost smiles.

"You don't know who I am, do you?"

"No. Why? Should I?"

She takes a step forward, bolder now. "Well, Mickey and I, we've made quite a few movies. Must be at least six or seven."

"Mickey? Mickey Mouse?"

An actual burst of laughter. "No. Mickey Rooney."

"Sorry," Constairs tells her. "I don't really get out much."

And then, all at once, it hits him. What a fool he's been. The way that if he couldn't find Oz, Oz would come to him.

"You're her, aren't you? Dorothy. Dorothy Gale." He stops, flustered. "Sorry. I mean you're playing her. And your real name. It's Janet? Jane?"

"Judy," she offers up. "And you must have a name too."

"Sorry," he says, extending his hand. "Constairs. Richard Constairs. I'm hoping, if my luck holds out, we might be working together."

She stares back, confused, her own hand limp.

"I'm a magician," he goes on.

And the way her face perks up at that. Like lightning in a bottle.

"A magician? Really? Can you show me a trick?"

"Sure. Any suggestions?"

She needs but a moment to think it over. "How about you make me disappear?"

Hearing her words, he's taken aback. He instantly thinks of Charlie. "Disappear? Why on earth would you wish for that? I mean, being an actress and all."

"Oh, not all the time," she explains, "just sometimes. You see, everyone else on the set, they've been doing it for years, vaudeville, or plays, or later on movies, and me, I'm just a kid. And sometimes, the way they all stare at me, like I'm holding everything up, and, and I don't know, sometimes it'd be nice to just get away from all that. To get away from all those eyes."

But it's her hands that he's been watching. The way they're wrestling with one another. A part of her may comprise an old soul, beyond any worries or cares, but clearly she's also a slip of a girl, barely keeping her head above water.

"And plus, if he couldn't see me, maybe he wouldn't say it."

"He?" Constairs asks.

"Mr. Mayer. He calls me his little hunchback."

"Not without a tongue he won't."

She looks back, startled, then starts to smile. "You could really do that?"

"Just say the word."

It's one thing that all of us tend to forget. Just how cruel a young girl can be. But then, with a shrug, she forgoes his offer, opting for mercy instead.

"But really, I shouldn't complain," she insists, "not as long as they let me sing. They can stare, and laugh, and call me names, just as long as I get to sing."

"Well, then. I guess I'd better leave you to it."

With that he gives her a little bow, as if she's royalty. "Here's hoping we meet up on the set. Share a flying monkey or two. And if you change your mind about Mayer, don't hesitate to ask."

Turning, he plunges back into the darkness, only to halt mid-stride.

"One last thing. That song you were singing. Are there words to go along?"

"Of course."

"Then why weren't you singing them?"

She shrugs, as if the answer's right there. "Because they always make me cry."

9

HE FINDS HIS way back to LeRoy's office. Learns that he's left for the day. That despite having made a half-dozen calls, there's still no appointment with Mayer.

Thanking the woman, he heads for home. Strolls along, all but blind, to a bus stop. But although his body may go through the motions, his head, his heart, are elsewhere. Still back with the girl in the gingham dress, and her wordless song of sorrow.

He's used to noticing women. To feeling interest, or just plain lust. But what he registers now towards this almost-stranger has nothing to do with all that. No, he decides, this deserves another word. A better word. Wonders if compassion would fit the bill. Because, with one look, you can see it all, the whole arc of her life playing out. Those first rays of hope, already dimming, the disappointments that will take their place, and, finally, the darkness itself, waiting at the end. And in sensing that, you want to reach out, try to deter that fate, all the while knowing that it's hopeless. That there are some things in life, like life itself, that not even magic can change.

It's getting towards dusk when the bus lets him off. A twilight stroll through fragrant hills. Radios playing, mothers calling their kids, dinner plates being laid on the table. There's a single light burning in their cramped bungalow, luring him in like a moth, and he finds Charlie there, stretched out on the couch, pretty much just how he'd left him that morning. Or nearly so. This time around he's paging through something. One of those fifteen-cent pulps. An alien creature, tentacles writhing, grabbing hold of a toothsome blond.

"Careful," he warns him. "You'll rot your brain."

Charlie just shrugs. "Like it's not too late."

Launching his hat towards a potted palm, Constairs retreats to the kitchen. Pours an inch or two of amber into a squat tumbler.

"You OK?" Charlie calls out.

He carries his drink back into the light. Throws himself down on the armchair. Pretends to not notice the cloud of dust that billows out from the cushion.

"Sure. Why do you ask?"

"I don't know. You just seem a little down."

Up. Down. Sideways. So many choices in life. Except, of course, they're not really choices, more in the way of decrees.

"So. Charlie. Think you could teach someone else how to do it? How to be invisible?"

He tosses the pulp onto the floor. Somehow manages

to sit up. "Teach someone? I can barely work it myself."

"Not full-on invisible," Constairs amends. "Just that other thing you do. Where people can still see you, they just don't *notice* you."

"Oh. That." He scratches his head, then yawns. "I suppose I could give it a shot."

"And if it worked, and then you took this person and put them in front of a movie camera, what do you think would happen? Would you still see her there? And if so, would she look different somehow? Flat, or washed-out, or drab?"

"Man," Charlie points out, "you are just full of them tonight, aren't you? All them What-Ifs and Might-Have-Beens."

Constairs takes a stab at his drink. Remembers why he seldom drinks Scotch. Then reminds himself that, on some nights at least, it's not about the taste. And maybe Charlie's right about all those What-Ifs. What do they really get you? He already has his own make-believe son, doesn't need a make-believe daughter.

"Any more RSVPs?"

"A few," Charlie says. "A couple by mail, one by carrier pigeon, and the last one showed up right after you left, it was like this miniature fireworks show. Almost set the rug on fire."

He thought he'd smelled it, coming in. A lingering whiff of sulfur.

"Which makes it, what, eighteen?"

"Nineteen by my count."

"You know, at this rate," Constairs admits, "it could be a real bust."

They take a moment to think about that. Neither one breaks out in tears.

So instead he takes another sip. "Guess we'll find out tomorrow night."

SO WHAT EXACTLY is a Longshoreman's Hall, and why is there one in North Hollywood?

There are no burly men with prominent tattoos. No bodies being tossed overboard. Not even a glimpse of tumultuous waves, or endless miles of ocean. But there is this. It was cheap. Not as cheap as the Elks Lodge, mind you, but nearly twice the size, and as for anything in Hollywood proper, you can kiss your wallet goodbye. Plus there were all the intangibles. The connotations, thick as tar. Just mention the word longshoreman, and there's a hint of skullduggery. Of menace. Back alley deals, and soiled wads of cash, and double-crosses that are actually triples. A place where history can be made. Where revolutions are born by C-section.

Which is why he insists on manning the door. Greeting every arrival in person. Shaking a hand, and meeting an eye, and sizing each specimen up. Reminding himself, if reminder is needed, of what an unruly mob they comprise. That in spite of what's often said about cats, and their reluctance at being herded, there is no more varied or cantankerous lot than a gathering of magicians.

There are wizened mages, stooped by age, eyes milky with cataracts, who have spent the last decade just scraping by, card tricks at bat mitzvahs and birthdays. Young hustlers, hair thick with pomade, their suit-coats smartly tailored, always on the look-out for the next big break, the con that just can't fail. Men and, yes, the occasional woman, hailing from Lebanon, from Budapest, from the backstreets of Taipei, some with impeccable English, some just point-and-nod, all lured by the glittering promise of fame, or at least a steady paycheck. Put them all together, combine their acumen, and realize that within that room is found the wisdom of the ancients. Six millennia's worth of craft and lore, human suffering and toil.

For that is the other thing Constairs can spot, with every new guest he encounters. A question never once spoken aloud, and yet asked nonetheless. How will you exploit me? What trick is up your sleeve? What lies will you regale me with, even as you rob me blind? Put anyone else, any group, any trade, all together in one location, and you'd hear laughter, commiseration, the sound of walls coming down. And yet here, tonight, it's all quiet suspicion, a deathly-still reserve, everyone out there watching their backs, and ignoring the faces that surround them. Which means it's all up to him. That somehow, in the next few minutes or hours, he'll have to bring them together. Convince them that, despite their suspicions, they're surrounded by friends, not foes.

"So much for a bust."

Charlie is smiling, his cowlick at full-mast, convinced that all is well. For him it's just a night on the town, and a chance to show off his new suit.

"Any clue as to a headcount?" Constairs inquires.

"I lost track at a hundred."

And then comes a yanking at his sleeve. Are there any more chairs in back? Some skeleton in a threadbare black suit, with his great-grandson propping him up.

"A chair? Yes, of course."

He conjures a Stickley, and then its companion. The escort deserves one too.

It takes him ten minutes to traverse the room. To hack a way through that crowd. Everybody's got their questions, or pleas, each more desperate than the last. He'd always found pride in being a magician, the very picture of cool self-reliance, and is only now sensing the awkward truth that lurks behind this misconception. That they're just a bunch of three-year-olds, the next best thing to helpless.

He finally reaches the shoddy stage. Homes in on the podium. Finds that a small wooden hammer awaits him, just the thing for dealing with children.

He raps once. "Excuse me."

The hall grows louder.

"Excuse me."

One man in front glances up.

"EXCUSE ME!"

It is the Voice of Jehovah, or at least that of Moses. A sudden quiet fills the room. Everyone's staring at the stage, the tall figure stationed there.

"If you could all please take your seats, we can get this underway."

Two or three minutes are spent finding chairs. It's the first day of school yet again. He waits for their silence, hoping for pin-drop, contenting himself with a murmur.

"My name is Richard Constairs. Many years ago, when I was sixteen, I applied to join the Guild. I'd just achieved the Fourth Protocol and felt I was more than ready."

The murmur grows louder. Perhaps a handful, there in that hall, had managed to master the Fourth. But to do so at such a young age?

"Instead I was rejected," he continues, "but, of course, I was never told why. At which point I decided to head out on my own, and let the Guild be damned. In the intervening years, I have found the Guild to be close-minded. Parochial. Shamelessly hierarchal. An embarrassment to our craft. But it wasn't until I arrived here, seeking opportunity, that the veil was pulled from my eyes. That I realized that the Guild was not just misguided or ineffective, but had in fact become outright evil."

A dozen voices ring out all at once. Men are rising to

their feet. Constairs summons up a dampening spell, and the hall is returned to silence.

"Some of you may agree with me. Some of you may not. Everyone here will receive two minutes to say whatever they see fit. We'll start with the first row. No interruptions, please."

Their very first victim, or perhaps guest of honor, is a middle-aged man out of Philly, who, it turns out, had arrived on the Coast just a few weeks ahead of Constairs. Short, squat, with thinning dark hair, he is anything but prepossessing. A quiet man who seems ill at ease addressing that large of a crowd.

"Just like everyone else in this room, I'd been hearing all the rumors. Good, steady work, and decent pay, and not having to work nights anymore. Which, when you've got a family, starts to mean a lot. So now they've got me working audio, the studios that is, cleaning up sound-tracks or what have you, and I could put up just fine with the boredom, or the way the boss lords it over me, but the truth is, between the Guild fees and the union dues, and the fact I never apprenticed, I finally had to take a second job waiting tables, just to make ends meet." He pauses, shrugging in defeat. "So much for not working nights."

Finished, he shuffles off the stage. There's a smatter-ing of applause. As he passes by the next man up, he receives a quick pat on the back. And then it's another story, and another one after that, the details varying not nearly as much as the way each tale is delivered. Some, like the first, are quiet vignettes, you have to lean in and listen, hear that unspoken hint of despair hiding behind each word. Others are harangues, delivered at gunpoint, a voice that fills the hall, egos so big and unruly it's a wonder the stage holds up. Still, whatever their differences, it's clear before long that they all share a consensus. The Guild is a parasite, plain and simple. The question being how to send it packing without killing off the host.

"Look, it's obvious."

The man is built like a fireplug. Or make that a long-shoreman. Disproving the myth that magicians are slender, and always wear dinner jackets.

"Anyone else," the fireplug bellows, "a plumber, a cop, he'd belong to a union, guaranteed. And he'd get to vote on who's running the show, all the way up to the top. But can anyone out there tell me who runs the Guild, or who voted him in, or how much he gets paid? No, of course not. Because we're just the peons, right?. The guys who do what we're told."

"But you can't have a union unless you have strikes," someone shouts.

"A strike?" the man chuckles back. "Sure. On all that giddas I got tucked away."

Constairs raps the gavel. It's time to regain control.

"Gentlemen and gentleladies. Let's pause for a moment to see where we are, to see what we've accomplished. In less than an hour, we've reached a consensus. Agreed on the following points. One, that the Guild can no longer be trusted. Two, that some new organization must be created to take its place. And three, that unless we establish our power to strike, to withhold our talents as a bargaining chip, that organization will be toothless. That, my friends, is the good news."

Everyone begins to nod in agreement. Not bad for an hour's work. Maybe they should all head home, get while the getting's good.

"Which means it's now time for the bad news."

You can almost feel the whole room deflate. A balloon shaking hands with a hat pin.

"The bad news is we're magicians."

He pauses a moment. Lets that sink in.

"The most cynical, suspicious, self-centered souls on this or any planet. We don't join unions. We don't form clubs. We are not the Three Musketeers. And our motto should be 'All for One, and One for Me, and By the Way, None for You."

A few of them grumble at this summation, but there's no sign of outright denial.

"Show of hands," Constairs continues. "How many of you can honestly say you've never stolen a trick? Bad-mouthed one of your brothers? Gotten a gig, somebody else's, by lying a little, or passing on rumors, or just being an all-around heel?"

He stops. Scans the crowd. Not a single hand appears.

"But don't feel bad about it. That's what magicians

do. Get paid to be dishonest, to pull the rug over everyone's eyes. Maybe this will sound naïve, but when I found out the Guild didn't want me, I thought that someone else would. A mentor, a partner, call it what you will. Only to discover that being a magician, you're a country of one. That the last thing any of us are willing to do is help out the competition. To make anyone else look good.

"So before we go any further, or start throwing around words like union, let's all take a moment. Turn to the person on your right, on your left. Look him in the eye. Ask yourself, if his plate was empty, would you share whatever's on yours? Because if the answer isn't yes, then let's just head home now."

"THAT'S THE LAST of them."

They'd taken an old shoe box. Carved a slot in the cardboard top. Torn up a few sheets of foolscap and passed the scraps around. And sure, just about anyone there could've conjured up actual ballots, but there was something pure, untainted, about not using any magic. To admit that, for once, it wasn't about their skills, their Talent, but the person they'd decided to be.

"And the count?" Constairs asks.

"113 Yes, 22 No," Charlie tells him. "Pretty much a landslide."

"And out of those 113, how many really mean it? Will lay themselves on the line?"

He greets that with a lopsided grin. "You always got to spoil things, don't you."

They have the hall till a quarter-to-twelve. It is now eleven-thirty. A man with a push broom and grey coveralls is giving them the stink-eye.

"Your friends. They all go. Who going to clean up this mess?"

Constairs take a slow, deep breath. Reaches up and snaps his fingers. The chairs, the trash, they're all suddenly gone, the room is now pristine.

"Hey," the man exclaims. "How you do that?"

"Just magic," he replies.

10

"RICHARD CONSTAIRS?"

He'd had the phone installed just two days ago. Never thought it might actually ring. Or that, if it did so, it would happen to be at such an ungodly hour.

"Speaking," he manages.

"My name's Thompson," the voice declares. "I work for Mr. Mayer. Mr. Mayer will see you today, two o'clock, at his main house. I assume you're available?"

"Available? Sure." He starts to fumble for pencil and paper. His brain is still half-asleep. "What's the address anyway?"

"A car will pick you up at half-past one. At your residence, if you'd like. Be aware, however, that given the current circumstances, Mr. Mayer might need to cancel at the last minute."

"The current circumstances?"

There follows a pause, brief yet pungent. He's clearly failed some test.

"You do get a morning paper, I hope."

"Yes," Constairs tells him, lying.

"Well, then. You might want to read it."

HE STEALS A paper from a neighbor's porch. Tells their cat that he'll bring it right back. The article's buried on page thirteen, beneath a slew of ads. Tom turkeys for sale at twelve cents a pound, just in time for the Holidays.

GUILD DENIES WALKOUT

Constairs begins to read.

And in doing so he soon discovers that Hollywood's in a pickle. People are calling in sick, it seems, if they're calling in at all. And not just any people, but those who claim to be magicians. As a result, a mere three days in, the wheels have ground to a halt, with the studios heads all growing nervous, eyeing their bottom lines. And looking, of course, for someone to blame, a few heads to knock together.

The Guild, for its part, claims complete ignorance. Why shoot the Golden Calf? Leaving rumors of a shadowy presence, a new player in the game.

"Was that the phone I heard?"

This from Charlie, out in the kitchen, brushing his teeth at the sink.

"The phone?" Constairs lobs back. "I must have slept right through it."

"And since when do we get a paper?"

"Since never. But now that I'm President of a power-ful yet mysterious fraternal organization, it seems I ought to stay well-informed."

But while he may affect a blithe disregard, he is, in fact, a bit nervous. Life consists, he'd learned long ago, of trying your damnedest to budge an immovable object. Then desperately scrambling to outrun the same as it suddenly plummets your way.

"I'm starting to wonder," he admits with a sigh, "if our walkout was all that smart."

"It's not like that's your fault," Charlie points out. "They're the ones who voted for it."

"Yes, that's the theory."

Constairs had never found a mentor, but he knew how the process worked. Knew that warning their wards of the dangers they'd face had always been part of the package. All the ways the world would betray them. How people would let them down. But the ultimate admon-ishment, the one that stung the most, was when a mentor revealed his own flaws. Admitted that he too was a charlatan, just like everyone else.

He watches as Charlie retreats to the armchair. Stares at him in disbelief.

"What are you trying to tell me? That you monkeyed with the vote?"

"Don't worry. We would have won, no matter what," he assures him. "I just made it more resounding."

But even to his ears, the words sound hollow, a curtain yanked aside. Sometimes we grow up in pieces. Sometimes all at once.

"I swear," Charlie tells him, "the way you act sometimes, it's like I picked the wrong horse in this race."

Constairs pretends to study his paper. All he sees is a jumble of words. It's not as if he hadn't warned him, told him this moment might come.

"The wrong horse," he finally echoes. "As if there's ever a right one."

THE CAR ARRIVES ten minutes early. Constairs is waiting out front. The sight of a limo on that humble cul-de-sac far better than a visit from Santa. He nods towards blinds now scissored half-open, more curtains tugged aside, then disappears into its shadowy depths, black leather and a glint of chrome.

To reach Oz you must first cross a forest. Fight your way through the trafficked throng. And only then will you find yourself climbing upwards, to where the air is more rarefied. They pass by palms. Lavish mansions. Driveways guarded by wrought-iron gates. With each glimpse, each oasis, surpassing the last, an endless game of who outdoes who. Eventually the road narrows. The houses drop away. A mile-long stretch of switchbacks and scrub, home to coyote and cougar. One last view of a blue Pacific, one last gate to endure, and then the

Emerald City beckons, only it's white instead.

The white of angels, brought to earth. Of sun-baked walls in Spain. With red-tile roofs, and turquoise pools, and deep green expanses of lawn. When you sell dreams for a living, this is the dream you live, but seeing it all, so polished, so perfect, it rings a hollow note. Because, in essence, it's just another back-lot. A place that isn't real. And dwelling within it, calling it home, surely makes one unreal as well. Just like a magician who's learned the trick, seen the back side of the mirror, the wealthy, the privileged, must bear their own burden. They're immune to their own spells.

A man in black escorts him in. The ceilings are twenty feet high. Their heels clicking on Moroccan sandstone as they wind through endless halls. Mayer's study—one of many, no doubt—is perfectly appointed, a tribute to knowledge and culture and class, with barely a nod to Mammon. Left alone, Constairs scans the shelves. Notes a volume of Aleister Crowley. How odd to find a dear old friend at home in such a setting.

The nap is so thick he hears no footstep. Just the sound of a throat being cleared.

"Constairs, isn't it? Thanks for making it out."

Standing, he takes the proffered hand. Finds skin as smooth as satin.

"On the contrary. Thanks for the invite."

Mayer, it turns out, is built like a penguin, one stuffed in a burgundy suit. A short, well-rounded pug of a man, exuding an easy bonhomie. Grey hair slicked back, sparse up on top. An owlish pair of glasses. The air of someone who's been in the trenches, and now knows just how lucky he is. Constairs had come there wanting to loathe him, to cast him as enemy. Can't decide if finding him likeable instead will only make his job that much harder.

"Can I get you anything?" Mayer asks. "It's a little early for a drink."

"No thanks, I'm fine."

Mayer takes the desk, of course. Constairs settles back in his chair. The light of a desk-lamp catches Mayer's glasses, hiding his dark eyes.

"LeRoy said you asked for five minutes. I'm willing to go a full ten. But being honest, you'll have an uphill battle, with the way I feel about magicians. Especially now."

"And who's to blame you," Constairs concedes. "No one can stand us, including ourselves. We're an arrogant, self-centered bunch of cheats, no two ways about it."

Mayer stares back, saying nothing.

"But even so, we can still be useful."

The light on the lenses shifts a bit. He takes that as a good sign.

"Now this thing in the paper," Constairs continues, "people calling in sick, sure, it's an inconvenience. But the real problem, the underlying conflict, it's been there since day one. All along, you've been dealing with the Guild in good faith, making them your partner. Only problem is, the Guild doesn't really represent your working magician. Never has, never will."

"According to you, at least."

"No, according to them. And frankly, you, MGM, all of the studios, you've only made things worse."

Mayer leans back, consulting the ceiling. Toys with his left cufflink.

"And how did we manage that?"

"By treating us like we all have the plague. Like we're some dirty little secret. When every twelve-year-old kid in Poughkeepsie knows damn well you've been hiring magicians for years."

Mayer slowly shakes his head. If only life were really that simple.

"There are intricacies, Mr. Constairs. Things you wouldn't understand. If I, if any of the studios were to align themselves with magicians at this late date, they'd merely earn new enemies. Not to mention the fact that such a gesture would be a tacit admission of guilt. An acknowledgement of the fact that we'd been in the wrong all along."

"And what if I told you that wasn't a problem. That you had your very own Get Out of Jail Free card."

"I'm afraid I don't understand."

"You're shooting a major production. *The Wonderful Wizard of Oz*. So why not announce, for the very first time, that magicians are running the show. That every special, every trick, will be one-hundred-percent real magic. You'd be getting a jump on the other studios. Turning a problem into a plus. And if you think Technicolor will be a big draw, just imagine when you send out a hundred magicians, one for every premiere. All the ways you can market this thing, turn it into a real event."

There are, of course, two kinds of silence, and both of them speak volumes. One being the silence of total indifference, of having nothing to say.

And the other?

"I trust," Mayer finally pronounces, "that you've mentioned this to no one else."

"No, of course not."

"And you seem to be suggesting that you hold sway over these magicians of yours. That you know what they think, how they feel."

"As much as anyone can."

Back to the cufflink, and the dark stone inside it. Obsidian or perhaps an onyx. A moment later a smile, sly and knowing, steals across Mayer's face.

"I'm beginning to wonder," he tells Constairs, "about the timing of all this. I find myself with a labor shortage, delays in post-production, and suddenly a man shows up, claiming he can fix all that."

"No more farfetched," Constairs suggests, "than some Russian immigrant kid making it big. One day he's sweeping gutters and the next he's calling this home."

He watches as Mayer finds his feet. Swings around the desk. Yet again he offers up his hand, the same hand that once held a broom.

"You'll hear from me in a day or two. In the meantime, please keep this to yourself."

"Sure. And you can do me a favor too."

Hearing the rancor behind those words, Mayer tries to retrieve his hand. But Constairs merely smiles back. Grips it even harder.

"You ever call her a hunchback again, you'll wake up as Quasimodo."

THIS TIME, THE ride seems to take a bit longer. Traffic has picked up. Constairs tries putting the time to good use, reviewing their brief exchange.

Unlike certain hot-tempered magicians, the kind who make nasty threats, Louis B. Mayer is a businessman first, and a businessman last as well. Somebody who'd lie down with the Devil himself if it kept his empire afloat. Which means, in all likelihood, he'll simply ignore Constair's little gaffe. Do a little digging of his own. And soon discover that his visitor's offer is really more of a bluff. Claiming to speak for a couple hundred magicians, and just praying that they'll go along.

But it's not just them Constairs has to win over. It's the person who's waiting back home. A kid who's just had his eyes pried open, courtesy of You-Know-Who. On the surface, Charlie's trick was remaining unseen, hiding in plain sight. When in fact that blindness worked both ways; a willful refusal to see all the bad stuff, the pettiness, the dishonesty, the deceit. People like Charlie, they needed a north star, someone they could look up to. The problem being, this time around, he'd gotten stuck with Constairs instead.

He watches the limo pull away. Finds his way to the door. Feels a sense of trepidation as he steps into the foyer.

"Charlie?"

It's that certain kind of echo. A house with no one home.

"The bastard's back," he says anyway. "More disillusionment, served up cold."

It takes all of two seconds to conduct a quick survey. The bird has indeed flown the coop. Maybe to merely run a quick errand, or maybe gone for good. He circles around, returns to the front door, gently swings it shut. Only then notices that Charlie's one pair of shoes is still tucked next to the closet.

That's odd, he thinks to himself.

And then a darkness, deeper than night, closes all around him.

11

His FIRST CLUE is the smell.

Close. Dank. Just shy of musty. The odor of dear Mother Earth. Suggesting that he's somewhere deep underground, in a cavern or perhaps a mine shaft. But a mine shaft in California? Then again, they did have that Gold Rush, and not so long ago, and yet he's fairly certain that had been miles away, in the hinterlands farther north.

Still, if he's all that eager for answers, he could just open his eyes. Take a quick look around. Only both lids are composed of lead, weighing in at several pounds each, and really, the darkness, it isn't so bad. Almost soothing, as a matter of fact. Which apparently means it's up to his ears to provide a bit more incentive. A high-pitched squeak, quick and nervous, a sound from his childhood, something burrowing away in the cellar as he lay awake at night.

Something with teeth, and a tail.

Just like that, his eyes snap open. He's suddenly wide awake. There's an iron spike inside his skull, throbbing with each heartbeat. His first impulse is to reach up, check for wounds, see if the spike is real, but then discovers that his hands are lashed in place, with what feels like leather straps. Straps attached to some kind of table, rough-hewn planks of wood, a primitive cousin of the cork-lined number they'd used in Karla's act. Only this isn't an act, is it? No, it's all too real.

He gaze reaches out. Finds cold granite. Large blocks that look hand-carved. No windows, or at least none that he can see, nor any sign of a door. Still, it's hard to catch the details, because the place is so poorly lit, just a couple of torches in crude iron sconces, casting their oily glow. Plus, there's the fact that his head's lashed down also. He can barely twist his neck. Someone could have tucked the Taj Mahal, or perhaps the Tower of London, right there behind him and he wouldn't even know it.

And then those same words—the Tower of London— ring out like a gong. He knows this place from a picture book. It's his childhood yet again. An artist's rendition of the original dungeons, way back in the good old days.

"You awake? Finally? Thought you were dead over there."

And that voice, it's better than any gong. His heart floods with gratitude.

"Charlie? Is that you?"

Then all at once, elation is gone, replaced by keen disappointment. "Damn. So they got you too."

"Looks that way, don't it."

He'd known the Guild would strike back somehow, but had hoped they'd be wearing kid gloves. Maybe come at them with a cease-and-desist, or put some pressure on the studios themselves. But this? Not for the first time, nor for the last, Constairs has made a bad call.

"Well" he promises Charlie, "give me a second to get my head back on straight, and we'll be out of here in a jiffy."

The straps should be a piece of cake. It's the door he's worried about. Reinforced, most likely, with a few binding spells, or perhaps a Ketterling Seal. Ignoring the pain inside his head, he sends out a quiet summons. A handful of Nimble Fingers perhaps, just the thing for buckles and locks.

Nothing happens.

He sends out a second call-to-arms, fireworks and trumpets blazing. Imploring, demanding, that the Universe listen, bends to his will, like always. But Fingers or Faeries, card tricks or feints, they've all taken a vacation. Abandoning him in his hour of need, without cause or explanation.

"You OK, boss?" Charlie finally inquires. "Or are we still in that jiffy of yours?"

A bead of sweat works down his face. The throb in his skull pulls a cartwheel.

"It must be this room, this place," he replies. "My magic doesn't work."

TIME PASSES. TIME crawls. Time creeps like molasses, each second recast as an hour. The only proof of its sluggish advance being the gradual cessation of pain.

And then, from out of that endless expanse, there arrives a visitor. Not the jingle of keys, because jingles are jolly; a festive, holiday sound. So call it instead a tolling of keys, the dour bells of a funeral mass, a signal that their time is up, that their jailor is at hand. Hearing it, Constairs lifts his head, or at least he makes an attempt, then catches the discourse of metal on metal, of key uniting with lock. The hinges are almost theatrical, like hinges always are, and as the massive door starts to swing open, he can feel a cool draft of air.

"Don't tell me we have company."

It was supposed to sound breezy and off-hand. Instead it's a raspy croak. This business of keeping a stiff upper lip; like magic, it no longer works.

"Why?" a voice answers back. "Are you two tied up?"

He's the man who will sell you insurance. Set you up with a mutual fund. A plump and pasty blob of flesh, nondescript as a blank sheet of paper. In honor of their medieval theme, he should be wearing a jerkin, but instead it's a deep blue seersucker suit, sized for someone much leaner. The Old Glory tie-pin. A ring from the Shriners. A set of teeth, clearly false. If, like they say, we're defined by our enemies, Constairs suddenly feels quite small.

"You're the bad guy?" Constairs asks. "Really?"

"Until someone better comes along."

He takes a few steps, moving just out of sight. His next words are directed to Charlie.

"Still, I'm sorry you had to get involved with all this. And just so you know, whatever he decides on, you and I can make our own deal. There's no reason you should have to pay for his mistakes."

Driving a wedge between them? Constairs already took care of that.

"Hey! Milk-Fed! Leave the kid out of it. This is between you and me."

"Very well," he says, turning back to Constairs. "Then let's put our cards on the table. This setting, as I'm sure you've noticed, we plucked it from out of your head. Mildly unpleasant, to say the least, but there's much nastier ones waiting up there. And your magic. Thanks to a dampening field we've developed, it's now completely useless. You can't cast a single spell."

"And I'm guessing you can't either."

The man merely shrugs. "Why would I want to? You've already been rendered harmless. And yes, you're right, thanks to the field, I won't be able to employ any enhanced torture, but something tells me, in this case, more conventional techniques should prove sufficient."

Well at least they seem to agree on one thing. Constairs is an abject coward. One of those saps who runs for the ether if a dentist just walks through the door.

"Fine, fine," Constairs admits, "you've made your point. You've got a really big stick. But I thought, the way these things generally work, there's a carrot thrown in there too."

The man moves closer. Extends his hand. Finds an errant lock of hair. Brushes it back from Constairs' forehead, in a gesture that's almost tender.

"A carrot? Yes, of course there is. You can choose to join us instead."

That spot on his face, where he'd been touched, it suddenly feels ice cold.

"And who exactly is 'us'?"

Pulling back from the table, the man starts to pace, tracing an arc on the floor. In his wake he disperses a floral bouquet; not cologne, but more like perfume.

"Ostensibly, it would be the Guild. Why not use what's already there? A worldwide network of field branches, business ties, backroom connections. And as for who's really pulling the strings, that never need concern you."

Start out with that accent of his, coloring every word. Then throw in Carl, his Teutonic good looks, and probably dozens more just like him. What had started out for Constairs as a personal grudge, or a fight against petty corruption, was suddenly looking like something else. A struggle against true evil. A shadow from the east.

"I don't know," Constairs finally replies. "From the

sound of it, you'd be asking me to work blind. To maybe even betray my country."

"Your country?" the man teases back. "You have only one country. It's name is magic. It's what you live and breathe. Everything else is just window-dressing. A disguise you put on and take off."

If they're all as persuasive as this one, then the threat is alarmingly real. In a world plagued by want and deprivation, everyone's seeking a savior. Even one with a silly moustache.

"I'll need some time to think things through. To talk it over with my friend."

The man reaches down and pinches his cheek.

"Take all the time you need."

PUT TWO PEOPLE together. Throw in some bars, or some chains. Let them see just how fragile it is, the line between life and death. Then sit back and listen as they both speak their hearts, lay out a final confession, a litany of their mistakes and misgivings, the botches they'll leave behind.

For Constairs it's all the slip-ups that he's made. Actions colored by regret. How the road taken has been filled with potholes, stray dogs that he's clipped by mistake. While with Charlie, it's all the things he *hasn't* done, the chances he never took, because, in the end, his fear was too great, his self-doubt too crippling. All of which means that being there, in that dungeon, it's really a shot at redemption. A chance to do the good thing, the right thing, even if it's the last thing they do.

"So how you holding up?" Charlie wonders.

"By a thread, and it's not even silk," Constairs replies.

For the past few minutes, he's had this itch, the same place where Milk-Fed had touched him. Almost as if the rest of his body doesn't want it around anymore.

"I mean, dying itself, that I can live with," he goes on. "It's the torture part that's got me spooked."

"So maybe we play along," Charlie suggests. "Pretend to say yes. Not only do you skip the torture, but maybe later, down the road, one of us gets a chance to do some real damage."

Hearing that, he wants to shrug, only he's still tied down.

"Sure, that sounds good. In theory. But somehow I suspect, people like this guy, they know when 'yes' means 'no'."

He stares out at the nearest wall. God, he's sick of granite.

"And then there's you. I feel like a heel, dragging you in here. This was my war, not yours."

"Hey, nobody dragged me in here," Charlie insists. "And if it's really as bad as it's starting to look, that makes it everyone's war."

A war, Constairs chooses not to point out, that they're about to lose. He'd like to find some glimmer of hope, something to cheer them both up, but apparently, this time around, it's Charlie's turn instead.

"Hot damn," he declares. "It worked."

"What worked?"

"I just turned invisible."

Constairs tries confirming the fact. All he gets is a kink in his neck.

"How'd you manage that?" he asks. "With their dampening field and all."

"Hell if I know," Charlie admits. "Maybe because, with me, it's not about spells or incantations, it's just some switch I got inside me."

"Sounds plausible. Still, not to rain on any parades, but where exactly does that get us? You're still strapped to a table, I take it."

"Maybe. Maybe not."

There's a second of silence, fraught with tension. What's he got up his sleeve? Then suddenly Charlie is standing before him, barefoot and now visible.

Constairs blinks in surprise. "I thought I was the magician."

"It's something I've been working on for a while. Kept it under my hat. Figured if I could pull off being invisible, intangible shouldn't be that much more of a stretch."

Anyone else would be bragging by now. Patting himself on the back. But Charlie, of course, still insists on being Charlie, aw-shucks and golly-gee.

"And I don't suppose you can do both at once?" he hazards.

"Not yet, but I'm working on it."

It takes but a moment to set Constairs free. His body is one giant knot. He finds himself actually envying Charlie, and the supple resilience of youth. And, to be honest, his discomfort doesn't end there. He's spent years in the spotlight honing his craft, earned his right to top the bill. Charlie's new Talent may well save his life, but it's not doing much for his ego.

Working in tandem, they scour the room, looking for any weak spots. A secret way out that an eight-year-old Constairs had discovered decades ago. But the walls are solid, the door is locked, and there's no sign of a hidden passage, just squeaks that persist with no rats to produce them, and torches that never burn out. Inconsistencies that both would gladly trade in for a few sips of tepid water.

"Well, we ain't hog-tied, but we're still in a cage. What do we do now?"

"That's obvious," Constairs tells him. "At least one of us has to get out of here. Spread the news about the Guild. And if that someone's invisible, it would make his job a whole lot easier. So when Milk-Fed shows up, or one his flunkies, I'll do my best to distract him while you slip out the door."

"And leave you stuck here?"

"Look, Charlie, I made this mess. For once I can do

the clean-up."

The two men eye each other. Charlie falters first. Lets his gaze drop to the floor, and shrugs his bony shoulders.

"Fine, boss. Whatever you say. And what do we do in meantime?"

Constairs finds a seat on the cobbles.

"What do you think? We wait."

AN HOUR PASSES, maybe two. Or perhaps it's several lifetimes. When they both hear the rattle of keys growing closer, each thinks they're imagining it. From his perch in the corner, a few feet from the door, Charlie gives him a quick nod. And then, like that cat with the mile-wide grin, he slowly fades from sight.

Constairs takes a deep breath. Holds his body stock-still. Whoever is about to pay them a visit, they'll assume that they're both still strapped down, that there's no need for caution, or stealth. That the small patch of darkness, there on the floor, it's a shadow, and nothing more. As he listens, key finds lock. Tumblers tumble. Hinges acquiesce. All the tiny surrenders that play out, just to open a door.

As before, there's the barest hint of a draft. And with it, a cloying fragrance. A scent that makes him want to recoil, recalling a stranger's touch. It's him, Milk-Fed, Constairs knows in an instant. Back to gloat, and wheedle, and taunt. Only maybe, this time, he'll escalate, and his touch won't be nearly as gentle.

A couple of steps, heels on granite. Then a pause before the third. A realization, palpable almost, that something is amiss. Knowing he can stall no longer, Constairs springs to life, that irrelevant shadow now expanding, exploding, into a full-grown man. But you have to give Milk-Fed credit. He doesn't panic or flinch. Out of nowhere a gun appears in his hand, but he's far too calm to use it. Merely takes a step back, beyond Constair's reach, and levels it as his chest.

"Spark and powder. That's real magic. Move, and you'll find out."

Ignoring the words, Constairs glances past him. Sees that the door's still ajar. There's a crack wide enough to let a rat by, maybe even a scrawny kid.

Milk-Fed seems to read his thoughts. His eyes dart right, then left.

"And the boy?" he hisses. "Believe me, I won't ask twice."

What's it feel like, getting shot? Any worse than Karla's knives? All it will take is a single step, at which point he'll find out.

But before any step, any twitch, any blink, the room erupts in chaos. The gun, grey metal and black consequence, is no longer aimed at his chest. Seems instead to be struggling with its owner, a dog that won't stay leashed. And there. That glimpse. It looks like Charlie. A flash and nothing more. Not any kind of deliberate act, but rather a falter or hiccup. Suddenly the gun tilts upward, aiming towards empty air, and he can't tell which occurs next. The sound of a gunshot, ringing out, or the sight of Charlie, now fully visible.

Milk-Fed stares at him, shocked and frozen. Charlie stares right back. Only Constairs is left to add two and two, to realize that Charlie had willed himself intangible at just the right instant, letting the bullet pass harmlessly through him. And now? He watches as Charlie's hand reaches out. Tries to shove Milk-Fed aside. Only that hand, no longer solid, passes right into his chest. Panicked, he stares down at his arm, buried just past the wrist. Reacts then by reflex alone. Wills it tangible again.

The sound is worse than any gunshot. Worse because it's *moist*. Add in a cry of sheer agony, and it's almost too much to bear. Milk-Fed collapses to the floor, a gaping hole in his chest. Gazes up at the shape now standing above him, not quite visible. Not a man, not a boy, not anything human, just the outline of one instead, defined by a cloak of bright red blood, of bone and viscera. Only then, as Constairs watches, that unseen shape takes form, and once again it's only Charlie. Charlie the Visible Boy.

The two of them, the two still alive, just stand there, staring blankly. And oh, the weight of that one look. A lifetime of regret, of self-castigation, earned in a single moment.

"I, I … I didn't … I wouldn't," Charlie moans. "That

wasn't supposed to happen!"

He pinches his eyes shut. Starts to sob. Smears the gore across his face.

"Charlie," Constairs cries out, embracing him now. Sharing the blood, the blame. "Charlie, it's not your fault."

The tears that serve to wash his face. The sobs that wrack his body. Constairs holds on, giving him time, even knowing how precious time is.

"Look," he tells him. "I know it hurts. That you want it to hurt even worse. But we can't stay here. They're coming. And if we don't get out of here now, all that hurting, it'll just be pointless."

Charlie looks up, blinking. Forces some air in his lungs.

"I can walk, I think. But you'll have to lead the way."

Once they pass through the dungeon's door, the illusion sloughs off like dead skin. Instead of the Tower, that grim pillar of stone, they're in some kind of aircraft hangar, one that houses a few private planes, waiting to pierce the sky. The place is eerily quiet, no sign of anyone there, the ghostly calm of an MGM back-lot, awaiting the actors, the lights.

"You think, between the two of us, we could manage one of these planes?"

Charlie actually tries to smile. It looks more like an open wound.

"Give me a minute, OK?"

But apparently they don't have a minute. Both turn as they hear the sound. A screech of tires, a squeal of brakes, an engine at high RPM. The car circles around the tarmac, comes to a halt by the hangar. Three men spill out, moving as one, the pack mind already in place.

Constairs nods to Carl, clearly their alpha. Delivers a grim smile.

"Decided you need reinforcements?"

"No, they're just here to watch."

Constairs glances back at Charlie. Sees the wreck that he's become. Maybe he can't undo what just happened, but at least he can make someone pay.

"Fine," he tells Carl. "Let them."

A bolt of light lances out of his body, fueled by an awful anger. Anger at Carl, anger at Milk-Fed, but mostly anger at himself. It's obvious now he'll never know goodness. His magic will never be white. But at least he can meet the darkness head-on, and sometimes drive it back.

He stares across at the smoldering husk. One down, two to go.

The man on the right, he tries manacles. The other prefers a muzzle. As if they think they can lock him up, silence his spells for good. But a quick Latherton renders them useless, as frail as tissue paper, and then it's a Kromsky enveloping both, turning their minds inside out. He can actually see the thoughts fleeing their heads, like rats on a sinking ship, till at last all that's left are two empty vessels, ready to be filled again.

He levitates their bodies five feet off the ground. Clears his throat, addressing their Master.

"Here are your toys. They should still work. Sorry about the first one. But be aware, should you send any more, I might not be as gentle. As of now, you stand on notice. This is our turf, ours alone. And don't be surprised if, one of these days, we pay a call on yours."

But bluff, bravado, that part's easy. It's everything else that's hard. Taking someone you care for, someone who's shattered, and mending them back together. His magic depleted, he hunts down a rag. Moistens it at a spigot. Uses it to clean Charlie up, wipe down those last bits of Milk-Fed, still clinging to his clothing, his skin.

All the while knowing that the real stain will never be excised.

12

THE NEXT DAY.

Constairs awakes with the advent of dawn. Takes a quiet peek into the bedroom. Confirms there's still a lump on the mattress, its breathing slow and shallow.

When they'd finally made it home last night, he'd done a stupid thing. Decided it would be a good idea to make sure Charlie got drunk. No, not like that, not a rollicking drunk; to rollick requires too much spirit. More one of those dismal, determined sedations that take the place of saying goodbye. And to whom was Charlie bidding farewell? To his innocence, of course. His entire life he'd been a good person, and now he was something else.

In finding that bottle, dispensing its contents, Constairs had sought two goals. The first one, all too obvious, being to numb his companion, to lighten his melancholy. And the second? Sometimes, when you wake up hungover, it's actually a blessing. The pain in your gut, for a while at least, eclipsing the one in your heart.

Time passes. The sun ascends. Constairs might doze

off a little. The next thing he knows he's gazing up at a shadow, back-lit in the bedroom door.

"Charlie," he exclaims, springing up off the couch. "How are you feeling?"

"Like something I stepped in."

A weak cup of coffee, diluted with milk. Toast burned to almost black. With both of them finding comfort in their shared task, bringing the corpse back to life, all the while tip-toeing around it, yesterday and its aftermath.

"Anything in the paper?" Charlie finally asks.

"It's still too early for that. And I wouldn't be surprised if, with the Guild's connections, the story gets buried completely."

Buried? Not the best choice of words, given the circumstances. And one that leaves Constairs asking himself if the two bodies they'd left behind are already in the ground.

"You must thing I'm a real milquetoast," Charlie tells him. "Getting so upset."

"No, of course not. Not at all."

But his reply goes unnoticed. Now he's the invisible one.

"I mean it's not like I've never been around death," Charlie continues. "Back on the farm, or whatever. Slaughtering hogs, or putting down dogs, or chopping the head off a snake. But this. This was different. I don't care how evil they were, they were still people, like us."

"People, yes. Like us, no. You owe yourself more

credit."

Just like before, the words bounce off. It's clear he *wants* to hurt. Desperately trying to restore his worth by proving how deeply he suffers.

So he tries another tack.

"I'm sure, with everything going on, chances are you've forgotten, but tonight's our follow-up meeting. And I'd feel a whole lot better if you were up there at the podium with me."

Charlie refuses to meet his eyes. Stares down at the floor.

"I don't know," he eventually offers. "I'm thinking I need a vacation."

"A vacation?"

"From all this. From magic. From you."

Constairs can't seem to get enough air. The room, it's suddenly smaller.

"What?" he stammers. "Why?"

Charlie spins round, facing him now. The numb indifference is gone.

"I thought I wanted to be like you. Maybe now I've changed my mind. The guy I killed, I didn't want that, it was just an accident. But you?" He pauses. Shakes his head in disgust. "You were actually smiling."

Constairs recalls the joy he'd felt. Admits that it's probably true. Knows that Charlie has sniffed out something inside him, something he's always kept hidden.

"But that's what magic is," Constairs counters. "Turning one thing into another. Taking all that spleen, that spite, and somehow making it do good."

Charlie finally lifts his gaze. Stares into his eyes. How can someone who can't be seen be the one who sees so clearly?

"Do good," he shrugs back. "Maybe. Or maybe that's just what you tell yourself so you can sleep at night."

THE TURN-OUT IS better than last time. Constairs should be walking on air. Instead there's a gaping wound in his chest, even worse than the one that killed Milk-Fed. He's tempted to slip back out the door. Knows damn well he can't. There's too much at stake, too many lives, to give up on what he's started.

As for the crowd, they're abuzz with excitement. The three-day sickout is over. With a few men let go, some retaliatory scheduling, but little more in the way of payback. They'd delivered their warning to Hollywood: ignore us at your peril. And shown their opponents, still consigned to the shadows, just what they were capable of. One man, exploded from the inside out. Another reduced to ashes. A missing plane, stolen from Palmdale, later found in an empty field.

Everyone's eyeing Constairs with new respect. He's proven he can play hardball. But the last thing he feels like doing is gloating, or celebrating what had to be done. He'd already decided, lying awake last night, that his best recourse would be silence. That with no solid proof that the Guild was involved, or yoked to a far greater evil, all he could do was to play things down, continue to frame their struggle as a simple labor dispute. Eventually someone, probably Constairs, would hand-pick a small cadre. An inner circle of skilled adepts who will guard their turf from attack. And perhaps, one day, make good on his promise, and launch an assault of their own.

But in the meantime?

A hollow man, a stuffed man, he finds the podium. Gazes out at a couple hundred faces, yet to suspect he's mere fraud.

"Gentlemen, ladies, please take a seat. I have some good news to share."

This time there's no need for a dampening spell. Everyone is all ears.

"Two days ago, I met in person with none other than Louis B. Mayer."

A babble of voices fills the hall. Constairs waits for it to die out.

"At that time I presented him with a proposal, one with mutual benefits for both ourselves and the studios. We would select one film, one major production. Agree that every single effect in that film would be achieved through magic alone. Use that commitment as a brand of honor, a declaration to the world that it is through magic, and magic alone, that the full promise of the cinema would be realized." He pauses, letting the tension build. "That film, of course, will be *The Wonderful Wizard of Oz*."

The crowd erupts in shouts, in jeers. At last, the Promised Land. Not just the prospect of steady work, but a glimpse of something far greater. Respect.

"I have yet to hear back from Mr. Mayer," Constairs tells them, "but I believe he is leaning our way. And with your permission, I'd like to sweeten our offer, give him one last nudge. Not a concession, mind you—our days of surrender are over—but rather a proposal that will guarantee our stature, now and in the future."

Bait the hook. Tug the line. Hold out for the strike.

"When you or I pay to see a film, do we make our selection based on who the hair-stylist is, or the costume designer, or the gaffer? No, of course not. We hear that lion, roaring away, see those letters, MGM, and trust they reflect a level of expertise, a commitment to quality, that makes their names all but meaningless. This is the beauty of the studio system, a factory where dreams are stamped out, and isn't it time that we magicians stole a trick from Mr. Mayer?

"Not by forming our own studio, mind you, but a clearinghouse instead. A place where miracles happen. Where wizards are real, and monkeys can fly, and a girl wears ruby slippers. And where, not coincidentally, we control the production schedules, and the pay-scales, and determine who's best suited for any particular job."

A voice calls out from somewhere in back. "Are you saying no names in the credits?"

"Oh, your name will still be there, bigger than ever, not that you'll really care. Because from here on in you'll be part of a team. A family. Something bigger than just yourself. All along it's been our fate, our curse, the reason we've stayed small, the fact that as magicians, we've gone it alone, every man for himself. Only now, when you're some old codger, with a great-grandchild in your lap, you can look him straight in the eye. 'Were you a magician?'" he'll ask you. 'Even better'," you can tell him.

"I was an Illusionaire."

THE CALL COMES two days later. Mayer wants to see Constairs again.

By then his roommate has already moved-out. Declines to tell him where to. Nor does Charlie bother explaining how he can afford it, paying for a place of his own. With anyone else, given his Talents, the answer would be simple. A quick trip down to the nearest bank just in time for the teller's lunch break. But this is Charlie, after all. The next best thing to a saint. Far more likely he's staying at St. Thomas, trading chores for a cot in the basement.

Constairs thinks about that on the drive up. About

honor, and about thieves. How, if you end up derailing a life, you're expected to make things right. He wonders if Mr. Mayer has his own demons. His own reasons to stay up at night. Even admits he'd be tempted to ask him, only it might nix their deal.

"Mr. Constairs, it's good to see you."

It's the same study where they met before. The same handshake, smooth as silk.

"So I've been reviewing our staffing quotas," Mayer says, clutching a thin sheath of paper. "And our attendance is back in the ninetieth percentile. Some of your doing perhaps?"

Constairs offers up a bland smile. "You still seem to think I'm some mastermind. When really, I'm just a third-rate magician."

"But a humble one, nonetheless."

Mayer leans back, still gripping the papers. The cufflinks are gold this time. Constairs can see him, a kid, five or six, toying with his favorite marble.

"After considering your proposal, I've decided it has some merit. To be honest, the post-production work, the specials, they've always proven a major headache for the studio. And if a man comes up to me and says here, let that be my problem instead, then, of course, I'll listen to him. Still, there remains an enormous amount of details that would have to be worked out first."

Constairs finds himself hesitating. This is the moment of truth. And if it turns out he's made the wrong play, he'll have even more to regret.

"And what if I told you," he responds, "that the details don't mean a damn thing. That you've got to cut your ties to the Guild, even if we can't strike a deal."

Mayer stares back, eyes narrowing. At least he's got his attention.

"Pardon me if this seems intrusive," Constairs goes on, "but you're Jewish, aren't you?"

"Not devout," he admits. "But yes, I was born into that faith."

"And I assume you've been following what's happening in Europe. Germany, especially. The National Socialists. The unrest."

"Of course. Where do you think half our people come from? In fact, at times, you could say we've been guilty of make-work. Finding any excuse to hire on more émigrés."

"Then you owe it to them, and maybe yourself, to send out a few feelers. Find out where the Guild's funding is coming from. Who's really running the show. Because, unless I'm mistaken, their ultimate goal is to hijack the industry. Start altering content. Swaying the general public. Don't get me wrong, but here, in Hollywood, you've got the most persuasive propaganda machine in human history. And they want to make it theirs."

With a man like Mayer, his silence is coin. A sign he's been listening. A high compliment when coming from someone who is more often listened to.

"But you have no proof, I take it?"

"Proof? Of course not. I'm a magician. I make stuff up for a living."

This provokes the hint of a smile. The Wizard is amused.

"Well, you've given me even more to think over, Mr. Constairs. As if I already don't have enough. Still, I do have a line on several people that are good at digging things up. Perhaps I'll give one of them a call. In the meantime I'm hoping that you, your people, might be willing to meet with mine. Discuss some of those pesky details you just told me don't really matter."

Mayer rises to his feet. Constairs joins him a second later. He's already halfway to the door when Mayer's voice sounds out.

"And one last thing."

Constairs stops. Turns.

"That word, 'hunchback', it's not quite right. It sounds much better in Russian."

Constairs thinks that over, then nods.

"You should tell her that sometime."

13

THERE'S NOTHING SADDER than a wrap. The end of a good long run.

He'd first felt that melancholic bite many years ago, during his brief stint as an actor. How a handful of strangers could all come together, each pretending to be someone else, only to discover that, through repeated performance, they really had been transformed. And apparently this same magic took place when it came to making a film as well. That even though the process was so disjointed, with scenes often shot out of sequence, a bond was still formed, a deep understanding, between cast and crew, one that an outsider could only guess at.

An outsider like Richard Constairs.

Oh, they'd all done their best to pretend they were welcome, this new crew, these Illusionaires. But it was obvious, right from the first day of shooting, that they lived in two different worlds. Actors and actresses worked from within, mined their own dreams and desires, while with a magician it's all surface gloss, tricking the eye, not the heart. Plus the sets were already cramped and crowded. The last thing they needed were gawkers. More spectators, however well-intentioned, watching them muff their lines.

And the Illusionaires? Most of real work would now be theirs, once the cameras were idle. Altering backgrounds, adding detail, assuring that a witch would melt, or that a cadre of monkeys might fly. Reaching into the film stock itself and bending emulsion to human will. And yet still there'd been moments, sometimes whole days, when they'd been present on the set, forced to work side-by-side with an actor, finding a language in common. But out of that discord, that turbulent marriage, something new was emerging. An ungainly child called Art.

Not that Constairs had been granted much of a chance to view this process firsthand. He'd arrived in Hollywood as a magician. Had wound up a mother hen. Or perhaps more like a much-needed midwife, aiding an awkward birth. Imagine a world without any blacksmiths, only now there were suddenly plenty, with all the confusion and friction you'd expect from such a social upheaval. Soothing ruffled egos. Deciphering legalese. Pretending to speak for all magicians, only to muff his lines too. And as a result, he'd been far too busy to snatch up any of the plum assignments. Had contented himself with just one project, one prize he couldn't pass up.

"Can I get you something to drink?"

She's in her twenties, most likely. Hired on just for

one day. Probably hoping that someone will see her, sign her up and make her a star.

"That would be wonderful," Constairs replies. "A Boodles martini, dry."

They've taken one of the larger sound-stages and gussied it up for the party. An acknowledgment that after nine months of toil, the last frame of film has been shot. Bunting and streamers. Colored gels on the spotlights. A punch-bowl as big as a fountain. When you've spent a small fortune on the film itself, why skimp this late in the game?

"You're a hairdresser."

It's one of the Munchkins, three sheets to the wind, stabbing a finger his way.

"Afraid not," Constairs tells him.

"Costume designer."

"No. Sorry. I'm an Illusionaire."

"Figures," he tells Constairs' belt buckle. A second later he storms off. When the girl returns, martini in hand, Constairs thanks her for not being short.

Drink in hand, he commences to wander. Wishes he had a companion. And yes, of course, he'd invited Charlie along and, of course, he'd been duly snubbed. He's only seen him twice since their parting, almost a month ago. Once to ask him a special favor, and a second time to check out his new mentor, a shaman from New Guinea, skilled in astral projection.

And didn't that sting, meeting his replacement? More

than a little, in fact. Because he was the one who walked out on people; people didn't walk out on him.

By accident, or perhaps fate, he's drifted to the front of the room. A spot where the lights are brighter, the music louder, and the real stars congregate. That handful of people whose names will appear right after the lion roars. He's barely had a chance to connect with the cast. They're from one world, he's from another. Just that conversation he'd had with Burt Lahr one day, sharing stories of their vaudeville high jinks.

And then, at last, he spots her there, almost lost amongst the others. A tiny figure, still half a girl, staring up at her fellow performers, wearing a dazed smile on her face, as if she's mere fan instead. It could be Kansas, it could be Oz, it could be Hollywood, but he has the feeling, wherever she lands, that look will remain the same. That no place is the place she lives.

That no place is her home.

Feeling dazed, he slowly pulls closer. Jostles his way through the crowd. Eventually he's standing there, no more than a few feet away.

"Remember me?" he asks her, words buried in the din.

"Sure. You're the magician."

"That's right." He throws a nod to their surroundings. "How about we find someplace quiet?"

She shrugs back in confusion. "Like where? Maybe the moon?"

At that point he does what he knows best. Tickles at the odds. Suddenly they're all alone, on another sound-stage, this one quiet. For perhaps a second, her eyes grow wide, her face betrays confusion, but then she surrenders to the moment. Surrenders, in fact, to him.

"You know all the good tricks, don't you?"

"And some of the bad ones too."

The gingham is gone. It was all just for show. She's wearing a gown instead. But somehow, on her, those grown-up clothes, they look even more like a costume.

"So that song you were singing, last time we met, I finally heard the words. And you were right. If weren't such a cold-hearted bastard, I would've been crying too."

"You? Cold-hearted? I doubt it."

"Don't."

It comes out sounding way too harsh. Warnings often do.

"Anyway, I had to see you one last time. I've got a couple of things to tell you. First off, there's a friend of mine, or at least he used to be. Said he might be willing to teach you a trick or two, ones that will help you get by. You know, when all the cameras, the people watching, get to be too much."

"A friend, huh? Well, he'll have to get past the studio first. They keep a close eye on me."

"With him that won't be a problem."

She takes a moment to think that over. "And what's the other thing?

"This."

Just like that, he's holding something. Or maybe holding isn't the word. Because no one can really hold onto light, not even a magician.

Seeing his gift, her face lights up. Her cheeks shine back, twin rubies.

"It was you," she exclaims, short of breath. "The first time I saw them on the set, I asked everyone where they came from, who made them. But they wouldn't tell me. Said it was a secret."

"No. You don't understand."

"Understand what?"

"The ones you wore, the ones in the movie, they were just a prop. A fill-in. But these are the real ones. The ones that can take you home."

"Take me home?" she asks, confused.

He nods down towards his offering. A glow so bright he has to squint.

"When I first read the book I didn't get it. What going home really means. I thought it was merely hiding out in the past, pretending you could never grow up. But since then, something happened. Now I finally see. All of us have to grow up, no matter how much it hurts. And home, it's the place we all come from. Where we all wind up in the end."

Leaning forward, he sets them down. Near her feet, where they belong.

"Maybe there will be angels there. Maybe it's just

dark. Either way, at some point, we all get a chance to find out. But until then?" He stops. Sighs. "I wish I could promise that you'll have a good life, an easy life, but I think we both know that's a lie. And at least this way, if things get bad, you'll always have place to go."

He pauses a moment.

"A place you can call home."

A MOMENT OF darkness. A cessation of sound. A sensation that's not quite movement. The girl in the sequined gown stares out at the crowd that now surrounds her.

"Where the heck you been?" asks Scarecrow Ray. "I thought you'd snuck out or something."

Only then does he notice the pair of slippers. The way they almost seem to glow.

"Careful," he says, whispering now. "If LeRoy catches you sneaking off with those things, he's liable to dock your pay."

HE RETURNS TO his house, still empty. A house meant for two, not one. Checks a few spells—no visitors, please— then gropes his way to the front door. He'd meant to leave the porch light burning, could conjure it on in a jiffy, but somehow stumbling around in the dark seems like the right thing to do.

As he passes through the entry, he almost steps on it. Some kind of object, paper-thin, lying unseen on the hallway floor. Cursing, he fumbles for the lamp, summarily ending its slumber, only to spy a small envelope, courtesy of the slot in the door.

He picks it up. Checks the return. Some place he's never heard of. With a contemptuous flick of his wrist, he rips one edge clean open.

Bastard –

Cleaning up Hollywood. Good for you. You can clean yourself up next. And what's all this gimcrack about illusions? You must mean delusions instead.

We need to talk. Soon. And not by phone or psychic channels, but in person mind you. I'll call you when I get into town. In the meantime, work on saying you're sorry, only like you really mean it.

Karla

P.S.—I'm pregnant

P.P.S.—It's yours

1963

14

EVERYONE CLAIMED IT was some great honor, being invited down to Langley. Then again, they said the same thing about dying for your country, and he'd managed to avoid that so far.

"Sorry he's running late. Sure I can't get you some coffee?"

He knew said coffee would be Government Issue; tepid, weak and foul. Ever since his first sip of the real stuff, years back in Vichy France, Folgers just wasn't the same.

"No," he tells the woman, smiling. "I've been trying to cut back."

It had been six months since the news first broke: a major shake up at the CIA. Dulles was out, Markley was in, more heads were bound to roll. And roll they most certainly did. Connors, Mankewitz, that guy with the stutter, an Assistant Deputy Aide. Like witnessing one of those Politburo purges, something Stalin might've pulled in his heyday. By then just about everyone in Division 12 was taking bets, setting up pools, predicting who'd be next, barely able to hide their glee at seeing their rival in such disarray. Still, that was the way things worked in DC. First you're up and then you're down. And as soon as things looked like smooth sailing ahead, better update your CV.

Not that he was worried, of course. After twenty-odd years and three administrations, Charles Overton was a fixture. As unnoticed as the drapes in Lincoln's Bedroom, and as likely to be replaced.

All of which makes it a mystery. Why he's been summoned there. The fact he's now staring at the very same face he'd seen in *Newsweek* a few days back.

"Overton? Thanks for making it out. It's a pleasure to finally meet you."

"The pleasure is all mine."

In color, in person, Markley looks younger. Like he's his own understudy. None of that steely gravitas he likes to trot out for interviews or photo shoots. Just your average mid-management salary man in charge of the Tulsa office, ten years shy of the gold watch and pension, with his wife and his two-point-five.

All of which makes Overton that much more wary. Never trust a bland, smiling face. The same hand that's now making meatloaf out of yours could stab you in the back tomorrow.

"Claire didn't get you any coffee?" Markley asks.

"I respectfully declined."

Markley leads the way back into his office. Overton is

underwhelmed. Everything about that room—the square-footage, the décor, the Naugahyde upholstery and Paul McCobb knock-offs—is exactly what you'd expect from some G-17, way further down the pay-scale. Ever since his placement, Markley's been boasting about how he wants to establish a new CIA, one that's leaner and meaner, more focused on results than rank. But this? This is closer to penury. The cell of a monk, not a spook.

Finding a seat behind his desk, he motions towards a chair.

"You know, I thought this day would never come. Breaking bread with Charles Overton."

"You make that sound like major news."

Markley smiles back, shaking his head. "And there you go again. Pretending that it isn't. Pretending that you're just some anonymous minion, pushing paper and collecting a paycheck." He nods in what could be admiration. Could be something else. "But that's always been your MO, hasn't it? Hiding in plain sight."

That guy who runs the Tulsa office. He's brighter than you think.

"Well," Overton counters, "I wouldn't call it hiding exactly."

"Don't get me wrong. It wasn't meant as a criticism. Where do you think it came from, this little crusade of mine? For years we'd had our eye on Division 12, trying to keep track of who's who, and then we finally realized, the guys on top, the ones with the fancy offices and the big salaries, they're not really calling the shots."

Overton doesn't admit that's true, nor does he deny it.

"That thing about knowing your enemy," he observes. "You seem to take it seriously."

"But that's just it," Markley insists. "We shouldn't even *be* enemies. The OSS, the Illusionaires. Sometimes I wish I could go back twenty years and keep it from happening. Whatever it was that got us both on the wrong track. That left us thinking we weren't on the same side."

Whatever it was? Meaning he doesn't know. But Charles Overton does. After all, he'd been there.

"And it didn't help," Markley goes on to admit, "what happened after that. Those eight years of Eisenhower, back-to-back, and then throw in Joe McCarthy. 'Are you now or have you ever been?' No wonder you can't stand us. We were part of all that."

When someone's this eager to take the blame, to start declaring mea culpa, they're usually hoping for absolution, a salve for their troubled conscience. But government agencies don't have a conscience, least of all the CIA. Which means Markley's show of contrition, it's just some kind of ploy.

"Well," Overton concedes, "it's good of you to reach out. Admit your mistakes. And you certainly had your comeuppance, didn't you?"

"Yes, we certainly did."

The Bay of Pigs. Operation Zapata. Call it what you will. The biggest fiasco in the last hundred years, as engineered by Langley. Two years later and they're still on the shit list, a rift that has yet to heal, with Kennedy determined to limit their power, a dog on a very tight leash.

"Which means," that dog adds, "whatever happens, we can't afford to mess this up."

Overton glances across the room. His eyes lock onto Markley's.

"Mess what up?"

"A new assignment. The biggest, the trickiest, we've ever been asked to tackle. Pull it off and, God willing, we'll be back in the President's good graces. Fail, and there's serious talk of having the Agency permanently dismantled. Mothballed."

"And why are you telling me this?" he wonders. "So I can get the champagne on ice?"

Markley leans forward, ignoring the jibe. Pins both elbows to his desk. For a moment he's no longer The Man in Charge, looking more like a scared little kid.

"How many of your people can you really trust? With a secret, or even your life."

Overton doesn't hesitate.

"All of them," he replies.

"I wish I could say the same." He lowers his gaze to a thin sheath of papers, neatly stacked on top of his blotter. "But after these last two years—the loss of morale, the infighting—I'm not sure who I can count on. Especially with something like this."

"So what are you saying? You want us to vet them for you? Enforce a Spell of Silence?"

He glances up, taken aback. "You can really do that? I thought that was just more talk."

"Oh, we can do it," Overton concedes. "It's more a question of if we'd want to."

Restless now, Markley leaves his desk. Prowls over to the room's sole window. Stares down at the parking lot, five floors below, all that Detroit gleaming back.

"Well, I have to admit, something like that, sure, it would come in handy, but you're missing the whole point. What I'm talking about would be a partnership. A full collaboration. The kind of thing we should've been doing since Day One. We'd cover the groundwork, the staging, the logistics. All the things we're good at. And your team, Division 12, you'll provide the magic. Because if ever a job needed that extra something, this one is going to be it."

"A partnership. A collaboration." He studies the man at the window. "Every time those words get tossed around, I wish I'd never listened. How do I know this will be any different?"

"You don't," Markley tells him.

Finally. Some honesty.

"But at least I can give you my word."

The smart move would be to tell him no. To let things

run their course. To sit back and watch yet another fiasco, perhaps even worse than in Cuba. Because if they do help, lend their own special skills, and in doing so ensure success, they will have empowered their oldest foe, and squandered their current advantage.

And if he says yes instead?

"You know, you still haven't told me what this assignment of yours is. That might make all the difference."

Leaving the window, he circles around. Parks himself just a few away.

"Any chance I can get you to run that spell first? I can't risk this being leaked."

Just for a moment, he's tempted to walk. How dare Markley question his silence? But, in the end, his pride gets the back seat. Curiosity takes the wheel.

"If you'd done your homework, you'd already know—you can't work a Spell of Silence on yourself. But I can offer you something even better."

Markley stares back.

"I can give you my word too."

Despite its modest trappings, the room's probably swept twice a day. Which means, whatever secrets are shared there, no bug will pass them on. But in spite of that fact, Markley now moves closer, till his face is mere inches away. And when he finally responds, his voice just a whisper, the words are more felt than heard.

"You want to know our assignment? We have to kill JFK."

15

HE'D NEVER BEEN one for politics. All those infinite shades of grey. Backroom deals, and quid pro quos, and promises made to be broken.

And besides, why focus on petty disputes, when you lived in a world like ours? A world that had proven, time and again, that true evil walks the Earth. His first trip abroad with the Abraham Lincolns. Fighting the fascists in Spain. And the slow realization that off to the East, darker forces were gathering strength. Yes, Hitler was a demagogue, could bend huge crowds to his will, but the greatest threat of all would prove his penchant for the occult. His willingness to summon up arcane powers that would make splitting the atom, building some bomb, seem like children playing with matches.

As for Allied Command, they'd been all but useless, their heads buried in the sand. And so it had fallen on a ragtag band of magicians, Illusionaires one and all, to face the threat head-on. Midnight raids on Nazi covens. Waffen SS reduced to dust. Rumors of an invisible man, one who could walk through walls, and able to uncover any secret, or drop in on the Fuhrer himself. For those left back home, consulting the headlines, the war had only two fronts; the German threat in the European theatre, and the Japanese in the Pacific. When, in fact, it was on a third front, all but hidden to the public at large, where the fate of mankind would be ultimately decided.

With the aid of their spells and, of course, all those bullets, the Allies eventually triumphed. Leaving evil to slink back into its lair, where it could fester and wait. America was now ascendant, left undamaged by the war, and the government could finally acknowledge its debts, and give credit where credit was due. Just as the wartime OSS was recast as the CIA, President Truman had reluctantly agreed to create Division 12. The place where magic happened. All that remained was appointing its leader, just back from his stint in Europe, a twenty-five year old pacifist civilian by the name of Charles Overton.

In retrospect, this seemed an elaborate joke. A sheep disguised in wolf's clothing. Giving a man who couldn't brook violence a chance to run the show. Within days Overton would set up shop inside a refurbished broom closet. Abolish all titles, all ranks. Award his recruits with what they, what every magician wanted, a chance to break a few rules. By then, the Red Scare was in full swing. Blacklists were all the rage. And the men and women of Division 12 were expected to follow their mandate, hunt down the very same socialist agitators that had inspired the Illusionaires in the first place.

Eight longs years of playing the game. Of giving, but not giving in. Handing over the occasional minor offender, mostly loudmouths hungry for fame, while never quite betraying the Movement itself, or the ideals they all held dear. Over time, Overton and his Division 12 became a running joke. Had watched their funding and influence dwindle. And everyone knew, with Eisenhower on the way out, they'd soon be facing an ugly choice. A red-baiting, lantern-jawed lummox named Nixon who had them in his crosshairs, or some spoiled rich kid straight out of Boston with an accent as thick as clam chowder.

And then the impossible happened. The rich kid actually won. And Charles Overton, who'd never thought much of politics, found himself walking twelve blocks through the snow to hear him take the Oath of Office. Moms and dads in their winter coats. Kids riding high on their shoulders. The glare so bright it was near biblical, angels come down to earth. For way too long, there'd been that feeling, a feeling of promise being squandered. Of knowing that, sure, America was on top of the heap, but what would we do about it? Because power, like magic, it had to be used. To be given an outlet, a purpose. Otherwise it would start to sour, milk left out on the kitchen counter.

The crowd stretched across the Capitol Mall. Eager. Hopeful. Restless. And at its head, up on that stage, stood a man in his crisp blue suit. Cocky as hell, he ignored any jacket, said no to a hat, or to gloves. Seemed so alight with their expectations he could catch fire any second. The wife, dark-haired, stationed beside him. The judge in his formal black robes. The crazy belief that one single man could somehow pull it off. Be their hub, their axis. The fulcrum point for change. Insisting that now, at this moment, this instant, we could find a new beginning. Asking not what's in it for me or you, but what would be our privilege to give.

And sure, three years in, there'd been disappointments. Opportunities fumbled, or lost. A reminder that our leaders, our very best, were just as flawed as the rest of us. But how often do we get to see it? To see a man outgrow himself? To make mistakes, and blunder along, and eventually find something better, all the while knowing that the fate of mankind is resting in his hands. For Charles Overton, holding that weight, that burden, seems incomprehensible. Too much for any one man. Only to now discover something that's even harder to grasp.

That the fate of that one man, the man at the top, could be resting in his own.

NEXT STOP IS the basement.

But first, en route, there's a metal detector. The latest in X-ray scanning. A full-body search that gets a little too chummy as it ventures below his waist. It's obvious that the word has gotten out somehow, that he's there from Division 12. And if they can't refuse to let him by, they can make sure he wishes they hadn't.

And at the end of all this rigmarole? Three inches of steel plate. What looks like a door that belongs on a bank vault, because that's precisely what it is. In a highly sensitive, top-secret move leaked to the *New York Times*, the Agency had decided, two years back, to transfer all of its records—a half-century's worth of spycraft, analysis and innuendo—into a more secure facility whose whereabouts have yet to be revealed. And as a result, approximately ten thousand square feet of cold, dank, windowless vistas had suddenly come up for grabs.

Or at least till Stan Lansky moved in.

"You the guy from upstairs?" an intercom barks, with an accent that reeks of Flatbush.

"I guess so," Charlie replies.

"Hold on. I'll buzz you in."

Said buzz is worse than a Norelco. Each one of his fillings sings back. A second later the door swings open, its hinges mercifully silent.

Lansky, it turns out, could well be a tailor, twenty dollars to let out your seams. Short, rotund, with a balding pate, and glasses perched on his scalp, not his nose. Not that Charlie has any right to pass judgment. He doesn't look like a spy either.

"So you're here about the Camelot thing?" Lansky

asks.

Camelot? The reference seems apt enough. And the Agency does love its code-words.

"Honestly, I'm not sure why I'm here. One second I'm there with Markley, learning about stuff I'm not supposed to share with anyone, maybe even including you, and the next he's taking some hush-hush phone call, shoving me out of his office, and claiming there's some guy in the basement that'll fill me in on the details."

Hearing this, Lansky nods to himself. "Like I said. The Camelot thing."

He's got a desk, Charlie guesses, probably buried beneath all that paper, but chooses instead to bustle right past it, in search of something better. A quick jog past those tall metal shelves. A right at the mimeograph. And just like that they've entered the Rec Room of some small private college in Vermont. Scooting around the foosball table, Lansky nods towards a sagging couch. Feeds some coins to the vending machine. Promptly snatches up two ice-cold bottles of Coke, then hands one to his guest.

"I've read it works wonders on an old engine block. Just imagine what it does to your stomach."

Undaunted, each man risks a sip. Like they say, it's the pause that refreshes. Lansky parks his sizable rear onto a second couch, even rattier than the first.

"So what do you know about Jack Kennedy?"

Charlie tries to be objective. "Apparently not enough."

"Don't feel bad," Lansky tells him. "Nobody does."

He takes another sip of Coke. Fails to stifle a belch.

"But at least you must know the obvious stuff. Youngest president we've ever had. All those games of touch football and tennis, or maybe it's sailing some yacht. The very picture of health, right?"

Charlie starts to open his mouth. Lansky cuts him short.

"Wrong."

The word just hangs there, suspended in mid-air.

"Our Commander-in-Chief, the most powerful man in the world, he's practically a cripple. Alright, maybe not FDR crippled, but not that far off either. Wears a back-brace every day. All those hot baths and massages. And there have been times, more than a few, when he had to use crutches to make it to his morning briefing."

Charlie nods back, digesting all this, conceding it's probably true. Like most Americans, he'd known in some vague, unspecified way that the President had health issues. That his back acted up now and then. But the smile, and the tan, and the freshly-pressed suit, that's what really counted. That's what the whole world saw.

"Still," Lansky admits, "if that was the only problem we faced, you wouldn't even be here. What do you know about the Addison's?"

He really ought to get out more. Pay attention to that place called The World.

"It's a defect in the adrenal gland," Lansky goes on.

"Normally no big deal. He's been on hormonal supplements for years, which pretty much keeps things in check. So maybe the Addison's was some kind of trigger, or else it was totally random, but either way he was diagnosed a couple months back. Advanced adrenal cancer."

"How advanced?" Charlie asks.

"He might live long enough to win a second term. No way will he ever serve it."

All men die, whether vassal or sire. Every story, every legend, has to end. But knowing that fact was one thing, and seeing it out there, perched on the horizon, drawing closer by the day, that was another thing altogether. For a moment Charlie just sits there, mourning both man and dream, or at least until, weary of waiting, the question asks itself.

"But wait. Why kill a man who's already dying? What would be the point?"

"Kill a man?" Lansky echoes back. "What are you talking about?"

"Markley told me that was your assignment. You're supposed to kill JFK."

A burst of laughter rends the air.

"Kill him? Hell, no," Lansky insists. "We're just supposed to help him fake it."

"SO AS SOON as the diagnosis was confirmed, he had us start running polls."

They're both on their second bottles by now. Their engines are sparkling clean. And Charlie still can't decide what he feels, relieved or just plain confused.

"But obviously we had to be careful," Lansky explains. "We couldn't just come right out and ask. So we had to couch it all in hypotheticals. Historical analogies. If, God forbid, President X had to die, what was the best way to do it? Slowly fading, day by day, betrayed by a failing body, or go out instead as a warrior? To die the same way that he'd lived, in the bright sunshine, surrounded by his fellow Americans."

Charlie nods back, still perched on the couch. "Put like that, it's obvious."

"That's what we thought too. But still we needed proof, numbers. Something we could count on. And boy, did we get them. A thirty-point spread. If Kennedy dies by tumor, the country feels only despair. Profound loss. But if Kennedy dies by some whacko's bullet, then everyone comes together. Vows to make sure that he didn't die in vain."

"So then what? You rammed it down his throat?"

"What? No way. I mean, who do you think was pushing this whole thing? Calling the shots from day one?"

He watches as Lansky abandons the couch. Plods on over to a second vending machine. Drops in two quarters, punches some keys, then waits for the jackpot to drop. A couple of packets of stale Ritz crackers, sealed in cellophane.

On his return flight, he tosses one over. Overton snags the line drive.

"So I get the feeling," he tells his guest, "that you're one of those guys who doesn't much go for politics. So let me boil it down into two words that anyone can relate to. The first one is 'legacy.'"

He starts to paw away at the wrapper. For a tailor, he's pretty clumsy.

"The way it works with presidents, it's all about that second term. Because the first four years are a dress rehearsal, especially if you're a novice like Kennedy. Hence the Bay of Pigs. A disaster that would've sunk most administrations, but they didn't have glad-handing Jack. And to give the guy credit, he's a fast study, he's learning on the job, and if he were to win that second term—which all the polls say is a shoe-in—then he's free to push his agenda, fashion his legacy, for years, more like decades, to come.

"But then he sees all that fading. He won't be there to see things through. Which means that he has to set things up so it'll happen all on its own. Be willing to die a martyr's death, just like the good Catholic he is, and trust that Johnson will finish the play, win one for the fallen hero. And it's not like LBJ needs all that much of a boost. He already knows how to work Congress much better than his boss, and any fool who tries to cross him will be spitting on St. Jack's grave."

Overton samples a cracker. Thinks about what he's just been told. Thinks about his own legacy, and how this meeting might turn out to shape it.

"You said there were two words," he reminds Lansky. "What's the second one?"

"Vanity," he replies.

He pauses to brush a few crumbs off of his shirt. With that couch, they'll have company.

"Being President, how many times a day do you think he's photographed? A hundred? A thousand? But I dare you to find a single shot where he doesn't looked poised. In control. You know, he'll sometimes change his shirt out, two or three times a day, just to look his best. And that thing he does, almost a tic, that thing about patting his hair. Making sure every strand is neatly in place, ready for the very next flashbulb."

"So he's vain. So what?"

"So this. Beneath all the rhetoric, the lofty ideals, the President is in love. In love with a guy named JFK. And he'd do anything to keep his public from seeing him in a moment of weakness, or pain, or despair. Because then they'd know he's human, when really, he's a god."

He'd encountered his share of men like that. One in particular came to mind. The kind of man that, when passing a mirror, can't help but steal a look.

"Fine," Charlie tells him. "You paint a convincing portrait. I can almost believe he'd actually do it, die the right way, the hard way, if he were given the choice. But that still leaves one question unanswered."

"Which is?"

"Why all this talk about faking it?"

Lansky smiles, clearly pleased. His guest has been paying attention.

"Because that's the last piece of the puzzle. The one that's missing from the box. To get what he wants, to get results, he knows he has to die a cruel death. An ugly death. But at the same time, he has a family. Three children that he worships, a wife he supposedly loves, despite how much he sleeps around. And the last thing he'd ever want to do is put them through all that. Seeing him gunned down in the prime of life, slaughtered like something out of a feedlot."

"And so you need an illusion," Charlie suggests. "A death that's carefully staged. Give the people their hero, their martyr, but let the man live on."

"Exactly. And who knows? Maybe all he'll win are a few brief months, but at least they'll be together, as a family. Without the whole world watching them, sullying their grief."

Put like that, it sounds almost noble. An act of charity. But Charlie knows that, just like always, there are wheels within wheels within wheels. For twenty-five years he'd followed his compass, lived by his own rules, pretending to swallow the company line, then doing what he knew was right. But this? This would be terra incognita. A whole new level of complicity. Telling the Big Lie, rewriting the facts, in the name of a much greater truth.

"This thing you're planning, Camelot's end, have you got a timeframe yet?"

Lansky merely shrugs.

"Nothing's set in concrete. We're shooting for this fall. We want to give Johnson plenty of time to pass a first round of legislation."

This fall. So soon. Just three months out. Three months that would feel like a lifetime.

"I'll need a few days to think things over. Then I'll let you all know."

16

BY THE TIME he makes it back to his place, the streets are growing dark. A late-summer dusk, the air close and humid, what they used to call firefly weather.

But fireflies, they were made for kids. For people who sit on their porches. And in a place like DC, in a time like the 60s, everybody is way too busy. Busy thinking about the latest crisis, some blow-up in the Sudan, or maybe that unwanted gift from France, a conflict in Southeast Asia. Still, that's the price one pays for power. For daring to rule the world. Because every crown is a crown of thorns, no matter how much it sparkles.

The brownstone is quiet, and still smells like breakfast. He'd forgotten to crack a window. Had gotten too used to having someone else do it, after he'd left for work. It's been three weeks and counting since Mark had gone, one last cardboard box clutched in his arms, with both of them staring down at the floor, rather at each other. There'd been no fights, no recriminations; they'd both been so reasonable. Practically sawing the poor cat in two, only who gets the bigger piece? All the while knowing that it wasn't some pet, but their hearts they were hacking apart.

There's a hunk of cow still tucked in the freezer. The rest of last night's baked potato. Everything he needs for a bachelor supper, wolfed down in front of the Zenith. But the thought of eating, or eating alone, is enough to turn his stomach. Without even thinking, he crosses the room, fumbling in the shadows, then finally locates the telephone, his lifeline to the world. He hasn't seen Karla in what feels like months, and he should have to look up the number. Only somehow his fingers know what to do, even if the rest of him doesn't.

Five long rings. A voice, out of breath. Any port in a storm.

"Yes?"

"Hey, K. It's me. Charlie. Got any plans tonight?"

WHEN KARLA HAD shown up in Hollywood, all-too-visibly pregnant, it had caused quite a stir. Not that expectant mothers, married or not, were all that rare in California. But how many of them had been foolish enough to dally with a magician, and how many of those same magicians were as famous—or should that be infamous?—as Illusionaire Richard Constairs?

By then, of course, Charlie had moved out on his own. Was a distant spectator at best. Bearing witness, just like everyone else in town, to fights so caustic they soon became the stuff of legend. Constairs, for his part, refused to even consider marriage, or own up to being a father, and while Karla herself didn't much want a baby, still, it was tucked there inside her. And rather than just seek out an easy solution, abortion or eventual adoption, she seemed strangely determined to bring the child to term. To abandon her life on stage. To declare to the world, or merely her foe, that after boasting of how he'd taken care of things, blocked any chance of conception, Constairs' magic had failed him in such a spectacular fashion.

Day by day, her passenger grew. Day by day, the future darkened. Giving birth to a child was always a gamble, let alone at a time like this. A time when evil, malignant and dark, seemed ready to claim the field. The baby, dubbed Randall, appeared nonetheless, screaming like a banshee, and Karla spent the next two years pretending at motherhood. No more knives or black fishnets. Warm milk and soiled nappies took their place. With Constairs providing a roof, a bed, but not much in the way of affection. His focus was on the Illusionaires. Securing their place in the world. A world that hung on the edge of war, as the Germans advanced into Europe.

And then, one day, Karla heard the call, one more pressing than even motherhood. People, her people, were being gunned down, or shipped off to labor camps. Constairs, they agreed, would hire a girl, a live-in to raise the child, thus freeing his mother to cross the Atlantic and put her skills to use. And Charlie? In spite of his young age, his abhorrence of violence, he'd flocked to the cause as well. Would never forget that winter night, his first drop behind enemy lines, or the meeting with Karla that followed days later, in a churchyard outside Arles. What? You? Here? They'd laughed, they'd hugged, just like old friends, though really they were still almost strangers. Their lives both touched, for better or worse, by a man named Richard Constairs.

Only then, over twenty years later, their paths had crossed again. Charlie, for his part, was now with the Division, had lived in DC for years. While Karla was no longer throwing her knives, but manufacturing them by the truckload, having taken control, shortly after the War, of one of West Germany's premier foundries. With Berlin in tatters, and its coffers torn open, opportunities were at hand, especially for someone with her special talents, and a ruthlessness to match.

But regardless of where the money had come from, she'd put it to good use. And about a year back, she had moved into Georgetown, deciding to set up shop. Without even blinking, she'd bought up the Carlton, an elegant boutique hotel, then claimed the entire top floor for herself, what she called her Washington Office. The only problem being, to use the elevator, you needed an access code, one which, unlike with her phone number, he always seemed to forget.

"K—it's your dinner guest. What's that damn code

again?"

"Some spy you make. It's 2114."

Fine. Next time he'll give her a real surprise. Float up through the floor instead.

A ten-second ride, silent and smooth. A ding as he reaches the top. Once the doors open, his nose starts to twitch, enticed by the smell of a steak or two being seared in a hot skillet. Following that scent down a plush corridor, he spots the entrance to her suite. Notes that the door's been left half-cracked, anticipating his arrival.

She's parked in front of a four-burner stove, a glass of red wine in her hand. A black leotard and a loose white T, both splotched with what looks like oil paint.

"I never knew this place had a kitchen."

"I had them put one in. Got tired of ordering room service—the asparagus was always limp."

A few quick steps across travertine tiles. He bends down to give her a hug. She responds with a pair of those fleeting cheek-kisses they like to dish out in France.

"As usual, you look wonderful."

"Hah!" she responds. "I'm a mess."

Her version of mess, needless to say, is something most women would die for. As pronounced as his talent for not being noticed, only hers works in reverse. And yes, there is grey amidst the black, and you can't overlook the wrinkles, but on her they only improve the view, give poignancy to the picture. Remind him that the reason we value beauty is precisely because it's so fleeting.

While the steaks rest they catch up on old news, flitting from this to that. He's there for some reason, that much is clear, but she knows better than to ask what it is.

"Sorry to hear about Mark," she ventures.

"That makes two of us."

He dabbles at his glass of wine. Can barely taste the stuff.

"I mean it's not like I had any grand hopes," he admits. "I knew he wasn't the one. But still, you miss it. Coming home to find someone there. Someone you can talk to."

He pauses. Studies her for a second.

"And then there's you. Don't you ever get lonely? Want a body there in bed, even if it's the wrong one?"

"Not really," she responds. "That's the beauty of having spent time with Richard. You realize that sometimes, being alone, it beats the alternative."

They eat outside on the small balcony, with the traffic their version of Muzak. Just enough noise to distract from the carnage, the sound of them gnawing away. And as for those steaks knives, they're better than sharp. So sharp they're almost scary. Probably some miraculous space-age alloy her engineers had discovered last week.

"Twenty-five-hundred feet per second."

"What?" she asks, glancing up.

"Twenty-five-hundred feet per second. That's the average velocity of a bullet as it exits a rifle barrel. And just think about what happens when that same slug hits a body."

"Damn," she says, fork in hand, "Thanks for ruining my steak."

"Not that I'd really know," he goes on. "Not personally at least. Because after that one time, that time back with Richard, I made a promise to myself that I'd never be the one. The one who pulls the trigger, or throws the knife, or makes the bad thing happen. No, I'd just let somebody else shoulder all that. Keep my own hands clean."

"Charlie …"

"No, no, let me finish."

He stares out at the city. The distant lights of the Capitol.

"I must've told you a dozen times. Back in '44. That time I broke rank, went off on my own, went off the reservation. By then the front was less than a hundred miles outside of Berlin, everything was chaos, confusion, and I knew this was my one chance. Before he crawled off to some retreat, some bunker, where maybe we'd never find him."

The smell of cordite and spilled kerosene. Concrete pounded back into dust. Close his eyes, and it's all still there, there till the day he dies.

"And I did it, K. I did it. Just me and him and a couple of goons who have no clue that I'm there. And it would have been so simple, so easy, to just reach out, grab one of their service revolvers, point it at his head. End it right there. But I couldn't. I *couldn't*. Even knowing that it would all be on me, every person, every prisoner, every mother and child who'd die because of what I did. No. Strike that. Not what I did. What I *didn't* do."

He leans back then. Takes a breath. Lets it out again.

"All of which means, what they're asking now, it might help make up for that."

"They?" Karla asks, her face in the shadows. "Who's they?"

"I can't tell you."

"Then how about what they want?"

"I can't tell you that either."

She casts a sigh, a sigh of disgust. DC and its rules.

"Fine. What can you tell me?"

"Just this. What they want, what they're asking, like I said, it should help balance the scales. Or at least maybe tip them a bit. Only somehow, there's this voice in my head saying look behind the curtain. Like I woke up in Oz instead of Kansas, and they're planning on pulling a fast one."

"And this voice. The one in your head. You believe it?"

"Sure," he admits, "a little. Or maybe it's just me doing it again. Being a pacifist chicken-shit."

He watches as she takes her fork, then pokes at a piece of lettuce. Trying to decide if it looks better here, or maybe over there. Cheer up, he wants to tell it. I know exactly how you feel.

"So you asked me what it's like," she finally says. "Sleeping alone every night. But thing is I don't. Because unlike you, I used that knife, or a gun if I had to. Didn't think twice about it. Didn't realize, all these years later, how crowded a bed could get."

She drops the fork to her plate.

"So act or don't act, kill or abstain, there is no right or wrong. Just all of us living from day to day, making it up as we go along."

Talk about cold comfort. Then again, it's better than none.

"Still," she offers, "if it turns out you get in over your head, that you need some help, some back-up, just remember I'd be more than willing to lend a hand. That I've even made it a point to keep my clearances up to date. You know, just in case."

"Thanks, but really I couldn't."

For the briefest of moments she looks disappointed. Recovers just as fast. "And what about Richard? Burying that hatchet?"

He'd be in his sixties by now. Probably using a cane. And the last thing Charlie would ever admit is that he might need his help.

"Fine," she replies, reading his face. "So that's not an option either. Well, there's always Door Number Three."

He stares back, caught by surprise. "I thought you said he wasn't ready. That really, he's still just a kid."

"You're right. I did. Still, he'll have to grow up sometime."

Pausing, he thinks that over. Knocks back the rest of his wine.

"Take it from the kid I used to be. Growing up, it's not all that grand."

17

HE SPENDS THE next day in his office, tying up loose ends.

Not that there are all that many to deal with. Summers tend to be a quiet time, especially in DC, a place where the heat, the mind-numbing torpor, drives people out of town. And, to be honest, Division 12 has never been that kind of place, a place where showing up, looking busy, carries all that much weight. Half the staff, they work out of their homes. The other half's caught up in fieldwork. Sometimes it gets to feeling almost ghostly, the vacant desks, the empty corridors, as if they'd managed to set up shop, provide all the necessary trappings, only to then somehow run out of money before they could hire on any help.

So maybe Karla was right after all. Maybe they did need new blood. And even though Randall might've never grown up, he'd be in his twenties by now. Older, in fact, than Charlie had been when he'd first hooked up with Richard. In a way it would be almost fitting, like passing on a curse, to take on an innocent, sheltered soul and show him how life really worked.

The afternoon drags on, like afternoons do. He can't keep his eyes off the clock And it's not until after he wraps up his third call—a rumor that Castro, with unrest on the rise, is starting to employ santeria—that he finally realizes what's up. That the reason he's so busy clearing his desk, opening up his schedule, is because he'd already decided. Decided to take the assignment. To work with the morons who've made his life hell for the past decade or two.

And that voice up in his head? Well, it's not like he's ignoring it exactly. Just putting it on hold. Going in with his eyes wide open, on the lookout for anything hinky. If the Agency's on the up and up, and they buy Kennedy more time, then maybe it'll signal the beginning of a brand new era, old rivals now working together. And if it turns out instead to be some double-play, one of the CIA's dirty ops, then he'll finally have the ammunition he needs to sideline them once and for all. Whichever it is, thumbs up or thumbs down, he'll only find out by playing along, but at least he knows the perfect guy to sign up for riding shotgun.

Charlie the Invisible Boy.

Because it's something he'd found out years ago, back when he'd first met Richard. Being invisible, it's not just about them not seeing you. It's about you finally seeing them; every pore, every blemish, every lie. When someone doesn't know you're there, they become their real self. The disguise goes away, the belt gets loosened.

The dog is off his leash. And you, unseen, can take your time, take all the time in the world, ignoring that advice you got as a kid: it's not polite to stare. Oh, the things he's seen, over the years, they'd be enough to burn your eyes out. The dark and private places we go when we think nobody's watching.

Which, in the end, means he's perfect. Or at least the perfect spy. Because you never know who somebody is until you've seen the things they hide.

"SO RUMOR HAS it you've decided to come on board."

"Or at least provisionally."

For better or worse he's back with Lansky, in his bank vault that thinks it's a rec room. Apparently Markley is out of the country, attending an Interpol conference, leaving his minions, Lansky included, to muddle along on their own.

Said minion gives him a baleful stare. His left brow creeps up an inch.

"Provisionally?"

"It looks we'll be working together, so I might as well level with you. I know what we do, it has consequences, sometimes unfortunate ones. But I also need to know that the people I work with, they'll try to keep them to a minimum. That our goal is to save lives, not take them."

Has he just been speaking Swahili? Lansky shakes his

head, bemused. "Listen to you. You sound like a goddamned Quaker. And did you give them this same run-down when they first hired you?"

"Actually, I hired myself," Charlie tells him. "Got in on the ground floor."

He watches as Lansky thinks that through. Runs the numbers in his head. Finally determines that this must have been when Charlie was still teething.

"You're looking at a guy," Lansky finally replies, "who can't even make it through *Bambi* without crying. I have no problem saving lives. But realize it's not me you have to convince. It's Markley."

"I know. I'm working on it."

Lansky shuffles across the room, searching through both pockets. Feeds two quarters into the slot, and then reaches past the frosty glass door. The pyramids were built on a ration of beer. Rome on sour red wine. But the key to the current Pax Americana are a few million gallons of Coke.

Lansky pops open both bottles. Hands one over to Charlie.

"So, I assume you've been thinking it over," he says. "How to kill a president."

Charlie scolds him with a look. "That's not how *Bambi* ends."

"You're right," Lansky admits. "Let me rephrase that. How to not kill a president, but make it look like we did."

"Actually, no. I haven't. I've had other things on my

mind. So how about you tell me what you've come up with so far, and I can poke holes in it."

Lansky takes a slug off his Coke. "Doesn't that sound fun."

They've decided the hit, he goes on to tell Charlie, will take place in public. The bigger the crowd, the better. And if possible, the event should be televised too, increasing both its reach and its impact. It turns out that Kennedy has already scheduled a series of early campaign appearances for the fall, most of them focused on the Northeast, with a quick swing south that will include Texas, a state crucial to his reelection. Several members of his cabinet, including brother Bobby, have tried to talk the President out of this foray into potentially hostile territory, and are especially concerned about Dallas, a hardscrabble town that always leans red, with its share of gun-toting yahoos.

All of which makes it the perfect setting for a staged assassination.

"And what's even better," Lansky notes, "is the fact that they're planning on a motorcade. And nothing gives JFK a bigger thrill than riding with the top down. Just like a little kid."

"So I'm assuming you figure on using a rifle. Or maybe someone in the crowd with a handgun."

"The Secret Service will be running two teams. No way could anyone on foot get past them. So, yeah, it'll have to be a long-gun. And the route will include lots of two- and three-story buildings, all with windows facing the street. Perfect spots for a sniper's nest."

"Which leads to an obvious question," Charlie points out.

Lansky waits for him to go on.

"This sniper of yours. Who does he actually shoot? If it's Kennedy, you could probably fake a wound, convince the people in the crowd. But then you've got the SS agents, the Dallas Police, the medical team at whatever hospital they rush him to. How are you going to fool them? Or do you honestly think you could fill them in, let them know it's staged, without somebody eventually spilling the beans."

"Which is where you come in," Lansky counters. "Division 12. The guys who can work miracles."

"You'd need a miracle alright."

"How come?" he asks back, almost taunting. "I thought that was one of your specialties. Clouding men's minds or whatever."

Like most things in life, it was all Richard's fault. Him and his Illusionaires. After twenty-five years of hoopla and hype, and shameless self-promotion, the public had finally become convinced that magicians really could do just about anything. Cure cancer. Right wrongs. Get rid of that bathtub ring.

"Sure," he tells Lansky, "we have Talents that can scrape memories, or plant false ones. And when it's a case of working one-on-one, the process is virtually flawless.

But as soon as you try to manipulate multiple subjects, things get complicated. Everyone processes memory differently. They use different cues, different triggers. Attempt to alter twenty minds, and you'll end up with twenty different recollections, hundreds of points where they don't coincide. Conflict with each other instead."

"So we keep them separate," Lansky suggests. "Never give them a chance to compare notes."

"But this will be an assassination. They'll be hearings, inquests, reports. If there's even a few slight discrepancies, people will still be throwing around conspiracy theories fifty years from now."

Lansky polishes off his Coke. Scrambles from the couch. Finds his way to the pool table and snatches up the white cue ball.

"And what if we find another way to kill him? Something quieter, more discreet?"

"Like what?" Charlie wonders.

"Like poison?"

"There'd still be a body to examine. A body that wouldn't be his."

"Then how about a body that *can't* be examined. Use a bomb instead."

"Unless you get the charge just right, they could still work up an ID. Off his teeth or fingerprints. And any bomb that would generate that much damage, it would kill too many others. The SS detail, anyone in the car, maybe even a few bystanders."

Lansky rolls the ball towards a pocket. It misses, then rebounds back. A sign from God that whatever they come up with, it isn't going to work.

"We keep coming back to the same basic problem," he bemoans. "We need two Kennedys. The real one, the one we save, and the fake one who we kill."

Two Kennedys. It's just that simple. Why hadn't he seen it before?

"What's that?" Lansky asks him.

"What's what?" he replies.

"That expression on your face?"

"I don't know," Overton replies. "I don't have a mirror. But I do have an answer. I know what we have to do."

"Oh, really."

A pound of condescension. A gallon of contempt. It's obvious nothing riles Lansky more than someone else getting there first.

"Sure. We have to build us a golem."

18

It was something he'd found out years ago. You don't need to be an expert. Just know how to find the one person who is, and ask them a lot of dumb questions.

He'd recruited Vadoma Bihari back in '59. What had seemed like a coup at the time. Much like a language, or even a cuisine, magics were regional, unique responses to specific demands that defined a people and their culture. And he'd noticed that, for whatever reason, the Division was lacking anyone with Roma blood. A deficit that, he'd decided one day, it was about time to address. Like any group that lacked worldly power, that was subject to hatred and hardships, the Roma had resorted to more arcane means to guarantee their survival. And even now, centuries later, people still feared the Gypsy's curse.

So he'd asked around. Done some digging. Enjoyed a couple of lovely weeks, hiking the Carpathian mountains. And had eventually tracked down dear Vadoma in her humble one-room cabin. Over tea and stale *buchty* he'd laid out his terms, sticking to simple pidgin, only to discover that her English was nearly flawless after several years in London's North End. *America? Hamburgers for breakfast? Do I look like I need a job?* But beneath all that bluster, her scowling black brows, he could tell she was intrigued. Relished a chance to challenge the world, to take on the competition, to prove herself the Queen of Dark Arts, and Mister don't you forget it.

As part of their deal, he leased an apartment. Flew her over, a seat in first class. Only to discover he'd left one box unchecked, that one about playing well with others. Because Vadoma obviously didn't. Within two weeks, three people had quit, four more were thinking about it, and every day, every hour, was some new test of wills. Yes, her technique was brilliant. She could out-cast them all in her sleep. But the problem was, she let everyone know it, whether they cared to or not. Things reached a head on a Friday afternoon, with her turning Sally into a toad, then refusing to turn her back again until she'd consumed a few dozen flies.

A farewell, not fond, on the following Monday. Another flight, coach this time around. They hadn't spoken a word since then, but they'd kept tabs on one another, Charlie in his broom closet, Vadoma in her latest digs. Rumor had it she was now in New York, working with a fellow adept, a former surgeon, Dr. Stephen Strange, who'd trained under the Ancient One. Hearing that, he couldn't help smiling. How long is that going to last? But when he finally reached her by phone, her tone was surprisingly warm. Yes, she'd love to see him. Her place, of course, not his. And as for this hush-hush project he's got, or answering a few questions, well, honestly, who wouldn't want to help out an old friend?

An old friend. Is that what he is?

He bids her goodbye. Makes a second quick call. Books a flight on the next puddle-jumper.

BLEECKER STREET.

This is his second visit here, the first being years ago. And he can still recall how taken he'd been, swayed by its grubby charm. Frantic jazz pouring up from some basement, with a crowd spilling out on the sidewalk. All those scruffy kids clutching their guitars, busking for spare change. He never did track down his target that night, a Voudon priest fresh up from Haiti, so the trip became a vacation instead, a night off from staid DC.

And this time around? It's not like the place has changed all that much, or at least in any way you can see. Yet still there's a stagey feeling now, like a smile held too long for the camera. Because the first time you tell a joke, sing a song, do anything ad lib, it's new. Fresh. But the second time around, or the third, or the forth, well, it may be new for all of them, but it isn't new for you. Which might explain what happens to any performer, what had happened, in fact, to Richard. Fake that freshness long enough, and you end up faking yourself.

He passes by her address twice. It's really that nonde-script. A door, once white, but now not quite, with no number, no placard, no clue as to what lays just past it. Which is, of course, classic Vadoma. He knows for a fact that she's stinking rich. Keeps a trunk filled with Krugerrands. Could probably afford to buy the whole block, its residents included. But she's always had a soft spot for dumps, for dives, for tight little cubbyholes, and, like a fox, if she's not out hunting, she's only happy when in her den. Especially when that den, however squalid, is so well protected.

Protected in this case by a standard Hobb's Wall. Something to keep out the riff-raff. No real problem for a guy with some Talent, even one as inept as he is. With a quick swipe he sends it packing, begins to climb the stairs, then realizes the Wall was just a feint, a straw man standing guard. All at once, the steps start moving, he's on a treadmill, not a mere flight of stairs, one that's moving ever faster, forcing him to pick up the pace. He could, of course, refuse to run. Call her bluff and see what happens. Only he senses there's something behind him, something that's hungry and mean. Knows that if he stops or stumbles, it'll be on him in a second.

One moment he's lunging, running full speed. The next he's merely standing. The air still coursing through his lungs, his heart still pounding away.

"For an old man, you're in pretty good shape."

She's taking her sweet time looking him over. Like a

kid with a lollipop.

"Forty-three's not old," he gasps.

But as for her, any kind of number, he'd given up long ago. Knew that if you checked her file, you'd find three separate birth dates listed there. Knew too that if you had the right skills, the right eyes, you might see that they're not in some ratty little walk-up off Bleecker Street, but maybe up in her hovel in the mountains, or some posh new spot London-way, or any one of a hundred locales where a gypsy might decide to hole up.

But real or not, he finds a chair. Or rather it finds him. Could swear it lets go with a gentle sigh even as it swallows him up.

"Still, you look good," she concedes.

He doesn't bother responding to that. No need to tell her the same. That between her eyes, as black as coal, and her cheeks, as sharp as diamonds, and the wicked curls, and the vulpine leer, and that ripe plum of a body, he almost feels like switching sides. Seeing how the other half lives.

"And how are things going?" he asks, nonchalant. "With the new partner and all?"

She already has a chair of her own. Makes it look more like a throne.

"You know I don't do partners."

"Then let's find a better word," he offers. "Victim maybe?"

There is now a porcelain mug in her hand. Most

likely tea, knowing her.

"Stephen and I, we have no illusions, about ourselves or about each other. Which must sound odd to someone like you, a former Illusionaire."

"Guilt by association?" he asks back. "Actually, I was never an official member. And Richard and I, we haven't crossed paths in years."

Somehow she'd snuck in a second mug, resting there on his armrest. He watches as the steam slowly rises, backlit by the afternoon sun.

"Still, we could sit here all day, couldn't we? Poking away at each other. But technically I'm here on the company's dime, and I hate to cheat the taxpayers."

"Yes," she agrees. "That project you mentioned. I suppose you should fill me in."

So he does. A run-through he's rehearsed a dozen times, editing it in his head, and which, nonetheless, still sounds like the plot of a movie you'd have to pay someone to watch. All the names are redacted, the details suitably blurred, just two old pros picking things over, in a world composed of what-ifs. And because she's a pro, all she does is listen; no questions, no interruptions. Waits until he's finally finished before mounting her attack.

"So. Charles. How long has it been? Since we last saw one another?"

"Three years and change. Call it four."

"I suppose that makes sense. It would take quite a

while for someone to get so stupid."

He waits for her to continue.

"A golem? Really? And this is your brilliant solution?"

"Well, at least it's a start."

"And what is a golem, we ask ourselves. We turn to the past for answers. Scour the Talmud, the Old Testament, centuries of arcane folk tales. Learn that, like with most things, there are disagreements, discrepancies, old grudges and arguments, but that, in the end, we can all settle on one thing."

She pauses, catching her breath.

"The golem is a hunk of clay."

It seems like a good time to sample his tea. He can taste a hint of licorice. Probably some blend of eleven herbs and spices, smuggled in from the old country.

"And?" he finally says.

"And? And? And you tell me this body, or what's left of it, they'll perform an autopsy. So explain to me what happens when they break out their knives, and start sawing away, and find out that, wait, this is not flesh and blood we have here, no it's more like ..." Another pause. She glances over. "What is that stuff they give them? The kids in their nursery school?"

"Play-dough?" he speculates.

"Yes!" she declares, slapping her chair. "Exactly. They find nothing but Play-dough."

He can feel his ramparts starting to crumble. Puts on

his best brave face.

"But everyone knows, that thing with the clay, it was just a metaphor."

"And what is magic *but* metaphor? One thing pretending to be another. And yes, with the right spell, you can convince the clay, for a while at least, that it can be flesh and blood. But that spell, it only reaches so far. It's not meant to deceive the whole world. The men with their scalpels, their knives."

Put like that, it makes perfect sense, and he's a perfect fool. Which is, of course, the problem with experts. They show you how little you know.

"But wait," she tells him. "There's more bad news."

Of course. Isn't there always?

"Maybe, somehow, you make your spell stronger. The clay becomes true flesh and blood. But it won't be *his* flesh and blood. His face, his fingerprints, any scars, his blood type. So many ways they could look at this body and know it isn't his. Because golems are meant to be less than human. To lack faces they can call their own."

Just for a second, he feels a spark. That old, familiar anger. Of all her skills, this one was foremost—the art of getting under your skin.

"So how about we come at it from a different angle?" he suggests. "Seems to me most folk traditions have tales of people creating duplicates. Doubles. Maybe that's where we need to look."

She's about to take another sip of her tea, but her arm

freezes instead. The sound of the traffic, the catcalls, the horns, not as loud as the gears in her head.

"Yes," she says, her head slowly nodding. "Yes, of course. A changeling."

A legend, a myth, even older than golems. A very part of the human subconscious. That hunch, that suspicion, that something's not right, that your loved one isn't really your loved one. Usually it's an infant or child, stolen away by the Devil, with something left to take its place, something sly, and cunning, and evil. Or maybe you prefer your nightmares more modern. A B-movie at some drive-in. That pod tucked away in a shed out back, waiting to turn into you.

She glances up. Studies his face. Sees the glimmer of hope he now harbors. But whether she replies out of mercy or malice, it's impossible to say.

"No. Don't you dare get all optimistic. I already see many problems."

"Problems? Like what?"

"Like why do you think, with a changeling, it almost always involves a child? The person, the self, it has had less time to form a connection with the body. But a full-grown man? Perhaps the somatic bond is too strong. Which means that your double, your duplicate, it would be not just a physical copy, but also share thoughts, memories, all the thousand little things that make us who we are."

"But you're not sure."

"No, of course not. Which brings us to another problem. Different magics, different traditions, they seldom work well together. Like people, like you and I even, they can get their backs up. Have a spat or two. Maybe even get so angry they end up sabotaging one another."

"Why? Are you feeling tempted?"

"Some poor fool who works for the government?" she shrugs back. "I have bigger fish to fry."

Which would mean, for once, there'd be no bickering. No back-talk or petty squabbles. Just a chance for her to prove her mettle, even if she couldn't go bragging about it. Because that would be the sticking point. The one thing he'd have to make clear. That once she finds out who their subject is, she'd have to keep her mouth shut.

"So what would you need to pull it off? Assuming you even can."

"Trying to make it a personal challenge? Really, Charles, you're so transparent."

She whisks both mugs back into the ether, though his had been barely half finished. Sits there a moment, her face a blank, thinking his question over.

"We'd need some clay, or just plain soil, from a place he's connected to. A place with which he feels a strong psychic bond, perhaps wherever he was born, or a homeland that he treasures."

An emerald isle, surrounded by sea. "That shouldn't be a problem."

"But that will account for simple bulk. To personalize our body, that will require more work. It's been a while since I've browsed any changeling spells, but most, I recall, require an actual physical artifact. A lock of hair. A few drops of blood. And considering our subject will be a man, not a child, I'm thinking it might be smart to include a few drops of semen as well."

"Assuming he hasn't run out."

The two of them study each other. A smile plays at her face.

"Charles, are you trying to tell me something?"

"More like trying not to."

"Fine," she promises. "But you do realize, sooner or later, the cat will be out of the bag."

But is it the cat that has nine lives, or the one that needs a skinning? Maybe he can figure that out during his flight back.

"Still, there is one last thing," he tells her. "One potential hurdle."

She'll probably end up laughing at him. He's used to it by now.

"You said there's a chance, with this duplicate, it might not just be physical. That they might end up sharing some mental traits—his personality, his memories, what have you."

"Yes. It's possible."

He thinks back on a promise he's made. All the ways it's shaped his life. Wonders, as always, if it's kept him shackled, or kept him free instead.

"And what about his soul?"

19

"YOU WANT *WHAT*?"

Well, at least he's got Markley's attention after three days of hide-and-seek.

"It's all there in the requisition report," Charlie explains. "And we're really hoping, given our timeframe, you can expedite the request."

He'd known all along it would prove a hard sell. That the Agency would balk. That exploding cigars and poisoned lipstick, that was all fine and good. But mention something as shocking as sex and you'd have all hell to pay.

"Look," Markley tells him, "everyone in this administration, all the way down to the maids, we've got our hands full, keeping his indiscretions out of the public eye. And now you want us to, what, start checking the trash for used condoms?"

"Or you could ask him for a sample. Just like a doctor would."

He watches as Markley shoots out of his chair. Heads on over to that same tired window. Almost like he's expecting a brand new view; palm trees not Pontiacs.

"Plus there's the whole religious aspect to think of. The fact he's a card-carrying Catholic. And here we go trying to sell him on this crazy scheme of yours. Voodoo and black magic."

"Actually, that shouldn't be a problem," Charlie points out. "Pope Benedict's edict of 1917 officially declared there was no inherent conflict between magic and Catholicism. That both were created and sanctioned by a just and loving God. Plus Kennedy, he had no problem with magic back during the Missile Crisis. Why do you think we're all still here, and not glowing in the dark?"

"Look," Markley insists, "there's got to be another way. One that will achieve our goals while maintaining presidential dignity."

"Dignity? Come on. In a couple of months you'll be pumping a body full of god knows how many slugs. How dignified is that?"

Markley pivots from the glass. Tries to stare him down.

"You have two days to find an alternative. Otherwise you're fired."

Just like the Man Behind the Curtain, all bluster and empty threats. But Charlie had actually been on the set. Taken a good long peek.

"You're not my boss. You can't fire me. Hell, I don't even work here. And I've got back-channels to the Oval

Office that you couldn't even dream of. So the simple fact is he'll hear our proposal, either from you or from me. All you have to do is decide which is better, getting credit or running away."

TWO DAYS LATER the word comes back. JFK is onboard. And Markley's patting himself on the back for realizing when to fold.

Now if only Vadoma Bihari could prove as cooperative. After their first meeting back in the Village, she'd launched into her research. A painstaking process that, to gauge by the whining, is more work than a doctoral thesis. For one thing she keeps insisting on original sources. Is constantly flitting off somewhere—a night in Beirut, a quick stop in Krakow, even a trip to glorious Pittsburg—always claiming she's on the verge of some breakthrough, and all on Joe Public's dime. Some days would find her practically manic, convinced she could pull it off. And the next it was nothing but dour pronouncements, more Slavic doom and gloom.

Compared to all that, working with Lansky, it was practically a dream. An ordered world where you made up a list, and checked off each item, one by one. Would they need a place to conduct their spells, to house their almost-golem? He booked a small cabin over at Camp David, provisioning it with food, clothing, and a small security detail, sworn to secrecy. A bit of Irish soil? Two days later it arrived by air freight, labeled as fertilizer. But Lansky's true genius was only apparent once Vadoma had started pestering him on the phone. Two drams of Snakeroot, preferably Croatian. A bone from an ox, slain by moonlight. And a sordid collection of paperback bodice-rippers, which she seemed to tear through like candy. Watching them at it, thrust and riposte, he could see he'd created a monster. An old married couple who were secretly thrilled to see who could outlast who.

And then, of course, there was the clincher. A small package, hand-delivered by courier. They'd routed it through the Department of Agriculture, declaring it fresh seed, proof that even some faceless bureaucrat could have a sense of humor. Still, seeing it there, wrapped in brown paper, the joke began to fall flat. To become instead a kind of reminder that even Kennedy was just this, just a man. Once, on assignment, Charlie actually touched it. Handled the Shroud of Turin. And even though, by then, all the experts had declared it a fake, a bit of wishful thinking, it had touched him back anyway. The thought that all that faith, all that belief, all those lives forever altered, it all came down to a few faded stains, human sweat on a cotton rag.

But such thoughts, such reveries, there's no time for them now. Not when they're mere cogs. Part of a cold and indifferent machine that will soon rewrite history. Culling a list of cranks and subversives, the Agency's fingered their man, a make-believe assassin hand-picked for the job, gunning down a fake president. The patsy's name is Oswald. He's a communist devotee. And somebody who, as fate would have it, is already employed in a building located along the motorcade's route. On November 22, he'll punch out at lunchtime, suddenly feeling tired, only to come to an hour later with a rifle in his hand. Staring down through a third-story window at a man he's just sent to his grave.

November 22. Barely two months away. Which is why he's been pestering Vadoma for weeks, trying to pin down a date for their ceremony. And then, finally, she makes the call: they'll gather on September 3rd. At 2:16 that morning, Mercury will pass out of retrograde, which, she decrees, should all but guarantee that their project will meet with success. All along it's been her baby, one she claims she can birth on her own, and that having anyone else around will only be a distraction. A hindrance. But Charlie puts his foot down. Insists he owes Lansky a front-row seat for putting up with all her nonsense. Owes himself another one, considering he's the putative father.

Charlie and Lansky drive up from DC together. Discover they both love Stan Getz. End up playing that game with the license plates, making up acronyms. Meanwhile, for Vadoma, still back in New York, it's a one-hour flight on a Cessna, her passing the time with another romance and flirting around with the pilot. Swinging by a small rural airstrip just a few miles from the Camp, Charlie finds he's almost nervous. That old dilemma from junior-high: will your two friends get along?

He loads her bags into the trunk. She takes a seat in back. Studies Stan, still riding shotgun, then finds a winsome sigh.

"I must say, I was hoping you'd be more attractive."

He thinks that over a second. "You know, so did my mother."

"Terrible, isn't it," she laments. "The way life disappoints us."

There's a snafu at the Camp's main gate. Some papers got lost in transit. Which gives all those guys standing around in their uniforms an excuse to act important. At one point they insist on checking the trunk, find the bags of fertilizer stashed there, only to have a lively discussion as to the best way to green up a lawn. Someone finally puts in a call to Langley, their bonafides are confirmed, and within the hour they're parked at the cabin, deciding who's stuck with the couch.

Charlie offers to take the bullet. "Really, it's OK."

"OK?" Vadoma scoffs. "More like pointless. It's not like any of us are going to sleep tonight. We all have to do our vigil."

Stan looks up from his spot on the couch. He's already hit the pretzels.

"A vigil? And how's that supposed to work?"

"Work? A vigil is a vigil. We stay awake. We do not

talk. We focus on the task at hand. The more we think, and believe, and imagine that it's so, the more likely it will happen."

"There's a name for that," he points out. "It's called magical thinking."

"Yes. Exactly."

Whoever stocked the pantry, they really enjoyed their nitrates. A five-pound chub of pimento loaf that's probably army surplus. And maybe he's just a little dazed, a little out-of-sorts, but every time Charlie glances over, sees it sitting there, livid and pink, he's reminded of what's still out in the trunk, and what it might soon become, and any thought of food, of dinner, it sends his stomach crawling.

In the end, they settle for cheese and crackers. A few stilted attempts at small talk. It's finally starting to sink in, to feel real, this thing they're about to do. As dusk settles over the forested hills, Stan and Charlie revisit the Dodge. Begin to haul in the canvas sacks, surprised by how heavy they are. They've already procured a fold-up gurney, now set up in the largest bedroom, and one by one they saw open the sacks, sharing a dull kitchen knife. Within seconds the air is thick with it, the smell of soil, of earth, the very same earth that could bury a man, or bring one to life instead.

"And the weight?" Vadoma asks. "It's the same as our subject?"

"According to the shipping invoice," Stan tells her.

"Then again, this is Ireland we're talking about."

As they empty the sacks onto the gurney, Vadoma flits back and forth; carping, cajoling, a tad more here, and don't you dare go spilling any. Because soil is heavier, denser than flesh, the body will be slightly smaller, only achieving its final size once the transformation is complete. Clutching a plastic spray bottle, she nudges them both aside, wetting the dry soil as she works, molding it into shape. First the left leg, then its mate. A pair of arms comes next. Almost as if her body, her hands, are sharing a precious secret. Reminding the clay, lifeless and cold, that it can be something else.

Alive.

The head, of course, she saves for last. Her touch becomes almost tender. Five or six pounds of Kerry's finest, caressed into a skull. Finally she pulls back. Regards her work. Nods in satisfaction.

"Now the personal touches, yes?"

Charlie unfolds the white envelope. Tips it towards her open hand. A few locks of hair come tumbling out, chestnut brown, with a trace of russet. Leaning forward, she lets them spill, find a home on the earthen pate.

"May his hair grow."

Next up it's Stan, awkward as always. Patting his way through his pockets. A final, audible sigh of relief as he finds the small glass vial. Passing it over, his hand almost slips, a bridegroom fumbling the ring, or at least until Vadoma reaches out, snatching it from his grip.

She finds the right spot on his chest. Upends the tiny vial. Even though the clay is already damp, it swallows each precious drop. Almost as if the soil is thirsty, has a heart of its own, waiting.

"May his blood flow."

And then it's back to Charlie. Another vial, this one a bit larger, a bit more difficult to obtain. As he passes it over, their eyes meet, but Vadoma refuses to smile. She's too caught up in the moment, the spell. This chance to play with fate.

Unscrewing the lid, she tilts the vial. A few milky drops ooze out. That spot where legs and body meet, the place where life begins.

"May his seed sew."

And already it feels different somehow. It's not just a pile of dirt. More like a vessel that's filled with intention, with an overriding purpose. All three of them glance at each other, unsure of what they see. A hint of pride, of a job well done, leavened with their misgivings.

"So now what?" Stan wonders aloud.

"Now we vigil," Vadoma tells him.

She has them adjust the gurney a hair. His head has to point due north. Then oversized candles, fragrant with beeswax, are placed at the four compass points. The lights are killed, the fridge unplugged, the bedside clocks go dark. EM fields, she explains, can mess with the spirits, keep them at arm's length. At her insistence, they leave the bedroom, stake out the main room instead. The act of creation will brook no witness, no gaze to probe its depths. Unrolling a scroll, what looks like old beach bark, she starts to teach them a chant. Their lips, their tongues, stumbling over odd sounds, snatches of Lakota Sioux. Probably the first time that a golem, a creature born of the Ashkenazy and their shtetls in Eastern Europe, has been coaxed to life by a song of the First People.

The night grows dark. The Camp falls silent. Two owls converse in the distance. The flickering dance of yet more candles, playing out on the ceiling, the walls. Sometimes the chant is one they share, actual words being spoken, while other time it's a taut length of rope they follow deep into themselves. Which is probably the whole point. Inside, outside. Me, other. All the boundaries start to blur. Creating a place where soil and flesh can mingle, forget it's not one and the same. A moment comes when he looks up. Sees Vadoma seated there. Only somehow now she's a twelve-year-old girl, the one she must have been way back when, already looking regal. And then, a minute, or an hour, or a lifetime later, it's Stan who's been transformed. Turned into some kind of creature, three eyes and a pair of horns.

And through it all, imagined or not, a single question looms. What's happening in the next room? Because, of course, they can feel it. Can hear it, taste it, too. Something deeply intimate, personal yet also transcendent. Kind of like your two best friends are in there, having sex, and you're trying your best not to notice. And should they be tempted to take a quick peek, Vadoma has already read them the riot act. Made them swear on their mothers' graves. Explained just how flighty the spirits could get, how they hated being interrupted. *It's like a soufflé,* she'd told them, scowling. *You don't ever open the oven. Just one look, no matter how tiny, and you ruin the whole thing.*

So is it the longest night of his life? If not, it at least feels like it. Longer even then that one in Lyon, with him hiding out in a graveyard, surrounded by the SS. He supposes, at times, he must drift off, steal a bit of what passes for sleep, only to wake up to find that it's still dark, that their vigil is still in place. But perhaps this is a good sign. Births are supposed take a while. To bring both parties pain. A lifetime's worth of suffer and struggle, foretold in a single day.

Only then, it finally happens. His eyes open to other than darkness. A tentative light, pale as weak tea, stealing through the curtains. To his left, Stan is sprawled out on the floor, one shoe off, one shoe on. To his left, Vadoma is sitting cross-legged, as limber as a cat.

She gives him a quick once-over. He must look pretty awful.

"Ah. You're awake."

"If you say so."

He reaches up and feels his hair. Tries patting it back into place.

"So—you been in there yet?"

"And spoil the big surprise?" she shoots back. "We make this baby together, we take our first look together too."

But at least their wait is a brief one. Already the sound of their voices has prodded Stan awake. Sitting up, he rubs his eyes, then takes stock of his feet.

"That's weird. Usually, when I do that, it's the left one I leave on."

Laces are tied. Quick trips to the bathroom. Mirrors consulted and then ignored. It's not like they're stalling exactly, but no one's in a rush either.

"Alright," Charlie says, content to play bad guy. "Might as well get this over with."

The door to the bedroom is still ajar. One candle still burning, if barely. Someone will have one hell of a time getting all that wax off the carpet.

And the gurney?

The man atop it is naked, with a slender, athletic build. Skin that's tanned, lightly burnished, though it's never once seen the sun. There's a small red line on his abdomen, an appendectomy scar most likely, and a scuffed spot just below his right knee, left perhaps by some poolside spill. She'd already told them that he would be sleeping, and so, yes, his eyes are closed, a look of calm, of tranquil surrender, you would never see in public. But it's not his expression that catches his eye, that makes Charlie gasp out-loud. It's the face itself, the parts, the pieces, ones he's never yet seen this close up.

There, to his right, he can feel Stan stiffen. Hear the sudden intake of breath. But it's Vadoma who surprises him most. He'd never once seen her falter.

She stares down at man they've made, recognizing who he is. The look on her face, that glassy-eyed stare, giving way to consternation.

"Oh, Charles," she says, her voice barely there. "What have you gotten yourself into?"

20

"WELL, IT WORKED."

They're gathered around the kitchen table, staring at the remnants of breakfast. Scattered rinds of blackened toast. Scrambled eggs, or else they're erasers. What's probably his third but might be his fourth cup of Maxwell House. Nothing but props, put there to convince them that today is just any other day.

"Worked?" Stan counters. "That's an understatement. I bet even Jackie couldn't tell them apart."

He pauses for one last bite of toast. Glances up towards Vadoma.

"And if we ever do this again, and I make some joke, or rude comment, or do anything at all to suggest you're some kind of flake, just tell me to please shut up."

But it's almost like he hasn't spoken. Like the words had slipped right past her. With her displaying the same shell-shocked expression she'd worn since that moment back in the bedroom. The moment when all three of them caught their first glimpse of whatever it was they'd created.

"I don't think that will be necessary," she finally replies.

"And why's that?" Stan asks.

"Because we won't ever do this again."

It would almost be better if she just did just blow up. Threw a fit, or went storming off. Because this thing she's doing now, this quiet fury, it's even worse than instant coffee.

"Maybe we're looking at this all wrong," Charlie suggests. "Maybe it *didn't* work."

He's hoping his comment will serve as a goad. A way of breaking down her wall. But instead it's Stan who opts to respond, filling an awkward silence.

"What do you mean?"

"It's been an hour, maybe more, and he, or it, or whatever pronoun you use, hasn't moved an inch. So what if it's just this lump of flesh? Dead weight, with nothing upstairs?"

Stan takes a moment to think that over. Finds an indifferent shrug.

"Well, to be honest, what does it matter? A lump of flesh is all we need. And really, if it's unconscious, or comatose, or outright brain-dead, that will make transporting it, securing it, that much easier."

And then he seems to catch himself. His eyes lock onto Charlie's. A look that excludes the third party there, as if she no longer exists.

"Sorry. I guess, before I go any further, I should ask

how much she knows."

"Nothing," says Vadoma, staring down at the table. "She knows nothing at all."

STAN DECIDES TO take a walk. Makes himself scarce for a while. And maybe, with him now out of the way, they can finally clear the air. As suggested by Charlie, they move outside, find a pair of old Adirondacks. A cedar porch overlooking that wooded ravine. A bird feeder, catching the sun.

For a minute, or maybe two, they share a not-quite-companionable silence. A belated acceptance, on his part at least, of all the ways he's managed to botch things up. Still, that's how life works, isn't it. No one starts out with bad intentions, or decides to do someone else harm. They simple take the first logical step, then the next, and then the next. A slow, incremental descent into blindness, only noticed in retrospect.

"Really, Charles. How could you?"

"I guess things just got out of hand."

She stares out at the bird feeder. Seems to notice it's all but empty.

"So why do you think, back in the 50s, when you first tried to hire me on, I ended up being such a monster?"

"I don't know. I guess I just figured that was you being you."

"Me being me?" She thinks that over. "Yes, I suppose. A little. And, of course, it was flattering—for a peasant girl, born on a dirt floor, to be offered a job overseas, working for the Americans. But still, a part of me knew it would never work out. That I could never be that kind of person. Someone who could take orders, do what she's told, look the other way. So instead I made myself insufferable. Became someone you had to fire. Burned that bridge so badly it kept you away for four years."

A second glance at the feeder, a feeder that's now full.

"And this is how you say hello?" she continues. "How you welcome me back?"

"Look, I …"

"No! Shut up! This is me talking. You just sit there and listen. This thing you're doing, whatever it is, it's bigger than all of us. Which means, if it goes wrong, like things always do, they'll come looking for people to blame. And who better to blame than me? Or no, let's say a miracle happens, this scheme of theirs actually works, then still they'll come from all over the world, saying c'mon, make me my golem." She pauses. Blows out a lungful of air. "Don't you see? Either way I'm screwed."

He'd been hoping to break down a wall. Hadn't expected a floodgate. Hadn't realized that, for her at least, success might be worse than failure.

"Look, you're right. I should've spelled things out. Given you a choice."

With that she stares back, shaking her head. A look

that's almost tender.

"Not just me, Charles. You needed one too. A chance to tell them no."

She reaches down. Fingers her chair. Scrapes off a bit of dried duff. The very same chair, for all he knows, JFK might have used once or twice.

"Duplicate presidents, and secret schemes, and God knows what else going on. This is not you, not the Charles I know. That man turned his back on illusions. And if you try to play their games, to be as clever as they are, they will crush you in a minute."

Words of wisdom, delivered too late. He tries for a bluff smile.

"I appreciate you caring. Wasn't sure you even could. But the problem remains, this thing we made, what do we do about it?"

"We could end it now," she says, cold-faced. "Breaking the spell would be easy."

He feels a sudden surge of unease. Hopes it doesn't show. "I was thinking more of waking him up. Seeing if anyone's in there."

"Waking it up? I'd advise against it. The process can't be rushed. If it were a typical golem, it would already be awake, fully conscious, ready to do your bidding, since you are technically its master. But this hybrid we've cobbled together? Creating the organs, the viscera, is a simple process, or at least in comparison. But if it's matter of duplicating the brain itself, all those miles of neural pathways, it could take days, even weeks."

"Weeks? You've got to be kidding."

She glares back, affronted. "You know I do not kid."

And then a reprieve, however brief. Both turn their heads at the sound. A flutter of wings, feather-light, as a finch lands on the feeder.

"Besides which," she tells him, "before he wakes up, there's something you have to do."

He waits for her to go on.

"Sometimes you say 'it', sometimes you say 'he.' You have to make up your mind."

ONCE STAN RETURNS, they come up with a plan. He'll return the Dodge to Langley. Drop Vadoma off on the way back out, just in time to catch her flight. Unless, of course, they decide to elope and live happily ever after.

As for Charlie, it's more ersatz coffee, and using his Grown-Up voice. Making a series of calls to Walter Reid, where he lines up an off-duty nurse who, at the drop of her hat, will drive up to Maryland. Their creation, their golem, might well be unconscious, but still needs a fair bit of tending. An IV drip, a catheter insert, sponge baths and daily rotations. Once he hangs up, Charlie calls the Division, has Heidi run a quick check. After confirming his volunteer's clearance and scanning her employee reviews, he decides there's at least a fifty-fifty chance she won't go spilling the beans. *Guess who I just gave a wipe-down to, and yes, it included down there.*

Their nurse, Thomkinson, can't make it up till Thursday, which gives him a day to kill. A day to catch up on all that lost sleep and think about what Vadoma had said. Of course, he's in way over his head. It's become his standard MO. A consequence of his special talents, the way he can walk through walls. Unlike most people, he can blunder along, get in all sorts of trouble, knowing full well that if things go wrong, he can blunder right out again. That, if he chooses, nothing can touch him. No cage that can hold this bird.

But still, there are all sorts of walls out there, some of which we build on our own. Little ways we trick ourselves into caring, when we know that would be a mistake. Five or six times he visits the bedroom, wondering if things might've changed, finding instead the same inert form, the same eyelids, always closed. And it's not like their creation is soft and cuddly. A cat or a guinea pig. Something you'd find any need to fuss over, or feel you have to protect. So why does he have to keep reminding himself that less than twenty-four hours ago it was just a few bags of dirt. Remind himself that, in the end, it isn't a person, a human being. Just a little bit of stagecraft, or in other words, a lie.

Thomkinson, it turns out, is built like a fullback. Could take him in two out of three. A Sumo in her pressed, starched whites, displaying not a trace of makeup. When she catches her first look at Patient X, she doesn't even flinch, leaving Charlie to figure out how to say something without actually saying a damn thing. He makes a few vague allusions, loose lips sinking ships, then hands her a card with his private, scrambled number written on the back. If he moves, he tells her, call me. If he doesn't move, call me then too. And if a cadre of men, all speaking Russian, should happen to break down the front door, you will first administer a fatal dosage of insulin, and then, by all means, call me. Assuming you're still alive.

He procures a sedan, a one-way rental, for the hour-long ride to DC. Arrives at his broom closet just shy of noon, expecting to find minor chaos. Thanks to his latest project, the one he can't talk about, he's been remiss in his administrative duties, and even a place as relaxed as Division 12 needs the occasional memo from on high. But he soon discovers there are no crises waiting. No fires, large or small. He checks in with Heidi, asks about her kids, swaps a few recipes, then confirms that his calendar's empty. That Charles Overton, at the ripe old age of forty-three, has at last achieved true corporeal non-existence.

So why is someone knocking on his door?

"Sorry," Heidi whispers, just her head poking in. "He showed up out of the blue."

"Who did?"

"Markley," she hisses back.

And with that he blusters his way on in. Begins to survey their surroundings. His suit, his tie, his very presence jarringly out of place.

"Wow. They weren't kidding, were they? It does feel like a closet."

"Feel?" Charlie echoes back. "No, it really was one. Or two actually. Originally there was a pair of them, back-to-back, but I had them knock down the wall."

"Still, not much in the way of a view," his guest notes.

He decides to conjure one up then and there. Ramla Bay, just off Malta. He'd never dare claim to be a real magician, but at least he could manage that much.

"Well," Markley says, admiring the waves, "I guess I stand corrected."

Which must be why he doesn't sit down. Decides to stay on his feet. Or maybe he's too good to use the one chair, a ratty old Ames with casters.

"So, sorry to drop in like this, unannounced, but I just got through talking to Lansky." He stops. Lowers his voice. "I assume we're secure in here?"

"The only people who'd be listening in, they'd probably work for you."

"Sure. I suppose you're right. Anyway, after what he told me, I'm here to apologize."

The word is so unexpected Charlie has to repeat it out-loud. "Apologize?"

"For doubting you. For putting up roadblocks. Bad-talking you to our boss."

No one apologizes in DC. You might as well slit your own throat. The only question is, should he just play along, or call him on it now?

"Well, thanks. I appreciate that."

"And now that you've done the heavy lifting, it's time we did our share."

"Your share?"

"You know. The upkeep, the maintenance. Keeping it alive and kicking."

He'd like to see them give it a try. Risk walking through that door. Wonders how many field-ops Thomkinson could take down before she even broke a sweat.

"Actually," Charlie tells him, "Dr. Bihari said to give it some time. That if we try rushing things, we'll just shoot ourselves in the foot. Plus, there's something you need to know before you go any further."

Markley nods back, feigning interest. "Which is?"

"Don't say 'it', say 'he'."

21

THE CALL COMES two days later. The one he's been waiting for.

But he only realizes that's what he's been doing—waiting—once Heidi patches it through. That everything else in the interim has just been killing time.

"Overton here."

A second of dead silence. The curse of a scrambled line.

"Mr. Overton? It's me. RN Thomkinson. You said I should call if things changed."

And that one word. *Changed.* He can already see him, cold and lifeless. Just a few sacks of dirt after all.

"What is it? What's wrong? He's not …" He stops. Hesitates. Discovers he can't say the word.

"Awake? As a matter of fact he is. And putting up quite a ruckus."

A ruckus? It's one of those words from a *Times* crossword puzzle. What your grandparents might say. "You mean he's conscious? Actually talking?"

"Talking? Sure, he's talking. Talking up a storm. Only

trouble is, the more he does, the less sense he ends up making."

HE SIGNS OUT for a car from Transport. Throws in his overnight bag. With luck he'll be outside the District before rush hour hits. For a moment he's tempted to contact Stan, invite him along for the ride, but ever since Markley's impromptu visit, he's decided to be more cautious. It's obvious now he's no longer a joke, that guy with the private broom-closet. That thanks to their project, its unlikely success, he's got what everyone wants. A president you can keep on a leash, or at least the next best thing.

Still, knowing all this, he'd taken a few steps. Played it smart for once. Markley had barely left his office, taking his aftershave with him, before Charlie found himself back on the phone, tracking down their latest new hire. The kid's name is Kevin Something-Or-Other. Just a few years out of high school. One of those loners they insist is autistic when really, he's just shy. Either way, it's probably that reclusive streak that accounts for his unique talent, throwing some of the most formidable shields anyone has seen since the War. At Charlie's prompting, he'd driven up Camp David. Spent an hour or two at the cabin. Nothing and no one would be getting inside, not unless they knew the magic words.

And no, they're not Open Sesame.

He'd also spent a long afternoon in the Division's crypt, breathing dust and dodging cobwebs, engaged in a crash course on everything golem, like he should've done weeks ago. It turns out that, yes, it's apparently true, that offhand comment Vadoma had made. That whatever is waiting back up at cabin, he's not just a duplicate, he's a servant, a slave. Someone who'll indulge his creator's every whim, no matter how arbitrary. In theory, that power should belong to Vadoma, she'd done the heavy lifting after all, but instead she's decided to just walk away, to abdicate that position. So will it then become his by default? The texts refuse to answer. Just as Charlie himself can't decide if he's ready, ready to become someone's master.

The men at the Camp's gate scan his ID. Nod him through, barely noting his face. A reminder that sometimes without even trying you can still be invisible. Thomkinson's car is parked in the carport, a Volvo with sagging springs, but there's plenty of room on the side of the road, underneath that big-leaf maple. Stepping out onto the shallow ditch, he takes a calming breath, only then realizing how nervous he is, what feels like first-date jitters.

First date? Really? He thinks back to that lump of dirt, lying there in the gurney. Just this once, if he gets the cold shoulder, he won't take it personally.

As a courtesy, he raps on the door, rather than just

barging in. Has barely finished his shave-and-a-haircut before Thomkinson yanks it open.

"Thank God you're here," she exclaims.

Her blouse is ruffled, one button yanked loose. Her white bonnet pulled askew. He'd thought she could pass for invulnerable, but apparently he was wrong.

"Are you OK?" he asks, stepping inside. "I got here as soon as I could."

"I'm fine," she insists, despite her appearance. "He was getting so worked up, I was afraid he'd pull his IV. So before he could, I slipped 10 CCs of Demerol into the bag. That calmed him down in a hurry."

His eye strays back down to that one missing button. She catches the way he's staring.

"Lots of men do it, start grabbing like that. Must be something about the uniform."

Charlie decides to let it go at that. Glances down the carpeted hall. The house is dim, the bedroom's shut, the whole place eerily quiet.

"You want to check on him," Thomkinson continues, "you go right ahead. I moved him out of the gurney yesterday. Thought he might appreciate a real bed. And yesterday was his first meal to speak of, strained peas and a banana." She pauses. Hesitates. "One thing I did notice though. Whenever I move him, for a wipe-down and such, it seems to cause some pain. I'm thinking he might have some kind of back injury. Maybe a slipped disk."

Courtesy of a certain PT boat, stationed out in the

Pacific.

"Thanks," he tells her. "I'll take it from here."

Even though there's no real need for silence, he creeps back anyway. The faint sound of his shoes, Thom McAns, scuffing away at the short nap. The room is cool. The curtains drawn. The gurney folded up in one corner. A bed is now lined up against the wall, just beneath the room's sole window. The man inside it is no longer naked, he's wearing cotton pajamas, one sleeve rolled up to accommodate the plastic tube running from his IV bag. And though it's only been a couple of days since Charlie last had a gander, his face, his whole body, looks different. More comfortable, more lived in. The contrast between a stiff new suit, fresh off the rack, and one that's been worn once or twice.

Moving closer, he sees both eyes are closed. The patient is fast asleep. Only then, as if sensing he's no longer alone, one lid creeps up a hair.

"Which?"

"Which?" Charlie says back.

"Which one?"

His voice is a rasp, its blade long dulled. Each word seems to cost him something.

"Four brothers—Karamozov?—No, not them—They were Russkies, right?"

The man in the bed tries to lean forward. Comes up with a grimace instead. He's focused on Charlie, staring outright, as if he knows who he is.

"Joe? That you?"

Joe, the eldest of the Kennedy boys. Killed years ago, during the War.

"Sorry, sir. It's not Joe. You can call me Charlie."

His eyes bulge a little, hearing this. "Charlie?—Victor Charlie?—That's what they call them—The little gooks in their lampshades."

How much, Charlie wonders, is the Demerol talking, and how much is what's playing in his head. A feature film, forty years in the making, only it's been sliced into pieces. Past and present, real and imagined, all dancing across the screen.

"Sir, how much can you remember?"

He makes a noise. What could be a laugh.

"How much can I *not* remember?"

With that he falls back. Closes his eyes. And yes, even presidents snore.

IT WAS SUPPOSED to be a quick over-nighter. Instead he stays three days. Three whole days of playing Humpty Dumpty, trying to un-break that poor egg.

He begins by tallying up the pluses, all the things to be grateful for. His lump of clay is still alive. Even pawing the hired help. And instead of being brain-dead or comatose, he's a functioning human being, with thoughts, and feelings, and memories, and that cartoon accent of his. Only somehow, all those parts, those pieces, they don't quite make up a whole. At times he's completely lucid. He really is JFK. While other times, the things he comes up with, it's like some surreal dream. More dead relatives dropping by. Long pauses and odd word choices. A loopy, starry-eyed way of talking, like he's still in the fourth grade.

Still, each day he seems a little less lost. He's getting better at faking it. But the one thing that never goes away, that seems built into the package, is an ever-present sense of detachment. Proof that he's not all there. Even though he's slowly coming around to realize that there's a man called John Fitzgerald Kennedy. That this man is the thirty-fifth President of the United States. That he and this man seem to have the same body, the same face, the same past and perhaps even the same future. And yet somehow, it doesn't register. He doesn't seem to care. Doesn't question how this came to be, or how he should feel about it.

One morning, in the paper, they both note a brief headline. An announcement that there's a White House news conference scheduled for that same afternoon on TV. A few hours later they're side by side, watching JFK, the way he fields each question with disarming ease, never once missing a beat.

"He's really good at this, isn't he?"

"Yes," Charlie tells him. "You are."

"And he seems like a good person too." He stares for

a moment at the flickering Zenith. His ghostly alter-ego. "Do you think that's just an act?"

"I don't know," Charlie admits. "I think with a lot of people, being good, doing the right thing, it starts out as that, just an act. But then at some point, if they're lucky, they become the person they've pretended to be. Discover that they really are good."

"And you think that will happen with me?"

Leaning forward, he flips the switch. Watches the screen go black.

"I'm not sure, but I sure do hope so."

They take short walks on the quiet back trails. Both wear homburgs and dark glasses. Camp David, it seems, is all but deserted, but he can't risk his guest being spotted. Or maybe staying hidden, running away, it's no longer a viable option. The next day, after lunch, a car shows up, so drab it's conspicuous, and Charlie watches through shuttered blinds as four men start to climb out. They have that look, mid-level Langley, sporting last week's five-dollar haircut, and he almost feels sorry for them as they shuffle towards the cabin.

Or at least try.

Kevin's shields are not standard issue. They're linked to hyperspace. And whoever attempts to slip past one will instead find himself deflected, moving away at a perfect right angle to whatever object it encloses. For five or ten minutes the two of them watch as the agents grow ever more flustered, then finally retreat back to their sedan, left to lick their wounds.

But as comic as the interlude seems at first, it casts an ominous shadow. The wheels are turning, and much sooner than he'd expected. Everyone's lining up, taking sides. And if you want to talk, to negotiate, you send two men. But four instead? Four men means the talking is over.

Thomkinson is already in town, on her one day off. He waits until the sedan finally leaves, then calls his golem into the kitchen.

"Do me a favor will you? Fire up that front burner."

It takes him a moment to work the knob. He's still a bit of a klutz.

"Is that good?" he asks, once it's lit.

"Perfect. Now put your hand in the flame."

Still smiling, he starts to obey.

"No!" Charlie calls out, grabbing his arm. "I didn't really mean it."

He stares back with a wounded look. "Then why'd you tell me to?"

It's like talking to an eight-year-old boy. What people used to call simple. Only this boy, this simpleton, could be running the world one day. He nods towards the kitchen table. Both of them sit down. Already the look of dismay is gone, it's back to that vacant smile.

"I have to go away for a bit," Charlie explains. "Find a safer place for you to be. The nurse should be back in a couple of hours, and if it looks like I can't return in a day or so, I'll send someone special to keep an eye on things. Someone who can keep you both safe. Does that sound OK?"

"Sure, I guess."

For a moment he studies those ice-blue eyes, so free of guile, or deceit. Wonders if we'd all be better off if our leaders were just like him.

"While I'm gone, I want you to promise. Promise you'll be good. Stay indoors, and mind the nurse, and don't go touching her anymore. And if any strangers show up, and try to tell you what to do, just remember you don't have to do anything you don't want. That I'm the only one who can order you around, and only if I have to."

"And you promise you'll be back?"

"Yes, I promise. But before I go, there's one last thing we have to do. Give you a name."

He shakes his head in confusion. "But I already have a name. It's Jack."

"Well, sure, that's what everyone else might call you, but I'm not them, am I? So this will be a special name, one that just you and I will know about. Any thoughts on what it should be?"

Vietnam. The Space Race. Nuclear annihilation. Seeing him, it's obvious now, none of that matters as much as just one thing. Getting the answer right.

"Buttons," he finally announces, bouncing a bit in his seat.

"Buttons?" Charlie says. "That's a funny name."

His eyes gleam back, full of mischief.

"Not for a bunny it isn't."

22

HIS WHOLE LIFE Charlie had been a loner. That island they write poems about. Shuttled from house to house as a kid, hand-me-downs that never quite fit, people that took him in out of kindness, or to get a farmhand that worked for free. Out of all of them, Richard had been the closest, the closest to being a father, only look how that had turned out. Big fat letters scrawled on a blackboard, his lesson for the day. CARING = GETTING HURT = WHY BOTHER? Write it twenty-five times in a row.

All of which makes what's happening now feel like one of life's little jokes. The fact that at the ripe old age of forty-three he's been saddled with a kid of his own.

Traffic is backed up on I-81. Some kind of fender bender. Red tail lights and a blurry windshield, both thanks to the late-day drizzle. The dashboard radio drones away, but he doesn't even notice, thinking instead of what comes next, what new wrinkles he'll encounter. Will his make-believe son remain eight-years-old? Will his brain catch up with his body? Will somebody sneak him into the Oval Office, give him a script to read, or stick him inside that big black limo and pump him full of lead? So many options, so many outcomes, but not a single happy ending.

By the time he makes it back to the Division, the place is almost deserted. Just a few stray birds, loners like himself, with no one waiting at home. He scans through the memos from the last few days, sees that things are still quiet, thanks a God he doesn't believe in that Heidi still has his back. Then it's another trip downstairs, punching in the four-digit pass code, only this time around it's not knowledge he's after, but more like an escape hatch.

Camp David has clearly been compromised. He needs a new safe house. Somewhere he can stash his golem and buy them both a bit more time. Technically the portal is government property, which means that he'll be stealing. But he's the one who'd found the damn thing, and shouldn't that count for something? Seeing it there, tucked away on a shelf, you wouldn't waste a second look. Some kind of scroll, a bit of cheap kitsch, like you'd find in a Chinese market. But unfurl that scroll, take a good look, and you're staring into the abyss. A passageway to anywhere in the world. A door that leads to elsewhere.

He tucks the scroll into his pocket. Takes the stairs back up. Leaves a note on Heidi's desk, thanking her for five good years. He could drive back right then, hit the Camp after nightfall, but that might draw too much attention. Provoke a phone call to the wrong person, not that there's really a right one. So instead he heads to his apartment, parking a few blocks away, grateful that, thanks to the rain, the sidewalks are almost deserted. One of the features that had sold him on the place was a second entrance tucked out back, one you can't watch from the street, and once inside he keeps the lights off, feeling his way by Braille. He waters the house plants. Collects his old mail. Eats a can of chili, still cold. Lies down on his bed, the bed of a stranger, and waits for sleep to claim him.

The drive back up is uneventful. The wet weather has moved further south. At least once a minute he checks in the mirror, looking for signs of a tail. But apparently there's no need for one. The trap has already sprung. Pulling up to the main gate at David, he sees the same familiar faces, only this time around they don't bother smiling, or nod him on through like always. His clearance, it seems, has been revoked. The order came through yesterday. Conveniently issued just a minute or two after he'd left for DC.

He decides not to raise his own ruckus. What would be the point? He thanks the man, pulls a one-eighty, then drives a mile or two. Finds what looks like an old logging road and parks there, out of sight. Taking off cross country, he hikes back towards the Camp, the only visible signs of his passage a footprint, or the occasional bent branch. Once he spots the wire fence, he lowers his density, slipping past the electrified strands, insubstantial as a breeze. His only real concern are the dogs, but they're kept penned most of the time, and the odds of them latching onto his scent are practically non-existent.

When he finally finds their cabin, there's no sign of Thomkinson's car. And, far more distressing, no sign either of Kevin's defensive array. Has the Agency found its own adept? Is Kevin working both sides? Or had they found the right pressure point and forced his coopera-tion? Whatever the reason or explanation, the point is officially moot. Slipping through the cabin's rear wall, he conducts a quick walk-through. No clothes, no food, the cupboards are bare, the floors have even been vacuumed. Magic elves in their Monkey Ward suits, making it all go away.

Hiking back out, he's silently fuming. A day late, a dollar short. And every time he's made a move, they've already made theirs' first. He used to be a good spy. Not great, but decent enough. Maybe it's time to get off his ass and try being one again.

CIA HEADQUARTERS. LANGLEY, Virginia. If you're going to break into a government building, why not set your sights high?

And sure, security's bound to be tight. Professional pride, or what have you. But any lock, any alarm, any moat or drawbridge, they'll only keep out what they're *designed* to keep out. Only no one's designed like him.

8:15 on a Tuesday morning. Tomorrow is now today. He takes public transit to the nearest bus stop, then covers the last block on foot, weaving his invisible way through the stragglers, now officially late for work. All the external paraphernalia—the perimeter fence, the CC cameras, the kiosk and electric gate—are, for him, no problem. Which means his first real challenge comes at the entrance itself. That big revolving door. Awkward enough to negotiate, even for your average commuter, but doubly so when it's up to Charlie to stay out of everyone's way.

He stands there watching, timing the spin. Waits for a break in the crowd. Slips into the wake of a middle-aged woman, clutching her leather briefcase. Turning, she seems to stare right through him, as if somehow sensing him there, and then, just like that, they've both entered the lobby and he quickly darts away. An elevator car would be way too risky. He takes the stairs instead. Then realizes that his echoing footsteps, they're like a homing beacon. Finally, in the end, he takes off his shoes, opting for stocking feet. Stubs his toe on a concrete step and mouths a silent curse.

Because he's important, because he's in charge, Markley's office is on the top floor. But at least, thanks to that previous visit, Charlie knows his way around. Leaving the stairwell, he tracks down a bathroom, then slips his shoes back on, confident that the wall-to-wall carpet will serve to mask his steps. There's a chance, he knows, that he'll find Markley there, parked behind his desk, thus denying him a chance to root through his papers, or find anything worthwhile. Still, he's counting on the Director's oversized ego, a constant need to be seen, to insure he'll be at some morning press briefing, or testifying to the House.

The door is closed, good sign number one. Last time, he recalls, it was open. And there's no hint of voices bleeding out from behind it, good sign number two. Passing through drywall and stainless steel studs, he leans forward, then peers around. Sees that the office is indeed empty. As quiet as a prison cell. Which will, of course, be Charlie's next stop should he be detected.

A desk, standard issue, three drawers to a side. Two extra-large file cabinets. Probably somewhere in excess of two thousand sheets of paper, versus one pair of stigmatic eyes. He starts by ensuring some privacy. Fuses the door lock shut. A simple matter of inserting his hand and increasing its density. Once that's done, there's no need to maintain his invisibility, and a moment later he shimmers into view, then circles around the desk. He has no idea what he's looking for. No idea if it even exists. A fat file folder, stamped Top Secret, with one of their absurd code names. Operation Dead Ringer.

He finds instead an Operation Foxtrot. And Landslide and Freefall and Pointless. A couple dozen crazy schemes to outfox the Russians and put Khrushchev on the run. But flipping through each folder, he starts to realize that these very same Ops are now defunct. Suspended. That they'd either been abandoned midway through, never quite brought to fruition, or else were never even initiated in the first place, considered too risky, or impractical, or insane. Once he's worked his way through a couple of drawers, he decides to switch tactics, tackle the file cabinet instead. Finds a lot of outdated correspondence, notices from the GAO, plus five or six take-out menus, places you can order in lunch.

Somehow his legs find him a chair. He sinks down, his head now spinning. Floored by this latest look past the curtain, and a glimpse of nothing at all. Because it's almost as if all those reams of paper, the files, the photos, the reports, are just there to look impressive. To take up space. Almost as if Markley himself, the whole Agency, is just one big game of dress-up. As insubstantial, it seems, as Charlie himself.

The Man Who Isn't There.

"Jesus," Stan blurts out. "How'd you get in here?"

"I walked through the wall, how else?"

Stan's looking at him as if he's a ghost. Then again, maybe he is.

"Look," he tells Charlie, "if anyone sees you, finds out you're here, we're both toast."

Once he'd left Markley's office there was nowhere

else to go. Because, in the end, you have to trust someone. You can't fight a war on your own. Finding a seat on Stan's old couch, he idly glances around, wondering if there are any more surprises waiting to trip him up.

"Toast?" he asks. "How come?"

"They hired you to do a job. You did it a little too well. And then you had the nerve to pull that stunt, that shield you put on the cabin."

Charlie shrugs back. "Just protecting what's mine."

"Not yours. Ours."

He studies the man with the goatee and glasses. Has he made a huge mistake?

"Before you decide whose side you're on," Charlie tells him, "you might want to listen to something."

And maybe he's hoping that by sharing what he's found, saying it out-loud to another, it will somehow become more real. Less outlandish. Only this time around, it's not working.

Once he's done, Stan simply stares back. He can't quite swallow it whole.

"So what are you saying?" he finally replies. "He's just some kind of straw man?"

"A straw man. A fake President. Who's to say what's real anymore."

"But that's crazy. Bat-shit crazy. I mean, this is the CIA we're talking about. We're the guys who know what's up."

"Really? Are you sure?" Just for a second, Charlie's

back in that office. All those useless stacks of paper. "It's a classic dilemma—who watches the watchers? And if Markley really is a shill, a figurehead, who would even know? There's no one looking over his shoulder."

Stan yanks off his glasses. Rubs at his face. His Tuesday is not going well.

"So what do you want me to do about it?"

"Just keep your eyes open," Charlie tells him. "Keep your *mind* open. Really, that's all I'm asking."

As if that's not bad enough.

"And what about you?" Stan wonders.

"I'm going to make sure the package is safe. Somewhere out of harm's way. And then, assuming I'm still in one piece, I'll tackle the real question."

Stan just sits there, waiting him out.

"Because if Markley really is a puppet, then who's pulling his strings?"

HE SLIPS BACK out of the building. Retraces that morning's route. Finds the Rambler right where he left it, parked outside a crowded shopping center. He's got that thing going on in his head: everyone's in on the plot. That little old lady, that mom and her kids, that dog yipping in the front seat. He'd once asked Richard, did he ever lose track, what was real and what was illusion. Can still remember the way he'd grinned back, a smile that was almost cruel.

It's all an illusion, kid.

He eventually finds the highway. Pretends he knows how to drive. But somehow the process, all those dotted white lines, it's more than he can manage. After almost rear-ending a station wagon, he pulls over for a quick cup of coffee, only to discover that being wide awake is worse than being half asleep. Traffic thins out once he hits the back roads, the sky's already dimming, and he figures he's got a half-hour tops before he makes Camp David. His final, last-ditch, Hail Mary attempt to save Buttons from the Bad Guys.

Unless the Bad Guys find Charlie first. Rounding a curve, he taps the brakes. Tries them a second time. Starts to pump away in a panic, only nothing seems to happen. As luck would have it, he's on a downhill grade, not that steep but steep enough. His eyes lurch down to the little white needle, already pinning sixty.

Well, he thinks, sighing out-loud, so much for that Hail Mary.

And with that he yanks the wheel to the side, plunging off the road.

23

HE'S SURROUNDED BY total darkness. Or maybe total is a lie. Off to his left, the sky looks bruised, more purple than true black.

And speaking of bruised. He hadn't willed himself to become unsubstantial; no, his body had acted alone, an instinctive reaction which had saved his life, but extracted a price nonetheless. He reaches down. Feels the branch. The way it's shooting straight through his left leg. Chances are when he'd finally rematerialized, his flesh had re-formed around it.

So all he needs to do is just run the film backwards, like a thousand times before, only taking his time, doing it in stages, trying to not lose too much blood. The trick, he'd discovered a while back, was to find that sweet spot when the tissue wasn't quite solid, more like a gelatinous mass of pink pudding, stuffed inside the balloon of his skin. At one point he almost passes out. Tells himself to buck up. Because the process would hurt a whole lot worse if the branch had gone though his head.

Once it's over, and his splinter is out, he lets himself

rest for a minute. Listens to the sounds of the night, a screech owl shrieking away. Back in Caton, when he'd lived with the Schusters, he used to gather them up. Rats and field mice, voles and gophers, whatever varmints he could find, carrying them out into woods, where they at least had a little cover, a chance they might survive. His sympathies, of course, always lying with the victim, the prey, the thing that ended up getting eaten, whether it scurried along on four legs, or walked upright on two.

Eventually he sits back up. Somehow manages standing. Starts to fumble his way uphill, searching for the Rambler. Normally he'd just become insubstantial rather than fight it out with all those brambles, but he's afraid if he risks it, goes low density, his wound will open back up. Nearing the ridgeline, he finally spots it, a two-lane ribbon of asphalt, then follows the road to a wounded oak, and the bird cage wrapped around it. The engine block is now riding shotgun. The windshield just pebbled glass. The fumes of spilled gasoline so heady, so strong, it's a wonder they haven't combusted.

He reaches down. Pats the hood. Rest easy, valiant steed. Then takes a moment to consider his options, glancing both right and left. The Camp would be closer, much less of a hike, and he'd already snuck in once. Could probably lay low in their old cabin, with no one being the wiser. But the problem is, that would be hiding, and he doesn't feel like hiding anymore. Is sick and tired of fighting his battles by pretending he's not there. He pops the trunk, still intact, and retrieves his soft-shell suitcase. Finds his way back to the road and begins to follow it south.

LIFE FEELS DIFFERENT, he'd learned long ago, when somebody's trying to kill you.

Colors are brighter. Sounds are louder. Everything is amplified. As if someone has taken your whole damn world and cranked it up a notch. And sure, some of that's just adrenalin at work, the old game of fight or flight, but to claim this alone explains how he feels would qualify as a lie.

Like that leg of his. With every step, there's a sharp jolt of pain, some guy with a very dull knife, only instead of bitching and whining about it, Charlie's grateful for the company. Because, if it hurts, that means he's alive. That his body is still complaining. That existence wants to torture him further, hasn't yet tired of the game. And as long as it hurts, he won't fall asleep, won't nod off in mid-step, and can instead engage in the kind of top-flight, brilliantly insightful tactical analysis that has served him so well up to now.

Is somebody really trying to kill him? *Step.* Sure, accidents happen, but both the Agency and the Division itself have pretty robust vehicle maintenance schedules, and the timing is rather suspect. *Step.* So who might this somebody be? *Step*. Someone with enough expertise to not only rig a brake failure, but to somehow assure that it would occur later in his trip, where the topography and road conditions would be more likely to make that failure a fatality. *Step*. And why had this someone acted out now? *Step*. Between leaving Stan's dungeon and retrieving the Rambler, barely forty-five minutes had elapsed. Not enough time to order, let alone implement, an intervention. Which meant that the kill order, if that's what it was, had already been in place, and not the result of what he'd told Stan that afternoon.

Up ahead he spots a pair of headlights. He scrambles off the road. Waits, invisible, as the car speeds past, probably bound for Camp David. Whoever had rigged the accident, they'd want to be first on the scene, to insure the proper outcome and check for any loose ends. Loose ends like a missing body. At which point, they'd then initiate a search, with at least two teams sweeping the road, probably bringing along some bloodhounds, and stopping to check the shoulder at regular quarter-mile intervals. Still, all that would take a while to coordinate, organize, which means he has a good four or five hours, or maybe even till daylight, to do what he needs to do. To disappear without a trace.

And once he does? They'd known exactly which buttons to push. How to get him onboard. A dash of patriotism, a dollop of outright flattery, and, most importantly, the promise of a chance to redeem himself, to make up for past mistakes. As clumsy as the Agency is, as laughable, as square, they know how to get the dirt on people. Even people like him. Given what he'd found in Markley's office, he could always just sit back. Let things run their course. Watch as this latest scheme of theirs blows up, just like all the rest, leaving both him and Division 12 smelling like proverbial roses. Because sometimes the smartest thing you can do is doing nothing at all.

Only then, instead of a two-lane road, he sees a man staring back. A man so trusting, so gullible, he'd set his own hand on fire. And he knows, at that moment, doing nothing at all is no longer a viable option.

HE COUNTS FIVE more cars, all headed north. A few delivery trucks. A buck, a four-pointer, crossing the road, silhouetted by a sliver of moon. When the eastern sky first begins to grow lighter he decides he's just seeing things, refusing to accept that his trek might soon end, that his trial is truly over. But no, it's true, that's really a road sign, one he'd passed on the way in. And if memory serves, which it seldom does, there's a gas station over the rise. A place to procure some food, some drink, and maybe even place a call.

Earl's OK Service. Not good, not bad, just OK. There's a cardboard sign taped to the screen door, claiming they open at seven. His watch, a Timex, took quite a beating. Insists it's still 10:38. He finds a spot on the curb out front and waits for someone to show.

That someone, maybe Earl, pulls up a half-hour later. Parks his pick-up in the shade. Takes a leisurely five or ten minutes to get things opened up. Then, when he heads for the restrooms out back, Charlie slips through the screen door, grabbing a bottle of Nehi soda and a package of white powdered doughnuts. Last stop is the register. He'll need change for the phone. Decides at the same time to slip a few bills into the drawer, just to prove he's still one of the good guys.

The sugar hits him all at once. He feels like a junkie. As he makes his way to the booth out front, his hands have started to shake.

Somehow he still knows her number by heart. Dials it and then waits.

"Hello?"

Her voice sounds like a pack-a-day, even though she doesn't smoke.

"K? It's me. Charlie. Sorry to call so early."

He can hear her thinking about it. What calling early means. When she speaks again, she's wide awake, and her words and clipped and clear.

"What is it? What's wrong?"

"That thing I mentioned last time I saw you. It blew up in my face."

"How bad?"

"Bad enough. I'm supposed to be dead."

It isn't the first time they've been here. Probably won't be the last. All those tight scrapes, those narrow misses, and still, they're both vertical.

"So what do you need me to do?" she asks.

"Well, first off, whatever you've got in the way of security, promise me you'll double it. And if anyone contacts you, especially from Langley, just play dumb. You haven't heard from me in weeks."

A sigh of impatience, like wind in the lines. "Fine. I get it. What else?"

"Have you still got that dead-letter drop? You know, the one we set up?"

"Of course."

"Next couple of days, you'll see a package. And sorry, it'll be handwritten. I should've had something prepared in advance, but this whole thing, I've been one step behind from the get-go."

"Stop beating up on yourself."

He thinks about the hole in his leg. Would that qualify?

"Anyway, I'll spell out what's been going on, though you'll probably think I'm crazy. And if I don't get back to you in a day or two, should suddenly fall off the radar, it'll be up to you. Get it out to whoever you can. Make a big, fat royal stink."

"And what about some real help? Me, or maybe that third-party we talked about?"

"No. No way. It's bad enough I've dug my own grave. No one's climbing in here with me."

He watches as a car pulls up. Stops in front of the nearest pump. Two guys, mid-thirties, both sporting crew cuts, in lightweight summer suits.

"Look, I'd better go. Any last-minute questions?"

"Yes," she tells him, sounding miffed. "Is anyone else in on all this? Someone I can trust?'

He thinks about that. Eyes the two men. Why the hell is he smiling? "Just this kid I met last week. Goes by the name of Buttons."

24

GETTING BACK DOWN to Langley is a bit of a challenge. Or maybe he's just getting old.

Because there's no transit, public or private, serving rural Maryland, he has to get creative. Wait there at Earl's, with the day growing warmer, till the right vehicle comes along; an open-bed truck, the back filled with melons, probably headed for DC. Somehow he drags his body onboard while the driver steps out for a coffee, then realizes he'll be cuddling up with a couple hundred volleyballs.

Soon enough they're on their way. The truck is over-loaded. As a result, every pothole they hit feels like they've found the Grand Canyon. Judging by how it's carrying on, his leg is now infected, and when he reaches up, checks his forehead, the skin is hot and dry. If this were the Good Old Days, and there was a bullet lodged in there, he could coax it out, no problem. But trying to corral a bunch of germs, it's really not in his skill set. So instead he decides to just lie back. Crushes a melon or two. Feels the ripe sap staining his slacks, mixing with dried blood. And every time he starts to drift off, another jolt jars him awake.

The next thing he knows, they're no longer moving. They're here, wherever here is. Apparently he'd been so beat, so exhausted, he'd managed to fall asleep. Peering through the wooden slats, he can see that they're surrounded. More trucks, some new, some old derelicts, all lined up at a big loading bay. Still half-asleep, he clambers back out, almost slipping on a moist melon rind, then begins to weave his way through the logjam, engines idling their exhaust. If this is, in fact, somewhere in the District, then he'll have to backtrack. Find another ride headed east. Not as easy as it may sound for a man who can barely stay upright.

Unseen, he starts to wander the streets. Spots a place he can go to ground. An abandoned hotel, its windows smashed, the front door long since gone. And though he's tempted to make his way inside, pass out then and there, he forces himself to keep on going, till he finds a five-and-dime. He grabs some canned food, chili and stew. New clothes to replace his torn suit. Risks a perilous trip behind the pharmacy counter, where they keep the antibiotics. Every item he grabs is just one more burden, one more thing to make disappear, and he keeps glancing down, checking his stash, making sure he hasn't slipped up somehow.

Back at the fleabag, he pops four pills. Chases them down with some chili. Tells himself he should change his clothes, and then closes his eyes instead. But if his body finds the rest it needs, his mind keeps running in circles, clawing its way through places he's known, times he's been on the run. Marrakesh. The smell of dry dust. Three days in a spider-hole. Or else that screw-up in Amsterdam, everyone's cover blown, the SS with those dogs of theirs, trust no one, not even yourself. After almost twenty years, twenty years of fat and happy, he'd thought he'd paid his dues in full, that his running days were over. Only to find there in no respite. Someone's always on your tail.

He wakes up at some point in the night. More water and more pills. Then, just like that, the sun is up, as the city shudders awake. He checks his leg, already less tender, then tries on his new clothes. Realizes he's passed the crisis point, that it's all downhill from there. Greyhound, it turns out, has a direct to Virginia. The next one leaves in less than an hour. Slipping onboard, he hides in the head, Pinesol and a whiff of old puke, and his heart barely even skips a beat when somebody pounds on the door.

"Occupied," he yells back.

WHEN HE REACHES Langley, three hours later, he feels like an old pro. Like his previous visit was merely a warm up, or call it a dress rehearsal. Step one finds him waltzing on through the front entrance, assuming gimps can waltz. Then it's a quick hobble straight to the stairwell, though this time he heads down, not up, forgoing a visit to the boss, preferring his minion instead.

Stan, he discovers, is still having breakfast, or perhaps it's an early lunch. A bagel, smeared to death with cream cheese and topped with what smells like lox.

"Watch out—that's guaranteed fish breath."

Lansky actually jumps a little. Almost drops the bagel.

"What the…?" he launches, wheeling around. "Wait, is that you?"

"None other," Charlie replies.

Stan tries to stare in his direction. He's off by a good three feet. "Well, come on," he tells his guest, "get visible already. You're starting to creep me out."

"Visible? Why? So some guy upstairs, pinned to his screen, can spot me talking to you?" Charlie shakes his head. "No thanks. From now on I'm being careful."

Stan just scoffs at that. "Look, if I was out to get you, I could've already pushed the right button. Had a half-dozen goons down here, guns drawn."

"Or maybe I beat you to it. Materialized my hand inside of yours, and now the bones are more like toothpaste."

This is what's known as a stalemate. Both sides have barred their fangs. Now it's time for some hearty butt-sniffing, followed by wagging tails.

Charlie nods towards the bagel Stan's clutching, a

gesture that goes unseen. "How about you share some of that," he suggests, "and I'll tell you about my day."

Stan fishes up a second bagel. Anoints it with cream cheese. Then leans back, his face a blank, prepared to play the skeptic.

At least he waits until Charlie has finished before deciding to pounce. "And do you have any proof that your crash was deliberate? That it wasn't an accident?"

"No."

"Or that, if it was, the Agency is somehow responsible?"

"No."

"Then what do you expect me to do?"

And all at once, Charlie is angry. Angry enough to draw blood. This little man, in his little room, never once risking his hide.

"Just tell the truth," he spits back. "Assuming you even know how."

Whatever is left of Stan's smile disappears. For a moment he looks almost crushed.

"Was any of it real?" Charlie plows on. "The so-called tumor, the faked assassination, having two presidents, or have you just been feeding me bullshit from day one?"

Stan reaches up and plays with his glasses. Finally finds his voice.

"I've seen the medical records. What were supposed to be his X-rays. But granted, all of that could've been faked. Especially considering what you claim you found up in Markley's office."

"Not claim. Saw."

Stan just bats that aside. "Look, if you're really shopping for someone to blame, why not make it yourself."

Now it's Charlie's turn to fall silent. He waits for Stan to go on.

"All we wanted was a little smoke and mirrors. Some way to distract from what we'd already planned, claiming he'd been shot. But no, you had to be a show-off. Come up with something better. Sell us on this golem idea, just to prove it could be done.

"And sure, at first, Markley's a roadblock. Only then he sees the light. Sees that if this crazy scheme of yours actually works, we've got a second President on call. One that's hard-wired to follow orders from the person who brought him to life. The only question being, who is that person supposed to be? Me, or you, or some Hungarian witch with her candles and magic spells."

"Actually, it's me."

"And you know this how?"

"I did a little experiment."

For a moment Charlie sits there, trying it on for size. The thought that he's as much to blame as Stan, or even Markley. Sure, he'd started with good intentions. Had tried to do the right thing. But in the real world, wherever that was, all that mattered was the outcome. The consequences.

"You do realize," he finally points out, "that this gives

you guys a motive. That maybe once I'm out of the picture, you get to play daddy next."

"Play daddy?" Stan asks back.

"You must have seen him. Talked to him. Realized what he is."

"Oh. That." He shrugs once, nonchalant. "Actually we've been working with him. Bringing him up to speed. The psychologists, they now peg his mental and emotional development at around age twelve, maybe even thirteen. Or at least on one of his good days."

"Working with him? Where?"

That's the thing about stalemates. They're never meant to last. And just like childhood itself, they soon become obsolete.

Stan digs up a smug little grin. "I'm not sure I should tell you."

And then, without even quite knowing why, Charlie lets himself be seen. Lets his face, with its scratches, and that ear, torn and scabbed, and the two days of stubble, and the baggy tracksuit, and yes, even that smile on his face, lets all of that do the talking.

"Jesus," Stan proclaims, his own face slack, "you look like shit."

Which is probably quite true.

"So I assume," Charlie tells him, "that just like me, you've been working the angles, trying to see where all this goes. Does Markley, or whoever's in charge, order our double to ride in that limo, make him take the shot?

Or does he off the real JFK, and then put his puppet in the White House? But the thing is, either way, I can't accept the outcome. I don't know how, I don't know why, but somehow we've created a person. A human being. Which means we can't let either one of them die. Because, if we do, we'll really be killing ourselves."

They take a moment to study each other, now that they finally can. In spite of himself, Stan starts to smile, then shakes his head in dismay.

"Damn," he says, giving way to a sigh. "So much for that nice, fat pension."

25

THE CIA LOVES its hidey-holes. Its secret little places. And because Charlie's in charge of Division 12, he's even been to visit a few.

Some are located in distant locales, safely beyond extradition, dank hell-holes where questions were asked, free of judicial restraint. Others call the Grand Ole USA their home. And one, or at least according to Stan, is tucked away in the Hudson Valley, a former prep school just outside Red Hook which had recently been repurposed. You won't find it on any map. Officially, it's not there. The perfect place to stash someone who isn't quite there either.

Charlie gives himself a solid week, a week to recuperate. To take advantage of his own hidey-hole, a place to rest, to heal. Shortly after the end of the War, weary of backstab and intrigue, he'd decided he needed a safe house, a place he could let down his guard. Had found precisely that in a drab, unassuming one-story Queen Anne in the suburbs just outside of Richmond. Agatha lived in the house itself. A certified crazy cat lady. And also a sorceress of uncommon skills, just the person to keep out the riff-raff. And as for Charlie, his needs were few, in terms of floor space or décor. Just that shop out back, a glorified shed, where he could hang his hat.

He eats real food. Tends to his leg. Takes walks at three in the morning. Tries not to think about how close it is, the twenty-second of November. With yellow legal pad in hand, he composes his notes for Karla, still marveling at how absurd it all sounds, even though it's mostly true. That the fate of the country might very well rest on a couple of sacks of dirt. At one point he's tempted to call up Richard. Let him in on the joke. Let him see how his one-time dream, a society of magicians, has managed to yield such strange fruit. How wishing, pretending, telling outright lies has become a national pastime.

Finally, on a Tuesday, six days out from Dallas, he leaves the safety of his refuge, wondering if he'll ever see it again or if fate has other plans. It's a two-mile walk to the nearest train station, and it feels odd being out in public, that awkward process of steering past people when they can't tell that you're there. After an uneventful ride north, he climbs off at the Red Hook stop, girding himself for a much longer walk on a series of quiet two lane roads. The trees, mostly oaks, are crimson, not green, the air carries a whisper of winter, and whenever he stops, rests for a moment, he can hear the geese overhead. He wonders if it's mere coincidence that they've chosen the fall for their mission or if, on some level, they know that's the right time. The season for felling a king.

It's getting towards dusk when he spots the school, brooding away in the distance. Quarried stone walls, and a blue slate roof, and an iron gate spanning the entrance. A pair of men in hunting jackets are standing just past it, more of a statement, a nod to tradition, than any real deterrent. But that dog? Already he's whining, a big German Shepherd, straining away at his leash, prompting Charlie to reach into his pocket and snatch up his rabbit's foot. Tossing it down with a flick of the wrist, it bounces once on the pavement. Suddenly decides it's a real live rabbit, one that bolts for the overgrown grass.

The Shepherd lunges, ignoring him now. The leash wraps around someone's leg. By the time they have it all sorted out, he's a half-mile down the drive.

Up close, the place looks downright evil. A bed-wetter's worst nightmare. Four or five generations of refined blue-blood stock, tortured into compliance. Scanning the windows, he counts three floors, tries to read the story they tell, finally deciding that the most honored guests are most likely kept up top. With his density this low, he probably doesn't have to worry about tripping any alarms or sensors, but still, it pays to play safe. Ignoring the ornate door up front, the garish twin colonnades, he slips around to the back instead, steering clear of the raked gravel paths. Don't mind me, he silently voices. I'm just the hired help.

Rounding the corner, he spots it at once. A much newer service door. Leaning forward, he pokes his head right through it, then gives the place a gander. One cook working a four-top. Another prepping dessert. A pair of women, servers most likely, and a dish-washer, lost in his suds. Too many bodies, moving too often, to risk a direct approach. Pulling back out, he moves further north, a good ten feet at least, where a second peek reveals a big storage room, lit by a single bare bulb. Slipping inside, he pauses a moment, removes his clunky Highland walkers. Slips into a pair of ballet slippers, what the spies are all wearing this fall.

Passing through an interior wall, he leaves the store-room behind. Finds himself in a two-story great room, a fire burning away in the hearth. Although the place could house a small army, it currently holds but two; a pair of sturdy-looking men in shirtsleeves, playing a round of gin rummy. Wafting by them, he conducts a quick recon, finds the rest of the downstairs empty, then climbs a staircase to the second floor, testing each step for squeaks. Once there, he's expecting a nurse or two. Guys with clipboards, wearing white lab coats. Anything but what he finds, a lot more vacant rooms.

By now he's growing suspicious. Was Stan's info out-of-date? Have they already moved the package elsewhere, perhaps to the White House itself? Before he can jump to conclusions, he mounts a last flight of stairs, spots one room at the end of the landing, its door cracked open a hair.

Ghostly, he travels down the hall. Peers through the narrow gap. Sees a room, an office, dimly lit, overwhelmed by a massive oak desk, and lying there before it, stretched out on a rug, a man contemplating a chessboard.

Charlie doesn't really play the game. Has found he much prefers *Go*. But it's obvious, even to a novice like him, that white is in serious trouble.

"Can't the good guys ever win?"

Hearing that, the man looks up. Sees his visitor, visible now. Watches as he closes the door, ensuring their privacy.

"Charlie," he says, grinning away. "I thought you fell down a hole."

It takes him a moment to climb to his feet. That ornery back of his. Then comes the handshake, surprisingly firm, the grip of a man, not a boy. Feeling that, seeing his face, Charlie senses the transformation. In the couple of weeks they've been apart, he has now become JFK.

"I know, I'm sorry," he tells the man, "I meant to check in a whole lot sooner. Things got complicated."

His golem nods back with a been-there look. "Believe me, I know the feeling."

There's a small loveseat and accompanying side-chair stationed across from the desk. By silent accord they both sit down, making sure to steer clear of the chessboard.

"So, I promised I would keep you safe," Charlie tells him. "A promise I didn't quite keep. But at least I got here soon enough to try and make up for it."

The man stares back, confused. "Make up for it? How so?"

"I'll get to that in a second," he says, "but first, I've got a question. The man who told me you were here, told me how to find you, he claimed the choice was yours. That you came here willingly."

"Of course."

"But why?"

If anything, his confusion grows. He sits back, searching for words.

"Well, that's what you do, isn't it? When your country calls, you answer. And when they explained how the President was sick, and all the ways that someone like me, almost his twin, all the ways that person could help out, I ... I don't know. I just felt like I didn't have a choice."

Put like that, it almost makes sense. Charlie bulls ahead anyway.

"Well, now you do."

He reaches into his back pocket. Extracts the tiny scroll. The moment it hits the open air, it immediately doubles in size. Clearing a space on the small coffee table, he begins to unfurl both ends, exposing a foot or two of frail rice paper, dyed black with a thin white margin.

"What the devil is that?"

"Take your finger," he tells him. "Place it anywhere

it's dark."

Charlie watches as he does just that. The finger is swallowed up whole. All at once he pulls back, shaking his hand, making sure all five are still there.

"It's like that hole I thought you fell down. Only this one's real."

"Not a hole," Charlie tells him. "More like a passage-way."

"Passageway to where?"

"Anywhere you want."

Charlie leans forward on the loveseat. Wonders how much time they have left. Knows the two men downstairs will be on some kind of schedule, and could show up at any second.

"Look, if you stay here, with them, your life is at risk," he continues. "I should know—they tried to kill me. But using this, we can disappear, go somewhere they'll never find us."

"How?" he asks, looking askance. "We wouldn't even fit."

"The passageway will expand to whatever size is needed. You could drive a car through there."

The man stares into that patch of darkness. A little shard of elsewhere. Seems almost tempted to take the plunge, but then leans back, shaking his head.

"Sorry. I can't."

"Why not?" Charlie shoots back.

"If you really have to ask, I couldn't explain it to you."

But that's just it. He already knows. Doesn't need an explanation. The promises we make to the world, or sometimes just ourselves.

"You realize, of course, I could order you. Order you to use it."

For a moment he sees it, there in the man's eyes. A sudden flash of anger. "Order me? Like that trick you pulled back in the cabin? That time with lighting the stove?"

"Yes. Exactly," Charlie admits, still regretting his act. "And I could do it again, believe me. But I won't. Not if you promise me two things."

Poker-faced, he waits him out. A bad back, but no shortage of spine.

"Next week, the President is scheduled to fly down to Texas. Four stops in a single day. Finishing off with a final motorcade ride going right through downtown Dallas. And if they start prepping you for that trip, even hint at a campaign appearance, I want you to stall, lie, do whatever it takes to keep from riding in that limo."

He doesn't say yes, doesn't say no. Merely points out the obvious.

"You said two things."

"You're right. I did. Promise me you'll hang onto the scroll. That you'll use it if you have to."

"And if it turns out I don't?"

Charlie waves that aside. "I don't know. Keep it as a souvenir. Or, hell, just stick it an envelope, unaddressed, and put it in the mail. It'll figure out how to find me."

He knows he's already outstayed his welcome. This was supposed to be a quick fly-by. Leaving the loveseat, he heads for the door, or at least till his host calls out.

"Wait. Hold on. What if I have to get in touch?"

"Send your regards to Texas."

The almost most powerful man in the world blinks back in surprise. "Texas?"

"Where else?" he asks back. "If you won't let me stop this train from the front end, I'll have to try it from the caboose."

26

RICHMOND TO DALLAS. Over one thousand miles. Plenty of time to think.

So he does. Starts things off with a flashback to when he was nine, living with the Thompsons, and the first time he'd ever ridden a bike, or more like the first time he'd crashed one. Only to find his brain switching gears, with him now in that crazy Hollywood restaurant, the one shaped like a hat, and the next thing he knows he's downed a flying monkey using only a butter knife. And then finally, thanks to the scenery scrolling by, he harkens back to a road trip, that long weekend with Mark in the Badlands, scrambling along those weathered draws, sharing the same water bottle, and both realizing without saying a word that they'd somehow become more than just friends.

But all that is what's on the surface. The clutter, the chatter, the chop. What he's really hung up on are the Big Questions, the kind that require capital letters. Ones that involve words like fate, and duty, and free will, or at least until you finally admit that you don't know what any of

278 BRIAN T. MARSHALL

those words really mean. That the longer you stare out that window, past the grime and the smear of dead bugs, the less you're sure where it is you're headed, or why there and not someplace else.

And it's not like he regrets what he's done. Stripped off those training wheels. Allowed his creation, his golem, to steer his own course, determined to do the right thing. Because as soon as you accept the first tenet, that he does, in fact, have a soul, then you have to accept the whole package. Grant him autonomy. Nor does he wish that he'd gone one step further, aimed right for the top, somehow slipped past multiple safeguards and penetrated the White House itself, waiting patiently for one of those rare, precious moments when the President is all alone, and only then pleading his case.

Sir? Sorry to barge in like this. But my name's Charlie, and I'm a widely-ridiculed, seldom-believed eccentric federal employee who's here to warn you of an insidious plot that may or may not involve your life and safety, assuming it's not already threatened by a terminal illness you may or may not actually have.

With luck, they'd have to adjust their timetable. With luck, the cell would be padded. Or perhaps all he'd get was a nod and a smile, proof that JFK was in on it too. That the President knew full well of his double, that this double would be publicly slaughtered, and that, with his demise, the real Kennedy would earn a chance to die in peace. Or, conversely, it's a double play, with the

President kept in the dark, which meant that he'd be killed instead, and Buttons would take his place. It reminded him of some fiendish Zen koan. Pretzel logic through and through. If JFK knows, yes, he'll believe you, so why risk your life to tell him? But if he doesn't, of course he won't, because in the end, who would?

And Dallas? Dallas is just a long shot. The thing you do, pointless or not, when you can't do the anything else. Still, he'd been around long enough to know that even long shots sometimes pay off. That the same improbable massaging of odds that was the very basis of magic could also play out in the real world, assuming such a place even existed.

A blocked fuel line in the big black Lincoln. A sudden case of the sniffles. An unexpected rain shower that would force them to raise the top, and thus obscure the target. Any or all of them but a quick spell away if you happen to be a magician. For the first time in ages, he actually does it, wishes that Richard were there, all of that bluster, that sheer arrogance, called into duty once more. But there is no Richard. No Karla. No Vadoma. No one to help him now. Just an empty seat on a bus that's nearly, grinding its way ever southward.

DALLAS IS DRY and dusty, even in late November. A hardscrabble town with a chip on its shoulder, and the state's highest homicide rate.

And if you had to pick which American city most despised the man in the White House, Dallas might well top the list. Like most of Texas it trended red, the spilled blood of old Sam Houston, and even with Johnson serving as his VP, Kennedy was a hated man. According to Stan, half of JFK's people, especially his younger brother, had tried to talk him out of the trip. Insisted that it was too dangerous, that the risks outweighed the rewards. While Jack, with ego front and center, had taken their pleas as a challenge.

Once the Greyhound is parked and empty, Charlie quietly slips outside. Ducks into a bathroom stall, then steps out, fully visible now. There are four or five hotels scattered near the station, and he chooses the seediest one, a sprawling, one-story study in stucco, AC units hanging off like old scabs. The bed talks back when he tests it. The carpet crunches underfoot. Still, with Friday just two days off, he tells himself it'll do.

He grabs a newspaper from the lobby, fingered-over that late in the day, and soon discovers there's a big map inside, with the motorcade's proposed route. The late-morning drive will begin, he learns, with a long, straight shot from the airport, one that will probably draw few people, only to finish in downtown proper, where the real crowds will form. And sure, posting the details like that, it makes perfect sense. It's a public event after all. So why does it feel like something else; a provocation, or even a dare?

Extracting the map, he returns the paper. Rings the service bell. Asks the man with the permanent scowl if he can glance at his phone book, maybe get some change for the booth out front. Checking the listings, there's only one Oswald, no first name, just a 'V', and he chides himself for not listening more closely as Stan had prattled away. Once in the phone booth, he tries the number, then waits for 'V' to answer, finally learning that she's an elderly woman who should buy a hearing aid. So either he's got the last name wrong, having only heard it once, or else the sniper has no phone, or requested that his line be unlisted.

He goes to bed early. Pretends to sleep. Gets up well before sunrise. Eats a bad breakfast at a small greasy spoon and sets out for downtown. Like with most cities it's a north-south grid, a nod to The God of Straight Lines, and within a few minutes he spots a street sign that corresponds with a name on the map. Glancing upwards, he begins to count, eyes scanning right and left, noting every potential site, places with some kind of cover, and good, clear sightlines to the streets below. Finds himself giving up after a block or so, having already spotted several dozen.

And escape routes? Normally this would be a factor, cutting down that number by half. But with the way Stan had described it, the shooter, Oswald, wouldn't even care. Would be acting under orders, ones reinforced by some kind of drug or post-hypnotic suggestion, with no thought of pursuit or capture. Plus, there's the motorcade's path through downtown. The way it's been laid out. With a series of turns, some broad, most tight, that would all but force the limo to decelerate. To give a shooter even more time to track an already slow-moving target.

Hearing someone describe the set-up was one thing, or perusing a simplified map. But walking it firsthand, surveying those streets, it soon became obvious. This wasn't a parade, or a public appearance. This was a shooting gallery. The perfect place to take a life, and in doing so change history. And seeing it now, seeing the truth, the question almost screams out; how deep does this thing go? Because there was no way in hell the Secret Service would sign off on such a debacle. Not unless they were in on it too, complicit in his death.

He spies some kind of park, or plaza. A glimmer of green grass. Finds a bench, a bit of shade, and tries to think things through. All along, he'd been hoping to pull an end-run. Contact the Service directly. Pray they'd find him convincing enough to at least cancel the event. But now? He watches as a black-and-white cruises by, probably scouting the route in advance. Realizes then that he has only one option left. One last thing to try.

"I'D LIKE TO see whoever's in charge."

The Desk Sergeant looks him over, trying to find the right box.

"May I ask what this is about?"

"It's about that thing tomorrow. That thing with the President."

The Sergeant's brow creeps up a half-inch. Charlie knows the look well. Sure, like most walk-ins, he's probably whack, but it never hurts to be sure.

"Mind if I get a little information first?"

He asks the usual questions. Charlie answers back. At one point he surrenders a fake ID, a Texas driver's license, which he'd had the foresight to procure before ever hitting the road. It's obvious that the Sergeant has found his box, tucked him safely inside it, but protocol and ass-covering demand that he at least go through the motions.

"Sir, if you don't mind taking a seat, someone will be right with you."

There's a short stack of *Watchtower*s there on the table. So much for Church and State. He picks one up, starts to thumb through it, reading up on eternal life. Thinks about the next twenty-four hours, an eternity of their own.

"Mr. Myers? I'm Detective Watts. Would you mind following me?"

Watts is slender, mid-forties range, with no hint of southern cornpone. A quiet man just doing his job, free of bluster or bravado. The fact that he's a full Detective, it throws Charlie a little at first, but then again, with the upcoming visit, they're probably short on staff. With a place like Dallas, still rough and tumble, not much caring who does what.

He follows Watts down a short corridor, then into a brightly lit room. Notes the long metal table, bolted to the floor, and the mirror stretched along one wall. And then there's that notebook, the one in Watts' hand, the way he's keeping its cover closed.

"So what'd I do?" Charlie wonders aloud, nodding at their surroundings. "Rob a bank?"

Watts looks over. Fakes a smile. "Just making sure we get some privacy."

As if he's out to prove his point, he shuts the door behind them. Then motions towards a pair of metal chairs, bolted down as well.

"So apparently you've got some concerns about the President's appearance tomorrow."

The trick to playing stupid, it's like pretending to be drunk. Make sure you don't overdo it. Just enough to convince the other guy he's two steps ahead of you.

"So three, four weeks back," Charlie tells him, "I went to this meeting in town. Was supposed to be all about cutting taxes, sticking it to Uncle Sam, but pretty soon I realize, these guys, they're just plain pinko. Sharing the wealth, and what's yours is mine, and all that lefty shit. So anyways, I ride it out, wait till they all take a break, and then, just like that, I'm out the back door, ready to head home."

He waits for Watts to start taking notes, but instead he merely sits there. One of those cops who actually listens instead of just writing things down.

"Only this guy," he goes on, "somehow he's beat me to it. Is already out there, having a smoke. So we get to talking, this and that, and before you know it one of us says why don't we go grab a beer? And what the hell, I'm in-between jobs, I figure that sounds alright, so me and him, we hit up this place, one that's just around the corner.

"But you know how it is with beer. There's no such thing as just one. And before long, this guy, he starts getting hammered, spouting all kinds of shit. How he used to in the Army. What a bad-ass shot he is. How pretty soon the whole damn world will be lining up to pin him with a medal. So me, I just sit there, lapping it up, or at least till I finally decide to call his bluff. Ask him straight-out, what the hell's he talking about. And he just looks back, with this funny little smile, and then he's whispering three letters. JFK."

Charlie leans back with a satisfied grin. Like a dog who's just fetched the paper. Waiting for Watts to pat his head, maybe even give him a treat.

"And this man," Watts finally asks. "Did you happen to get his name?"

"Oswald. Not really sure if that's first or last, but you

guys can figure that out." He pauses. Scratches his head. "Oh, yeah, and that was another thing. He said he had this job right on the route they'd staked out. That he could scope the whole thing through his window. Like it was proof, from God or whoever, that he was meant to do it."

"But you did say he was intoxicated. Starting to ramble. What makes you think, the things he told you, he wasn't just making them up?"

"I don't know. Maybe it was the small shit. Like the way he kept talking about his rifle, some kind of Italian army surplus job, left over from the War. Like it wasn't just a gun, no, it was his friend. Or maybe more like his girlfriend."

Watts pauses to think that over. Charlie feels a tug on the line. What might be the first clear indication that he's finally set the hook.

"Fine," Watts tells him. "You decided to believe him. So why wait till now to say anything? You said this was weeks ago."

He turns away. Squirms a bit. A kid who's been caught out.

"Look. Coming in here, it wasn't easy. I'm not too partial to cops. And frankly, the world would be better off if somebody *did* put him down."

He delivers this with no hint of shame. Just laying out the facts.

"Only somehow it didn't sit right," he goes on. "Him

having kids and all. And if by me waiting, it makes your job harder, what can I say? You get paid either way."

He wants to leave Watts a little bit angry. Angry people get things done. Even if the only reason they do so is to prove some asshole wrong.

"Well, Mr. Myers, we certainly appreciate you coming in. And we'll take what you've said into full consideration. But just to be frank, I feel I should tell you we already have a suspect we're about to take into custody."

It takes Charlie a second to find his voice. "Really? You mean Oswald?"

He watches as Watts reaches down for his notebook. Flips the cover open. Slowly shoves it across the table, assuring him a better view.

"No, not Oswald."

And Charlie finds he's looking down at a photo of his own face.

27

COUNTING IRON BARS.

Each bar is roughly two feet in length. And given an approximate ceiling height of eight feet, that would account for a total of four horizontal rows in the entire cell wall. Estimated row length? Let's say ten feet. And as for the gap between bars, there's probably an industry standard based on average hand size, but for now let's assume it's in the neighborhood of three inches. Which would mean four bars per foot, forty bars per row, and about one-hundred and sixty bars in total, not accounting for the lock assembly and the fact that he has a headache.

And sure, he could pass right on through those bars. Leave any time he wants. Even track down whatever two-faced bastard had decided to rat him out. But being in a jail cell, in this pit of a town, is exactly where he belongs. His punishment for screwing up yet again, and finding himself out-maneuvered.

There is, of course, no clock on the wall. Nothing resembling a window. No way of knowing what time it is, except for the growl in his stomach. Meaning it must be getting on towards five, six o'clock in the evening. Late enough, dark enough, he won't even have to become invisible. Can just melt instead into all those shadows, the cool November air. And then what? Yes, exactly, nail on the head, that's the million dollar question. *And then what?*

Piece by piece, step by step, his faith has been dismantled. His blind assumption that, in the end, the good guys always win. Only to be replaced by ... what? A hunch, a hint, a slow realization that there's something at work out there. Not a God, not some devil, nothing quite tangible, more like a blind, dumb force. An obstinate insistence that whatever happens, it will happen a certain way. Call it fate, or destiny, or whatever word you favor, it'll just laugh at that label. And then quietly go about its business, churning out history.

So is it magic? Not by a long shot. Or at least not the kind he knows. A polite exchange wherein the world is nudged in the right direction. No, this is more some grim, dark march, as inexorable as death. And all we can do, as humans, it to pretend. Pretend we have some say. Pretend we can do anything but stall, and dither, and make some noise, and, in the end, surrender.

Because one thing is clear. This force, inclination, whatever it is, it wants Jack Kennedy dead. Will pull any lever, move any mountain, to see him in his grave. Maybe it finds hope offensive. Maybe it hates bright lights. Maybe it has some higher purpose we mortals will never fathom. From its very inception in some dank cave, humanity has known both; those few brief moments of promise, of progress, and the plummet back into the pit. So call it a cosmic thermostat. The swing of a pendulum. We've had our idyll in the sun, and now it's back to the shadows.

He reaches out. Grabs hold of one bar. Watches his hand pass right through it. Decides it's probably time to head out for the place he's going next. A much larger cell, the one we all live in, and the one we can never escape.

THE NEXT TWELVE hours pass like a dream. Or call it a nightmare instead. One of those beauties with the endless hallways, and the doors that are always locked.

First off it's a trip to the airport. Twenty minutes or so by cab. A parking lot with slots to spare, and a terminal that's almost empty. Invisible, he passes on through it, heads for the tarmac instead, finding a sprawl of assorted out-buildings, which he will search one-by-one. Fifty-gallon steel drums, stacked on wooden pallets. A couple of biplane crop dusters. A man, confused, who is left to wonder why that door opened all on its own. But no sign of a Lincoln limo, standard or armor-plated.

He hunts around. Finds the main office. Starts digging though paperwork. Makes no attempt at stealth or silence, by now he's way past caring. Finally, he uncovers an invoice, with his answer in neat black type. They'll be bringing the limo in by plane. Turns out it flies in Air Force One, along with the President. Which means, by the time it arrives, the place will be crawling with agents, maybe even the very same ones who tipped off the Dallas PD, leaving Charlie with absolutely no chance of rigging a breakdown.

Door number one? Locked.

Another cab ride heading back into town. The same guy behind the wheel. A few pathetic attempts at small talk which Charlie just ignores. He can't risk going back to the hotel. It could be under surveillance. Instead he has the cabbie drop him off downtown, just a block from the motorcade route. The critical portion, their killing field, only covers five or six blocks, and it's barely after midnight. Plenty of time to go door-to-door, searching for his sniper's nest.

A third of the buildings are vacant. Dallas must be in a slump. And as for the rest, they're a random assortment, private and public mixed. There are rooms piled high with cardboard boxes, cramped offices, crammed with desks, all of them probably too heavily staffed during business hours to allow for a shooter's presence. A competent sniper, a professional, would've scoped his lair out in advance, verified that the windows weren't sealed shut, checking out the angles and sightlines. But Oswald? Charlie scours each sill for cigarette butts, dusty smudges, any sign of a recent visit. Finds only rats, searching like him. Probably with more luck.

Door number two? Locked.

And then, at about three-thirty, he has an inspiration. Decides to flip things on their head. Instead of avoiding all those late-night patrol cars, he'll cozy up to the next one he spots. Loiter outside it, just within earshot, eavesdropping on their dispatch. A half-hour later he finds his prey, an idling black-and-white, then learns that they've issued an APB. That the hotel is indeed being watched. That some helpful Agency drone has notified the locals that their quarry can become transparent. This being the case, the Dallas PD have decided to contact the County. Four teams are on the way. Drug-sniffing dogs that, just this once, will be hunting for flesh and blood.

Door number three? Locked. And with him on the wrong side.

He'd been hoping that, at the very least, he could physically intervene. Run out in the street once the limo appears, maybe force the motorcade to detour. But with those four teams working the crowd, the chances of that are now nil. And thanks to the dispatcher, he learns of another wrinkle. They're reassigning their beat cops. Pulling them from scanning for open windows or signs of a potential sniper, and moving them street-side instead. And no, the irony isn't lost on him. The fact that this means his very presence will be helping Oswald out. With Charlie stuck serving as stalking horse, or more like his accomplice.

Helpless, he watches them start to arrive. The early birds, seeking out worms. With their bland, vacant faces, and cheap paper flags, already hungry for blood. At every choice spot, the ones that are shaded, or that offer an open view, clots have begun to form, and with each new body, milling about, staying hidden grows that much harder. Turning, he stumbles into a man. Almost trips and falls. Watches as the man then wheels around, pig eyes scouring the crowd. And that dog. Not a K9 unit, not by a long shot, just somebody's scrawny rat terrier. Trailing him down the sidewalk, nipping away at his heels.

Somehow he finds an alley. A milk crate for a seat. Squatting down, his vision dims, his headache sharper now. Just for a second, he lets it all go. He's visible. He's solid. Just another failed human being, like everyone who surrounds him. Only then, out of nowhere, a man appears, shouting in Cantonese. Waving a folded cardboard box as if he's shooing a fly. He tosses out a word in English. What might've been 'police.' Lurching upwards, Charlie's on the run, fleeing back into the street.

A toe-head kid in overalls, ice cream dripping down his chin.

His mother, still in curlers, sucking away at her Kent.

And from somewhere behind him a tinny speaker, worse than a dentist's drill, blasting away with Hail to the Chief in an endless reel-to-reel loop.

This is what he'll die for. This is what he'll redeem.

This is the world he'll leave behind, maybe better, probably worse.

With a cry of desperation, Charlie throws himself into the crowd. Trips over a boot, a small piece of Texas, and then he's on his knees. He no longer cares if people can see him. He now longer cares at all. Would gladly swap places with the man in the limo, just minutes from his death.

Or perhaps someone already has.

Revived by that thought, he's moving again. He's been in this place before. Looking up, he spots it, that green knoll ahead, the promise of peace and quiet. One step, two step, three step, four. He's almost there. Almost there. And then, another man out of nowhere, or no, it's more like two, lunging towards him, arms outstretched, their faces in a panic.

He thinks about letting them pass right through him. Only somehow he stays solid. A human touch, no matter how brutal, is what he needs right now.

A glint of gold. A wall of blue. That final moment of impact. All three of them are tumbling down, down onto the sidewalk.

And right then, right on schedule, the very first shot rings out.

28

A WEEK HAS passed. It should feel better. But some wounds never heal.

For those who have lived through the past few days, there will always be remembrance. The sight of Cronkite, blinking back tears. A black horse with no rider. A three-year-old boy, standing alone, bundled up in his Sunday best. We think that myths are ancient things. That we all live in the present. How odd it is, then, to wake up inside one, to watch the tale play out, to know we're part of something huge, the slaying of a kingdom, a king.

But seeing them line up in the bitter cold, stretching on, block after block, you had to wonder, had to ask, where had they been the last three years? How many had voted for the other guy, or passed around the same stale jokes, or had never much cared, one way or another, if he lived or died. And now? Now, in death, he's above all that, has transcended all fault, all blame. Taken his place up on that cross, like the one who came before him.

Which means, in the end, he got what he wanted. A brief walk in the sun. No slow decline, no ugly truths, no awkward reckonings. And forget about Oswald, or grassy knolls. Gunmen, lone or not. John Kennedy had but one assassin, and his name was John Kennedy. A man who discovered that when it comes to heroes, America prefers hers dead. Fly too high, and of course they'll hate you. Do their best to bring you down. Whether through scandal, or backroom intrigue or sometimes even magic. So all you can do is harbor hope. Take that final gamble. Bet you'll accomplish more as a corpse than a living, breathing man.

BUT WITH ALL those millions in the streets, at least one man is missing. A man too shattered to join the crowds, to face up to his own failings.

Sometimes, when Charlie wakes up, he knows that he's been back. Back dreaming of the very same moment, playing out again and again. Him splayed out on the sidewalk, one shoe missing, his arms pinned to his side. Then hearing that shot, the second one this time, and sensing it's somehow different. Darker. More final. Around them, the crowd is surging. Screams, and yells, and shouts. The growl of all those angry horses as the limo speeds away. Only to be followed, eventually, by a much slower ride, with the two cops up front, and their prisoner, cuffed in the back. So insignificant now, so beside the point, he doesn't even merit a siren, or the play of the light-bar up top.

It's chaos back at the station. Everyone's placing bets. The haters hoping they'll get good news, their counterparts silently praying. Seeing Charlie arrive, an afterthought almost, they stick him in his old cell, then proceed to forget about him, forget he's even there. With him so deep in his own forgetting he barely notices where he is. Sometime later, the next day maybe, they finally come around. Unlock the cell door. Tell him that he's free to go, that all charges have been dropped. Dropped. Just like the man in the crisp blue suit. Just like that flag at half-mast.

Back out on the sidewalk, he blinks at the sun. Wonders why it has bothered to rise. Wonders too about what comes next, that other shoe yet to drop. Theoretically They, whoever They are, have gotten what they wanted. Killed the President. Which means Charlie should be irrelevant, no longer a 'factor at play.' Then again, he knows the score, could manage to name a few names, and the one thing the guys with their crew-cuts can't stand is leaving any loose ends. Another free brake job? A jab with a hypo? Really, it doesn't much matter. Now that he's heard the gruesome details, what that second shot had done, he figures whatever they try on him, it can't be any worse.

No anonymous Greyhound for the trip back. This time he takes the train. Hoping the hypnotic clack of the rails will lull him into a stupor. But as for forgetting, forget about that, because it's obvious no one else can. That dull grey look you see in each face, whether porter or passenger. Like someone reached right into their chests and grabbed hold of their hearts. Riding past backyards, he can see all the flags. The battered cardboard signs. Bidding farewell to the guy with the accent, the one that they never could stand.

He arrives home to find five dead houseplants. A big stack of mail by the door. No clue as to how many times he'd been searched, or if they've bugged the place. He feels as empty, as void of hope, as he did back in the War. Those first few years, sour with defeat, when Hitler, the Nazis, had seemed invincible. But, of course, their fortunes had eventually turned, just like fortunes always do. And so, he knows, this darkness will pass, the world will continue to turn. The trick being what to do in the meantime.

Because meantime is all we've got.

"So I was wondering when you'd show up."

He hadn't wanted to tip Markley off, so therefore no appointment. Just an unscheduled visit from the Invisible Boy. The guy who can walk through walls.

"Mind if I have a seat?" Charlie asks him.

"No, of course not." He nods towards the nearest chair. "Still, that won't do you much good, will it. Not unless you become solid."

"Meaning what—you can shoot me then? Fine. Problem is I'd bleed out. Make a big mess on the carpet." He settles down onto the chair, then shrugs. "Besides which, if you'd wanted me dead, we'd be having a séance right now."

The two of them study each other. Had it really been less than three months? Sometimes it feels, with him and Markley, they'd been hacking away since forever. Two lonely souls, two sides of a mirror, waiting for their Godot.

"So you must be pretty happy," Charlie hazards.

"How so?"

"Your thing. Operation Camelot. Talk about a rousing success."

Markley tries his best not to smile. Just not his very best.

"Actually, there were a lot of fumbles, places we slipped up. Like that Oswald fiasco. He was supposed to just slip off, crawl back into the woodwork, and then we'd take care of him later. Only instead he screws up, gets arrested. Has the nerve to get himself killed."

Charlie nods back in sympathy. "I guess that's the price you pay. Working with amateurs."

He now wears that word as a badge of honor. A declaration of what he is. An admission that, twenty-five years ago, he'd made a huge mistake. Don't ever try to out-trick the tricksters. You'll only trick yourself. Become the very thing you've been fighting, complicit in their crimes.

And does Markley sense this sea change? If so, he breezes past it. "Just so you know, I'm expecting a call at eleven. So if you have anything to …"

"Two questions," Charlie barks back.

He pauses. Thinks that over. "Sure. I owe you that much."

"Question one: who do you work for?"

He takes a moment to study the ceiling. "Actually, that's a bit of pickle. Because technically, the Agency, we're a branch of…"

"Who do you work for?"

He shakes his head, chagrined. "What, you mean you want a name? It doesn't work like that."

Leaning back, his voice grows dreamy. He ponders the view from on high.

"Your old friend, Richard, he figured it out, though it took him a while to catch on. Thinking he could clean up Hollywood, make it his turf. Only every time he'd win some skirmish, things would get worse somewhere else. Because whatever it is, whatever it wants, it always gets it in the end. And all you can do, all anyone can do, is pick sides. Decide whether they want to be a winner, or a loser."

"And that's what you are? A winner?"

He shrugs, the answer obvious. "You came to me, not vice-versa."

"And what if I told you, it's already in place. A pretty much textbook dead man. And if anything happens, if I don't check in, there'll be a major media dump."

"Well, of course you'd have a trigger," he admits, his voice still calm and relaxed. "It's not like you're some novice. And even though it's doubtful anyone would believe your story, that it wouldn't become just one more of a hundred whacky theories about who killed JFK, why should we take the risk? No, it's in both our interests to just let things be. Stay quiet and stay alive."

And could Charlie really do that? Wear a muzzle the rest of his life? It's one of those things you can only find out once you've gone ahead and tried it.

"Fine. Question two. Which one?"

This earns a sly little grin. "Really?"

"Really."

"Well, that's the problem," he concedes with a sigh. "When the boss isn't even human, how do you know what it wants? It's not like you got a memo. And I swear, it kept going back and forth, right up till the very end. Off the real one. Off the fake. There were pros and cons each way. And it didn't help, knowing your coin toss, it could change the whole world forever."

The very same toss he'd had to make at least a dozen times.

"So what happened?"

"We decided we couldn't gun down our puppet. He was worth too much alive. Which meant that it should've been the real JFK riding in that limo."

"Should have?" Charlie asks back.

A single short buzz from one of three phones. Markley glances down at his desk. When his eyes return, lock with Charlie's, the same sly smile is back.

"Sorry. I really do have to take this."

"No. Wait. Hold on," Charlie demands, rising from his chair. "All I need is a yes or no. Was it JFK or not?"

Markley reaches for the phone. "Sorry. That's classified."

HE PICKS UP his car from the lot down below. Drives home on auto-pilot. His arms, his legs, all doing their thing while his brain flies around in circles.

So a while back he'd skimmed through an article, probably in *Scientific American*. A valiant attempt to explain particle physics to your average man on the street. Not much had stuck, it usually doesn't, but he still can recall the gist. The fact that with sub-atomic particles, sometimes they'll act one way, sometimes the other, but if you try to figure out which, the very act of observing them somehow messes with the outcome. That, in the end, some things, maybe even all things, are, in fact, unknowable. That the facts, the truth, the world we live in, are as elusive as Charlie himself.

He parks on the street. Climbs up three flights. Slips

his key into the door. From what Markley's said, his life's not at risk, there is no shoe to drop, but caution, fear, are by now old habits, and habits are hard to break. So maybe that's why he doesn't see it. Almost crushes it with his foot. A plain brown manila envelope lying beneath the mail slot.

He stops. Stares. Carefully toes it. The mail isn't due for three hours. And what's even stranger, the envelope's blank, there's no address, coming or going. No postage even. Finally picking it off the floor, he holds it to his ear. Gives it a gentle rattle. Hears the rustle of paper on paper, and suddenly he knows.

He grabs a knife from the kitchen. Carefully opens one end. Watches as the scroll tumbles out, landing on the floor. Without even thinking, he snatches it up, eyes scanning the envelope, only to notice a sheet of white paper still tucked away inside it. He yanks out the sheet. Reads what's there. It only takes a second.

Charlie—

Like the man said, ask not

Buttons

29

HE THOUGHT HE spoke passable Spanish. Had gotten by just fine in Buenos Aires. But apparently, in Argentina, what they use is gentler, more refined. A lilting tongue, almost a song, with a hint of old Castilian. While here on the island, it seems like every third word, it's *chinga*-this and *chinga*-that.

Still, the place is beautiful. Lush beyond belief. Especially once you leave Havana, and find your way into the back country. Winding dirt tracks, more footpath than road, snaking up into the mountains. Rounding a corner to find a small stream, meandering through a ravine. And everywhere the signs of life, of people living off the land, only not in an ugly, abusive way, but blending in with nature instead. The tiny patch of tended earth. A burro lashed to a tree. A couple of kids, wild as banshees, tearing through the *selva*.

Which means it's no wonder he's been taking his time. Moving along at a snail's pace. Content to pursue his prey in slow-motion, one grudging clue at a time. A word overheard in a tiny cantina, him invisible, listening in. Some hot tip that will soon turn to ashes, revealing another dead-end. The fact is he doesn't want it to cease. This dance, this game of gotcha. Because, once it's done with, once the music is over, he'll be back at square one. Staring out at an empty horizon, wondering what comes next.

Up ahead he spots two men, resting in the shade. Sharing a bottle of what might be water, might be something else.

"*Buenas*," he calls out.

"*Buenas*," they toss back.

They share a few comments about the weather. They ask him where he's from. He names the same country that's on his fake passport, the one he'd cobbled together back home. And then, no rush, he finally decides it's time for the today's dead-end.

"I'm looking for a stranger, like me. Another German maybe. Has anyone passed through lately?"

The two men eye each other. One of them finally speaks.

"An old man?"

"Maybe."

He nods up the road, if road it is. A chicken wanders by.

"The blue house with the tree out front. A half-klick, maybe more."

He nods his thanks. Steers clear of the chicken. Starts to climb once again. Can feel their eyes boring into his back, asking a thousand questions. Still, those questions, answered or not, they come with the territory. Every time you follow a trail, you leave one of your own.

Ten minutes later he spots it, tucked up into the slope. A squat little box of stacked cinder blocks, painted a bright turquoise. Two big windows face out towards the road, but both of them are shuttered, even though the house is well shaded and there's no reason to block the breeze. Pausing, he feels his heart beat faster, or maybe that's just the climb. Reminds himself that hope, expectations, are always out to betray you.

A flight of steps, each one rough-sawn, leads up to a covered porch. A door, solid pine instead of screened panels, glowers back his way.

Three quick raps, brusque but friendly. The silence stretches on. He's almost ready to turn around when he hears the hinges squeak.

"Si?"

It's a woman, he sees, of average height, with a slender, almost fragile build. Dark hair that falls just past her shoulders, the tresses streaked with grey. But there's something about those streaks, that hair, that carries a hint of falsehood. Just like her glasses, which are heavily tinted, even though the room is dark.

"Yes," he tells her, sticking with Spanish, "I was hoping I could take up a few minutes of your time."

Hearing those words, her whole body stiffens. Or maybe it's not what he's said. More like an accent he can't quite disguise, the country they both call home.

"Might as well let him in."

This second voice, it comes from behind her. English, not Spanish this time. And as for the accent, those broad, flat vowels, it pretty much puts theirs to shame.

The room is tiny. The air is close. Faint daylight bleeds through the shutters. There's a man in the corner, in a wicker chair, dressed in white cotton pants and shirt. His hair, unlike hers, is solid grey, quite possibly from a bottle. A bushy mane that bears no sign of his formerly tight coif. But what really stands out is the steel-wool beard. His nod to Hemmingway.

Charlie just stands there, too numb to speak. The hunt is finally over.

"Good afternoon, Mr. President."

The man nods back, slow and easy, as if he's seen this coming.

"So who are you? One of them?"

"Them?"

"The bastards who tried to kill me."

Charlie thinks that over. "No. Not really. Though, being honest, I might've have made their job a little easier. Or at least at first."

And then he hears a sound, right behind him. A sound he knows all too well. The sound of a revolver being cocked, one that's old, or in need of a cleaning.

He sees the way the man's gaze moves past him. A subtle shake of the head. That thing, that habit, handing out orders, it can be a hard one to shake.

"No, honey, it's alright. We won't shoot our way out of this one."

The gun is returned to a dresser drawer. Three glasses are filled with iced tea. Kennedy tops his off with a shot of rum and Charlie does the same. There's almost a congenial feel to the air. He senses they've both been lonely. Alive, yes, but at what price. The bargain that they've struck.

"The beard looks good," he tells his host. "You going to take up writing next?"

"And who'd ever read the damn thing? Part of the deal is I stay dead. Invisible."

Invisible. Just like Charlie. He turns to Jackie next. "And I thought you were staying in Europe somewhere. One of those isles off Greece."

"It's been hard to keep up," she admits. "One week I'm pretending to hide out, a grieving widow in some photograph, and the next I'm back here, hiding for real, both of us feeling like outlaws." She abruptly stops. Seems to hear her own words. "Still, it's better than what could've happened. What *did* happen, for some."

All three fall silent for a second or two. Another shadow in the room.

"So, sir, I have to ask. How much did you know?"

Kennedy shifts a bit in his rocker. That bad back or something else.

"All of it, at first. How they wanted me out of office.

How I had a choice. They fake my death and I take a powder or else they kill me outright."

"Not a bad deal," Charlie offers. "Considering your health."

"My health?" He suddenly shoots forward, almost spilling his drink. The old man in his rocker is gone. Jack Kennedy's speaking now. "All that crap, the tumor, the cancer, that was all bullshit. Just something they could feed the troops. A lie they could all buy into."

"And your double?"

Calmer now, he takes a breath. Shakes his head in regret.

"That's when the whole thing blew up. Those morons in Division 12. Should've known they'd come up with some half-assed scheme, something to gum up the works."

Charlie leans forward. Sticks out his hand. Kennedy stares back, confused.

"Charles Overton. Executive Director, Division 12. Or at least I used to be."

You have to give him credit. He actually drums up a smile. Extends his hand, the grip firm and solid, almost like he's running for office.

"Did I just use the word moron?" he asks.

"Don't worry. I've thought the same thing."

The two men eye each other. Both revisit their drinks.

"One last question," Charlie finally says. "When did you find out?"

"About this double of yours?" He shrugs, as if embarrassed. Reluctant to come clean. "So we'd just touched down in Dallas. They were getting the limo unloaded. And I was still up in Air Force One, all alone for once. Only then, out of nowhere, someone walks in, me barely noticing, and or at least until I decide to look up, and guess what, it's me looking back."

He shakes his head, still marveling at that, not quite sure it really happened.

"So, of course, I'm pretty flustered, trying to make sense of it all, and when he tells me there's been a credible threat, that I have to take cover at once, I don't question it, don't think twice. Just do what he says, hide out in the head, until I get the all clear."

It's pretty much what Charlie had figured, with a minor tweak or two. He shaves another inch off his glass, barely tasting the rum.

"So when they thought they were killing you, they were really killing him."

"Not much of a loss," Kennedy replies. "From what I heard, he was just smoke and mirrors."

Without even thinking, Charlie's hand shoots out. Grabs Kennedy by the wrist. The glass, half-empty, tumbles down, shattering on the floor.

"Don't you say that! Don't you dare say that! You owe him your life, goddamnit. I'm still not convinced it wouldn't be better if they'd killed you instead of him."

And so it's finally front and center. The thing he'd

come there to say. The thought that's been haunting him, day-in, day-out, ever since those shots rang out.

He can feel Jackie cringe, stung by his words. The way the man in the rocker freezes. Kennedy finally clears his throat, staring down at the pool on the floor.

"I'm sorry to hear you feel that way. You sound pretty torn up."

"You're right. I guess I am."

It takes but a minute to clean up the mess. To separate glass from ice. All of them tiptoeing around the raw wound he's now left in their lives. Is he embarrassed? Mortified? Does he want to crawl off and die? Yes, of course. But if he'd never spoken his piece, he knows he'd feel much worse.

"So what's next?" Kennedy wonders, pretending that everything's fine. "You're the one who writes his book? Blows my cover all to hell?"

"No. Of course not. The country still needs a hero. In fact, if you let me, I'd like to help. Despite the things I said."

It's finally Jackie who speaks up next, sensing the olive branch.

"Help? How?"

Just for a second, he becomes transparent. They both pull back in alarm.

"You're the guy who can disappear," Kennedy says. "Now I know why that name was familiar."

"But invisible's not what you need. What if I told you

there was a way, something I could teach you, where people, they could still see you, interact with you, only they won't *notice* you. And that if you learn how to do it, you could go anywhere in the world, do anything you want, and all they'd see was a man and his wife. No one they'd recognize."

He can't miss the look they share. A look that's almost hungry. After all that time hiding out in their shack, to see the world again.

"Well," Jackie says, still cautious, still leery, "that would be wonderful, of course. But knowing how you feel about things, why would you even bother?"

He's already lashed out, for better or worse. Spewed his spleen across the floor. Now it's time for what comes next, extending an open hand. He glances up at the man in the rocker, a man just as flawed as he is, and finally decides, decides just like that, to get rid of the crap he's been carrying.

Out goes the hatred. Out goes the guilt. Out goes the judging, the harping. If he can manage to forgive himself, he can forgive anyone.

"Why?" he asks the room, the world.

"Because he'd want me to."

1969

30

2.7 POUNDS.

No, it doesn't seem like much, not in the grand scheme of things. Less weight than a bag of kitty litter or a gallon of two-percent milk. And also less weight, though he's never confirmed it, of your average human head, according to an article he'd read years back in a doctor's waiting room.

2.7 pounds.

But it turns out that if you realign the crystal deposition in a standard graphite matrix, the same kind they use in tennis rackets, or the heat shield of a space capsule, you can increase thermal dispersion while actually lowering the weight. Not by much, mind you. Given Apollo 11's mass and dimensions, and standard reentry velocity, it works out to—you guessed it—2.7 pounds.

Still, the fact remains; that 2.7 pounds means that much less weight they'll have to carry into orbit. That much less fuel consumed in clawing their way into space. Fuel that might come in handy later, in case anything should go wrong. And don't let the guys at the press conferences fool you—things are always going wrong. Like missiles blowing up while they're still in the gantry, or tumbling back down to earth, or having three astronauts, alive one minute, turned to nothing but ashes the next. Because, just like Kennedy promised, they were headed for the Moon, only not because it's easy. No, they were headed for the Moon precisely because it's hard.

And which is why, for the last year or so, Randall Livotski has spent five, six, sometimes ten days a week, running calcs, crunching numbers, herding molecules left and right, all for the niggling, far-from-glamorous goal of winning that 2.7. Increasing the odds that two months from now he'll look up at the night sky, catch a glimpse of that big hunk of green cheese, and realize that three guys, one of whom he's actually met, are up there making history. And will they think about Rand, or the countless others, the ones who helped put them there? No, of course not. Just like no one ever stops to thank all the millions of cells that make up their bodies, their brains. But without those cells, those nameless nobodies, mankind wouldn't exist. Would still be just a handful of apes, cowering away in some cave.

STILL, ON OCCASION, a cave's not so bad. It gives you a place to hide out.

With most people out there, stuck in most jobs, it's all

about having a window. A hunk of glass you can try not to stare through while you're pretending to work. But for Rand, and half the guys at JPL, the basement is where it's at. Some drab white room, bathed in florescence, with no sign of a clock anywhere, the kind of place where they could nuke all of LA, and you wouldn't even notice. Sometimes Rand would even crash down there, not bother going home, just stretching out on this funky old cot he'd scored at the Salvation Army. Catch breakfast with his fellow night owls, bleary-eyed, as pale as ghosts.

But tonight, he decides, he'll go home instead. Sleep in an actual bed. Feed his goldfish, and water his houseplants, and maybe do a load of wash. All the things that normal people do, the same ones who stare through those windows. Only then something happens, like it usually does. He gets lost down some rabbit hole. The next thing he knows, the cleaning crew's out there, and it's almost two in the morning. Somewhere in the real world, wherever that is, it'll be time for last call. Scraping drunks off the floor, and calling for cabs, and waitresses divvying up tips. So at least Rand's got that much to be thankful for. At least he's not one of them.

It's a ten-minute drive to his apartment, assuming he takes the freeway. But thanks to that last cup of Vendo-mat coffee he's still copping a mild buzz. There's a longer loop home that skirts through the foothills, with its curves and dense chaparral, and on impulse he ends up hanging a right, downshifting the Bug into third.

Scattered homes tucked down long driveways. Guardrails hugging the road. A pair of eyes that gleam back from the shadows, some coyote out on the prowl. Barely a mile from downtown Pasadena, and already it's a whole other world, with safe, well-lit streets giving way to all this, a walk on the wild side.

Only then, from behind him, he catches a flash. The strobe of a red light. Most likely an LA Sheriff's patrol car, or maybe the CHP. Rand knows damn well he wasn't speeding, not on four measly cylinders, so they must be responding to some kind of call, most likely an accident. With the light growing closer, he hunts for a turnout. Spies only more curves ahead. If whoever's behind him keeps riding his ass, there'll be two fender-benders, not one.

Finally, at the crest of the hill, the road widens up a hair. And just past that there's some kind of turnout, what looks like a big open field. Hitting his blinker, he veers to the right, spraying gravel in his wake, only to find he's stalled the Bug, accidentally popped the clutch. Still, that's the least of his problems. Instead of continuing on down the road, his shadow has hung a right too, is now stopped behind him, ten feet or so back, his light rack still cycling away. Only now that Rand can get a good look, he sees it's not a rack. Just one of those smaller, magnetized numbers made for sticking up on the roof. And the car. There's no two-toned paint job, no decals, no markings, or at least none he can see. Just a plain, anonymous four-door sedan, the kind someone's dad might drive.

Rand watches in his rearview mirror as a man exits the car. Notes that the driver remains seated inside, with the engine idling away. For a moment he thinks about leaning on over, hunting through the glove box, finding his insurance papers, his registration, only to hear a voice in his head. No, don't move, it tells him. Keep your hands right there on the wheel. He can always claim, later on, that he thought you'd reached for something else.

So instead Rand just sits there, mannequin still. Watches the figure grow closer. It's been a warm week, and his window is down, and he can hear the scuff of each footstep.

Reaching the Bug, the man stops, then leans over. A big, white, beefy face. When he speaks his breath has a distinctive odor. Not bad, just stale somehow.

"Good evening, Mr. Livotski."

Hearing his name, Rand swallows once. His evening just got that much weirder.

"My name is Agent Thompson," the man says. "My partner is Agent Green. Sorry about the unorthodox approach, but we're hoping we could have a few minutes of your time."

There's aftershave too, wafting in through the window, but the smell is off just a hair. Almost as if it's perfume instead, and Thompson can't tell the difference.

"Can I ask what this is about?" Rand wonders.

"It's work related," Thompson replies. "I'd rather not

go into any details till we've reached a secured location."

It takes Rand a second to parse this out. They want him to go somewhere. And he suspects that if he does, they'll also insist on driving.

"And what about my car?"

"Feel free to lock it up. We'll drop you back here once we're done. Should take only an hour tops, and then you'll be free to go."

When someone uses the same word twice, it's usually misdirection. Rand knows that he's now entered a world where no one is really free. He can challenge them now, refuse to comply, and suffer the consequences. Or decide instead to play along and see where all this leads.

"Alright, fine," Rand finally says. "But I'll hold you to that hour."

He follows Thompson to the sedan, eying the man behind the wheel. Catches a glimpse of a lean, narrow face, topped with thinning hair. As Thompson opens the right, rear door, nodding for him to slide in, Rand is struck by a blast of warm air—Green has got the heater running. It's only once the door slams shut that he notices what's missing, that there's no sign of a lock mechanism, and he suspects that should he try the handle, the door would refuse to open.

Without a word, they abandon the turn-out, hang a right on the two-lane road. With the windows cranked up and the heater on full, the car is already stifling. About a quarter-mile up, there should be a side road, the quickest way back into town, which prompts Rand to wonder if they'll take that route, or keep climbing up the grade.

"So you said you were agents, but not who for. Anyone I might've heard of?"

The two men up front exchange a quick look. What could almost be a smile.

"It's doubtful," Thompson lobs back. "Just a few letters lined up in a row. You know, like JPL."

"Or NASA," Green decides to add.

From his perch in the backseat, Rand stares out. Spots the side road as it whizzes by. Pretty soon they'll be hitting the San Gabriels proper, LA's own mountain range, where open scrub gives way to forest, the kind of country where people get lost. He remembers, as a kid, the stories he'd hear, what went on up there in the boonies. The wild biker parties, the satanic cults, the bodies in their shallow graves. Never once dreaming that he might take the tour. Find out if the rumors were true.

"You know," he points out, without knowing why, "they have a name for it. When letters, initials, stand in for whole words. They're called acronyms."

"Acronyms," Green replies. "Sounds more like a disease."

Thompson nods. "Either that or some crossword clue."

But Rand's not thinking about crosswords. He's thinking about what comes next. What would happen if, on the next sharp curve, he reached up and grabbed hold of Green. With any luck, that might cause a collision, hitting the guardrail or a tree, with his new friends taking the brunt of the impact, thanks to the fact they're up front. Unless, of course, Rand's timing is off, and they sail right over the edge. Find out how far it is to the bottom of whatever ravine's waiting there.

"And this agency I've never heard of," Rand says. "It's got an office way up in the hills?"

"Not an office," Thompson counters. "More like a clubhouse really."

This provokes a chuckle from Green. "A clubhouse. That's pretty good."

But any amusement soon proves short-lived. The sedan has a sudden hiccup. There's a loud backfire, sharp as a gunshot, as the car begins to lurch.

"What the …" Thompson exclaims. "You forget to fill up or something?"

"No," Green insists. "Just look at the gauge. We still have half a tank."

By now they're barely moving. The cylinders rattle away. Rand watches as Green jerks the wheel to the right, trying his best to reach the shoulder. But all he gets for his troubles is another rude impact as the front tire enters a ditch. The angry screech of what must be the axle, scraping against the blacktop.

And then there's only silence.

All three of them sit there, sizing things up. The calculus has changed. Instead of one victim and two men in charge, they're now all in the same boat. A boat with a sizeable hole in the hull, and a porcelain tea cup for bailing.

"It's probably a block in the line," Rand offers. "That or a bad fuel filter."

The men in the front just stare at each other, ignoring his presence, his words. Almost as if they're still at it, still talking, only using their eyes, not their tongues.

"You don't think …"

"Think? No way. I *know*."

Like two puppets sharing the same strand of string, their heads both swivel forward, eyes now directed towards the deserted road, still bathed in the sedan's headlights. Leaning in closer, following their gaze, Rand can suddenly see it. A lone figure caught within that same wash, calmly walking toward them. Tall, whippet thin, it had come out nowhere, as if conjured by their fear alone, and Rand can actually smell it on Thompson, beneath his aftershave. The rough, raw stink of a trapped animal, knowing its end is near.

The figure does something with its hands. A bit of pantomime. Just like that, his two captors are suddenly gone, no longer flesh and blood. Rand pulls back— scared, confused—and then surveys the upholstery. All he finds are two piles of crumpled clothing. A fine powder that looks like sand.

He watches as the figure approaches. Wonders if he'll be next. If the process is painful, he tells himself, at least it seemed pretty quick.

Swinging around to the driver's side, the man pauses by the rear door. A moment later he yanks it open, calling out in a playful voice.

"Come out, come out, wherever you are. The cavalry has arrived."

Sliding out from the bench seat, Rand stands up, only to find himself swooning. After the stifling heat of the sedan, the night air is a slap in the face.

"The cavalry?" he manages. "I thought that was just in the movies."

"Of course. But so am I."

Rand takes a second to study his savior. Can see he's no spring chicken. A gaunt, weathered face, and a scatter of age spots, and the frost in his neatly trimmed hair. And those clothes. Back when he was still at Caltech, he used to cruise the thrift stores. Knew the look that fabric got when it had seen better days. Put all these hints together, and it points to a single word. Another one of those crossword clues he seems to be dropping tonight.

Relic.

"So just out of curiosity," the man asks Rand, "how'd they get you in the car in the first place?"

"They told me they were agents. I didn't want to make a fuss."

Hearing this, the man shakes his head. And that one shake says it all.

"Well, they had a flashing light," Rand explains. "Cut

me a little slack."

"And what about ice cream trucks? You go for rides in them too?"

It's increasingly clear, this rescue of his, it comes with a hefty price tag. Having to play the foil, the straight man, in somebody else's stage act.

"So before we go any further," the man tells him, "please accept a bit of advice. From here on in, you will trust no one. Believe no one. Accept no help from strangers. And whatever anyone tells you, it's probably a lie."

Rand thinks that over. Responds with a shrug.

"And I assume that includes you."

For the very first time, the man cracks a smile. At least he's found a quick study.

"No, I was talking about everyone else. Of course you can trust your own father."

31

THEY LEAVE THE sedan still stuck in its ditch. There's plenty of room to drive around it. And as for whatever's left inside, someone else can deal with that too.

Still, that leads to another quandary. How will they get back into town? Before Rand has a chance to ask, the answer presents itself. The car is huge, bulbous yet lithe, lots of chrome and sweeping curves, the kind of arrogant, self-assured ride they stopped making years ago. And just like its driver, now behind the wheel, it's a remnant from the past, a refusal to admit that life goes on. That all good things must pass.

"It's called a Phaeton," the man explains, even though no one asked. "Cadillac used to make them."

"And what about my car?" Rand asks back. "Think it'll fit in the trunk?"

"We can pick it on up on the way into town. You can follow me from there."

But follow him where, Rand wants to know, just one of a thousand more questions. Like who were those guys and who did they work for? And how was it they turned into sand? And why had his savior been parked there, just waiting, waiting for them to show up? All of them mere prelude to the biggest unknown of all. Is this man, this total stranger, his actual, flesh and blood father?

Within a few minutes, they've reached the turnout, and Rand motions for them to pull over. Twin headlights strafe his beat-up Bug, glinting back off the tiny rear window.

"And just in case you lose me," the man tells Rand. "We're headed for Karla's place."

Rand stares back, mulling this over.

"You know my mother?"

A knowing smile. The ghost of a laugh.

"Once, in the biblical sense."

FIVE YEARS BACK, his mother, Karla, had gone a little bit crazy. Decided to schedule a midlife crisis, just shy of her big Five-0. Resigning from her post on the Marlbourne board, she'd cashed out her extensive stock options, vowing to follow her son out west, whether he liked it or not. Gone was the posh suite of rooms in DC. She found herself a small bungalow. Had become just one more laidback Venice hippie in her sandals and 501s.

All of which means she now keeps her own hours. Often stays up half the night. But when they arrive, just a hair past four, her place looks dark and deserted. Rand shoehorns into a spot down the block—it's why he drives a Bug—then watches as the Phaeton idles, thanks to a crowded curb. Behind the wheel, his savior glares. Mouths what could be a curse. Finally decides, with no sign of traffic, to just double park, tickets be damned.

Seeing Rand's expression, the man merely shrugs.

"Don't worry. We're not staying long."

Well-worn redwood steps lead up from the sidewalk. Scattered clay pots are filled with flowers. Knowing his mom, knowing her temper, Rand decides to hold back. Lets his companion make the call, whether to announce their presence with just a light knock, or dare to use the bell. Only then, as if to deliberately thwart him, the man pats his pocket instead. Fishes up what looks like a key. Whoever, whatever, this stranger may be, he's obviously tight with his mother.

The deadbolt turns. The door creaks open. Her cat's waiting there to greet them. As the man bends down to give it a pet, something flies right past his head. There is now a knife, eight inches of steel, embedded in the narrow oak jamb.

"You missed," the man says, straightening back up.

"That's assuming I wanted to hit you."

Risking more punctures, they enter the foyer. Rand eases the door shut. Already his mother has found a desk lamp, coaxing it back to life. For a moment she inspects her not-quite-target, a cursory glance at best, and then her eyes lock onto Rand, widening in surprise.

"What's this?" she asks, challenging the man. "I thought we were going to wait."

"We were," he replies. "But nobody told them that."

His mother pauses, thinking that over. Gets that look on her face. The one she always seems to wear when things aren't going her way.

"And how many of them are we talking about?"

"Just two, mere flunkies. They weren't a problem. Still, the wheels have started to turn."

Turning or not, Rand's had enough. He's tired of playing catch-up. Ignoring the cat, the knife in the door frame, he takes a few steps towards Karla.

"Sorry to interrupt you two, but maybe you can fill me in. Those flunkies, they're not really flunkies anymore, just a couple of piles of sand. And this guy, the guy who did it, he claims to be my father. But you always told me he was dead. Has been for umpteen years."

Hearing this, she shakes her head. Trots out her side of the story.

"Dead? I don't think so. I mean I might've said that I wanted him dead, or maybe that's what he deserved, but I never once claimed that he actually *was*."

"So you're saying this is really him? My father?"

She nods towards their third party, silent until then.

"Rand, this is Richard. Richard Constairs. We used to work together."

By now the man is smiling, holding out his hand. But as far as Rand's concerned, it might as well be a dead fish.

"Work together?" Rand spits back. "I mean come on—he's a magician."

"So was I," she admits with a sigh. "A long, long time ago."

At that point she flips on a few more lights. Puts a kettle on the stove. Probably tells herself she's giving them time, time for some instant male bonding. But maybe Rand doesn't want to bond. Feels more like freaking out. If what they're claiming is actually true, then somebody up there is laughing. After all the things he's said about magic, and the people who dish it out.

Waiting for Karla, the man takes the loveseat. Rand opts for the couch instead. At least that leaves them a good ten feet apart, just in case he's radioactive. And despite what they're saying, Rand's not quite ready, ready to use the f-word. Admit that this man, this total stranger, is, in fact, his father.

But if said father can sense this refusal, he bulls ahead anyway.

"All along I'd planned on doing this right. Breaking things to you slowly. Because Karla has made it very clear, the way you feel about magic." He pauses. Shrugs. "But sometimes life, it forces one's hand. We don't get what we plan, or want."

But Rand doesn't need excuses. Just the salient facts.

"So what you're saying is you two, you've been deliberately doing it this whole time. Keeping me in the dark."

"Not by my choice, I assure you. But despite her

Talents, her own unique skills, your mother isn't too fond of magicians. And the last thing she wanted was me being around, being a bad influence."

"Did I hear that right?" she calls out from the kitchen, her head buried in a cupboard. "You're blaming it all on me?"

The man, Richard, denies this at once. "Not at all. Lord knows I have my own misgivings. Things that I regret. And I promise, once we're out of danger, both of you can feel free to wrack me over the coals."

With that, he glances out the window. The sky is no longer pitch black. Out in the backyard, just off the deck, a few birds are beginning to stir. Goaded along by his impatience, Karla ferries in their tea, then finds herself a place on the couch, thus serving as go-between. Just for a second, Rand can't help it, he's imagining them as a couple, a couple who'd met, and loved, and tangled, and created at least one thing. A person named Randall Livotski.

"Well, as long as we're playing true confessions," she announces, "I should probably come clean too."

She glances towards Richard, then drops her gaze, looking almost repentant.

"One of the reasons," she explains to Rand, "that your father was willing to lay low, stay out of the picture for so long, was because of you. The fact that you didn't seem to have any Talent. No hint of abilities."

"Crudely put," Richard observes, "but essentially

correct."

"And he'd always assumed that this was just bad luck on his part. That magic had skipped a generation, like it often does."

The man on the loveseat quickly leans forward. Almost spills his tea.

"Are you saying it was something else?"

Karla pretends he hasn't spoken. Keeps her eyes pinned on Rand. "You have to understand the choice I faced. The fact that I had no choice. I couldn't let you turn out like your father. I'd seen where that path could lead."

Richard's face is now an ashen grey. "Let me guess. A suppression spell."

"Wait," Rand says, his own mug forgotten. "What's a suppression spell?"

Even the words themselves sound weighted. Something you don't talk about. He throws a glance out to his mother, but it's someone else who answers.

"It's a process we're generally loathe to practice," Richard explains. "Like gelding, or sterilization. And it's not nearly as popular now as it was in its heyday, during the Salem witch trials. You, see, generally speaking, a magician's gifts, they first manifest in puberty. But if you can find a child early enough, perform the proper procedures, you can forestall its development for months, years. Sometimes an entire lifetime."

Rand turns back to his mother, not sure what to say,

or to feel.

"And you did this to me?"

She nods back. "Right after that first episode, back when you were ten, I took you to the hospital to have your appendix removed, remember? Only once you were under, it didn't stop there. I did what I had to do."

Which means, in a way, that she had saved him. Saved him from a curse. So why did it feel like something else, the worst kind of violation.

"So who'd you have do it?" Richard asks. "Anyone I know?"

"Karl Bischoff."

"Bischoff," he sighs back, disgusted. "The man is a total hack."

"Hack or not, he got the job done."

So what had he called it, Rand tries to recall. A sterilization, a gelding? Like what you might do with a dog, or a cat, to keep it more manageable. Part of him wants to get up, to leave, to forget these people exist. All the while knowing it wouldn't change much, that they'd still be his parents anyway.

"So that explains it," Richard finally says, nodding in comprehension.

"Explain what?" Karla replies.

"Why those two men were so eager to get hold of our son. Why their timetable has moved up. Bischoff is the worst kind of gossip, he can't keep his damn mouth shut. Which means, all along, our enemy must have known who Rand was, what was done to him. And what he still might be capable of."

"Which brings up a point," Rand interrupts. "You still haven't told me who those goons were."

Richard nods back, admitting his gaffe. "All in good time. Suffice it to say, for now at least, that you and I have something in common, besides just blood. That if those men, and the ones that employ them, have their way, then your precious Apollo will never reach the Moon."

If Rand thought he was already confused, this takes it to a whole other level.

"Apollo? The Moon? What are you talking about?"

Ignoring his question, Richard glances up, consulting the morning sky. The first hint of light, tepid and pale, has just found the kitchen windows.

"We haven't a second to waste," he proclaims. "They might already be on their way. And this time they'll send out some serious Talent, of that you can be sure."

Leaving the loveseat, he peers towards the street. Checks that the Phaeton is still there. But once the sun's up, and the neighborhood with it, someone's bound to call the police.

Wheeling around, he turns to Karla. "Your place in Big Sur, it's ready to go? Those new spells are in place?"

"Of course," his mother responds.

"Big Sur?" Rand's already springing up from the couch, determined to put on the brakes. "Just hold on a second. Look, I've got a job to go to. Something called a life. And I'm not about to drop all that just because you two say so."

The man, his f-word, just shakes his head. Stares back through pale grey eyes. With the first light of day, and a night without sleep, he already looks ten years older.

"Stick around here," he tells his son, "and you won't have a job *or* a life."

32

THEY WOLF DOWN a makeshift breakfast, then Rand calls into the Lab. Leaves a brief message with some nameless intern, explaining he won't be in. Ten minutes later they're on the road, headed for the 405, fighting it out everyone else, who are fighting it out with them. Pretending they're spies, they've taken two cars, and are using two routes out of town, hoping to confuse any potential tails on the off-chance they're actually followed. Plus once they reach Karla's seaside retreat, they'll want to keep a low profile, and Richard's ride, just like its owner, can hardly be called discrete.

Only that word—decided—it isn't quite accurate. Not when his father, if that's what he is, can make a suggestion sound like a decree. Growing up, Rand had gotten used to it. Having the boss drop in. Having a mother who'd be gone for weeks at a time, and then show up unannounced, with her own agenda, her own iron will, her own version of how things should be. Only now, suddenly, there are two of them. Two people who think they're in charge. Each one convinced that they know best, that everyone else should shut up.

Just getting through breakfast, it's like a minefield. One skirmish after another. You burnt the toast, you call this coffee, where'd you learn how to fry an egg. Almost like they're in a dance, a performance, one they've polished up over the years. Which, Rand starts to realize, is exactly what it is. When his mother had mentioned that they'd once worked together, he'd assumed she meant during the War, but no, this was apparently some kind of traveling act. A magician and his squeeze. Leaving Rand to decide which is more left field, the thought of his mother taking orders from anyone, or the prospect of her strutting around the stage in fishnets and a tutu.

And then there's the biggest quandary of all. Where does Rand fit in? They've been together for barely an hour, and already he can feel them. Those invisible tendrils, his bloodline, his clan, determined to reach out and grab him. Though no one's willing to come right out and say it, Rand suspects he was never intended. An accident they can now fight over, use as a weapon, a tool. One second they'll be focused solely on him, out to wheedle, or charm, or coerce. And the next they'll lock eyes, and everything else disappears, and it's just the two of them in the room. Not quite in love, not quite in like, but not quite hating each other.

Talk about frying pans. Talk about fires. How can you tell the difference? A few hours back, right across town, he'd pretty much been abducted. Shoved in a car, destination unknown, with somebody else at the wheel. And now, guess what, it's happening again, only with one major difference. Instead of two strangers for company, it's his parents this time around.

ROAD TRIP, PART One. Rand and his mother. Grinding their way up the Grapevine. Though thanks to her Porsche, a compact two-seater, it feels like they're flying instead. At his father's insistence, they'd left straight from her place, hadn't risked stopping off at Rand's, and so he has no spare clothes, no overnight bag, not even so much as a toothbrush. Just what he's wearing, the watch on his wrist, and a few presidents in his wallet.

Eyes pinned ahead, his mother speaks up, fighting it out with the engine.

"So you probably hate me a little."

"Yeah, you're right. I probably do."

Rounding a curve, they speed by a semi. It might as well be parked.

"But if you could have been there," she counters. "Seen what he was like. How arrogant, how self-centered."

"And yet you screwed him anyway."

He wants his words to sting her. To repay her for what she'd done. To have it out, one adult to another, instead of as mother and son.

"But just the one time" she insists, "and only out of spite. Just like that, he gave me the axe, after almost five years together, and I wanted to show him what he'd be missing. What he'd never have again."

"One time," Rand takes a moment to consider the odds. "I guess you guys were lucky."

Luck, of course, being a matter of perspective. Someone's good is the next person's bad.

"I probably shouldn't tell you this," she admits, "but it wasn't supposed to happen. Because Richard, without even asking, he'd done something inside of me. Something to make sure I wouldn't conceive. Which means, if he'd had his way, you wouldn't even be here, trying to decide if you hate me."

Another bombshell, another twist. The hits just keep on coming. The same man who might've just saved his life didn't want him around in the first place.

"And what about you?" he asks Karla. "Did you want a kid or not?"

"It someone had given me a choice, do you want to get pregnant or not, I probably would've said no. But once you were real, once you existed, everything felt different."

She hesitates then. Rand glances over. Sees the way she's gripping the wheel. Whatever hell he's going through, she's feeling the heat too.

"And, to be honest," she finally adds, "I wasn't quite done being spiteful. Because now I had a piece of

Richard, stuck right there inside me, and I knew I could shape it, fix it, find all the good parts and take out the bad. Or at least that's what I told myself."

"So that's when you decided to do it. That suppression spell of yours."

This is met by a shake of the head. "No, that was years later. And by then, he'd already made it clear, he wanted no part of you. I mean he helped out with the money and all, sent me a check once a month, but anything else, being a real father, it wasn't on his agenda." She pauses again, treading carefully now. "Plus there were other things going on. That whole ugly mess with Charlie."

"Charlie?" he asks back.

For a moment she focuses on the road. The white lines dashing by.

"If he ever gets insufferable, or too damn full of himself, just ask him to give you the lowdown on Charlie. That'll shut him up in a hurry."

ROAD TRIP, PART TWO. The Secret Rendezvous. By prior agreement, they meet up in Santa Paula, in the land of the citrus groves, only this late in the season the trees have been mostly picked clean. Both his parents are convinced they haven't been followed, prompting Richard to finally relax, deciding they can risk a stop at a diner that serves dishwater in lieu of coffee.

At that point Rand opts to swap cars. He doesn't dare play favorites. Knows if he does, he'll get turned into sand, or ventilated by some sharp object.

"So how was your ride up?" his father asks.

"No tickets," Rand tells him. "Which is pretty amazing, considering our average speed."

"And Karla filled your head, I suppose, with all sorts of intriguing lies."

"Intriguing, yes. Lies, who knows. So now it must be your turn."

A leisurely drift into the left lane. Turns signals are made for sissies. And why is the guy they just cut off honking his horn like that?

"Actually, I say let bygones be bygones. Spilt milk under the bridge. I'd rather we concentrate on the here and now, try to avoid getting killed."

"Fine," Rand chimes in. "Let's start there. Who or what wants us dead?"

His father just sits there, contemplating that question. What to say, and what to keep hidden. "I don't suppose you've heard of the Sorcerer's Guild."

Rand shakes his head in response.

"No, of course not," his father laments. "No one has anymore. And that's one of the things I truly despise about the path you've taken. As magicians, we acknowledge that science is real, both its benefits and drawbacks. But talk to a scientist?" He waves a dismissive hand towards the dashboard. "No, with science it's either my way or the highway. And all of you have been determined to deny our existence from the very beginning."

"So what do you want me to do about it? Apologize?"

His question is ignored. "Anyway, as to the Guild, it's pretty much been gutted, but the sentiment that fueled it, that lent it power, is still very much alive."

"Like those guys who picked me up."

"As I said before, they were mere flunkies. Not a Talent to their names. But more than capable of accomplishing their task, absconding with a helpless boy."

Rand's not sure which one is worse—the helpless or the boy.

"But why me? Why you? Why dead?"

"The 'me' because I've been a thorn in their side for going on thirty years. The 'you' because you're my son, a son who also just happens to have an in with NASA. And the 'dead' because they hate loose ends, and dead… well, dead is dead."

It's no wonder he ended up a magician. Every question leads straight to two more. An endless series of asides and digressions, rabbits pulled out of his hat.

"Alright, hold on," Rand tells him. "That's the second time you've mentioned NASA. What the hell do they have to do with any of this?"

"So you've been at that job of yours for, what, going on ten years. And in those ten years, how many accidents have there been? Or perhaps it was something more subtle. An unforeseen setback, or a budget cut, or an appropriations bill not passing. So didn't it ever make you wonder? Didn't it ever seem as if someone, or some *thing*, might not want us to reach the Moon?"

It's a warm spring day in sunny California. Why does Rand feel a sudden shiver?

"For years I was just a stage act," Richard continues. "An entertainer, playing for the house. But eventually I found another path, one with far more meaning. Realized that, in my own small way, I could influence events, shape outcomes, make the world a better place. But every time I attempted to do so, I could feel something pressing back. It wasn't quite human, that much was clear. Not even what we'd call alive. More like a force, a purpose, an immutable part of what is. And yet the oddest thing was it seemed to have some stake in us, in humanity and its fate."

"What? You mean like God?"

"I certainly hope not. Because if what I'd glimpsed was truly God, then I'd sign up with the Devil. I first encountered it in Hollywood of all places. Tracked it during the War. And now, for whatever reason, it's found a new focus on this Space Race of yours. It doesn't want man to reach the Moon. To claim it for its own. Because somehow, us venturing out into space, it's not part of its agenda."

Of course, it sounds like total nonsense. UFOs and little green men. For the very first time, Rand starts to wonder. Is this man, his father, all there?

"So how will this thing try to stop us?" he asks, shelving his doubts for now.

"I don't know," his father admits. "What we need is a good futurist. But much like the Guild, we magicians are scattered, blown to the four winds. Which is why, all along, I'd planned on eventually seeking you out. Enlisting your aid instead."

Meaning Rand could be useful, if things work out. Not needed, not loved, just useful.

"Look, I've got to be honest," he finally replies. "This is a whole lot to swallow. And if you were to contact NASA or the Lab, and tell them what you just told me, they'd lock you away somewhere."

The man at the wheel stares ahead. Shrugs his elegant shoulders.

"I know. Which is why, if you want Man to reach the Moon, it's up to us to make it happen."

ROAD TRIP. PART Three. The Arrival.

Even though he'd been born in California, had lived his whole life near the coast, Rand often forgets how strange it is, to literally live on the edge. A place where earth and water, land and sea, are in a constant state of war.

But being in Big Sur, you can't forget. It's staring you

straight in the face. All those arrogant statements in redwood and glass, barely clinging to windswept cliffs. At least Karla's place is east of the highway, where the hills are a hair more stable, and they follow her up an unmarked track that snakes through thick stands of brush. With each curve, each tight switchback, they gain a new view. Another glimpse of a roiled Pacific. Until finally, as the grade levels out, they spot their destination, a two-story hulk with weathered grey siding, tucked into a stand of pines.

They park Richard's Phaeton inside the garage, clearing the back wall by inches, then troop through the front door to find the house empty, smelling of dust and disuse. The place is huge, or at least by Rand's standards, with four spacious bedrooms upstairs, and in less than a minute they've each snagged their own, calling dibs on who gets the first shower. Between all three they've slept two hours out of the last twenty-four, but apparently someone has compiled a checklist that's much more important than bed.

"So what about your neighbors?" Richard asks.

"The Thompsons are a mile north," Karla tells him, "on the leeward side. Another couple I haven't yet met live a few hundred yards past them. I doubt we'll see either one."

"And the road we took is the only way out?"

"From here it climbs up over the ridge, then ties back into Highway One. And if we take that route, there's a one-lane bridge about a mile up. Easy enough to disable behind us, in case someone's on our tail."

"So," Rand asks, barely hiding a smile, "you two always this paranoid?"

His father refuses to take the bait. "Paranoid and alive."

"I'll head into town while you two clean up," Karla offers. "Pick up some food and supplies. Grab the Boy Wonder a change of clothes while I'm at it."

"And then what?" the Boy Wonder wants to know.

A pair of grey eyes glint back his way.

"We see about making you a magician."

33

THE NEXT DAY.

By the time Rand finally cracks his eyes open, it's almost ten hours later. Just what he'd needed after their all-nighter and the long drive up from LA. For four or five minutes he lies there, half awake, staring out through the bedroom window, contemplating a view framed by three gnarled pines, with a glimpse of the ocean just past them. In another world, he'd already be at work, knee-deep in his current project, but apparently that world is gone, for now or else forever. A disguise he'd somehow outgrown overnight. No more time for training wheels.

He wanders downstairs, stifling a yawn. His parents must still be crashed out. He decides to put the time to good use and make a second call to the Lab. Though JPL reports to NASA, and is theoretically government-run, the place still feels more like Caltech sometimes, a playground without any rules. He'd already left that message yesterday. Theoretically his ass is now covered. Still, it couldn't hurt to play it safe, clear it with Carl directly. Rand hasn't missed a day in forever, he's got weeks of PTO piled up, and all it takes is that one word—family—and Carl is wishing him luck. Take off till Christmas, he tells Rand. Maybe they'll be gone by then.

During the call, he'd kept his voice low, but apparently not quite enough. And he's barely parked the receiver back down before Karla is poking her head out. Matted hair and puffy eyes and the shuffling gait of a zombie. This from a woman who'd made the cover of *Fortune*, not once, not twice, but three times.

"You sleep OK?" he asks her.

She manages to nod back. "When I'm here, I always do. Must be the negative ions. And don't you dare play Mr. Science and tell me that's all BS."

"C'mon, I'm not that bad."

Then he pauses, gesturing towards their surroundings. The big redwood beams overhead.

"So this place. How come you've kept it under wraps? Never once mentioned you owned it?"

"Because, technically, I don't. As soon as it came on the market, I set up a string of shell buyers. Made sure not to leave a paper trail. Once you've been a spy, worked undercover, it becomes second nature. You always have to have a safe house around. A place where they won't find you."

He stares back at this woman, this stranger. A jigsaw puzzle brought to life. The more he learns about his mother, the less he seems to know her.

"And just to give you a head's up," she adds, "I might

be making myself scarce the next few days."

"Scarce? How come?"

"There's some contacts I need to talk to. Leads I have to check out." She pauses. Studies her son. "And besides, you and Richard need some private time. You've got thirty years of catch-up. And once that's over, maybe then you'll get it, why I left him in the first place."

"So why do you hate magic?"

Breakfast is over. Karla is gone. The dirty dishes are piled high. But rather than deal with the mess in the sink, it's time for the mess labeled Rand.

"Hate?" Rand shrugs back. "That's a pretty strong word."

"Then let's try another," his father suggests. "Mistrust perhaps? And I assume that whatever word we decide on, you would've learned it first from your mother."

"No," Rand insists, "it wasn't like that. She never told me how I should feel. Just let me figure out things on my own. Draw my own conclusions."

"Which were…?"

"That magic was a cheat. A shortcut. That you could either have the discipline, do the hard work, figure out why things happened the way they did, or you could just sit back and wait for the universe to do what you wanted. And it didn't help, all through school, that it was the jerks, the losers, who wanted to go that route. Who wanted the easy A."

He watches his father consider all this. Decide if he should feel insulted. Then, with a shrug, he lets it roll past him, just one in a lifetime of slights.

"I think I see the problem here. It's a question of semantics. Like most non-believers, you're conflating two things, assuming they're one and the same. Because magic, in part, is a body of knowledge, much like science itself, a logical system anyone can master, given hard work and sufficient time. And believe me, if you think that sounds easy, or consider it some kind of cheat, then just try earning your first protocol."

No, he feels like telling his father. You try earning two PhDs.

"But then," Richard adds, "there's a whole other side to magic. What we like to call Talent. A gift, a knack, dispensed at birth, through genes, or fate, or folly. I, for one, have a penchant for odds—I can alter them in my favor. While Karla, your mother, although she'll deny it, can manipulate EM fields. And no, it's not fair, who gets rewarded, and who gets stuck being normal, and to make matters worse, there are people like me, who are lucky enough to have both. A Talent in its own right, and a gift for learning the rest."

"Wait," Rand tells him. "Back up a bit. What's this thing about EM fields?"

"To the untrained eye your mother is merely someone who's good at throwing knives. But I've had those same knives come hurtling my way. Seen them do impossible things. And so I became convinced, years ago, that she was able to control their flight even after they'd left her hand."

"Then why not admit it's magic? It's not like she's breaking any laws."

"Some people would rather deny it. Who, or what, they are."

With that, his father consults his mug. Seems to notice it's empty. A second later there's a faint trail of steam, wafting up from inside it. Perhaps he'd felt lazy, didn't want to stand up, got a refill the easy way. Or perhaps with some people, when it comes to their Talent, it's about flaunting, not denial.

"So the other night," Richard continues, "Karla alluded to something. An incident involving you as a child, before Bischoff cast that spell."

Rand pretends at disinterest. "Sure. What about it?"

"I was hoping you'd tell me about it."

For a moment they both fall silent. In the distance the waves grind on. Sometimes you leave a scab in place and sometimes you tear it off.

"So I must have been nine, or maybe ten. We'd just finished moving again. That place she wound up buying in Rosemead, the one with the big front porch. And along with the new house, and a new woman to run it, she'd decided to splurge, get all new appliances too."

He waits for his father to speak, interrupt, but for once he chooses silence.

"So one day this refrigerator gets delivered from Sears, a Kelvinator I think they called it, the same one they showed in all the ads, the one with its own icemaker. But still, it was just a fridge in the end, no big deal, right? Only about a week or so later, I woke up one night, and I could hear this sound. A sound like somebody crying. And at first I tried to ignore it, pretend it wasn't there, but really, how could anyone do it, ignore a sound like that. So I got up, started to poke around, quiet as a mouse, and somehow ended up in the kitchen. Finally realized it was that fridge. That it was making this keening sound, like it was in some kind of pain.

"So the next morning, Karla gets up, she hadn't yet left for back East, and she finds me lying there, stretched out on the linoleum, fast asleep. Somehow I'd managed to pull that refrigerator out from the wall, yank off the back panel, find where this metal tube from the compressor had somehow gotten crimped, only I didn't have the right tools to fix it. Had finally given up, I guess, and just cried myself to sleep."

Just for a second, he closes his eyes. Ignores the wash of the waves. Recalls instead the sound from that night, a sound he'll never forget.

"After that it was like a door got yanked open. One I couldn't keep closed anymore. And I started to realize, all the stuff in the world, our machines, our devices, they're alive, just like us. Crying, or laughing, or chattering along, or sometimes even singing. But everyone else was deaf to all that, and only I could hear it."

His father clears his throat.

"And then you went to the hospital. And when you woke up, the voices were gone."

Rand nods in response.

"And did you ever, do you ever, wish that they were back?"

It is, of course, the very same question. The same one he's asked himself. Even though he knows that what he wishes or wants, it doesn't matter in the end. That there's no turning back, no second chances, no do-overs, taken or not.

"I don't know," he finally admits. "In a way it would scare me shitless. You can't imagine how loud it can get, really listening to the world. How you can't even hear yourself think."

Richard leans forward, pleading his case. Looks Rand dead in the eye.

"That's where the other side of magic comes in. Teaching you how to tame your Talent. How to come up with a filter, a switch, something that will put you in charge. But the very first step, assuming you take it, would be to cancel out that spell. Give you back yourself."

"And what if I end up changing my mind? Can we put it back in place?"

All this earns is a smile from his father.

"Believe me, you won't want to."

RAND WONDERS IF there will be candles involved. Incense and temple bells. But no props are needed, just him on the couch, finding his happy place. After two cups of coffee he's mildly buzzed, can't seem to settle down, and he feels as if he's some poor, dumb lug who's been asked up on the stage. Convinced to crawl inside a box and get himself sawed in two.

Or maybe put back together again.

For the first few minutes nothing happens. The room is deathly still. Somewhere behind him, his father is seated, quiet as a ghost. After a while Rand's breathing, his heartbeat, starts to fade away as well. A sensation as if he's falling through space, even though he's glued to the couch.

And then it's Sparky, staring back at him. That stupid grin of his. With that big white seam running down his side, and those cheesy plastic eyes, and the way his front paw, the left one like always, looks like it's hanging there, broken. Only Sparky, he seems pissed somehow, despite the way he's smiling, and now it's his mouth that's flapping around, making sounds, or more like words.

Hey there asshole, Sparky calls out. *You still remember me?*

Rand would like to say something back, only his

mouth doesn't work.

Yeah, that's right, now it's your turn. You can play mute for a while.

And then it's Rand's dump truck, the bright yellow one, the one he lost at the beach. But how can a dump truck look so upset? It doesn't even have a face.

I called and called, the dump truck wails, *But you, you just left me there.*

Look, Rand pleads, finally speaking up, *I went back. Looked everywhere. Some other kid must've found you.*

And then there are cartons, stuffed full of Play Dough, and those lame wooden blocks from Sweden, and his very first Erector Set, still in the original box. All of them lining up with their tales of woe, their grudges and their guilt-trips, and pretty soon they're comparing notes, seeing who got it worse, and it's starting to feel like they're forming a lynch mob, with him as the guest of honor.

And the noise. The squeaks, and groans, and growls, and hoots, like twenty cartoons all at once. All the sounds that Rand had learned to ignore, but who'd stuck around anyway, biding their time. Awaiting their revenge. Which means that his father had lied to him, this isn't a cure, more like an exorcism. A purge of all the nasty shit he'd tucked away and forgotten.

Hearing it, he wants to cry out. Hearing it, he wants to scream. To shout past the silence they'd forced down his throat, to finally find his voice.

So he does.

"Randall. Randall! Don't worry, I'm here. It's alright now, it's over."

His father is clutching him by the shoulders. Leaning over the couch. There's a look on his face that goes beyond anger, that registers more like outrage.

Rand stares up. Shakes his head. "Jesus, what the hell was that? A dream or …?"

"That was Karl Bischoff," Richard replies, "doing what he does best. Getting hired to swat a fly, and deciding to use a sledgehammer."

Rand sits forward, patting himself, making sure everything's still there. Wondering if the whole world has changed, or if it's merely him.

"And it worked?" he asks his father. "I'm cured, or whatever you'd call it?"

"The spell is broken," he nods back.

"So now what?"

The look of concern is starting to fade. His father takes a deep breath.

"You're no longer who you used to be. Now we find out what you've become."

34

THE REST OF the day is a total wash. It feels like his head's been ripped wide open. All those years, all those voices, torn out one by one, left to bake in the bright light of day.

Too tired to sleep, too wired to stand still, he decides to hike down to the shoreline. To follow a deer trail wherever it leads, hoping he doesn't get lost. The ocean he knows, the one he grew up with, had been a tame Los Angeles version. A gelding, like himself. Endless miles of dead-flat sand, the waves just barely lapping, a world of straight lines and long horizons, what you see is what you get. But up here, up north, the rules break down. It's a land of constant turmoil. A place not sure just which it is, a ballet or a battlefield.

Navigating through the knee-high grass, his eyes on the lookout for snakes, he finally realizes what feels wrong, or not really wrong, just different. He's alone. For the first time in a couple of days, ever since those red lights in his mirror, there's no one pushing him around, telling him what to think, or who to be. And not that he mistrusts them exactly, his mother or his father, but still, now that he is alone, he can see how easy it would be. To get sucked up, defined, by their angers, and their agendas, and their versions of whoever he is. To just go on being a gelding.

The further he follows the slope on down, the more he has to watch it, with those loose rocks scattered across the trail and not much in the way of footholds. Still, that's how it always works. You take a chance, pick a path, and at first it looks like smooth sailing. And by the time you finally discover the truth, it's too late to turn back. If anyone at JPL could see him now, playing hooky, hanging out with magicians, getting his head turned inside-out, they'd probably call the police. That, or maybe his parents.

Yeah. Right. His parents.

So sometimes when he's at the Lab, getting introduced to the latest new-hire, they'll make a comment, or get a look of their face, and suddenly Rand gets it. They think he's still an intern, a kid. And granted, he did end up skipping four grades, and got his first PhD at twenty, but maybe they're picking up on something else, something he'd rather not own up to. Maybe he is still a kid. Will continue to be one, right up until the day he dies, unless he finally does something about it. As to what that something might be, he's clueless. All he sees is a big blank place. The silence that was left behind when his father set him free.

IT'S LATE AFTERNOON by the time he gets back. There's still no sign of Karla. Granted, she'd mentioned that she might get scarce, but exactly how long does scarce last?

Richard, for his part, seems completely unfazed. She'll get back when she gets back. And in the meantime, he suggests to Rand, they can get to work on some magic. It's obvious his father has found a pet project, turning his son into him, and what better place than to start with the basics, a peek at Tennet & Swift.

But Rand, he's got a headache, and that's not just some excuse, probably thanks to the afternoon hike and his hangover from Bischoff's spell. Right after dinner, some awful canned chili, he disappears upstairs, planning on closing his eyes for a second only to sleep for nine hours. At some point he wakes up, not quite sure why, then hears the front door clicking shut. Figures it's either some random axe-murderer or something much worse, his mother.

Despite her late arrival, she's the first one up the next day. Scenting the house with her dark French roast, guaranteed to raise the dead.

"So I'm guessing that was you who got in late," Rand offers.

"Sorry. I tried to be quiet."

"No big deal. Only considering we're sort of hiding out, shouldn't we be more careful? Have an alarm hooked up or something?"

"There is one," she says, filling a mug. "Or three, if you're keeping tabs. Not to mention the various spells I've had installed over the years."

"I thought you didn't like magic," he counters.

"Not magic. Just magicians."

They putter their way through breakfast. Cold cereal and burnt toast. Eventually one more pair of footsteps navigates its way down the stairs.

"You two look like some TV show," Richard notes. "Biff getting ready for school."

Karla's on him in an instant. Don't you dare call her a housewife. "And why is Biff's father sleeping in? Did he get canned again?"

"No, just on vacation."

They carry their coffees out to the great room. The sun is just clearing the ridge. Dust motes dance in the thin shafts of light that spill across the floor.

"So I made a few calls when I was out."

Richard bristles at once. "Calls? From where?"

"If they're tapping the pay phone at the White Swallow," she replies, "then we've already lost the war."

That seems to shut him up.

"Anyway, I checked in with my contacts at NASA. And it's even worse than we thought."

Hearing this, Rand perks up at once. "You have contacts at NASA?"

"Just a few," his mother admits.

"But who? Why?"

For just a moment, her eyes find Richard's. A shared look, almost complicit. "When they hired you on at JPL, we thought it might be smart. Your father already had his suspicions about what was going on with the Space Race, and we decided it might come in handy, having some ears on the inside."

"Plus, as far as the government is concerned," his father explains, "I was already damaged goods. A left-leaning sympathizer, maybe even a full-on Red. We couldn't very well let my reputation spoil your budding career. Especially when that same career could become of enormous use, should my theories prove correct."

"So what did you do?" Rand wonders. "Put the screws on someone who worked there?"

"Of course not," Karla tells him. "Just nudged things a little, now and then, back when you were first vetted. When whatever you're fighting knows how to be subtle, you have to be subtle right back."

So is that what they're trying to sell him? Claiming they've been discrete? It feels more like they'd taken a bulldozer and driven it straight through his life.

"But thanks to all that," she continues, "we've got an inside line. And apparently, these last few weeks, there's been a string of malfunctions. Something to do with their computers."

"And that's the best this contact or yours can come up with? Rand asks. "Something with their computers?"

Karla stares back, a flesh wound at best. "I leave you two alone for one day, and already it's rubbing off. How to be obnoxious."

"Hey," he protests, nodding towards Richard. "I was doing just fine at obnoxious before I ever met him."

"So rather than bicker," his father suggests. "Let's try this from another angle. If you had to sabotage the upcoming mission, prevent them from reaching the Moon, how would you go about it?"

After all those years of trouble-shooting, it almost feels refreshing. To focus, for once, on what could go wrong, and actually *want* it to happen.

"Well, honestly," Rand tells him, "it's almost too easy, thinking of all the ways. All the thousands, millions, of tiny details that could somehow go wrong." He pauses then. Eyes his mother. Smiles back an apology. "But, yeah, the onboard computers, they've always been finicky. I mean half the circuitry in those things has yet to be tested in space."

"But these weren't the computers in the capsule," Karla points out. "These were the ones down in Houston."

"Of course. That's how the whole thing works. The computers, the control panels, every dial, every switch, they build two identical versions. The one that will actually ride in the capsule and the one that the astronauts train on. And if you really wanted to mess with any of it, you'd probably focus first on the trainers. See where the system is most vulnerable. Where the weak points are."

For the very first time, Rand starts to buy it. The chance there's a credible threat. As if thinking things through, saying them out-loud, has suddenly made it all real.

"And these glitches, these malfunctions," he asks his mother, "were they able to find them, to fix them?"

"That's just it. There seemed to be no pattern, no trigger, as to when things might act up. And half the time they would correct themselves, only to screw up again. Almost like someone was taunting them, determined to drive them crazy."

Someone or some thing.

"So let's assume," his father says, "that they go ahead. Launch the capsule, despite whatever troubles they're now having. Only to find that, at some point in the voyage, this computer of theirs malfunctions yet again. Would the ground crew be able to affect repairs from thousands of miles away?"

"I seriously doubt it," Rand replies. "From what it sounds like, they can't even fix the problem here on Earth."

"So if there were any hope of a rescue being mounted, it would have to take place in space."

Rand studies his father for a second. What exactly is he getting at?

"Look, it's not like calling up Triple A," Rand tells

him. "A computer's not a flat tire. And besides, the whole point is moot anyway. There'd be no way to reach them up there."

Richard nods back, playing at chagrined.

"Of course not. What was I thinking?"

35

IT'S HARD WHEN you're a genius. Even worse when you know you're one. After a while you become convinced there's nothing you can't figure out. So maybe, in a way, it's long overdue. Rand's day of reckoning.

After breakfast, Karla makes herself scarce again. More time for male-bonding. Which, in Richard Constair's book, means teaching his son some magic. Even with the suppression spell now cancelled, Rand seems to be plain old Rand, which most likely means if he once had a Talent, it's been banished for good. But don't fret, Richard tells him with a trumped-up smile. We can still show you how to be useful. How to make parking tickets disappear, or win that next hand of pinochle.

They start out with a single penny, Honest Abe stamped on one face. All Rand has to do is make sure with each toss, that same face keeps smiling back. There are no magic words, no incantations, no eye of newt required, just Rand deciding—or more like insisting—that it'll be heads every time. But as the minutes creep by, and the coin spirals upwards, only to be snatched in midair, it's as obvious as the nose on his face, something isn't right.

Isn't right because he's supposed to believe, believe that he can do it. When all along he knows damn well that things don't work that way. Fact or faith. Science or magic. It's no longer an abstract discussion. More like a rift, his own Grand Canyon, leaving him torn in two.

But you admit it, the odds are dead even, it could go either way.

Yeah. Sure. Whatever.

So why shouldn't it be heads?

Because it could be tails instead.

Not if you don't let it.

Meaning what? It needs my permission?

It's almost like Rand is back at Caltech, just in time for a Feynman lecture. Him grinning away at the head of the class, playing the quantum clown. And what is Bozo trying to tell us? That through our very presence, our attempts to observe any outcome, we end up altering that same outcome, no matter how careful we are. Only instead of this being a drawback, a failing, his father has made it his creed. Dedicated his whole life to cheating. To being Maxwell's Demon.

Still, that's what draws people to magic in the first place. The bait that lures them in. A chance to play God, to rig the game, but only if you believe. Not in facts, or rules, or a shared consensus, but solely in yourself. There's a reason why Karla can't stand his father. Why she gelded Rand with that spell. Thanks to the War, she'd already seen it, the dark side of believing. How one man could drag a whole world with him to the very brink of destruction. How certainty, knowing that you're right, is a poison, pure and simple.

So maybe the fact Rand's an abject failure, it should be a cause for celebration. A guarantee that, no matter what happens, he will never turn out like his father. Never tip the scales to his own advantage. Never call it, heads or tails.

AFTER AN HOUR they decide to give up. Rand is getting too frustrated. Even Richard, though determined to stay upbeat, is starting to fray at the edges. To admit that his son, his own flesh and blood, is utterly, hopelessly normal.

When Karla returns, she can obviously detect it, the smell of failure in the air, but decides it's better to opt for silence than ferret out the cause. Once they've all eaten, small talk and leftovers, Rand beats a retreat upstairs, tries losing himself in a paperback Heinlein he'd bought when they'd stopped for gas. For a while it works, he forgets his own troubles, gets lost in a land called the future, but after a while the words start to blur, and it's time to call it a day.

Moonlight stealing through the window. Sheets

scratching at his skin. At some point it must finally happen, him drifting off to sleep, but of course he doesn't know he's been out till he suddenly snaps awake.

A sound that could be a footstep.

A shape at the end of the bed.

A darkness leaning towards him, clutching something in its hand.

And then all hell breaks loose.

It's hard to say what hits him first. Probably the lights. The ones in his room, the floods in the backyard, what looks like the whole damn house, suddenly flipping on and off, like some kid with a bad stutter. Or maybe it's all the noise instead, that same kid going berserk. The wail of an alarm, a clock radio blaring, the coffee grinder and vacuum cleaner, and what must be Karla's stereo, blasting away downstairs, playing some kind of orchestral music, the perfect soundtrack to total chaos.

But no. Wait. There's a new distraction, upstaging all the rest. Because, somehow, there is now cold water, raining down on him from above. What must be some sort of state-of-the-art sprinkler system, mounted up in the ceiling. All Rand's wearing are his skivvies, and he's tossed off all the blankets, and within seconds he's drenched, soaking, and his teeth are chattering away, but once he looks up, up from the bed, being cold is the last of his worries. Because now there's a man, dressed all in black, standing just a few feet away.

He's wearing some kind of one-piece. What looks like

a neoprene wetsuit. But what really stands out is the item he's holding, a hypodermic, at least three feet long. At first, just like Rand, all the chaos must've thrown him, distracted him for a few seconds. Only now it looks like it's back to Plan A, pretending that Rand's a pin cushion. Ignoring the water, he circles around, almost slipping on the wet floorboards, and meanwhile Rand's holding up the wet sheet, as if it's some kind of shield. A second later the man lunges towards him, the needle snagging on the fabric, and now they're struggling on the bed, fighting for advantage.

He's bigger than Rand. Stronger than Rand. This can only end one way. And then, just like that, his limbs go slack. He's nothing but dead weight.

Rand shoves his body to the floor. Scrambles off the bed. Only then does he notice the knife in his back, buried up to the hilt.

"You OK?" Karla shouts, barely audible over the noise.

"Yeah, I guess."

And with that she spins back, facing the door. Two more figures charge in the room. Just like the first guy, they're dressed all in black, only this time there aren't any needles. Something must happen, as quick as a blur, and already one is stumbling. There's a second blade lodged between his shoulders, even though he'd been facing forward. The last one, the third, hesitates for a second. A second is all it takes. Another knife has managed to bounce off the floor, catch the man on the rebound, slicing the tendon in his left ankle, bringing him to heel.

"Basic field training" his mother yells. "Always leave one alive."

Grabbing the soaked sheet, she kneels down. Binds his hands behind his back. Uses the slack to secure his ankles, one already oozing blood. Rand watches as crimson fades to pink, thanks to the water pouring down.

But then she freezes, head aloft. Rand just heard it too. A brand new noise, only this one is different. It sounds sentient. Alive.

Her eyes find Rand's, and then the hallway. She mouths a single word.

"Richard."

With her in the lead, they sprint towards his room. The sound is growing louder. The angry cry of a frustrated child, only pitched a few octaves lower. Nudging the door to Richard's room, she risks a quick peek past it, so engrossed with whatever's waiting there, she ignores Rand stealing behind her.

Following her gaze up towards the ceiling, his eyes spot Richard first. Richard, who's standing upside down, as though it's the floor instead. And that thing next to him. It's squat. Charcoal grey. With a body about the size of a large dog, only it's smooth and hairless. There are three appendages, what might be legs, securing it to the ceiling, but every time Rand tries to focus on them, his eyes turn away on their own. It's almost like staring at some bright object, or squinting from the sun, only in this case it's an absence of light. A darkness not meant to be seen.

"What the hell is that?" he hears himself gasp.

"I don't have a clue."

The two figures, man and beast, are a few feet apart, showing no sign of a struggle. So how can Rand tell there's a war going on, that they're both fighting for their lives? There's a sound, a whimper, again like a dog's, like something straining at a leash. The one indication, the sole giveaway, of the forces now at play.

Only then, as Rand and his mother stare upwards, there's a hint of movement. One of the legs starts to writhe. The sinuous crawl you might find in a snake, or the arm of an octopus. And there, on its chest, something is happening, an aperture is opening up, one lined with teeth that look razor sharp, putting Karla's blades to shame. The limb leaves the floor, or is it the ceiling. Reaches out towards the mouth, fully open. A moment later the jaws clamp shut. There are no longer three legs, just two.

Disgusted, enthralled, they can only watch. Watch as it happens again. The thing consuming a second appendage, sucking it down in one gulp. Balanced on its remaining leg, it seems to hesitate, and Rand sees the effort on his father's face, the agony etched there. Finally the limb surrenders. Bends to Richard's will. Slips into the waiting maw, the body now floating in space. With an awful, rending sound, the last leg disappears, and in a final quick flash of viscera and bone, the creature swallows itself.

"So what the hell just happened?"

They are camped out on the downstairs sofa. Or maybe it's really a sponge. And if nothing else, Karla now has an excuse to buy herself a new one. As for the sprinklers, the lights, the noise, all that is but a memory, deciding to end as conveniently, as mysteriously, as however they'd begun.

"What happened?" Richard replies, still looking fatigued. "For once, the good guys won."

"And that thing?" Rand asks.

His father somehow finds a smile. Manages to look pleased. "Even if they come back tomorrow, and make shish kabob out of me, at least I'll die knowing I finally saw one. An actual Xyzecom."

"Well, I'm glad you get a new notch in your bedpost," Karla tells him. "And maybe, in exchange, you can help clean up this mess."

But it's not the house that has her riled. Rand knows better than that. It was those few seconds, back upstairs, when she'd gone and blown her cool. Had showed the world, or at least her son, how much she still cared for Richard.

"She's right, you know," Rand points out, providing a little cover. "She rolls out the red carpet, lets us stay here, and this is how we repay her."

"Fine," Richard tells them both. "I'm sorry, as if that makes a difference. But the point is we got something back in return. Something far more valuable that dry carpet, or a good night's sleep."

"And what's that?"

"Knowledge."

You can read it in his tone of voice. The self-satisfied look on his face. Dispatching that creature, whatever it was, had left him free to gloat.

"First off, we now know our cover is blown. That we need to find a new safe house. And if anyone here should take that to heart, I think she knows who she is."

He glances toward Karla. Karla glares back. "Is this about those phone calls again?"

"The timing does seem suspect. Even you'd have to admit as much, Still, thanks to your quick thinking, there's our crippled friend upstairs. And who knows what we may tell us, given the right persuasion."

"And you'd just love that, wouldn't you. A chance for a little payback."

For a second, Rand sees it, the look on his face. Something dark and predatory. But then, just like that, Richard casts it aside. Reigns himself in instead.

"Then, lastly, there's one more thing to consider. That the man had a hypo, not a gun. That they obviously wanted to capture Rand, to assure he remained alive. And how ironic that it was their very attack that revealed his true value."

"What do you mean?" Rand shoots back. "What are you talking about?"

"So who do you think provoked all that chaos? Sounded the alarm? It was you, your Talent, lashing out. Reacting instinctively."

Maybe his father is clutching at straws, trying to lay claim to his son. Or maybe Rand's just in a state of denial. Doesn't want it to be true.

"Look," he replies, still on the fence, "one time, as a kid, I thought I heard something. A refrigerator having a meltdown. But whatever happened tonight, it was totally different. Not even in the same league."

"Different? Of course, it was different, because you're no longer a child." Richard pauses a moment, studying Rand. Surveying his creation. "After this morning, I thought it was hopeless. I was ready to throw in the towel. But now, whether you like it or not, you've just proved it's true."

He smiles then. Lays a hand on Rand's shoulder.

"Proved that you're a magician."

36

THEY CHANGE INTO dry clothes. Brew some coffee. Make a few, half-hearted attempts to clean up all the mess. But when your house just ran into a swimming pool, there's not a whole lot you can do.

And as for Rand, he's almost useless, too lost in his own thoughts. Did he really just make this train wreck happen? Does he have some kind of power? One that's no good when it comes to pennies, but great at trashing a place. He's tempted instead to just claim it's a lie, something his father cooked up, out to convince Rand he was like his old man, that he had a Talent too. Or at least until he remembers that thing on the ceiling. The look on Richard's face. There are some things even he couldn't fake, and one of those is being scared shitless.

But then Rand recalls what happened next, once Richard was clearly winning. The way his father's initial fear had given way to a something else; a look of triumph, even joy, when he'd finally killed off his opponent. And there's a trace of that same expression this morning as he slowly climbs the stairs. The man with the hypo, he's one of the bad guys, he doesn't deserve Rand's mercy, but still, it doesn't seem right somehow, signing onto what comes next. Richard taking a stroll inside his skull. Seeing what secrets he can shake loose.

Only like they say, you win some, you lose some. Apparently it's already too late. Whoever or whatever had sent those men there had decided to take precautions. A few minutes later Richard returns, no longer looking so smug, and explains that their prisoner is but a husk, devoid of a past, or a self. Some nameless, low-level drone whose mind had been scrapped, and then issued a set of commands. There's even a name, Rand learns, for such things. They're known in the trade as Volitions. The will of an overseer, the will to power, rendered in flesh and blood.

Still, they don't need a confession, much less a roadmap, to read the lay of the land. Once again, their redoubt has been compromised. It's time, yet again, to flee. With the dawn still hours away, they decide they'll try heading inland, with no goal, no destination, just an urgent need to put a few hundred miles between them and their close scrape. Richard takes point, alone in his Phaeton. Karla and Rand ride the wake. If subterfuge failed them last time out, this time they'll rely on speed.

Headlights on a smooth black ribbon. A waning moon above. They're a few miles south of Gilroy when his mother finally speaks up.

"I know I already said this once, but I guess I should

say it again."

"Say what?"

"I'm sorry."

There's something dead smeared on the road. She deftly swings around it.

"You're sorry?" Rand scoffs in reply. "We're the ones who trashed your place. Or maybe that was just me."

But it's as if he hasn't even spoken. Like the blame is all on her. "I thought, you and Richard, you deserved some time together. A chance to get to know one another. Only I should've known he'd try it. That thing he always does."

"And what's that?"

She's running the heat—her hair is still damp—and the Porsche feels like a cocoon. A warm, safe place for sharing your thoughts, saying what can't be said.

"When we first hooked up," she tells Rand, "I was barely twenty. Convinced I was God's answer to the world, when I really didn't know a thing. And Richard he saw that. Used that. Made me what he needed. Because casting spells, that's not enough—no, he casts people too."

Cast as in sculpture, Rand can't help but think. Like something captured in stone.

"And you think that's what he's doing to me?" he asks, already knowing the answer.

"Look, I know I don't have a leg to stand on. Not after what I did, that spell and all. But just because I was in the wrong, it doesn't mean he's in the right."

As if anyone ever is.

"You know," he admits, "I almost said something, back when he started talking about that guy being a Volition. Being a husk, a shell, a pawn in somebody else's game. Kind of like me, I felt like saying. Someone you can order around."

"Only somehow you never said a word," Karla points out.

Staring ahead, he tracks Richard's taillights, leading them god knows where.

"No, you're right. I didn't."

FINALLY, NEAR NOON, his father pulls over, on a back-road just off 395. A sad motor court with a big neon sign, buzzing away like a trapped fly. Richard parks the Phaeton out back, where it can't be seen from the road, and Rand volunteers to pay for the room, being the least conspicuous of the three.

Cold cans of Pepsi from the vending machine. Hershey Bars and Almond Joys. Assuming they come out of this alive, they'll all have to visit a dentist.

"So we experimented a little on the ride over," Karla tells Richard. "Thought maybe we could see if what happened last night was just a fluke, or something he could control. Put to use."

"And the verdict?"

"He was able to turn the radio off and on. The same with the headlights and high-beams. But when he tried it with your car, nothing happened. Which could mean there's a proximity effect. That whatever it is he's doing, it's got a limited range."

"Yes, I was afraid that might be the case."

With that, he turns his gaze towards Rand. A lab rat, or else a son.

"And as it was happening, did you see or hear anything? Like those images you told me about, when we removed the suppression spell?"

"No, not at first," Rand explains. "But then, when I touched the Porsche's dashboard, made direct physical contact, it was like I could suddenly feel the car's pulse. The distributor firing, and the pistons at work, and the fan belt whirring away. I could even tell that the carb was off, running a little too rich."

"So much for German engineering," Richard replies. "No wonder they lost the War."

In spite of the strained attempt at humor, he can barely hide his glee. The rat has exceeded expectations. There's hope for his son after all.

But before he can question Rand any further, Karla springs off the bed. Begins to pace across the worn shag, hands clutched behind her back.

"Look, I know we agreed to wait a while. To not push things unless we had to. But if there really is a limit to

Rand's power, if he needs to make physical contact with whatever object he's trying to control, then I can't see any point in putting things off. In stalling any longer."

"No," Richard counters, "we'll only get one shot at this. I don't want to scare him off."

"Or maybe you're the one who's scared. Afraid of what he'll say."

Rand eyes one, and then the other. Tries to read the field of play. Up till then it's been Richard who's pushing things, and his mother who's riding the brakes.

"Excuse me," he says, breaking their silence. "But you're both doing it again. Making me feel like I just walked in halfway through the movie."

Karla seems to catch herself. Decides she's had enough pacing. Retrieves her damp towel off the room's sole chair, and parks herself on down.

"So what do you know about teleportation?"

"Only that it's impossible," Rand tells her. "But then again, so is talking to a car, or seeing some big, ugly thing on the ceiling decide to eat itself, so I guess I don't know jack."

"It's generally accomplished," his father explains, "through the use of a spell or incantation, but both the range and applications are quite limited. There is, however, one device that makes the process seem almost effortless."

"Device?" Karla says. "That makes it sound so ... mechanical. So cold."

"Fine. Then let's call in an artifact."

"Yes, an artifact."

"An artifact," Richard adds, "that could then be used to put both yourself and your power wherever it's needed. And, as luck has it, we even know where this artifact is."

"Which is," Karla points out, "the problem."

A few seconds ago it was open warfare. Now they're playing cute. As if they're both back up on some stage, polishing their patter.

"Let me guess," Rand offers. "It's locked up in a bank vault somewhere. Or buried in some pyramid."

"Even worse," his father replies. "It's in Ecuador. Only it's not the physical location that's the problem, it's the person it ended up with."

"You see," Karla adds, "the three of us, myself, and your father, and this particular person, we have some history going on. With me and him, it's not so bad, only a few minor spats, but when it comes to him and your father—"

"We haven't spoken in thirty years."

A lifetime of burned bridges. Of nailing each door shut. If this is what comes from being a magician, no wonder they're all disappearing.

"Which leaves us with only one option," Karla concludes. "Rand will have to go down there instead."

It's hard to tell who's more surprised, the father or his son.

"It's obvious," she continues, homing in on Richard.

"Who better to play go-between? To do what you can't do? And just think of it, your two worst mistakes, finally comparing notes."

Rand watches his father, cowed into silence, as he struggles to find the right words.

"I'm glad those mistakes can give you such pleasure. I wish they did the same for me. But obviously, the thrill of seeing me squirm, it's clouded your better judgment." He pauses then. Nods towards Rand. "They already tried to capture him once. They'll undoubtedly try it again. And the last thing we need is him fumbling around in some foreign country, helpless and alone."

"Which is exactly why it makes total sense. It's the last thing they'd suspect. And meanwhile, you and I will keep them busy, play the stalking horse."

Hearing all this, Rand finally gets it. Sees his mother's strategy. She's out to win him some breathing room, a little time away from his father. A chance to escape from under his shadow and finally think for himself.

"Sorry," Richard says, not sounding one bit, "I couldn't possibly allow it. I haven't found myself a son just in time to lose him."

"Then why don't we do the right thing for once. Let that son decide."

Taking sides. Rand had always loathed it. Ever since he was a kid. Which is probably why, thirty years on, he's managed to keep on being one. He glances towards Karla, nodding his thanks, then turns back to his father. Finds his eyes are suddenly useless, too timid to seek out Richard's.

"You know, I haven't had a vacation in forever. I guess I deserve one now."

37

THERE ARE NO direct flights from San Francisco. Rand has to swap planes in Houston. And peering down at that dusty brown city, home to Mission Control, he's reminded of everything that's at stake. The reason he's up there, breathing recycled air, and stuffing his face full of peanuts.

Because it's now Tuesday, June 29. Less than three weeks till the launch. Three weeks until NASA tosses the dice, praying that they're not loaded. If Karla's sources are on the money, they should probably scrub the mission. Take however long it takes to chase down this gremlin of theirs. But if there's one thing Rand has learned from his years at the Lab, it's that Big Things have momentum. That pride, and hubris, and just plain stupid defines the human race. So no, there will be no cancellation. No admission that things might go wrong. We are the good guys, after all, and the good guys always win.

Or do they?

The past two days, he's been cramming for finals, with Karla as his private tutor. Learning all he can about one of those same good guys, a man named Charles Overton. Long before the U.S. had entered the War, he'd volunteered to fight the fascists, whether it be Franco in Spain, or the Germans in occupied France. Had even fought, side by side, with Karla, back in her glory days. Just like her, he'd been blessed with a Talent; could render himself invisible, control his molecular density, literally walk through walls. And yet the real thing that had set him apart, that left him a perpetual outsider, was his unyielding moral rectitude. A righteous regard for meting out justice, for always doing the right thing.

Still, it's easy to parse right from wrong when you're squaring off against Hitler. Far harder once that struggle is over, and you're caught in its shadowed aftermath. Desperate for a new sense of purpose, a way to better the world, Overton had eventually agreed to lead a government program known as Division 12. A cadre of likeminded outcasts with Talent, and a foil to the CIA, the Division had been determined, from its very inception, to pursue its own agenda. To do that elusive Right Thing. The Suez crisis. The Bay of Pigs. Even Kennedy's assassination. Whenever the waters grew murky, or an unseen hand tipped the scales, somehow Overton's name would always pop up, just like the proverbial penny.

And then something happened. Some kind of rift. Even Karla isn't sure what. With a mere week's notice, Overton had resigned from his post, taking a few treasured prizes with him and then melting into the wind. For a year, maybe two, he'd stayed off the radar, playing the Invisible Man, only to finally resurface down south, in Ecuador of all places. Evil, it seemed, could take many forms, bear a host of consequences, whether it be thugs toting their chainsaws, or the cleared land they left in their wake. The Amazon basin, the lungs of the planet, now found itself under siege, and apparently someone, a mysterious presence, had decided to fight back. Sabotaged trucks. Dismantled bridges. Spirits that came in the night. Pretty soon the loggers were passing it on—beware El Diablo Blanco.

Which meant it had fallen on Rand and his parents to track that Devil down. To somehow find an Invisible Man in five thousand acres of jungle. For Karla, the way to proceed was simple; you set yourself a trap. The only trick being to find the right bait to tempt this particular beast. Yes, guerilla tactics are emotionally satisfying, but one man can't win a war, and the real fight, the one worth waging, would be fought in a different arena. It could be some boardroom, or a courthouse instead, or in the pages of *Newsweek* and *Time*. Battlefields that would only be accessed, secured, with lots and lots of money.

All it takes is a morning on the phone, in a quiet bar just outside Merced. Karla doing what she does best, pulling strings and calling in favors. The Deputy Aide in Quito knows a man who works both sides, one who can pass a message along to a certain reclusive party. All that's left is naming a figure. She barely hesitates. The first million payable when they meet. The second if he says yes. And as for Rand, he'll get his vacation, and a peek at the equator.

THEY TOUCH GROUND just shy of midnight. Twinkling lights on a mountain plateau. The air smells like wood smoke, and diesel exhaust, and another scent Rand can't quite place.

At the customs desk he pulls out his passport. Tries to look like an Alex Peters. Karla, it turns out, has had one for years, a second person for Rand to be. Part of him feels grateful for this, the fact that she'd shown so much foresight, planned so far ahead. While another part fears it's written up there, scrawled across his forehead. A single word. Pawn.

Passport stamped, he flags a cab. Gets dropped at a cheap motel. A credit line for a cool two million and here he is, stuck playing the skinflint. But if there's a they, and if they are watching, they'll probably focus on the swanker places, and if his current room does in fact have roaches, they stick to the floor, not the bed. At some point in the night he wakes up. Has a moment of blind panic. Can't remember where he is, or what he's doing there. If this is what it's like to be a real spy, he's almost glad he's just a pawn. Can forgive his mother for who she is, the way that she's turned out.

He grabs a light breakfast in the place downstairs. Black coffee and a sweet roll. He's midway through his second cup when a man decides to join him. Grabbing a chair from a nearby table, he plunks himself on down.

"Mr. Peters, I presume?"

His accent is faint, British it sounds like, though he'd otherwise pass for a native. A short, compact build, and dark, tawny skin. Hair so black it shimmers a bit.

"None other," Rand replies.

"I'm David," the man tells him, emphasizing the second syllable. "We're in luck. I was able to arrange for a meeting later today, on his turf, of course. Should be a short drive, only four or five hours. No washouts from what I hear."

"David," Rand says, second syllable also. "And what's your part in all this?"

"I'm what you might call an assistant, or perhaps a facilitator. Our mutual friend has been notoriously fickle about accepting outside donations. But given the source, their prior relations, he's decided to make an exception."

"How generous," Rand returns with a smile. "Being willing to take all that money."

The car is an old Land Rover, peppered with dings and dents. A layer of dirt, café au lait, skirts the bottom of the chassis. It almost seems a deliberate disguise, an attempt to pass unnoticed, but once they've left the paved streets of Quito, Rand realizes he's wrong. This is no affectation, no pretense, just a simple fact of life. What your vehicle ends up looking like when you live in a world filled with mud.

For a while they climb relentlessly upwards. It's like they're chasing the clouds. The landscape, the flora growing ever more barren as they slowly gain altitude. There are steep switchbacks. Sharp-edged hairpins. An endless series of perilous drop-offs. One blind curve where, out of nowhere, a rickety bus appears, with luggage roped onto the roof, and a driver who owns both lanes. After a while, Rand masters the trick. Keeps his eyes focused on the dashboard. There is no cliff just a few feet away. He's not about to die.

Only then, they cross an invisible line. What must be some kind of summit. The northern end of the Andes themselves, only here the peaks are rounded, with no sign of snow on the road itself, no ice to bar their way. From here on in it's down, down, down, a constant, almost sickening slalom, and with every curve, each minute passed, Rand can feel the world transforming. Grassy slopes give way to open scrub. Scrub is supplanted by trees. A rampant, joyous explosion of green, opening up before their eyes.

At some point they finally pull over for lunch. David has packed a feast. Pastries that he calls empanadas, and a block of salty cheese, and a sour fruit punch, not quite a wine, that's way too easy to drink. Topping Rand's glass, he delivers a lecture on the plight of the Amazon basin, not just the river, the jungle or climate, but the people who call it home. The way the *indigenos* had slowly overcome their distrust, learned that they now had an ally, this man who could turn into nothing at all, who would willingly fight his white brothers. And a man who waits for them up ahead, as a friend, or else a foe.

They pull into camp about three o'clock. The air is thick and stifling. Rand's clothes, his hair, every square inch of skin is already damp with moisture. He surveys their surroundings, such as they are, and almost feels disappointed. Notes just a few small huts arranged in a circle, with their thatched roofs and open sides. But then he stops. Recalls what he's learned. The stories that David just told him. The countless times they've been discovered, burned out, forced to quickly move on. For all of them, Overton included, impermanence was the name of the game.

The sound of their Rover wakes the birds. The camp seems to come alive. The late-day torpor giving birth to a small crowd, maybe a dozen men in total. Some, like David, are in city clothes, cargo shorts and button-down shirts, while others wear nothing but loincloths, with their bare feet and a few strands of beads. But there's one man there who can't help but stand out, only it's not due to his outfit. He's the only one, except for Rand, who tends towards pink, not brown.

"So you must be Alex," the man greets Rand. "I'm Charles Overton."

He's tall and lean, with a sinewy build, his blond hair turning to grey. A pair of glasses, gold wire-frames, gives him a scholarly look.

"Actually, it's Rand, not Alex. Didn't Karla fill you in?"

Behind the lenses, the man's eyes widen. It looks like he swallowed a bug.

"Rand as in Randall?" he finally replies. "As in someone's son?"

"That's right. Guilty as charged."

Still chewing that over, he nods past Rand, towards the one hut that's fairly private, with actual walls, and a door that works, and a couple of crude camp chairs. Following him in, Rand grabs one, as Overton does the same.

"All of this is starting to make more sense" he tells Rand. "How vague she was on the phone. She was probably afraid, if I'd known the truth, I would've hung up right away."

He studies Rand for a second or two, probably looking for clues. Anything, a nose or a nervous tic, that might link him to his father.

"So how's Richard doing?" he asks his guest. "Still a total asshole?"

"Pretty much. Then again, I'm not exactly an expert. I've only known him a week or so."

"With some people that's enough." He shakes his head, bemused. "So let me guess. You got tired of being an orphan. Finally tracked him down."

"Actually, he's the one who reached out to me. He thought I could help him with something. Only it turns out, just by being his son, it put a target on my chest."

Overton sits there, mulling that over, a light in those pale blue eyes. Eyes that have seen far more of this world than Rand could ever dream of.

"Collateral damage," he finally says. "That's one of his specialties. And just out of curiosity, did he ever bother to mention him, this kid he used to know? Went by the name of Charlie."

Charlie? Charles? Rand feels like a moron: it should've been obvious. One more loose limb on his family tree, and another mystery solved. And the reason, no doubt, why Richard had stayed home, agreeing to send Rand in his place.

"It wasn't him," he tells Overton. "It was Karla. She once said if I ever wanted to freak him out, play a guilt trip, I should just ask him about Charlie. About you."

For a moment they stare at each other, looking into a funhouse mirror. One a true son, one a mere proxy, both scarred by the same man.

"So what did he do that burned you so bad?" Rand asks Overton. "Or do I even want to know?"

"Thanks to Richard, I killed a man. Smelled, even tasted, his blood. Left me with a penance I'm still paying off, rotting down here in the jungle."

Rand had expected self-righteousness. A man who

saw himself as a hero. Anything but what he'd revealed just now, an anger focused inward. A decision to turn his back on the world, and finally on himself.

"It's funny," Overton goes on, "but at one point he sent me a letter. He was trying to explain, to justify, the way he'd treated you. How he'd refused to be your father. And he claimed that with me, I had been a test run, a chance to see if he could really pull it off, be there for someone else. Only once he realized what he'd done to me, it scared him off forever. Convinced him that the right thing to do was pretend he *wasn't* your father."

Was this the truth, or just an excuse? And did it even matter? The only thing Rand could say for sure is that Richard most likely believed it. That a lie, repeated often enough, becomes its own kind of truth.

And then, with a visible effort, Overton grabs hold of himself. Somehow summons up a smile, proving he still knows how.

"God, will you listen to me go on. It's worse than some soap opera. You come all this way to seal the deal, and end up with psycho-drama."

Leaving his chair, he finds a camp stove, an old Primus that runs on white gas. Fills a saucepan with bottled water and places it on the one burner. Striking a match, he cranks the dial, there's a quick burst of blue flame, followed in turn by a gentle roar that masks the sounds of the jungle.

"So Karla wouldn't tell me," he says to Rand. "What

you need it for."

"Does it really make a difference?"

He scoffs at that. "Yes, it does. To me. The last thing I need is one more of Richard's mistakes, hanging over my head."

"Well, if it's any consolation, it'll be for a good cause. He's convinced there's a chance that the Apollo capsule, the one they're sending to the Moon, could malfunction. Go off-course. And if so, we'd need a way to access it. Make the necessary repairs."

Overton blinks back. "You mean once it's launched? While it's up there in space?"

"That's the general idea."

But Rand's response falls on deaf ears. He's lost in his own little world.

"You know," he eventually replies, "I knew him. Knew both of them, in fact."

"Who?"

"Kennedy."

All those rumors, and stories, and crazy theories. Maybe some of them are true. And apparently Overton had met them both, Jack and his brother Bobby.

"So he was the reason" Overton muses, "the one who got the whole Space Race thing started. That promise to reach the Moon." He stops. Studies Rand for a moment. "And now you're telling me I have a chance to help make that happen. To cement his legacy."

"Maybe," Rand concedes. "Or maybe Richard's off his

rocker and everything will go just fine."

He watches as Overton leaves his chair. Fills two mugs with boiling water. Spoons some Nescafe into each one, and tops them off with condensed milk.

"Hearing all this," he finally remarks, "I'm almost tempted to forgo the money. The fact is I'd be willing to help the cause, even if it's for free."

Rand can't help but smile at that. "You sure do drive a hard bargain."

"You still haven't heard my final condition."

"And what's that?"

Overton takes a sip off his mug. "When you go back, I'm coming with you."

38

AT THAT POINT they should have an argument. Agree to disagree. Rand is supposed to bring back an object, not the person it belongs to.

But the funny thing is, Rand doesn't mind. He actually *likes* Overton. Finds himself drawn to this weird, tortured soul, hiding out in his overgrown jungle. Maybe it's because of what Rand has been, ever since he can remember. A pushover. A wimp. One of those people who hates making waves, go along and get along. And Overton? Overton is a professional crank, with a thumb for every eye, someone who's determined to swim upstream, to take on the whole world. Which, in a way, makes him Rand's alter-ego. The person he's never once been. The kind of jerk he might become if he ever stopped being so damn nice.

Plus, to be honest, he's a little distracted. His nerd-self is on red alert. Somebody's trying to sell him a bridge, and he's not sure what to do.

"C'mon. No way. That's it?"

Overton's clutching some kind of scroll, not much

bigger than a cigar. What looks like two pieces of lacquered wood doweling, with rolled paper stretched between them.

"That's it," he replies, deadpan.

"But there aren't any controls. No instrumentation. How do you turn it on? Plus the size is all out of proportion, unless you're Barbie and Ken."

Overton just shrugs back. "The size depends on who's using it—it'll get as big as you need. There's even a rumor that Hannibal used it to transport those elephants over the Alps. And as for controls, or knobs, or any of that nonsense, it doesn't need them. Operates by thought alone."

Rand moves a few steps closer. Holds out his hand. Overton passes his prize on over. And the moment that skin and paper connect, Rand could swear he feels it; a kind a vibration, almost a hum, as if the scroll is powered somehow.

"And where did it come from? Who supposedly made it? How long has it been around?"

"That's the thing, nobody knows. But there's another rumor, just speculation really, that some alien left it here while on a visit. Like how you might misplace your camera on a trip to Disneyland."

As Rand reaches out, tries handing it back, Overton shakes his head. "I'll let you have the honors. Otherwise you'll still think it's a trick."

It's like he's being offered a magic carpet. There must

be some strings attached.

"It's funny," he tells Overton. "When it was time to reserve my flight, Karla told me to book it one-way. Said that if everything went as planned, I wouldn't need to fly back."

He starts to finger the two dowels apart. The paper is razor thin. One wrong move, one slip of the wrist, and he'd literally tear it apart. Destroy the gift of the ages in the time it takes to sneeze.

"And how will it know where to take us?"

"Just imagine where you want to be."

"But that's just it," he shoots back. "I'm not sure where they are right now. What street, what town, what planet."

Overton shakes his head in dismay. "Christ, are you always this skittish? Look, all you've got to do is think about them. Picture their faces, or whatever. It'll figure out all the rest. Believe me, it's smarter than both of us put together."

Rand takes a deep breath. Spreads his hands. The scroll begins to unfurl. Stretching, expanding, no longer mere paper, no, now it's more like a river; an exuberant flow that spills to the ground, a splash of absolute darkness. Rand can sense what fills that void. Everywhere that ever was. A door so vast that even God can barely reach its handle.

He nods to Overton. Overton nods back. They turn to face the void. A second later they both leap forward and plunge into nothing at all.

KARLA SCREAMS.

Or at least Rand assumes it's Karla. The shower stall has pebbled glass, and all he can see is a blurred outline, but the hair looks right, and the curves are there, and already he's looking away. Watches as Overton does the same, smiling in spite of himself.

But to Karla's credit, it's not a girl scream. A sign of panic or fear. More like she was just startled a bit, realizing she had company.

"Rand," she calls out, killing the water. "I'm assuming this means you're back."

"You got it."

"And who's that with you?"

"Some guy named Overton."

"Charlie! It's great to see you."

"Likewise, K."

A hand reaches up and snatches the towel draped over the shower door.

"Give me a minute to get dressed, will you? Richard's out getting supplies."

It's another tacky motel room, tired drapes and a sagging bed. After rifling through the bedside table, Rand spies a slender telephone book, and learns that he's now in Likely, California, as unlikely as that might seem. A minute ago he was in the jungle. Now he's in the Golden State. Judging from Overton's blasé expression, it's something you eventually get used to.

And then Karla enters, in a cloud of steam, still toweling away at her hair.

"Charlie," she says, her arms reaching out. "It's been way too long."

They share a hug, brief but heartfelt. Rand would give it a 6.5. Two people who obviously share a past, but aren't too sure about the present.

"You're not even surprised," Rand points out to his mother. "You were hoping he might tag along."

Karla responds with an offhand shrug, admitting that's probably true.

"But how come? Just because it'll jerk Richard's chain?"

Overton must have a chivalrous streak. He steps to her defense. "It's been one of her pet projects. Getting us to bury the axe. She's convinced that, until we do, I'll keep on being a wretched cuss."

"Not just you," Karla points out. "Richard's almost as bad. And I still can't decide who it is you're both blaming—each other or yourselves."

But if a question like that can ever be answered, it'll have to wait. Out in the hallway someone is cursing, fumbling away at the door. With a few muttered words in a tongue long dead, the knob seems to turn on its own.

Richard enters, paper bag in hand, looking almost

harried. Only to freeze, his face now pale, as he sees who's sitting there.

"Charlie."

"Richard."

"Well, I'll be damned."

"Too late. You already are."

And the way their eyes are locked together. Those smiles, equally grim. As if two forces, push and pull, are caught in perfect balance. With his mother and father he's used to seeing sparks. The bickering and the digs. But this exchange is cold, not hot, no fire, merely ice, a spell cast thirty years ago, one that neither seems eager to cancel.

Richard is first to break their silence. "So I guess we've determined your selling price. A couple million, give or take. And this from a man who likes to claim he always takes the high road."

"Actually, as to the money," Overton replies, "I still haven't agreed to keep it. And if I do, it'll go to a good cause. Saving lives, not destroying them."

At that point, Rand turns to his mother. They exchange a wary glance. The room, their lives, the whole damn world is about to be held hostage. Transformed into a cheap stage-set where their feud can then play out.

"Hold on," Rand announces.

All three turn his way.

"As the only one here without any grudges, I now appoint myself in-charge. And Rule Number One is no pissing in the pool. If you two want to take potshots all day, fine, just do it on your own time."

Richard tries to look affronted. Overton starts to speak. Decides instead to keep his mouth shut once Karla glares his way.

"So the reason we're here," Rand continues, "is to maybe save three lives. Which means, for the next few weeks at least, we've all got to sign a truce."

"Alright," his father finally sighs. "So where do we begin?"

"Well, let's start with the scroll itself. What exactly is it capable of? It obviously works just fine here on Earth, but maybe not in space. Has anybody ever tried it?"

Overton responds with a chilly smile. "Tried being the operative word."

Richard begins to dig through their groceries. Retrieves a can of baked beans. "In 1402 Aldo Scarpini decided, on a lark, that he'd like to visit the Moon. Two days later his body was found, with the scroll still clutched in his hand. Based on the condition of the corpse, the freeze burns, the massive internal hemorrhaging, there are some who believe that he actually made it. That the scroll, once its user was dead, had returned them both to his study."

Hearing all this, Rand finds no comfort. He's seen what decompression can do.

"So assuming that's true, and the flight was successful, it's a big red warning sign. That unlike Scarpini, whoever tries next, they'd better wear some kind of spacesuit."

Karla perks up at once. "I hear Dior has a new line out. Perhaps they'll feature one or two."

"Or we could we cobble something together on our own," Overton suggests.

Rand just shakes his head. "Temps near absolute zero. The total vacuum of space. You want to risk that in some oversized baggie, you go right ahead."

"So we steal one instead," his father suggests.

"Actually, that's not a bad idea," Karla seconds. "From what I hear, security at the Cape is pretty spotty. They're more concerned about someone accessing the newer, cutting edge technology. And basic components like spacesuits, filtration, landing gear, it's almost public domain by now."

"And that brings up another point," Rand says. "Something I've been thinking about."

Just like that, three heads turn his way. He could get used to this.

"So far, this Talent I'm supposed to have, it's been your classic blunt object. I mean I can turn on the lights, or set off some sprinklers, basic caveman stuff, but who knows what'll happen if I try it on something as sophisticated, as complex, as an in-flight computer. Because now you're talking about micro-processors. Silicon chips. Things you'd need a microscope just to see."

"So what are you saying?" Richard asks. "That you're

not up for the job?"

"What I'm saying is I need practice. To see what I'm capable of. And the only place to really do that is on one of their flight simulators."

Two former spies and an aging magician, all experts in deceit. Rand can almost hear the wheels turning—who'll be first crack this nut?

"Maybe you can talk to the guys in charge," Overton suggests. "Arrange for some hands-on time. From what Karla told me, you're a known entity. You've worked there for almost ten years."

"Working for JPL is one thing. NASA's a whole different story. I show up there, asking for favors, a chance to play with their toys, and the next thing I know I'm in some locked room, getting grilled by a couple of monkeys."

"So just like with the spacesuit," Karla says, "we won't even ask for permission. Make it a black op instead. And considering our particular skills, that shouldn't be much of a problem."

She eyes Overton at the point. He glances back, meeting her challenge.

"I ran the Division. I out-rank you."

"Yes, but I have seniority."

"And I'm older than both of you put together," Richard points out. "Plus I performed for the Queen."

Rand considers his options. It's like ordering take-out Chinese. Only in this case he's the white rice, and each one of them is an entrée.

"It would feel too weird, breaking the law, with one of my parents watching. And if it comes down to who's most qualified, Overton wins by a length. Plus, out of all of us, he's the only one who actually met JFK. Which means, for him, it's personal. He deserves to get first crack."

Richard and Karla exchange a quick glance, agreeing it's time to concede. "At least let me do the legwork," she insists. "Track down some floor plans and schematics. It's one thing to show up invisible, another to go in blind."

Overton nods in agreement. "Fine by me."

And then he turns his gaze towards Rand. Seems to take his measure.

"So how soon do you want to give it a shot?"

"Before I can have second thoughts."

39

THEY TAKE OFF in the morning, still committed to staying on the run, with Richard insisting that a moving target generally beats a sitting duck.

As before, they'll take both cars, only Karla's sick of driving, and ends up in the Phaeton with Richard, trusting Overton with her Porsche. But rather than acknowledge what an honor this is, Overton decides to mouth off, pointing out that if they're really travelling incognito, they could rent less conspicuous wheels. Within seconds he and Richard are at it, like a couple of five-year olds, until Karla finally nips things in the bud, tossing Overton her keys. Just one more reminder how fragile their peace is. How they can barely stand one another.

But at least they'll be sticking to back roads, where the traffic should be light. And thankfully it's not like they're in a rush, no place they need to be, since even with Karla's contacts, it'll take a couple of days to round up the necessary intel. So in the meantime, it's Road Trip, Phase Two. Watching the world scroll on by. Tall pine forests, and lazy little creeks, and occasional glimpses of Mount Shasta.

"One of these days," Rand observes, "we'll have to lock you and Richard up in the same room. See who comes out alive."

Overton just shrugs back. "The smart money would be him."

Rand glances over, scans the hands on the wheel. The barked knuckles, the layers of callous. What looks like a scar, some old war wound, snaking along his left wrist.

"I shouldn't let him get to me," Overton continues. "Get under my skin like that. But he's just so arrogant. So smug. Like he's always got the answer, always knows what's best. I swear, hang around Richard long enough and he'll try teaching you how to breathe."

"Better than how not to."

Up ahead, there's a flash of movement. A deer darting across the road. As Overton slows, two more emerge, two fawns, still sporting their spots.

"So Karla, she filled me in a little," Rand says. "How this Talent of yours works. And according to her, you can project it, include other people, other objects."

Overton nods back. "When I first started out, I was pretty pathetic. Could barely work it on myself. But over time, I was able to get things wired. Get to the point where I could make a field, a bubble, about ten feet or so across."

"Which means, at the Cape, we'll both be invisible.

Able to walk right through walls if we have to."

"Yeah, that's the theory."

Maybe Rand blinks, maybe he doesn't. A second or two passes by.

"The theory?"

Another deer, this one alone. More curves and a patch of sunlight. Overton finally clears his throat, stealing a quick glance at Rand.

"I first noticed it a couple months back. Thought maybe I was imagining things. Told myself it could just be me getting older, or a bad cold, or something in the water. Anyhow, bottom line, it's been getting harder. Harder to maintain a field."

Great, Rand can't help but thinking. Superman without the Super.

"So what did you do about it?"

"I got by. Took less risks, less stupid chances, no more hot-dogging around. And I've been spending more time getting them trained, teaching the Quijos how to manage on their own, just in case I have to retire."

Retire. It's such a strange word. Not something that lone wolves do. No, they just find a spot in the backwoods. Curl up and wait to die.

"Does anyone else know?" Rand asks him.

"I'm pretty sure Karla suspects. Which might be why she waved that two million in my face. To get herself a firsthand look. A chance to mother me some more."

In the oncoming lane, there's a huge logging truck,

hauling twenty-foot lengths of felled timber. Going wherever tree trunks go once their time is up.

"So, you know that expression," Rand finally says. "about how, whenever one door closes, another one opens up. And then you realize, here I am, just learning about my Talent, and there's you, maybe saying goodbye to yours, and it seems, I don't know, almost fitting in a way."

Overton greets that with a grim smile.

"Easy enough for you to say. You're the one who got the right door."

SO THE THING about NASA, it's always been conflicted. Literally split in two. With its body plunked down in the middle of one state, and its brain stuck in another.

The brain, of course, is Mission Control, located just outside Houston. Because if Kennedy got a space center named after him, Johnson had to have one too. And the body, the place where they did the heavy lifting, threw their rocks into space, that was in Florida. Cape Canaveral. A few square miles of mangrove and palmetto, kissing up to the Atlantic. And clear on the other side of the country if you happen to be in California.

But for Rand and Overton that's no problem. They won't be flying the friendly skies. They've got a free ticket to anywhere in the world, good at a moment's notice.

Which means there will be no trip to the airport, just a solo drive for Karla, a four-hour haul to San Francisco while the rest of them cool their jets. She meets up with her contact in the Golden Gate Park. A courier's pouch is exchanged. And then it's back north, retracing her route, to return just after nightfall, still buzzed on Denny's coffee. All four of them scan through the documents. Discover their raid just got harder. That the spacesuits and flight gear are stored in Building Three's basement, with the simulators in Building One, which means that Rand and Overton will have to traverse the entire four-acre campus while remaining undetected.

The Cape operates on a standard, three-shift cycle, with graveyard, of course, being the quietest, and after accounting for the time zone differential they decide to depart around midnight.

They wait it out in their current digs, a motor-court outside Redding, with an AC unit set to stun and a TV that gets just one channel. They're all too jacked to think about napping, so instead it's a round of stud poker. Karla cheats. Richard cheats more so. Rand loses thirty cents. Karla cheers him up with a little gift, a kit she's put together, complete with two flashlights, assorted hand tools, and even a set of lock-picks.

"Just remember," she tells him, "slow and steady. Time is your friend, not your foe."

The room is too crowded to lay out the scroll. They find a quiet spot out by the dumpster. The same yawning void, the same pitch-black darkness, daring them to enter.

"You good?" Overton asks him.

"I'm good," Rand replies.

A moment later they both jump, disappearing into nowhere.

IT'S EASIER THIS time around, Rand discovers. He knows what to expect. A sudden lurch like a stuck elevator, caught between two floors.

He takes a moment to glance around, confirming they're in Building One. Eyes the spacious front entry, two stories high, the most open spot they could find. Even though it's a shade past three in the morning, with just a skeleton crew on-hand, they hadn't wanted to risk it, the chance of teleporting inside someone, killing them instantly. There are two men, their welcoming party, stationed at the reception counter. One of them stifles a yawn. His partner, in an identical white Arrow shirt, is working his way through a crossword.

Seeing them Rand feels naked. Exposed. Why don't they sound the alarm? He has to pause, to remind himself, now seeing only works one way. Still hesitant, he turns to his right, where Overton should be standing, then fights a second moment of panic, when he finds just empty air.

C'mon moron. Get a grip. It's called invisible.

On tiny little mousey feet they slowly cross the room, aiming for an open passageway that should lead to a flight of stairs. At one point the man on the left glances up. Seems to stare right through him. Overton had warned Rand, and more than just once, how likely that was to happen. How some sixth sense would tip people off, scream at them to look up, and the way, in the end, that they'd just ignore it, thinking everything's fine.

The door to the stairwell is closed, as expected. Overton starts to pry it open. And meanwhile Rand's gaze is pinned to the video cam mounted right above it. Yes, they are invisible, but their actions aren't, and so it's their version of Freeze-Frame. Some game left over from childhood. Breaking down each movement into steps so small, so incremental, they will hopefully pass unnoticed.

The trip upstairs should take two minutes. Instead it eats up ten. They're moving through jelly, or maybe it's tar, playing tag, only in slow motion. When they finally spot it, the first of the sim labs, Rand lets out a silent sigh. Finally something he knows how to do. They're back in his world, his scene.

All day long he'd been poring over the specs. Memorizing the right sub-routines. Which toggles to hit, in exactly what sequence, to engage the navigational array. And it doesn't hurt that with the Gemini program, he'd helped program their in-flight computers, has at least a rudimentary understanding of the modifications that they've made since. All of which means the real challenge won't be the equipment itself, the mock-up they've engineered. No, it'll be him. Rand. Seeing if he can use his brain, his Talent, to talk to all those semi-conductors. Seeing if those same invisible specks will bother to talk back.

"So what do you think?" Overton whispers. "Think you can pull it off?"

"We're about to find out."

Rand initiates a standard walk-through. A series of mid-flight maneuvers. The kind of minute course corrections that will keep Apollo dead on target. At first it all goes smooth as silk, there's no sign of drift or wobble, only then, for no reason, a red light starts blinking. The capsule is now off-course.

"But that's impossible," he mutters out-loud. "Nothing happened. Nothing changed."

Without even thinking, he reaches out. Almost kills the alarm. Then reminds himself that this would be cheating, that there must be another way. For a minute, maybe more, he just sits there staring. Staring at that stupid red light. Staring so long it's more like his heartbeat, the blood pounding in his head. And what if it really *is* all in his head? Acting on instinct, he blinks his eyes once. The light is no longer flashing. Only somehow he still feels that insistent pulse, telling him something's wrong.

And so he goes deeper. Where, he's not sure. What

feels like some kind of maze. A twisting, turning labyrinth that has swallowed him alive. There is no fear, no hint of panic, the chill of a bad dream or nightmare, just a quiet sense of what feels like awe that all this could exist. That he's a part of it now. Finally, inevitably, he finds what he's seeking. A place of pain, of hurt. Just like that refrigerator, all those years back, only now he knows what to do. How to make it better. He reaches out without a hand. Speaks while saying nothing. All at once the pain is gone. He's back in the here and now.

"Jesus. How long was I out?"

"I don't know," Overton replies. "Fifteen minutes, maybe twenty."

Rand tries standing. Almost blacks out. Unseen hands grab hold of his shoulders. He's still not sure which one is real, this place or the one he'd just been in.

"Give me a second," he tells Overton. "I need to get my bearings."

"Fine, but don't take too long. I can feel my field getting weaker."

Side by side, they retrace their steps. Climb back down the vacant stairwell. Rand is still feeling weak, woozy, and Overton doesn't seem much better. It's obvious that keeping them hidden is exacting a physical toll.

Leaving the building is a bit of a shock. Despite the late hour, it's warm. The heavy, humid air of the tropics, like a blanket you can't shed. On their journey across campus, they spy a handful of people, maintenance workers and hardcore night-owls, some busy at work, some lost in thought, others sneaking a quick cigarette. Building Three is located near the eastern perimeter, with the bay stretching out just beyond it, and if it weren't for their mission, the way they both feel, Rand might be tempted to pause for a second. Take time to admire the view.

Instead they try a side door. Discover that it's locked. Rather than monkey around with the lock-picks, Overton reaches into the knob. There's a muted squeal, barely audible, and the door decides that it's open. There is no main desk, no foyer, no lobby. Just a trip in a freight elevator. More cameras tucked into corners and eaves, seeing whatever they see. This late in the game, they've abandoned all stealth. It's get in and get out in a hurry. By the time that security knows they're around, they should already be heading home.

But should is one of those loaded words. As much about wishes as facts. And just like that, everything's going wrong, the whole world has turned against them. The suits, it turns out, have been moved from their locker. They're re-routing a plumbing line. So now it's an arduous room-by-room search, in a place that's as big as a warehouse. To speed up the process they decide to split up, each tackling one side of the building, but as soon as Rand strays a few yards away, he notices something's wrong. Realizes that he's not quite visible, yet he's not invisible either, more like a pale and ghostly outline, a shadow of himself.

Panicked, he almost turns around. Runs back home to Mommy. Maybe if they stick together, the outline will go away. But as pissed as he might be at Overton, someone else is on top of his list. A guy named Rand, who'd felt sorry for him. Who'd insisted he come along.

Oxygen tanks. CO2 scrubbers. Boxes filled with catheter bags. Everything but what they're looking for, a giant condom with arms and legs. And then he spots the blink of a flashlight. Overton signaling back. Apparently one of them finally got lucky, even if it wasn't Rand. He crosses the room at a full-on run. Nearly trips on a stray cardboard box. As he pulls closer, he can see Overton, the same milky contours as Rand.

"What's going on?" he hisses his way. "How come we can see each other?"

Overton ignores the question. Nods to a locker instead.

"Looks like we hit the jackpot."

Rand eyes three suits in clear plastic shells—not new, but the next best thing. Judging from the shoulder patches, they're left over from Apollo 10.

"Let's grab all three," Rand barks back. "And those oxygen canisters too."

Just like that, they're scrambling forward. Divvying up the spoils. Or at least until the overhead floods snap on, and the Voice of God rings out.

"*Unauthorized parties, you are now surrounded. Drop whatever items you hold. Then position yourselves face-down on the floor, with your hands above your heads.*"

Maybe it's the shock of hearing that voice. Maybe it's all those lights. Whatever the reason, the field is gone. They're both completely visible.

But if Overton has dropped the ball, at least he recovers well. It isn't a spacesuit he tosses down, more like something dark and hungry. Rand steals one last glance at their surroundings. Finally notices it hanging there. An overhead camera, trained right where he's standing, with a dead-on view of his face.

Seeing it, he leaps for cover. Plummets down into void.

All the while knowing, from here on in, he will be a wanted man.

40

RAND WAKES TO find an empty room. Sunlight streaming through the window. After crawling back in at a quarter-to-three, it's no wonder he's slept in late.

Running a hand through his cropped hair, he slowly accumulates clues. Tries piecing together what the world's been up to while he was sacked out. Clue one: a hastily scrawled note from Karla, explaining they're downstairs getting breakfast. Clue two: an addendum in Richard's elegant cursive, saying that Overton's disappeared. Clue Three: a trio of crumpled white spacesuits, draped over the back of an armchair. Confirmation, if needed, that whatever happened, it clearly wasn't a dream.

He parboils his body in the cramped shower stall. Dries off with the last clean towel. Tries reviewing their little adventure, or maybe make that a disaster. He's still not quite sure who he's more upset with, himself or his partner in crime. Knows only that from here on in life will never be the same. That every day, every moment, he'll be waiting to feel it, a pair of handcuffs ratcheting shut.

And, in the meantime, it'll be this. An endless series of squalid motel rooms. Life on the run, going in a big circle, and ending up nowhere at all. Not up to facing a smiling waitress, or a plate of greasy hash-browns, he heats some water on their dinky hot-plate. Fills a bowl with Cheerios. By the time the water's boiling, he's finished off his cereal. Is scooping some Maxwell House into a cup as his parents walk through the door.

"Finally awake," Richard observes. "We thought you might be in a coma."

"Actually a coma doesn't sound that bad. Better than a holding cell."

Grabbing the sauce pan, he anoints his pal Maxwell. Adds a splash of milk. Cup in hand, he retreats to the armchair, nudging the spacesuits aside.

"So what happened?" his mother wants to know. "And why wouldn't you tell us last night?"

Why? Because he'd been too embarrassed. Still felt the same way now. His very first chance at espionage and look how it turned out.

He nods towards the pile of white silk. "Well, the good news is we got what we came for. As you've probably already noticed."

Karla finds a spot on the mattress, just a few feet opposite him.

"And the bad news?"

He downs some Maxwell, scalding his tongue. Wishes

he'd added more milk.

"You know I always figured, once this was over, I'd just pick up where I left off. Go back to working with those new microfibers, or maybe some nice, juicy polymer research. You know, simple stuff. Geek stuff." He pauses. Risks another sip. "Only now, every time I go into a post office, I'll be looking for my picture on the wall."

Impatient as always, Richard leans closer. Filets Rand with his gaze.

"So what are you saying? Something went wrong? Stop beating around the bush."

"Yes, something went wrong, The deal was we'd be invisible, no chance of getting caught. Only, like everything else I touch, things got complicated."

Even he can barely stand it. That whining tone in his voice. Maybe the worst part of being around your parents is how it turns you back into a kid.

"Look," Rand continues, "he'll probably kill me if he ever finds out, finds out that I told you. But apparently Overton's losing his power, it sometimes goes on the fritz. And last night that's what happened. One minute we're invisible, the next you can see our outlines, and then, just like that, it's full exposure, we're standing there, clear as day. And, of course, there's a closed-circuit camera, catching the whole thing."

Karla tries her best to look upset. To convey some sympathy. But for Richard, it's just one more chance to prove he was right all along.

"Perhaps you should've listened to me," he tells Rand. "Picked a better accomplice. If I had been there, you can rest assured, things would've gone smooth as silk."

Karla silences him with a glare. Reaches out and finds Rand's hand.

"And what makes you so sure they'll recognize you? Make a positive ID?"

"The camera was only a few feet away, and they've got my photo on file. Eventually someone will make a match. It's only a matter of time. And at that point, I'm out of job, guaranteed. In jail, if they decide to press charges."

But if it's a pat on the back he wants, or a little commiseration, he's obviously in the wrong place. A place called Richard Constairs.

"Did you really think it would be that simple? That you could leave your life, see all that you've seen, and then just … just *stroll* back on into it, like you'd been on vacation?"

Rand can hear the contempt in his father's voice. The way he's taunting him. And just beneath it, something else, some kind of twisted pride.

"Like it or not, it's time to face facts. To finally accept the truth. It's not just the circumstances—where you live, or where you work, or what you've eaten for breakfast— that have changed. It's you. Your soul. Yourself. From here on in, you can't turn back. No, you can only go forward."

Rather than admit his words could be true, Rand turns back towards his mother. But instead of finding a friend, an ally, all he gets is a resigned shrug.

"As much as I hate to admit it, for once your father's right. Some things do change you forever. Like the very first time you take a life. Or create one, like I did with you."

It feels, at first, like they're ganging up on him. Making it two against one. But then he remembers the way it had felt, sitting there at that console. According to Overton, it hadn't been that long, maybe fifteen or twenty minutes. So why had it seemed like a lifetime? A glimpse of a whole new world.

"So I guess," he finally manages, "I should tell you about the other part."

"The other part?" Karla asks.

"Yeah. The part that wasn't a disaster."

But the harder he tries to do just that, the more he sees it's hopeless. That some things in life resist all words, refuse all explanations. Once, on a dare, he'd dropped some acid, back when he was at Caltech. Had ended up rambling on for hours into an old Sony tape reel-to-reel. Rand was convinced he'd gotten the goods. All the secrets of the universe. Only to find, when he played the tape back, it was nothing but gibberish.

"And that's kind of the way it seemed right then. Like I'd plugged into something big. For once in my life I was being the world, not just watching it go by."

His voice seems to falter. He stares down at the floor. Shakes his head in frustration.

"And now it's all gone."

Karla and Richard exchange a quick glance. Two conspirators, just this once.

"It's called the numinous," his father explains. "A connection with the Life Force. What Coleridge sought in his opium dreams, and what all us magicians live for."

Us magicians, Rand can't help but notice, not sure he likes how that sounds.

"And it's something," Karla decides to add, "that we tend to forget sometimes. Because when you're down in the trenches, tooth and claw, you can lose sight of the prize. Forget that there really are angels out there, along with all those devils."

From out of nowhere, Rand finds a smile. "Angels and Devils? Sure, if you say so. But what does that make me?"

"Just human," his mother assures him. "Which means you're a little of both."

Yes, he could see that. Accept that it's true. Only he's not sure it's quite that simple. Wonders instead if this thing, being human, is a constant state of war. The good side, the bad side, locked together forever, trying to decide who's boss.

"OK, sure," he finally tells them, "but you still haven't heard the worst part."

Mother and father both sit tight. Wait for him to go

on.

"When I was in there," he explains, "wherever I went, a part of me knew I should hurry up, that there was something we had to do, and we were on the clock. But another part of me, I swear, it didn't give a damn. Would've been happy to stay right there, there for the rest of my life."

And a part, he knows, that's still inside him. Still silently biding its time.

"It was like a peek at heaven," he goes on. "The perfect place that's waiting for us. Anyway, the point is, if I hadn't stayed there, blown things off so long, chances are we would've finished a whole lot sooner, before Overton's field could fail. And now it looks like he's out there, wandering around, probably beating up on himself. Meaning one of us should track him down. Let him know it wasn't his fault."

Richard merely shakes his head. Dismisses all that with a shrug.

"I wouldn't lose any sleep over it. That's always been his style. If someone in China happens to sneeze, he'll willingly take the blame."

"Or maybe," Karla suggests, her voice now clipped, "there's a bigger point to be made."

"Which is?"

"That Rand has already picked up on something. Something you'd rather not face. That magic has its dark side, just like any other drug."

"Drug?" Richard counters. "I think that's a bit heavy-handed. And drugs, need I point out, can prove rather useful, as long as you know what you're doing."

She turns to Rand. Studies his face. It's as if she can see it inside him. A darkness, a stain, spreading out from his heart, like the shadow you'd find on an X-ray.

"Yes, exactly," she finally replies. "As long as you know what you're doing."

41

ON A HUNCH, Rand checks first at the motel's front office. Tracks down the guy in charge. A grizzled old fart about Richard's age, only minus the attitude.

"Kinda tall? Wearing glasses? Yeah, he was in here first thing. Said he needed to stretch his legs a bit. Asked if there was any hiking around."

He whips out an old map, dog-eared but housebroken. Starts to stab away with his finger. It turns out that Redding is crisscrossed with trails, especially down by the river.

"The river?" Rand asks.

The man just stares back, shaking his head. "Yeah," he says. "The Sacramento. Maybe you've heard of it. Biggest one in the whole state."

And then his eyes narrow, lingering on Rand. "You a friend of his?"

Rand pauses, thinking that over. "Yeah. I guess I am."

"Good. It looked like he could use one."

〜

IT'S A HALF-MILE walk to the trailhead. There's even an official sign. And, being a weekday, just one car beside it, a steel grey Volvo wagon. Rand knows the odds are against it, running into Overton, but the day is warm, there's a breeze from the north, and a hike feels just about right. The thing you let your body do while your thoughts are spinning away.

And speaking of weekdays, once out on the trail, he finds his thoughts drifting back to the Lab. To the quiet routine he'd built for himself over the course of years. The rude shock of Monday mornings. Every Wednesday, climbing the hump. Skipping out early on a Friday afternoon, maybe grabbing a beer or two. Not a bad life, he has to admit, but not a great one either, just good enough to get by. Good enough you could always forget just how brief a life really is.

Only now, there's no more pretending. The illusion is cast aside. And as much as he distrusts Richard, and all he represents, Rand knows that he's right about one thing at least. Randall Livotski is dead. Maybe it happened back on that first night, with those two men, Thompson and Green. Or maybe later, at Karla's place in Big Sur, only this time she'd acted just a hair too late. A shot in the dark, a needle in the arm, in the end, did it really matter? All that counts is admitting that his old life, bad or good, is now officially over. A thing of the past.

Which leaves him with a question mark. Where does he go from here?

As if to mock his predicament, up ahead the trail splits. There's a narrow track that takes to the left, snaking up a rocky draw, and to his right a wider path, one that slopes gently downhill. Pausing, he contemplates his options. Decides to flip a coin. Only to find, after checking both pockets, that he's penniless.

"So what are you? The rescue party?"

Seeing Overton there, that's not what throws him. More like what's wrong with his face. This weird thing he's doing with his lips, his mouth, what could almost be a smile.

"Rescue party?" Rand tosses back. "I'm at least as lost as you are."

Pausing, they study each other. Not invisible, not anymore. "So believe it or not," Overton tells him, "there's this huge river over there. Must be a half-mile wide."

"Yeah, I heard," Rand replies. "It's called the Sacramento. Biggest one in the state."

Overton nods, digesting that. "You learn something new every day."

By silent accord they decide to keep walking, choosing the wider path. Neither one really caring where they end up, who's following or who's in the lead.

"Plus a while back," Overton rambles on, "I got my Disney moment. Saw a hawk, what looked like a red-tail, fly off with a big snake."

"And which one were you in this scenario?" Rand

wonders.

"I still haven't quite decided."

As they descend, the air's growing warmer. The hills look almost lush. Just the mention of that one word, snake, and Rand's already on the look-out. Scouring the trail a few yards ahead, listening for that telltale rattle.

"So before we go any further, I need to apologize."

Overton shoots him a look. "*You're* apologizing?"

"It was a classic idiot trap. One you fell right into. All along you'd been warning me, your Talent was messed up, things could go sideways in a hurry. And then I mess with our timetable. Get lost down a rabbit hole."

"OK, sure. But that still leaves me an idiot."

"Maybe. Or maybe we both are."

A careless step. A few loose stones. Rand starts to lose his footing. All at once, a hand darts out, steadying him in place.

"Thanks," he tells Overton.

And maybe it's due to that moment of contact. As if a wall's been breached. All Rand knows is that this is the moment. Time to finally pop the question.

"So what exactly was it?"

"Was what?" Overton replies.

"One day you're the guy in charge. Call the shots at your own agency. And then, just like that, you decide to quit, disappear overnight."

Overton's face does something then. He glances down the trail.

"I failed someone. Failed myself. Realized I'd lost my way. I thought it was me, running the machine, but the machine was running me."

A machine, just like JPL, or more like its papa-bear, NASA. A maw that was always hungry. And one that Rand had been feeding, day in, day out, for the last ten years of his life.

"And how do you pull that off?" Rand wonders. "Start over. Decide to be someone else."

"I guess you start by admitting the truth. That you're sick of who you are."

Some kind of bird, maybe Overton's hawk, is circling overhead. Riding the thermals, hunting for prey, a reminder that they'll never fly.

"No," Rand insists, shaking his head. "There's got to be another way. One that doesn't make you do it, be that hard on yourself."

"For some people. Not for you."

He stares back at Rand, his eyes now cold. There's no trace of mercy there.

"I was there when you blanked out. Saw the look on your face. The very same look I saw on Richard, years back, right before he killed two men."

"But I didn't kill anyone," he argues. "Just talked to a computer."

"No, you're right, you haven't hurt anyone. Yet. But that's the contract you make with magic. The way the whole thing works. Every time you make the world better, you make yourself a little worse."

"Worse? Worse how?"

"Just stick around—you'll find out."

Their warm summer day, it now feels tainted. Rand's eyes have been pried open. The very same trick that his father had pulled on a young Charles Overton.

"So what do I do? Just say no? Refuse to sign the contract?"

Overton stares back, looking bereft. He's finding no pleasure in this.

"Honestly, I doubt you could. There's too much of him inside you. All you can do is to try what I did. Try to thread the needle. To be the very best person you can be, for as long as you can be him."

ON THE HIKE back, they stay mostly silent. Rand is lost in thought. He's traded a world of sunlight and blue skies for a Xerox, muted grey.

Finally, with the trailhead in sight, he finds his voice again.

"So thanks, I guess, for the warning. I suppose I should be grateful."

Overton meets that with a shrug—no gratitude is called for.

"But just the same, I'm going to push my luck. Ask for another favor. Something you can work on when you're not being un-invisible."

Halting, Rand idly kicks at a rock. Half expects the rock to kick back.

"I think you're right. I can't stop now. The only way out is through. So I'm hoping you'll keep an eye on me in the meantime, make sure I don't cross any lines. End up like you-know-who. And don't worry, this favor, it won't be forever. Just until this thing is over."

You have to give Overton credit. He barely hesitates.

"Of course, I'll help," he tells Rand, "As long as you realize."

The wind is starting to pick up. There's a thin scrim of clouds to the north. Close your eyes and you can smell it, a mid-summer squall closing in.

Overton squints, studying those same clouds, then nods towards their motel.

"This thing will never be over."

42

THE NEXT FEW days feel like a jumble. Best of times and worst of times. Not just for Rand, or his companions, but for everyone on the globe.

On the one hand, there's a sense of giddy excitement. The launch is just a week off. Everyone and his brother are obsessed with Apollo, mankind's rendezvous with the Moon. Turn on a TV, pick up a paper, make a comment to some random stranger, and pretty soon you will sense it there, behind the doubt or cynicism. The human race now has a reason to hope. A sense of unity. In a world filled with warfare and racial strife, there's one thing that can bring us together.

But for Rand and the people he's sharing a room with, feeling good isn't really an option. They're all too aware of what could wrong, and what already has. Ever since their little escapade, they soon learn, NASA's been on high-alert, still trying to determine why anyone would steal a few used spacesuits, or how they'd vanished afterwards. And, in the meantime, security measures have been tightened at the Cape. There'd be no more playing around with computers. No games of hide-and-seek. The one bright light being that after the incursion, an unexplained string of ongoing malfunctions has suddenly come to a halt.

Does this mean that Rand had fixed the problem? Should they all exchange high-fives? Or is Richard's bête noir, his shadowy presence, merely enjoying some more cat and mouse? In a way, all the doubt, the constant uncertainty, mirrors what's in Rand's head, and he's starting to wonder if this is it, the way life will be from now on. A constant round of second-guessing. Of not knowing what is real. Finding threats where none exist, creating the foe you imagine.

Of course he can't say a word to his father. To question would suggest betrayal. So instead they resume their ongoing project, attempting to hone Rand's gift. To make sure that his Talent is ready should it be called on again.

They make use of the tools at hand. The motel is their lab. A small hot-plate, a vending machine, even Richard's precious Phaeton are all put to the test. But if Rand expects a repeat of that night, full immersion in another world, what he finds is more like a tepid bath, a dip in the kiddy pool. Trying to have a grown-up conversation with devices still stuck back in pre-school. Still, he knows better than to seem disappointed. They already suspect he's some junkie. And besides, he's working on his own theory, one he's not quite ready to share.

What is intelligence, after all? This thing we call a

mind? The consequence, the inevitable by-product, of any system of sufficient complexity. A heating coil wouldn't quite cut it. Ditto a car's solenoid. But obviously the computers at Mission Control had reached some kind of threshold. Had possessed enough depth, enough consciousness even, to respond to Rand in kind. So if he really means to test his power, to flex these new muscles of his, he needs to find the appropriate playmate. Someone who can meet him halfway.

"And where are you going?" Richard asks. "Giving up already?"

Rand grabs the Porsche's keys off the table. Returns his father's smile.

"If I'm not back by suppertime, Karla can write the obit."

REDDING SEEMS LIKE a nice enough town. All those trails and, of course, there's the river. But the one thing it's lacking, despite all its charms, is any kind of computer mainframe.

So instead he cruises around at random. Tries scouting transmission lines. He knows there's a dam up north at Lake Shasta, and they probably shunt power from there. Which means there would have to be some kind of sub-station nearby, most likely on the outskirts of town. He eventually spots a heavy-duty metal pylon. Two more located just past it. Then a dead-straight line of little tin soldiers, marching its way up the valley.

The station, once he tracks it down, is all but hidden behind a cinder block wall, one that's topped with three strands of barbed wire, and tucked behind a padlocked gate. It's as if they're convinced the whole world wants to sneak inside, risk death by electrocution. And Rand? Really, he'd much rather work at a distance. That it won't require physical contact. That all those thousand of kilowatts bustling along will pretty much speak for themselves.

He hunts for some shade, only there is none. They've gotten rid of all the trees. So instead, once he's parked, he just rolls down both windows and prays for an afternoon breeze. Lying back, he can hear the lines as they crackle, feel the tingle in the hair on his arms, like that storm that had passed through the other day, only this one is man-made. Another tribute to our all our smarts, like lightning in a bottle.

He closes his eyes. Lets his mind drift. Imagines a door swinging open. Catches a glimpse of whatever's behind it, aware of his presence by now. NASA's computer had been almost playful. A decidedly feminine vibe. Some kind of sprite, on gossamer wings, summoned not by a spell, but by science. And this place? This place is more like Guyville. Testosterone City. A bunch of dumb lugs, strutting their stuff, another day down at the yard. Knowing damn well if it weren't for them, the whole shit-show would grind to a halt.

Only then, they seem to notice Rand out there. Let go with a few loud cat-calls. It's not as if they're being outright hostile, more just egging him on. Within seconds, it all comes back in a rush. It's like he's a kid again. Facing every playground, every gym, every steamy locker room, all the torments they'd brought his way. He knows he won't win this crowd over with persuasion. No, he'll have to earn their respect. Play the old game of who's on top, and somehow make sure it's him.

Head held high, he saunters forward. Eyes the surly mob. Picks his first victim, some kind of transformer, as stout as a fireplug. Lunging out, he grabs at its housing, pins it to the ground, until somewhere down south, miles away, he feels a kind of hiccup. Realizes that half of the new shopping mall has suddenly blacked-out. Only then, out of nowhere, the tables are turned, someone's now grabbing at him, a series of relays, back-up power, determined to fill the gap. There's a second or two of tussling, he's down and then he's up, and only then does Rand finally get it, the thing he'd never understood as a kid.

Fighting, it's actually *fun*.

Who knows how long the melee goes on. An hour, or could be a day. All Rand knows is that he's laughing, grinning, having the time of his life. At various points there are more outages. He should probably be more careful. But the thrill, the sheer joy, of using his power is impossible to resist. For the very first time, Rand forgives his father. Can understand what makes him tick. Who could resist being a junkie if this is how good it feels?

Only then, just like that, something happens. It's like a whistle has been blown. The teacher announcing that recess is over, and there's a dark cloud on the horizon. Straining, he still can feel his new friends, only they're just beyond reach. Cowering. Stock still. Trying to pretend they don't exist. Praying that it doesn't find them.

Then, like them, Rand freezes.

Senses something there.

Feels a presence, crouching behind him. Cold breath hitting his skin.

So what if fear wasn't just an emotion. Something that came, and then went. Was more like a place, a place that has found you, and decided to swallow you up. There is no door. No sign of a window. Just a barren, featureless room. A room that you will never leave, that will hold onto your soul forever.

The breath grows stronger, there on his neck. A tendril reaches out. Gently snakes beneath his shirt, then steals across his nipples. *Come*, it whispers in his ear. *Come*, it pleads like honey. Come to where it's cool, and dark, and where no one will ever find you.

So sweet is that voice, he starts to swoon. He's already tumbling backwards. Back to the shadows that we called home, before we found the light.

The light.

All at once it's everywhere. Outside him, and within him as well. He can hear a scream, rending the air, the sound of pure agony. Whatever it is, perched there behind him, it tries its best to fight back. To reassert the darkness. And Rand knows he's that battlefield, imagined mere days ago, the place where angel and devil meet, to decide which one will claim him. Which one will get the prize.

And then Rand's back in this world. Still seated in the Porsche. The door is propped open and Richard's bent forward, glaring back at him.

"You idiot!" he lashes out at Rand. "And to think you're my own son."

"What … what was that?" he stutters, still shaking. "That place, the thing inside it?"

"I'll ask the questions here."

Still angry, he forces Rand out of the car. Makes him walk in a jagged circle. The heat of the day, the smell of the dirt, it all still feels unreal.

"So what were you thinking?" his father demands. "What was it that brought you here?"

"We weren't getting anywhere. Not with hot plates. So I decided to up the ante. And everything was going fine until …" He stops. Falters. Can't seem to find his voice.

"Did it ever occur to you that I might know what I was doing? That there was a reason we were taking it slow. Taking baby steps."

Rand doesn't try to defend himself. What would be the point?

"And do you have any idea," Richard goes on, "what might've happened if I'd showed up even just a few seconds later."

Only then does Rand pause, looking around. There's no sign of his father's car. So he must have used the scroll instead, borrowed it from Overton. Which means both of them will now know what an idiot he's been. What an idiot he still is. With the bright side being, his one consolation, stupid is better than dead.

"So how'd you find me? Know where to look?"

"You take off, close-mouthed and cryptic, and, viola, the grid goes down. It seemed like a bit much for coincidence."

Rand nods back, conceding his point. "And that thing?"

For a moment, his father gazes out towards the horizon. Finally blows out a lungful of air.

"So now you've met the enemy. Or even worse, more like felt it. The one who's been dogging me for the last thirty years, only it seems more like three hundred."

"But where did it come from? What does it want? Does it even really exist?"

"All good questions, for what that's worth. I'll let you know if I find any answers."

He pauses then, studying Rand. Shakes his head in

regret.

"But you meeting it, that's not what scares me. It's the fact that it's met you. Now it knows what you're capable of, what a threat you represent. And even worse, it's smelled you. Tasted you. And once that thing gets hold of your scent, it will never, ever let go."

And with that they're back in Overton's world. A world where things never end. Where no one can ever win the game, just forestall the eventual outcome.

"You think you're up to driving back?" he asks Rand. "We could pick the car up later."

He should probably thank his father. For showing up. Saving his life.

Instead he merely shakes his head. "No, I'm fine. The drive will do me good."

43

RICHARD WILL UNDOUBTEDLY get back first. He's using the scroll after all. While Rand is stuck with pavement and tires, and something called a speed limit.

Still, he's not complaining. He needs time to think things through. Or maybe, in this case, he could use something else, time to *not* think about things. Not think about an icy cold breath, working its way down his spine. Not think about that slimy tendril, how hungry it had seemed. Thanks to it, he now knows what it feels like to die. To let go of this world. Finally realizes that no matter what he thinks of his father, whatever his flaws or failures, he will never be truly evil. Not when compared to some things.

As he passes through Redding he can still see them. The leftovers from his little outing. Blinking traffic signals, and darkened storefronts, and utility trucks on the move. He hadn't meant to cause this chaos. Hadn't known he even could. Only now is he feeling the ripples he'd left; the spoiled food, the fender benders, the missed appointments and disrupted lives. Compared to the monster he'd encountered, Rand was strictly a light-weight. Too stupid to know any better. But intended or not, the fact remains, any blame rests solely on him.

He can feel that weight when he enters their room, back at the motel. The look that Karla gives him. The way that Overton just sits there, silent, holding back his I-told-you-so. Without a word, Rand closes the door. Sets the keys on the bedside table.

Richard greets him with a cautious smile. At least someone's not pointing fingers.

"Glad you're finally here. We've been trying to decide what to do next, in light of what happened back there."

"And do I get a vote?" Rand wonders aloud. "Or am I now officially in the doghouse?"

"Doghouse?" Overton replies. "Try the pound, why don't you."

Karla almost snaps at that. Decides to hold her tongue. Only somehow, for Rand, her quiet disappointment stings more than outright anger.

"There's no denying it," Richard admits. "You've left us in a jam. Now that you've been found out, scented, all of us are at risk. At the very least we'll have to leave town. Find lodging somewhere else."

"No. No way," Overton counters. "Not another damn motel. I'm sick of sharing towels."

"And you have a better idea?"

"Yes," he tells Richard, "I do. Back when I was with the Division, I established a string of safe houses. Remote.

Secure. Easy to defend. Last I heard, they were still being maintained, thanks to our friends at Langley. And if we're really stuck with each other for a few more days, we can at least have our own rooms."

"And there's one of these houses nearby?" Karla asks, finally joining in.

"Four, maybe five hours from here. Just a few miles north of Big Sur."

Then Overton pauses, seeing their expressions. "What did I say? What's so funny?"

Rand realizes he's actually smiling. That things no longer feel quite as bleak. Maybe the answer to Absolute Evil is a touch of the absurd.

"All along, I could swear we've been running in circles. Nice to finally get some proof."

THE TOUGHEST PART of their trip to the coast comes right at the beginning. Deciding who's going to draw the short straw and get stuck driving with Richard. Someone so clueless, so self-absorbed, that he thinks this should count as a privilege. But once they're packed and ready, Overton surprises them all. Volunteers to ride shotgun. Probably because he's so pissed at Rand, even Richard sounds like an improvement.

It's getting towards dusk as they hit I-5. The peaks to the west are now shadowed. Yet the stifling heat of a midsummer day is still seeping up through the floor-boards. Behind the wheel, his mother is silent, she's barely spoken a word, leaving Rand to wonder if this is deliberate, her form of punishment. A reminder that sometimes the absence of words says more than any word can.

"Then again, that's all my fault."

Her admission comes out of nowhere. Something private, given voice by mistake. Probably part of some ongoing conversation, conducted inside Karla's head.

"Fault?" Rand replies, turning her way. "What are you talking about?"

He can hear her hesitation. Some thoughts aren't meant to be shared.

"Growing up, I let you pick your own path. Decide what you wanted to study. Which meant it was always science or math. No time for fairy tales."

"Fairy tales?" he repeats back.

"Or maybe myth is a better word. You know, one of those stories that have been around since forever, the kind that nobody wrote. That just somehow write themselves."

One by one, the cars on the road, they're starting to turn on their headlights. Little white cones that guide them along, leading the way back home.

"And the thing is," his mother continues, "the people in them, the gods, or the kings, or the heroes, they always know what's going to happen to them, they've been warned time and again, but still, they go ahead and do it anyway. The one thing they shouldn't do."

Hearing this, Rand wants to protest. "What—you think that's me?"

But it's like his question doesn't exist. Like it's only her own voice she hears.

"It started with Richard, back in Hollywood. Him butting heads with the Guild. And how he was convinced, it wasn't just people, human beings, that he was up against. No, it was something else. Just sitting back. Pulling the strings.

"And then, all those years later, it was Charlie's turn. The way they tricked him into doing what he did. The lies, the pretending. Only to have the person in charge, Markley I think it was, finally admit that he was just following orders. That something else was calling the shots, had been all along."

For just a moment, her eyes leave the road. Find Rand, a few inches away.

"Which means, apparently, it's your turn now. Your turn to take on whatever it is. Only you're refusing to see the truth, realize you're the target instead. That all you are is a word, a footnote, in a book from long ago. The period at the end of a sentence, one you didn't even write."

He'd never once heard her talk like this. This was no longer his mother speaking. More like some seer, the voice of doom, making her grim pronouncements.

"Look," he insists, "it's not that bad. We still don't know what will happen."

"Don't we?" she replies. "Don't you see, this is why I did what I did. Tried to give you a normal life. I knew if you got even a taste of magic, you'd end up just like him. Just like your father."

"Could be," he admits. "But after what I saw today, maybe that's not such a bad thing."

She lets out a sigh, as old as the hills. She's heard it all before.

"You just don't get it, do you? If this thing wins, then wham, you're dead. No chance to do things over. And even if by some miracle you win instead, it doesn't matter, you've still lost. Because then you're stuck with what you've become. Just as evil, as toxic, as it is."

THEY REACH THE coast just a hair shy of midnight. Begin to scout around. It's been almost five years since Overton's last visit, and that had been in broad daylight.

Unmarked driveways. Gravel roads. Fire trails that lead to nowhere. They've probably woken up half the ridge when Overton finally spots it, a dark hulk lodged in a copse of trees, seemingly deserted. While the rest of them wait, barely awake, he conducts a quick recon, making sure they're the only guests. The last thing they need is sharing the place with some mole whose cover's been blown.

Once their host signals back an all-clear, Rand can get to work. Just like that, the alarms are nodding off too, and the place should be safe to enter. Overton reaches right through the front door, making quick work of the deadbolt, and then it's a scramble, upstairs and down. to see who scores the best room. But as for Rand, he merely watches, content to sit things out, finally settling for the smallest one, tucked away at the top of the stairs.

"So far, so good," Richard concedes. "Much better than a motel room. Lets' just hope that this time around our stay isn't quite as exciting."

Puzzled by that, Overton glances over. Richard goes on to explain. "During our last visit to the coast, they sent a Xyzecom."

"I thought those were extinct."

"Well, that one certainly is."

All through this exchange, Rand can sense something's up. They're both sounding way too friendly. Almost as if they'd signed a truce during the long drive over.

"So what's with you two?" he decides to ask. "Having a kumbaya moment?"

"I guess you could say that," Overton replies. "For once we're on the same page."

"And what page is that?"

"One with both our names on it," Richard tells him. "We've decided, if and when you head into space, I'll be going with you."

44

"DON'T YOU SEE, you'll need somebody with you. And that somebody has to be me."

There's never a good time to have an argument. But there sure are a whole lot of bad ones. And Rand's pretty sure, if you had to decide, this would qualify. Two o'clock in the morning, in a house you broke into, with your name on an APB.

"Sorry," Rand tells his father, "but if I do this, I do it alone. And the last thing I'd need is having you out there, breathing down my neck."

They're all sprawled out in the sunken living room, on a series of custom couches, these aligned in a rough horseshoe that surrounds a fire-pit, empty and cold. A space that feels almost palatial compared to their double at the Shasta View Inn. But along with their cramped quarters, they've left something else behind. Have finally escaped the oppressive dry heat of the Sacramento valley. Here, at the coast, it feels almost chilly, thanks to a summer fogbank. And all Rand wants to do is curl up in bed and bury his head in the covers.

But apparently Richard won't let him.

"At first I couldn't figure it out. Why our friend never acted directly. Why it always relied on flawed surrogates to carry out its schemes. Only to realize, belatedly I admit, that it wasn't by choice. That it *couldn't* enter our world. That there's something about its nature, its essence, that makes it impossible."

"But I could feel it there, back in Redding. Or are you saying I imagined all that?"

Richard shakes his head. "No, not at all. What I'm saying is that whenever you use your power, you go to another place. Call it the astral plane, or the fifth dimension, or whatever fool name you choose, the point is our friend can enter it also. Seek you out within it."

Rand turns first to Karla, who's stifling a yawn. Then next up it's Overton. He wishes they'd do something, say something, either convince him that his father's right, or else declare that it's all bullshit. Anything but what they're doing, forcing Rand to make the call.

"And let me guess," Rand finally says, "if that thing finds me in there, things could get pretty ugly."

"Yes, exactly. It could harm you, or kill you, or something even worse. Try to win you over instead."

Rand can still recall the way he'd been tempted. How incredibly sweet it had felt. To just let go, say no to the struggle, let the world pass by without him.

"So let's say it does go after Apollo," Richard posits. "And it's up to you to save them. Lord knows, you'll already have enough on your hands—you can barely control your power. But then just imagine that thing is in there with you, taunting you, goading you …"

"Fine," Rand offers, "then send Overton along. He can be my back-up."

But the man on the couch just shakes his head. "Me? I'm in even worse shape than you are. Can barely hold myself together. And as much as I'd love to show Richard up, for once he's actually right."

He turns to Karla, his last hope, but she's not biting either.

"Spacesuits and knives?" she shrugs back. "It doesn't sound, to me at least, like a very smart combination."

For a second he wants to challenge them both. Call them cowards, or something even worse. Unless, somehow, it's courage they've found, being willing to face the truth. And maybe he owes it to everyone there to finally do the same.

"Look, up until now, I've kept my mouth shut. Didn't want us to get too discouraged. But if somebody else's life is involved, it's time I spelled things out."

"What things?" his mother asks.

"Like what a long-shot it really is, this whole idea of a rescue. All the million things that could go wrong. I mean we haven't even tested any of the suits, seen if they're still functional. Have no idea if they'll still hold a seal, if the batteries will charge, if the radios are working."

Overton nods back, looking almost enthused. Doom

and gloom is his home turf.

"So we're basically working with army surplus. Anything else we should be worrying about?"

"What else? How about Point A to Point B. That scroll of yours works great if you're talking about here on earth. But with Apollo, she'll already be in mid-flight, travelling at 1,500 meters per second. Will the scroll somehow match that velocity? Synch itself up with its target? Because there's a whole lot of nothing waiting out there, and only one chance to get things right."

Rand stops. Hesitates. He's saved the worst for last.

"And then there's him."

He nods over to his father, not quite meeting his eyes.

"So how old are you anyway? Seventy? Seventy-five? Which means, if you were a real astronaut, they would've farmed you out decades ago. Weightlessness can mess with you big-time. Your coordination, your blood pressure, your heart. A lot of good you'll do up there if you suddenly go into A-fib."

But if that prospect frightens his father, he hides it well enough. His heart, assuming he really has one, is the last thing on his mind.

"So you're saying it's a suicide mission?"

Rand shakes his head. "Most suicide missions, you blow something up. At least get a little satisfaction. Only in this case, like it or not, that something might be you."

∽

THEY SAY THINGS always look better in the morning. For once they may be right. By the time everyone has finished off breakfast, they've mastered a state of denial. Acting as if they still have a chance while accepting they're doomed to failure.

After a thorough inspection of all three suits, they find them to be in good shape, inspiring Karla to drive to Salinas and the nearest Radio Shack. Each one, Rand explains, has its own compact battery pack, long depleted by months in storage, but he's fairly certain he can charge them back up, given the right supplies. If, in fact, he can pull that off, each suit should be good for three hours. More than enough time to make their repairs and zap back to Mother Earth.

Which leaves them with their second challenge. Coping with zero Gs. Learning how to get around when there's no up, no down, just sideways. For NASA it's an arduous six-month process. Training in B-52s. Sustained descents that produce a free-fall, and mimic what space flight will feel like. Only trouble is, Rand and Richard don't have six-months—the launch is in three days. And as for any spare aircraft lying around, they've somehow misplaced the keys.

So instead they're forced to improvise. Make do, or more like make don't. Let Overton employ what's left of his powers to lower their densities. Of course, it's not true weightlessness; like a feather, they'll eventually fall. But at least it will give them a taste of what's what should they actually wind up in space. It turns out that Richard is vertigo-free. Was born to wear a spacesuit. While Rand proves an expert at losing his cookies, one of life's little ironies. They start out indoors, just to be careful. Eventually move it outside. For the rest of the morning they're bobbing and swaying, trying not to get snagged by stray branches, and provoking rude squawks from the half-dozen jays that call the pines their home.

And as for the last, most troubling question, Rand is still short on answers. Hasn't a clue as to whether the scroll can rendezvous with Apollo. To do what it does is already impossible, transporting matter through space. Especially when it accomplishes that by somehow reading your mind. Taking a scrap of memory, an image, an idea, and turning it into a place. A destination. Still, even if it turns out they can't pull it off, sync up with a moving object, chances are they'll just be left floating in space, and thus able to return. Not a bad deal, especially when compared to the fate of the three men they'll leave stranded.

And it's thinking about them, Armstrong and his crew, that finally wins Rand over. Convinces him that should he go, his father should go with him. Not because he might save his life. Not because it makes much sense. No, the reason he gets to come along is because the story belongs to him. Like one on those myths, those fairy tales, that Karla had talked about, only in this case someone *did* write it. And for better or worse, for now and forever, that someone is Richard Constairs.

THAT NIGHT THEY build a small bonfire, tucked away in a quiet cove. A gibbous moon watches down from above, barely visible through the fog. In just a few days, that same moon will look different. Everything will have changed. Leaving behind something tamed, conquered, or else a memorial. A reminder of how we sometimes fall short, what Man can and cannot do.

The crackle of driftwood, not quite dry. The lap of the waves rolling in. For once, there's no bickering, no sign of strife. They're content within themselves.

"So why cheese?" Overton asks someone, or no one. "And why green, while you're at it."

"Cheese," Richard hazards, "because it comes in a round. That much seems obvious. As for the green, maybe someone liked Roquefort. Or perhaps it was Gorgonzola."

Sprawled out in the sand, Rand shakes his head. How exactly had it happened? A few days ago, put together like this, they'd be at each other's throats.

"And what if it really is made of cheese?"

All this earns is silence.

"No," Rand goes on, "I mean it. The shit I've seen, these last few weeks, things couldn't get much weirder. So who's to say it's not true."

Now it's Karla's turn to chime in. To take up the thread from her son.

"Actually, I did read something somewhere. Stock in Kraft has gone way up. Some kind of licensing deal with NASA, a percentage of gross sales."

"And speaking of gross," Overton replies, "I can just see it. Green Cheetos."

"Green Ritz."

"Green Velveeta."

All three of them turn towards Richard, hoping to coax him out.

"And where do you weigh in on all this?" Rand asks. "The public is dying to know."

Richard nods up at the house, a faint glimmer on the ridge.

"I think we'd better make sure the TV works. I'd hate to miss tomorrow's launch."

45

IT FINALLY HAPPENS on day three. July 19, 1969.

Countless millions had watched the launch, or listened to its soundtrack. Flown along with that flickering candle as it rose to meet the sky. And those same millions, and probably more, would be on hand for the denouement, the moment when a single footprint would change mankind forever. But in the meantime? In the meantime there's a whole lot of not much at all. History's longest commute. And could you really blame an adoring public if, on occasion, they'd taken a break, snuck in a quick nap, nodded off without meaning to, caught up in a sense of complacency, thinking nothing would dare go wrong.

And as it went for the rest of the world, so it went for them, tucked away in their coastal retreat, waiting for time to crawl by. A single instant of waiting, of anticipation, stretched over the course of three days. Meals were made. Dishes were washed. Books started, then set aside. And always with one of them glued to the set, in case something should actually happen. For a brief time, gathered around that bonfire, they'd found a kind of contentment. Had accepted each other, quirks and all. But now, with the waiting, it's back to square one; back to grousing and complaining. You're chewing too loud. You're breathing too loud. You're thinking too loud, thanks for asking.

But then, in a second, all of that changes. The sound of Uncle Walt's voice.

This just in from the CBS newsroom. Mission Control in Houston has announced what seems to be a minor malfunction in Apollo's navigational control systems. No word yet on the extent of the problem or when it might be repaired, but Flight Command has assured the public that the crew and capsule are otherwise fine, and at no risk whatsoever. We'll keep you posted as more details emerge. Walter Cronkite reporting.

They wait until Overton's out of the shower. Fill him in on the news. All four cluster around the set, its volume now turned down.

"Think this is it?" Richard asks Rand.

"If it were anything else, a problem with propulsion or life-support, I'd say wait it out. Get more info first. But the fact that's in navigation, the exact same point where the simulation acted up, that can't be coincidence."

A second later Karla springs up, grabbing the suits from the closet. Rand and Richard strip down to their scivvies, long past feeling embarrassed. It's a two-person process, slipping into the suits, taking care not to snag the fabric. Checking each gasket, each zipper and seam, then moving on to the next. Lucky for Rand, he's always been small, the perfect size for an astronaut, but as for his father, he can barely squeeze into the largest of the three.

Finally they're both suited up. A couple of big white marshmallows. All that's left will be locking their helmets in place, then confirming a tight seal.

"There's a sheltered spot" he reminds Richard, "about five by five, tucked behind the lunar module. That's what I'm going to visualize. Hopefully where we'll end up."

His father nods back, the very picture of poise. All those nights spent facing a crowd.

"So let's hope," Overton remarks, "this goes better than our last fiasco."

Karla's voice is tight. Clipped. "And that you both come back in one piece."

They've already cleared a space near the fire-pit, leaving an open swath of carpet. Overton reaches into his back pocket, and then hands Rand the scroll. With a flick of the wrist, he tosses it down, watching as it unfurls, and instead of the floor, a patch of tan shag, they're looking down into a hole. A void just as empty, as cold and uncaring, as the place they're about to go.

Rand steals one more look at the world, his companions. Knows it might well be his last. Then he reaches out for his father's hand, and together they plunge into darkness.

RIVETS. SIX OF them in a row. Little dimples in a patch of sheet metal. And beyond that some kind of cowling or shield, all but obscured by those shadows.

Wait. Shadows?

For a second Rand sits there, feeling stunned. Realizes they've actually made it. Crossed all those miles of barren space, only to land right on target.

But shadows, they can't exist without light. And all around him it's pitch black. Without even thinking, he starts to turn, seeking out that illumination. Or at least until his head's blown off by the brightest thing he's ever seen.

OK, Rand tells himself, now half-blind. That must be the sun. And on his other side? He turns back around, clumsy and slow, just like the Michelin Man, then finally spots his fellow blob, nudged up between two struts.

"Richard?"

Then it hits him. His radio is down. He's just talking to himself. Finding the right switch, he repeats his greeting, only this time around it sounds different. His voice is now coming from somewhere else, the tiny headset tucked into his ear.

"Richard? You OK?"

But Richard doesn't say a thing. Maybe he's off-line too. And then there's a second voice, there in his earplug, one he doesn't recognize.

"Mission Control, this is Eagle. We didn't quite copy that. Could you please repeat, over."

Shit. The very first thing he'd meant to do was swap out their frequencies. Otherwise, every word he and Richard exchange will be shared with the whole damn world. Kicking himself, he reaches out. Lets his mind make a minor tweak. From now on in, they'll have their own private bandwidth, with no one else listening in.

"Richard?" he repeats, third time the charm. "You're starting to freak me out."

Finally he hears a voice. A voice he knows all too well. Only there's something wrong, Rand can tell—a hint of tension, or what might be even fear.

"Yes, I'm here," his father replies. *"And unfortunately, so is it."*

"It?"

"Don't tell me you can't hear that. The way it's snuffling around. Must've been waiting all along, like it knew we were bound to show up."

Rand's never heard him sound like this. Like he's talking underwater. As if his mind if focused elsewhere, with only a shard left behind. Ignoring the fact that he's now weightless, that there's no more up or down, Rand starts to clamber his way on over, towards the lump in the bright white suit. One final lunge and they almost tap helmets. Rand peers through both layers of plexy. The sun's after-image is still so bright, all he can see is a blur.

"Are you injured?" he asks the blur. "Your suit seems

to be intact."

"Intact or not, it doesn't matter. My suit won't keep it out. So I suggest you get on with our mission. The thing we came here to do."

He's right, of course, that only makes sense. So why does it feel so wrong? As if turning around, ignoring his father, is the hardest thing Rand's ever done.

"Uh, Eagle. You still with us?"

Only then he catches himself. He'll need a new frequency. One that will link him back up with Apollo, and through them, to Mission Control.

"Eagle, can you read me?"

After a long pause, he hears a voice. The same one that replied before. Only now there's an edge, what sounds like honed steel, carving out each syllable.

"This is Commander Neil Armstrong, piloting Apollo 11. You are broadcasting on a secured wavelength. I advise you cease at once."

"Would that I could, Commander. But we have some business to discuss."

And then a third voice decides to butt in. Less steely, more just plain pissed. *"Unidentified party, this is Mission Control in Houston. Unauthorized use of this channel is a felony offense. You will clear this wavelength immediately or face full criminal charges."*

Now Rand finally gets it. He'll need one final tweak. A way to squeeze out Mission Control, keep them silent for a while. Because there's no way in hell he'll win

Armstrong over if it keeps on being a three-way.

"Commander, just to let you know, I'm temporarily blocking the signal from Houston. I'm going to need your undivided attention."

You can hear it in the silence that follows, Armstrong reviewing his options. All those months of training, of scenarios playing out, and never once one like this.

"OK, roger that, you've got my ear. Only this damn well better be good. And just out of curiosity, where are you broadcasting from? Why no signal delay?"

Rand is still gripping the scroll in his hand. Might as well put it to use. Reaching down, he finds the metal deck, then gives it three sharp blows. In the main capsule, just a few feet away, somebody's mind just got blown.

But you have to give Armstrong credit. It doesn't stay blown for long.

"You must be the guy who staged that break-in. The one who stole the suits. But how in the hell did you get out here? It's not like you stowed away."

"Look," Rand tells him, "that's irrelevant now. We both have a much bigger problem. That malfunction you reported in navigation, let me guess what's up. Your console is showing a course deviation, but the auto-pilot's not kicking in."

"What are you—psychic?"

"Not quite. While I was down there at the Cape, borrowing these suits, I had a chance to run some sims on your trainer. Saw the exact same thing happen. Which means not only do I know what's wrong, I know the way to fix it."

"Alright, I'll bite. How?"

"By ignoring the console for now. The course deviation, it's not really there. It's just a glitch in the software. And if you try to correct it, override the auto, then you'll really be screwed. Deliberately throwing yourself off-course with no chance of correcting it later."

He waits for Armstrong to mull that over. To fight every instinct he's got. The hardest thing to do in a crisis is doing nothing at all.

"So I'm just supposed to take your word on all this? Put our mission, our lives, on the line?"

You can hear it there, which way he's leaning. Rand decides it's time for a long-shot. "So Collins, I'm assume you're listening in."

Rand can hear Collins, their second-in-command, as he fumbles with his headset.

"Roger, this is Collins. And you still owe us a name."

"You're right. I do. This is Randall Livotski."

"Livotski? Why does that sound so familiar?"

"Down in Houston. That meet-and-greet. Two or three years back. I was the kid from JPL, the one who brought up Bullwinkle. Found out you were way into Jay Ward."

"Sure, sure. That's right."

"So maybe you can convince your boss that this kid is one of the good guys. That sometimes you listen to your gut, ignore what's in your head. In the meantime, I'd better check in with my boss too. Make sure he's OK."

It's only been a couple of minutes. Rand hasn't been gone all that long. But once he scrambles back across the bay, he discovers that Richard's unconscious. Dead to the world. Fighting back panic, he grabs his arm. Tries feeling around for a pulse. And when the suit proves too bulky for that, he checks out his helmet instead. Notices a faint trace of condensation inside it, proof that he's still breathing.

Still alive.

"Look, Armstrong, I can't stick around. The rest is up to you. But with your permission, I'd like to reach inside the console, fix that glitch of yours. At least, that way, you'll have functional navigation for the rest of the trip."

Just like that? Just like magic?

Rand pauses a moment, trying that on for size. For the very first time it feels right.

"Yeah. Just like magic."

He closes his eyes. Takes a deep breath. Forgets what and where he is. A tiny speck of gristle and bone, clinging to a tin can. Ever since they'd arrived, he's been hearing it there, the sound of something off. A complex system, a mind of sorts, sharing its pain with the world. Now he follows that trail, faint at first. Hones in on that melody. A single note, sounding out on its own, turning the whole tune discordant. Come back, he whispers, as if to a child. Come back, and we'll skip the spanking. Guide these three men to their goal. Do what you're supposed to do.

A moment later, Rand hears the change. A subtle shift in the music. Knows that whatever happens from there on in, at least he's done his part. Only now he senses a second sound, one that must have been there all along, but it's not the computer, with it silicon jungle, microprocessors humming away. No this is a raw and ugly screech, the sound of conflict, of mortal strife. Two animals fighting, talon and claw, fighting to survive.

"Armstrong, it's fixed. I've got to go. Give my regards to the Moon."

"Sure. And Livotski? Thanks."

HE CRAWLS HIS way back to Richard. It looks like he hasn't budged. Four limbs clinging to two metal struts, a rag doll, a thing with no bones.

And the sound? You'd think, being closer, that it would be louder, but it doesn't work that way. The struggle is taking place somewhere else, a place without space, or dimensions. By playing with their radios, tweaking the computer, Rand had already entered that world, but they'd been mere sorties, minor incursions, with no risk of real danger. So maybe it's time to get off his ass. Join his father on the field of battle. Face their foe, whatever it is, before it's way too late.

Only Richard decides to spoil all that. Has the nerve

to open his eyes.

"*Still here?*" he gasps, each word slurring. "*Can't get decent help these days.*"

"Hey," Rand tells him, "I saved their asses. What more do you want?"

The eyelids flutter, like two moths. He draws a ragged breath.

"*God, I've been such an idiot. I read the tea leaves wrong. This thing, it doesn't give a damn about your moon, or your mission. That was just the bait.*"

"The bait?"

"*All it ever wanted was the scroll. Or wanted it back, I should say. So it had to devise a sequence of events that would eventually force us to use it.*"

"But why? What good would that do?"

"*Apparently the scroll, it's not just a means of traveling through space. It can link dimensions as well. With it, our friend could go anywhere it wanted. Finally revisit Earth.*"

He stops. Surrenders to a cough. Rand tries holding him steady. That opaque patch inside his helmet, it's suddenly pink, not grey.

"And where is it now?" Rand asks.

"*Off licking its wounds somewhere. But don't worry. It'll be back.*"

"Good. I'm looking forward to a rematch."

With that, a gloved hand reaches out. Grabs him by the wrist. No matter how damaged his father may seem, his grip is surprisingly strong.

"*No,*" he insists, "*One of us needs to stay here. Keep it distracted. And meanwhile you can do something far more important. Get yourself and the scroll back home. Make sure it's someplace safe.*"

"And leave you all alone?"

The face in the visor does something then. Tries to find a smile. Midway through it changes its mind, decides it should be a grimace.

"*You know, if our foe had a hidden agenda, then maybe I did too. An excuse to finally re-enter your life. To see who you've become. And now that I've done that, watched you grow up, what's the point in sticking around?*"

Rand knows what his father is offering him. A chance to keep on living. Which may be the greatest gift of all, the only one that really matters. Unless, of course, there is another, one that matters even more.

Magic can persuade lead into gold. Coax up a pair of slippers. But even magic can't heal a soul, or trade regret for a chance at redemption. If, for once, his father is determined, determined to do the right thing, then it's up to Rand to grant him that wish, no matter how much it costs him. To give his father the gift he seeks most.

A chance to keep on dying.

"You know, they'll probably hate me for this. Even worse, I'll hate myself."

"*Give them some credit,*" Richard replies. "*Give yourself a little too.*"

He pauses. Coughs. Takes one more breath. There's

more blood on the plexy. A crimson splash, the sole sign of color, in a world of black and white.

"And at least I'll finally find out one thing. One thing I've always wondered."

Rand swallows. Glances away. "And what's that?"

"Is there really no place like home?"

46

IT'S A HAIR past noon on the following day. The tide's at its lowest ebb. The beach just a clutter of exposed rocks, still glistening from the surf. In shallow pools, things scamper and squirm, overhead the gulls squawk away, all of them focused on only one thing, the business of staying alive. It's hard to believe that someone would do it, volunteer to renege on this dance. Then again, that same sacrifice is why Rand's still here. Still tucked away among the living, and not in the file labeled dead.

Coming back, that had been his greatest fear. That they'd blame him for what had happened. That the one who survives, who does come back, will always carry the burden of guilt. His mother's tears, Overton's stunned silence, each one an accusation, or maybe more like a question mark, why Richard and why not Rand. Or for that matter, why not all of them? If any one person deserves to die, then everyone else does too, and perhaps it's merely a matter of luck as to who wins the lottery. Who flips the coin that makes the call, who decides if it's heads or tails.

But believing that, believing it's random, would be the ultimate betrayal. A way of declaring that his father's last choice wasn't much of a choice at all. Maybe he'd been driven by guilt or remorse. All those sins of his, finally catching up. Or maybe, for once, he had wanted to taste it, being his better self. Noble or venal, hero or heel, the point is they'll never know it, the reason he'd chosen to stay behind, to take the high road at the end. Whenever anyone meets a magician, they always ask him how. How he'd pulled off this or that trick, managed to fool the whole world. When really, all along, the how doesn't matter.

The only question worth asking is why.

As Rand watches, Karla picks up a shell, a small hunk of abalone. Part of some rainbow, shattered years back, only to wash up onshore. Sensing his gaze, she glances up. Gives him a smile, almost bashful.

"Hard to believe the last time we came here, there were four of us, not three."

Then she stops. Considers her words. Finds a more positive spin.

"Still, three is better than two."

And she's right, of course, Rand should look on the bright side. Be glad he's still alive. But deciding how you're supposed to feel doesn't mean you'll actually feel it.

"I don't know," Overton says. "What really throws me is all the rest of it. The idea that everything that happened—messing with the Space Race, all of us getting dragged in, maybe even me finding the scroll in the first place—was anticipated. Orchestrated. It's just too much to buy."

"But the point is Richard bought it," Rand counters. "And that's all that really matters."

A little too firm, or too forceful? For once, Rand couldn't care less. Because, even dead, Richard serves as their lodestone. The one that points the way. A path that will wind, and flirt with deceit, and yet always find truth in the end.

"So I've been thinking," he goes on to declare. "About whatever happens next."

Karla and Overton share a quick glance. They'd both sensed this coming.

"I don't know about you guys, but I'm sick of running. Hiding out from the world. And I don't care if it's some invisible whatsis, or the mucky-mucks over at NASA, I'd rather start dealing with things head-on, own up to the consequences."

His mother tosses aside her shell. Brushes some sand off her jeans. "And what exactly have you got in mind?"

"You're the one with all those contacts, right? So arrange some kind of press conference. Granted, I'm just some low-level grunt who works for JPL, but you'll manage to pack the room. And then I go full disclosure. Admit that it was me who snuck into the Cape, stole those suits. And if they want to press charges, fine."

"Sounds like someone wants to punish himself. Pay a little penance."

"Maybe. Or maybe, for once, I just want to do the right thing."

"And what about me?" Overton butts in. "I just sit back? Watch my cover get blown?"

"Look, I can keep my mouth shut. It's the rest of it they need to know."

Karla sniffs at that. "The rest of it?"

"What Richard did, who he was, and how he came through in the end. And the way, when those three guys splash down next week, they'll owe it all to magic. Because everyone out there, they're as stupid as I was, they think it's some kind of war. One thing or another, science or magic, you have to pick a side. When really, in the end, it's just knowledge. Finding out what works. Admitting that no one owns the truth, that we're all just stumbling around."

Overton stares back, still a bit wary. "And what if they don't want to hear that?"

"Then at least I tried."

A few more waves lick at the shore. A gull picks away at some litter. The scuttle of crabs, and the sound of an engine, a car grinding up Highway One. Would they really lock him away in a cell, or throw him a parade instead? The whole point being, if you do the right thing, it shouldn't matter either way.

Karla finally clears her throat. Nods over to her son.

"That still leaves one loose end."

"Yeah, I know," Rand nods back. "The scroll."

At first it had seemed too good to be true. A ticket to anywhere. And now it felt more like the ultimate curse, a burden they'd carry for life.

"There's always a chance," Rand points out, "that when he died, Richard took that thing along with him. And if it's gone, then maybe no one will realize the scroll's back on Earth, or what it's capable of."

Overton just shakes his head. Gives Rand with a wistful smile.

"You really think life is that convenient? After all we've been through?" He pauses, toying with a rock. "And even if whatever killed Richard is dead, I get the feeling, given its power, the scroll won't stay off the radar for long. That there will always be someone sniffing around, trying to get hold of it next."

"Which means," Karla adds, "that without even wanting to, we've put up a sign, bigger than any flag on the Moon. Declaring that, like it or not, mankind is now a player."

And with those words, all three fall silent. Let the weight of that settle in. Had they really managed to save the world, or just made it a more tempting target?

"A few weeks back," Rand finally says, "I did a little research. I wanted to find out who this jerk was, claiming to be my father. And maybe it's embarrassing to admit, but I'd never even heard about them. The Illusionaires. Never realized it was something people once craved. To be lied to. Put under a spell."

Karla nods back, remembering those days. How desperate they all were to believe.

"It's like Richard always said. A lie always beats the truth."

"So maybe that's what we give them now. Call it a lie of omission. One final illusion, the biggest one ever, pretending the world is safe. With no one suspecting the scroll exists, or how many bad guys are out there. And in the meantime, we can keep our eyes open, maybe scout out a few more recruits. People like us, who can keep their mouths shut, and have some kind of Talent to offer."

"I like that," Overton scoffs in reply. "The way you make it sound so easy. But take it from me, herding magicians, it can make cats look easy."

"Fine. So you can give me a few pointers. We'll call it Division 13."

But the moment Rand says it, he knows that's wrong. That someone deserves much better. That whatever happens, or where their path leads, it started with him, long ago. Reaching out, he takes his mother's hand. Grabs hold of Overton's next. It's up to them to carry on. To honor his crazy dream.

From here on in, they will share this one thing. They are now Illusionaires.

Now It's Your Turn

Reader reviews are the lifeblood of indie authors, ensuring our voices are heard. If you enjoyed the words you've read, please share a few more with the public, and take a minute to post a brief review on this book's Kindle page.

Also by Brian T. Marshall

Choosing the Dark

San Francisco. 1982. The hippies have fled, the punk are in turmoil, and a mysterious new illness is hitting the streets. But for Rob Walstein, fresh out of high school, his muse—and the darkness—are calling.

Breaking In

After a tepid East Side review, aspiring artist James Ibedson concocts an elaborate scheme. He will break into a museum. Risk his freedom, maybe even his life. Dare to challenge the works gathered there and hang a painting of his own on the wall.

Fleet

A man, lost and naked, on the streets of Manhattan. The retired linguist who realizes he's speaking an archaic Greek. And the young woman who befriends them both, launching an unlikely quest. From New York to LA, Nebraska to Delphi, Fleet travels a labyrinth, with a mystery as old as mankind lying at its very heart.

Printed in Great Britain
by Amazon

34710326R00274